For Cheryl Pientka, again and of course

Acknowledgments

With so much gratitude to:
Lucia Macro
Sophie Jordan
Leslie Ruder
And to you, dear reader.
Thank you! ♥

ENGAGED
TO THE
EARL

In later years Gwendolyn would look back to the moment she fell in love with the Earl of Westenbury, and smile.

"He was the handsomest man I'd ever seen," she would say. "When he walked into Almack's that evening, I was dancing with someone else and nearly stopped dead in my tracks. But I did see that he was looking at me too, and my heart seemed to lift, and soar—oh, like a bird in flight!

"After the dance was over, my partner—whose name I could barely remember, I was so giddy—he took me back to my relation the Duchess of Egremont. Standing next to her, it took all my self-restraint not to stare around the room, to search with my eyes for the handsome stranger. She was talking about horses, I think, but I couldn't tell you for sure. My mind was, well, elsewhere.

"And then Mrs. Drummond-Burrell—the haughtiest, most minutely correct of the Patronesses—came walking—no, *gliding* toward the Duchess and me, with *him* at her side, as if by magic, it seemed to me. A wish made manifest with all the incredible dreamlike logic of a fairy tale.

"He smiled, and I felt so joyful it was as if a thousand

lanterns within me were lighting all at once. And I smiled back.

"'Your Grace,' Mrs. Drummond-Burrell said to the Duchess, in that cool measured way of hers, 'here is, as you see, the Earl of Westenbury. He has just yesterday arrived in Town, and wishes me to present himself to you as a desirable partner for Miss Penhallow.'

"The Earl bowed, and oh, he was even more handsome at close range! He was wearing the dark knee-breeches considered *de rigueur* for Almack's back then, with a dark long-tailed coat and a beautiful snow-white cravat tied just *so*. And I could see that his eyes were a lovely deep green, flecked with gold, and that his hair was a tawny light-brown, cropped *à la Brutus*—also very fashionable at the time—and his shoulders were wonderfully broad, and—well, it was all a dazzling jumble of impressions and I'm not sure I was even breathing!—and then he was saying 'How do you do, Miss Penhallow' in that marvelous deep voice of his, and that was that.

"Love at first sight.

"Inexplicable, indefinable, practically indescribable.

"Yet there it was.

"It nearly hurt me *physically* to tell him that all my dances were taken, but, feeling myself very clever, I added, as casually as I could, that the next evening I was to attend Lord and Lady Mainwaring's ball.

"Imagine my happiness when the Earl immediately said that he was going as well, and might he secure two of my dances. I would have given him *all* my dances, but he could only ask for two, you see, because any more would have been considered dreadfully risqué. And then I had to wait twenty-three hours—yes, I counted them, I really did!—until I could see him again. And he danced so beautifully. He didn't step on the hem of my gown, or try to squeeze my hands in a vulgar way or bring me too close during a waltz as some other gentlemen tried to do and which made me absolutely furious."

Here Gwendolyn would pause, and into her eyes would come a look of warm nostalgia.

"The Mainwarings' ball took place two weeks after I arrived in London for the Season. After that, the Earl and I met at other gatherings, at assemblies and art galleries, at Vauxhall Gardens and Venetian breakfasts—every day, sometimes more than once!—and he would smile at me, and I'd fall in love with him all over again.

"And then suddenly the Earl disappeared. He was seen heading north in his curricle and four, traveling fast. I hardly knew what to think. He left no message for me. Where had he gone, would he come back, had he left me forever? I was beside myself with anxiety.

"Then, after what felt like the longest fortnight of my life, Hugo, my dear older brother Hugo, arrived! The Earl had traveled to Whitehaven, and formally requested from Hugo—he was my guardian, you know—my hand in marriage.

"'Is this what you want, Gwennie?' Hugo asked me.

"'Oh yes, oh *yes*,' I answered firmly. Rapturously. The Earl, I'd come to learn after our first meeting, had been for well over ten years one of the *ton*'s most eligible gentlemen, but hadn't found anyone he liked well enough to even consider marrying. And now he wanted *me*—as much as I wanted him! I didn't know whether to dance around the room like a zany, or collapse in a chair to try and take it all in.

"'You're sure?' Hugo said.

"'Yes, I am.'

"'It's all happened rather quickly,' he observed.

"'Yes,' I said. 'But Hugo, sometimes one just *knows*.'

"And of course Hugo had to agree with me, having been so fortunate in his own marriage. To have found his own true love."

Gwendolyn would nod wisely, and then go on:

"And so, in April of 1818, the Earl and I were officially betrothed. He gave me a ring, too. It had been in his family for generations—it was a gift from Queen Elizabeth to a previous Lady Westenbury who served as her Mistress of the Robes. Oh, it was so beautiful! It was made of gold, with a large, milky-white pearl in the center. Around the pearl were tiny, perfect rubies which made it seem to absolutely *glow*.

"When I was alone, I'd hold up my hand and stare at the ring. A symbol of my future happiness. No—my *present* happiness. I was engaged, I would tell myself over and over, and to the most wonderful man in the world.

"Engaged to the Earl."

Gwendolyn would look down at her left hand, and smile yet again.

Chapter 1

Whitehaven, England
Autumn 1811

"Christopher, may I talk with you, please?" Gwendolyn Penhallow said, and Christopher Beck, irritated at the interruption, brought his axe down with a *thunk* into a fat yew log and split it in two.

They stood in the long yard to the back of his house, where he'd come to chop wood—over Father's objections, who said it was a servant's job, not that of a gentleman—and all he wanted was to be left alone after yet another of Father's long-winded lectures.

So what if he'd been sent down from university? For "vulgar and pernicious conduct," according to the Chancellor, which was a high-minded way of describing the fights with his fellow students: those, that is, who objected to attending classes with a person of what they considered inferior birth, and who made their views known publicly and repeatedly.

As far as he was concerned, they deserved the black eyes and bloody noses. The damned haughty bastards. Who, incidentally, had *not* been sent down. He rolled another log into place with his boot and lifted his axe high.

"Christopher, *please*," said Gwendolyn, and with a scowl he lowered the axe and looked down at her. Gwendolyn lived next door and was his younger sister Diana's friend. She was just a girl, as uninteresting and annoying as Diana; he supposed they'd hardly spoken twenty words between them over the years. Which was fine by him.

"Well?" he said curtly.

"You see, I've had an idea."

"Bully for you."

"Will you *listen* to me?" she demanded.

"Apparently I must." He leaned on the axe handle and eyed her sardonically. "I am, as they say, all attention."

Gwendolyn, clearly deciding to take him at face value, said: "I must say I think it's quite a brilliant idea. You know, of course, that we're dreadfully poor?"

"No."

"Well, we are, and Mama's very worried, though she never says anything. But I can *tell*. And I do want to help! Diana says that an uncle of yours left you a great fortune, so I thought that you and I could get married, and then you could give Mama some of your money. I'm not asking for *all* of it," she added reassuringly, "just enough for our debts, and perhaps a new gown for Mama, and a horse for Percy, and some books for Francis, and something for Bertram's laboratory—oh, and Cook would absolutely love to have a new stove, and I do wish we could give more to the indigents' charity. Also—"

"Get *married*?" he interrupted. "Are you mad?"

"Of course I'm not mad," she replied, indignant. "It seems to me a wonderfully clever plan."

"In case you hadn't noticed, you're a child."

"I'm not. Girls *do* get married at fourteen."

She was looking up at him and suddenly it struck Christopher that her eyes were like great deep sapphire pools, sparkling with summer light. It also struck him that Gwendolyn Penhallow was, in fact, beautiful. Tall, willowy, with delicate features and bright golden hair and a mouth the color of a ripe peach. She was right: girls *did* get married at fourteen. To cover a rush of confused—confusing—emotions, he said sarcastically:

"I thought girls were supposed to wait for a proposal."

She waved a delicate-looking hand in the air. "Oh, who cares? Besides, wouldn't it be a splendid adventure? We could leave in the dead of night and slip away to Scotland! Gretna Green's only fifty miles away. I checked in our atlas. Just think of it," she went on, dreamily. "Married over the anvil, just like a hero and heroine in a romantic story."

Revolted, he said, "It sounds ghastly."

"I'd have to leave a note, of course." Gwendolyn's expression was still dreamy. "The heroine usually does. She leaves it on her dresser, and sometimes it's all splotched with her tears. Although you'd think the ink would run and make the note difficult to read, wouldn't you? I won't cry, naturally, but I do think a note is important. I'd hate for Mama and everyone to be worried about us. Would you leave a note for your father and Diana?"

Christopher straightened up, his mind racing. A note. What would he say? *Take that, you old windbag.* Father was always prosing on about university, the importance of getting good marks, the need to be prudent and cautious, how he was looking forward to Christopher joining him in his offices (a damned horrid stuffy place filled with people who sat around shuffling papers back and forth), and on and on till Christopher all too frequently felt as if he would explode with anger and impatience.

Now, picturing Father's reaction upon discovering that his only son had, at seventeen, embarked on a runaway marriage—a decidedly imprudent, incautious act—Christopher felt defiant glee overtake him. Ha! How furious Father would be. He tossed his axe aside.

"Let's do it."

Gwendolyn laughed and gave a little bounce on her toes. "Oh, Christopher, that's wonderful! It'll solve *everything*. Thank you *very* much. By the way, did you know we have a cousin in Scotland? He's a chieftain named Alasdair who lives in the Highlands. We've never met him but I'm positive he's one of those fierce, bloodthirsty sorts, so we'd probably better avoid that part of Scotland. Although wouldn't it be a lark to meet a real Scottish chieftain? Do you think he wears kilts every day? Will *you* start wearing kilts? I wonder if your knees will get cold."

Revolted all over again, Christopher said, "Focus, for God's sake. When shall we leave?"

"Oh, the sooner the better! And at night, don't you think? The moon will be full in a few days, which means we can travel more quickly. Also it will be more romantic that way."

Romantic or not, she was right about the moon making it easier to travel. And that it would be better to leave under the cover of darkness. What else? He'd need to pay for their coach fares, and for lodgings and food also. After they were married, they could travel further north, up into the coastal wilds of western Scotland (and, he supposed, bypassing her unsavory relation Alasdair). How much money did he have on hand? He thought about it. Probably thirty pounds or so. It was enough to get them away from here. And gone forever. No more useless arguments with

Father, ever again. No more university, either. Freedom beckoned—

Then he remembered something.

A small, minute, critically important detail.

Oh, bloody hell, but he was fortune's fool.

He told her, "I won't come into my money till I'm twenty-one. You can have it. You can have all of it. But not now."

Even as he said it, he saw the happiness fade from Gwendolyn's exquisitely pretty face.

"But that's *years* from now. That won't do at all. Oh, Christopher, we need it right away."

Well, that was that, then. His world closed in upon him again—his many failures, Father's disappointment and disapproval, Diana fluttering around him like a small maddening moth in a house far too big for just the three of them—and Christopher could feel his scowl returning, his brows drawing together, the quick downturn of his mouth. He shrugged, turned away, picked up his axe. "Sorry," he said, and didn't wait for her to leave before he brought the axe down into another yew log and sundered it in two.

As it turned out, Gwendolyn's brother Hugo arrived in Whitehaven a week after that and within a matter of days was betrothed to a fantastically rich heiress who lived just outside town, thereby neatly solving at a stroke all the family's money problems. Which was just as well, Christopher thought, because Diana had come trailing after him with the news of Hugo's engagement, and added in a low voice trembling with excitement:

"And Gwennie told me that her mama said that Papa asked her to marry him!"

He paused just outside the stable, stupefied all over again. The things girls said! "What the devil are you talking about, you nitwit? Father wants to marry *Gwendolyn*?"

"Gwendolyn? Oh, no, Christopher, how could you think such a thing? Papa asked Gwennie's *mama* to marry him! But she said no. Even though she's a widow, and Papa's a widower. Oh, Christopher, I do wish she'd said yes, she's the nicest, kindest lady in all the world! And then Gwennie and I would be sisters! And you would be her *brother*! We'd all live together in the same house, and maybe, someday, I could marry Percy—or Francis—they're so very handsome—though I can never tell which is which. I do wish they weren't identical twins! But then they wouldn't be themselves! They'd be somebody else! And then I wouldn't want to marry them."

"O God," said Christopher, nauseated to his very soul, then took one long step inside the stable and slammed the door in Diana's face. He brushed aside the groom's offer to saddle his horse and did it himself, doing his best to keep his hands gentle despite the anger firing up inside him again, and within five minutes he was on the wide sandy beach, bent low over his horse's neck, riding hard, half-wishing he could plunge straight into the turbulent blue-green waves and ride, like the mighty Poseidon in his mythical chariot, to someplace far, far away.

A few years after that . . .
Whitehaven, England
Winter 1815

"**O**h, Gwennie," exclaimed Diana, "isn't this the most beautiful gown you've ever seen?"

The two girls were sitting close together on a sofa in the large, comfortable drawing-room of the Penhallow house, poring over the current issue of *La Belle Assemblée*, all around them the cheerful sounds of a convivial holiday gathering.

Gwendolyn studied the illustration of an improbably elongated lady wearing an elaborate dress of striped silver gauze, its glossy silver-edged hem drawn up to the knee (boldly displaying the white satin slip beneath) and ornamented with a large cluster of artificial flowers. She was also wearing a gauzy silk headdress, a low-set wreath of brilliants, enormous ruby ear-bobs, half a dozen bracelets on each wrist, and had wide silver ribbons dangling negligently from her bodice—these additional adornments praised in the caption as the height of modish elegance. They may well have been, but to Gwendolyn the lady looked more like an overdressed actress in a bad play than anything else. But of course, taste was a subjective thing, and so to Diana she only said:

"Yes, very pretty."

"Do ask your mama to have it made for you! And you *must* wear it to Almack's! Everyone will be looking at you!"

Gwendolyn was sure they would, but perhaps not for the reason Diana imagined, and wondered, not for the first time, what it would be like to step into the hallowed halls of Almack's, that exclusive and supremely fashionable London institution. What it would be like to have her Season at last, after years of waiting. There was a time, before Hugo returned from the war, when the idea of a Season had been an impossible one. How different things were now—how infinitely better!

A burst of laughter near the mantelpiece interrupted Gwendolyn's musings, and she glanced over to see Hugo laughing at something his business partner, Mr. Studdart, had said. She let her gaze sweep around the room. It was lovely having her three other brothers home from Eton—and how tall they'd become, too, though they hadn't quite yet reached Hugo's great height. Percy stood next to Hugo, and Francis was talking to Grandpapa; Bertram, two years younger than herself, sat next to Hugo's wife Katherine on a sofa, his hand on her rounded belly and on his face a look of deep interest.

"Did you feel that, Bertram?" asked Katherine, and he nodded.

"It feels like an elbow, or a knee, kicking at me. How curious to think there's a person inside you, Katherine. Do you want a girl or a boy?"

She smiled at him. "I'll be happy with either."

"That's how I felt, Katherine dear," said Mama, who sat nearby with Mr. Studdart's new wife, Céleste, who had once been his housekeeper. Mrs. Studdart looked at Katherine, smiling a little, and Gwendolyn saw how her gaze went thoughtfully to Percy and Francis, and then to Aunt Verena and Aunt Claudia. Two sets of twins. Gwendolyn stared at Katherine wonderingly, then glanced over at the wide doorway as a movement there caught her eye.

It was Christopher Beck, coming into the room but only barely; he went directly to the nearby window and stood with his back to them all. He too had gotten taller in the past few years, and his hair was longer than when last she'd seen him, brushing dark and glossy against his white shirt-collar.

"Christopher didn't want to be here, you know," Diana whispered. "Father made him. He only got home today in time for supper, and already they've quarreled! Father asked why he couldn't be more like Francis and Percy and Bertram and do better at school, and then Christopher swore he wouldn't go back to university, and after that Father said he was slothful and undisciplined—oh, Gwennie, it was dreadful! They were positively *shouting* at each other. I was crying like anything and I could barely finish my dessert!"

Diana's eyes filled with tears and Gwendolyn patted her arm, though a little absentmindedly; she was seeing all at once how Christopher's shoulders had a rigid set to them, and how very still he stood, as if the subject of a portrait enclosed by the wooden window frame. If she were to sketch him she would use white paper and black charcoal, and the mood of the drawing would be . . . bleak. How lonely he looked!

Impulsively she got to her feet and went over to Christopher. "Hullo," she said with a smile. "I haven't seen you in ages. I'm so glad you could come."

He glanced down at her, his dark eyes resting briefly upon her face before turning away his gaze, out into the snowy, inky-black night. "Yes, it's always nice to have a guest who makes your brothers look yet more saintly in all their many accomplishments."

She nearly leaned away from the low, savage-sounding resentment in his tone, but replied stoutly, "*Nobody* thinks that, at least not in my family."

He shrugged. "If you say so."

That seemed unanswerable, so Gwendolyn turned her head to look out the window as well. How beautiful it was outside with the snow falling in great lazy flakes. How mysterious. Half-mesmerized, after a little while she said, "Christopher, do you remember the time we nearly ran away together? This would be the perfect sort of night to do it."

"In this weather? Don't be ridiculous."

"How odiously practical you are."

"More to the point," he went on, relentless, "even if we'd gone through with it, you still wouldn't have the money. My birthday's not for six months yet."

Gwendolyn was still watching the flakes descend. Dreamily she said, "I wonder what would have happened if we *had*? Do you suppose we'd be living in a snug little cottage somewhere up in Scotland?"

"If by 'cottage' you mean 'hovel,' then by all means. We'd be poor and unwashed, at each other's throats, and with two or three babies squalling at our knees. Very romantic," he said sardonically.

"Well, what a dreadful husband."

"Without a doubt."

At this surly reply Gwendolyn almost caught the black tenor of Christopher's mood, wanted to snap back angrily, but then, looking up at him, saw in his dark eyes a kind of remote desolation. And she realized, with a sudden sharp ache of sympathy in her heart, that he was *hurting*.

How could she help him?

Words wouldn't do much, she guessed, and might only make things worse. She wished she could brush aside the dark shaggy lock of hair that fell low onto his forehead, or even put her arms comfortingly around him, but instinctively knew that his pride wouldn't permit it—here in this room filled with other people.

So instead, she took a slow sideways step closer to Christopher, until her skirts brushed up against him, and using this proximity as a kind of concealment, she slid her hand into his and gripped it tightly. She felt him react with a kind of startled ripple throughout his body, as might a wild animal unused to a kind touch.

But he didn't pull his hand away.

They stood there in a silence that felt oddly easy and companionable. It was interesting, Gwendolyn thought, how merely clasping hands could create an instant connection between two people. Maybe, maybe, she and Christopher could become friends now. For years he had merely been Diana's aloof, irascible older brother, and then, during that time of the Penhallows' deep financial distress, someone she'd turned to for help. And he *would* have, if not for the issue of his age. That alone spoke to an essential kind of goodness within him, didn't it?

Gwendolyn didn't know when he'd have to go back to university—or *if* he was going back—but now, all at once, she was determined to make the most of his time here. Perhaps they could go riding together, or walk over to the harbor and see Hugo and Mr. Studdart's newest ship, or simply talk. She wondered if Christopher liked poetry.

She was just about to ask him when, from behind them, came a loud, long, shrill cackle.

Their hands came apart as reflexively they both turned to look over toward the perch where the Penhallow parrot sat, comfortably near the hearth and the recipient of its pleasant warmth. Aunt Claudia stood near, talking to him in her vague, amiable way.

"Do try, Rodrigo. Say 'I love you.'" Aunt Claudia held out a sweet rolled wafer and Señor Rodrigo only cocked his sleek green head and looked at it with visible contempt in his beady eyes.

"I love you," cooed Aunt Claudia.

Señor Rodrigo gave another loud extended cackle, then said, "Blimey."

"I love you."

"Blimey."

"I love you."

"Blimey."

Finally Aunt Claudia gave him the wafer, which he accepted in an outstretched claw. Greedily he ate it, scattering crumbs below him with total nonchalance, then fixed her with his gimlet eye. "I love you."

Gwendolyn smiled, and glanced up again into Christopher's face. He might have been looking at Señor Rodrigo but she was quite sure he wasn't *seeing* him; his expression was intent, arrested, inwardly focused. She said, curious:

"What are you thinking about?"

He didn't respond and Gwendolyn had to repeat her question. Finally he looked at her and slowly answered, "I hadn't thought about our silly little plan in years. But now I'm glad you did."

"Why?"

"Because you've given me an idea." He sketched her a rough little bow. "Thank you—and goodbye."

Something about this last word caught at her and quickly she said, "Where are you going?"

"To see an old friend."

With that, he was gone. Through the window Gwendolyn watched as his tall dark-coated figure disappeared all too rapidly into the black night, then she went over to Señor Rodrigo and held out her hand; he stepped onto it with the utmost affability and said, "Kiss me, you saucy wench."

Gwendolyn laughed, but still she wondered to herself: where exactly had Christopher gone?

A few years ago, Hugo Penhallow had let him work in his shipbuilding firm in the Whitehaven harbor, and now, with swift steps Christopher went to the house of an acquaintance he'd made during that time, an older, rather disreputable man who ran a collier-boat back and forth to Liverpool (and, possibly, also smuggled French spirits). A good-hearted fellow, Barnabas asked no questions and cheerfully agreed to take Christopher along on his next run which, as luck would have it, was slated for the very next day.

In the morning Christopher told his father that he was shipping out to Liverpool and from there to parts unknown, then endured with unusual forbearance the storm of paternal dismay and wrath which, predictably, broke over his head. When finally Father sat down in a chair, nearly gasping from the violence of his outburst, he said, "Don't go. Wait until June, and you'll have your money."

"I don't care about the damned money."

Father seemed to grow a shade paler. "You're a fool."

"I'm sure you're right. Well, goodbye. I'll write and let you know how I'm getting on."

"You needn't bother," said Father bitterly.

Christopher only shrugged, packed a few things in a valise, said a brief and hasty goodbye to Diana who, also predictably, burst into noisy tears, and made his way back to the harbor. He boarded Barnabas's ship, the grandiosely named *Golden Hind*, and took his place among the other sailors who, as uncurious as their captain, accepted his sudden presence without comment.

They sailed away.

"I would have liked to say goodbye to Christopher," Gwendolyn said to Diana, who, still with swollen eyes and a reddened nose, had rushed over to relay the stupendous news. "But I suppose," she went on thoughtfully, "he did say goodbye, in his own way. Oh, Diana, what a marvelous adventure! I do envy him."

"*Envy* him? Gwennie, how could you? Think of all the dangers! The discomforts!"

"I am," said Gwendolyn, a little wistfully, and Diana only stared at her, uncomprehending.

A week or so later, Katherine got a letter from their relation Henrietta Penhallow, the elderly, indomitable family matriarch in Somerset, who, along with other news, let fall the interesting tidbit that her former companion, Evangeline Markson, and her husband Arthur were planning an extended tour of Europe now that the war was finally over. They were looking forward to taking in the art and culture of France, Spain, Portugal, Italy, the German states, and—because Arthur was a Shakespeare aficionado and wanted to take his Evangeline to Kronborg, to show her the famous castle thought to be the model for the one in *Hamlet*—Denmark also.

"Oh, I'd absolutely *love* to see the castle," Gwendolyn said with longing in her voice. "Do you suppose it's a great dark hulk, very brooding and ominous? And I'd love to visit the Louvre—see the Rhine—go into Saint Peter's Basilica. *Everything*. Oh, Mama, do you think I might go too? May I write to Mrs. Markson, and ask? I won't beg, of course, or demand in a stupidly forward way—I'll just ask very, very politely."

Katherine lowered the letter which she had been reading out loud to the family, and looked curiously at Gwendolyn. "But Gwennie, what about London in the spring? You've waited so long."

"Yes, and I could wait some more," Gwendolyn answered, her enthusiasm for this new idea sweeping over her. "It's *such* an opportunity, Katherine! Only think of the museums—the galleries—the monuments—all the art I'll be able to see!"

"You could go another time," Bertram pointed out. "After your Season."

"Yes, that's true, but war *could* come again, couldn't it?"

"Here's hoping," said Percy, the future soldier, with a martial gleam in his eye.

Gwendolyn paid no heed to this unhelpful divagation. "Katherine, Hugo, you met Mr. and Mrs. Markson, didn't you, on your honeymoon trip to Surmont Hall? What are they like?"

"They're splendid," answered Hugo, as Katherine nodded agreement. "Very kind, and absolutely stuffed to the brim in the brain-box, both of them. Mr. Markson was at Oxford with Grandpapa, you know."

"There, you see?" Triumphantly Gwendolyn turned to

Mama. "They're practically another set of grandparents! Oh, please, Mama, do let me write!"

There was more discussion, and in the end, her mother agreed, and Mrs. Markson graciously said yes, what a pleasure it would be to have a lively young person accompanying them, and so in the spring, instead of going to London, Gwendolyn—without a single pang of regret for the Season which had launched without her—was on her way to Europe.

Everywhere she went, she looked, fancifully, for Christopher, but of course wasn't surprised not to see him— although she *would* have been astonished to know that at one point, while traveling in Italy, she and the Marksons passed, all unknowingly, within a mere ten miles of him.

Chapter 2

Christopher went from Whitehaven to Liverpool, and from there to Greece, where, beneath the bright Mediterranean sun, he found employment in the olive groves, finding the work tedious yet oddly satisfying. But in his heart he was volatile, unsettled, sore. More than once did he begin a letter home, then remember Father saying in an acrid tone, *You needn't bother.* Such letters were never finished. Instead Christopher spent his free time and what little money he earned in the *tavernas*, and on any given evening he might end up in a brawl or, more agreeably, in the arms of one willing woman or another.

When the picking season was done, he made his way to Naples, then Rome, finding work here and there, learning the language as he went, brawling and wenching as the mood struck him. Always was he disinclined to linger, his restless spirit driving him ever onward.

It was in the countryside outside Perugia, while he was tramping north along a winding dirt road, that he came across a large open pasture, within it a horse-training ring and a grizzled, middle-aged man gripping the reins of a handsome chestnut gelding in one hand. In his other hand was a long whip.

The horse was clearly nervous, shaking its head against the pull of the reins and trying to back away. But the man stood his ground and jerked at the reins, saying in a loud, rough voice, *"Stai fermo, bastardo! Stai fermo!"*

Stay still, you bastard! Stay still!

Christopher saw another man, old and frail-looking, leaning on the pasture fence, watching, watching, without saying a word.

Inside the ring, the man jerked again at the reins and when the gelding pawed nervously at the dirt, sending a cloud of dust swirling up and into the man's face, he struck hard at the horse's side with the whip and Christopher—who for all his life could never bear to see an animal mistreated, who hated bullies, and who had more than once recklessly plunged himself into misadventure because of it—felt a red haze of fury consume him like a flame to dry tinder.

Dropping his battered valise he bolted to the pasture fence and in a single fluid movement was up and over it, into the training ring and on to the other man before he had time to do anything but release the horse's reins and bring up his whip.

It should have been more than a fair fight, as the other man was bigger and stronger, but within minutes it was over, Christopher, in his fiery rage impervious to injury or pain, bringing the older man down with a sudden sharp blow to the jaw that had him sprawling, groaning, on the ground.

Christopher snatched up the whip. *"Sei il bastardo, dannazione a te! Alzarsi. Vai fuori di qui."*

You're the bastard, damn you! Get up. Get out of here.

The man did, struggling to his feet, casting over his shoulder black looks as he went to the road and walked away, limping. Christopher gave him back look for look until he was gone from view, then turned and with a massive heave threw the whip outside the pasture, deliberately sending it sailing within only a few feet of the elderly man still leaning on the fence. Useless old sod.

Christopher looked around the pasture and saw the gelding in a far corner, reins dangling on the ground. He took a few steps toward the gelding but paused when the old man said from behind him:

"Cosa pensi di star facendo?"

What do you think you're doing?

Half-turning, Christopher answered, *"Vedendo quel cavallo, vecchio pazzo."*

Seeing to that horse, you old fool.

The old man cackled. *"Sei il pazzo, giovanotto. Quel cavallo ha il diavolo in lui."*

You're the fool, young man. That horse has the devil in him.

"Anche io," Christopher said.

So do I.

He turned his back on the old man and without hurry, as if he had all the time in the world, slowly approached the gelding who lifted his great head, ears pricked suspiciously, legs gone rigid.

Christopher saw, now, the ribs showing beneath the red-brown flanks and wondered if deprivation was another training technique of that damned bastard—who himself had looked all too well-fed. Now he wished he'd gone after him and had the pleasure of sinking his boot into that broad arse and helping him on his way just a little bit faster.

With a long breath in and out Christopher tamped down the anger that wanted to flare up again, and instead fished into his coat pocket and pulled out the apple he had stowed there, plucked from an orchard a few miles back.

He was ten or twelve feet from the horse but stopped when it tossed its head and began to sidle away. So he took a knife from his pocket and, paying no attention to the horse, sliced the apple into four quarters. He bit into one of the quarters and slowly, slowly, ate it, and when he was done he looked up to see that the horse was watching him, still with ears suspiciously pricked.

He put one of the quarters onto his palm and held it out. "Want it?" he said. "Here. It's yours."

It took nearly an hour for the horse to cautiously come close. Christopher remained entirely still, holding his arm extended, determined to stand like a statue all day if that was what it took. With pity in his heart he watched the horse, with its wild, wary eyes, and murmured:

"Ciao, c'è un bravo ragazzo. Esatto, vieni a prendere la tua mela, è molto buona."

Hullo, there's a good boy. That's right, come get your apple, it's very good.

"Non ti farò del male, lo giuro."

I won't harm you, I swear it.

Finally the horse inched its way close enough to take the apple piece from Christopher's palm.

"Good boy," said Christopher softly. "Want some more?" With slow, casual movements he put another apple quarter onto his palm and the horse, which had retreated, carefully came forward again. He took the apple, and after that Christopher offered him the last quarter. He was close enough now to see that the bit was too large and had to be painful to the horse's sensitive mouth.

Bloody, bloody hell, he thought, furious, but suppressed—yet again—his anger, and looked again at the horse, who stood very still, looking back at him, and clearly ready to shy away.

"You poor fellow," he said in a quiet voice. "I'd like

to take that bridle off, and brush you down, and feed you properly. Will you let me?"

Christopher turned away and, still with the same casual slowness, began to walk toward the stable he'd seen at the end of the pasture. When at length he got to the open doors, he turned and saw the horse had followed him, although at a distance.

"Come on," he said. "Bridle off now."

And the horse came to him, tentative, nervous, but still letting him remove—slowly, gently, ever so gently—the bridle.

"Good boy," said Christopher. "Never again for that bit. Let's brush you now, and then to supper."

It took more than two hours to accomplish this. Christopher was glad to see there was plenty of hay and oats inside the stable, but was nonetheless practically shaking with anger by the time he emerged into the waning afternoon. The old man was still there, leaning against the fence as if it were propping him up.

"So," the old man said in reasonably good English, his voice heavy with irony, "you dismiss my trainer? Am I to thank you?"

"You're the owner?" Christopher demanded.

The old man nodded.

"Well, he was a damned bad one."

"Yes."

Taken aback at this unexpected agreement, Christopher said, "Why'd you have him then?"

Suddenly the old man with his wispy white hair and deeply lined face looked yet more frail, more sunken. The irony was gone. "I suppose, *giovanotto*, you would like to thrash me as well?"

"I—ah—"

"Perhaps I deserve it." The old man gave a long, low

sigh. "Why did I have him, that reprehensible man? It is because I lost my two sons. They went with General de Beauharnais into Russia, and never came back. So you see, I have no one. Only this horse, and the half-dozen others, in the stables beyond." He gestured toward a larger outbuilding behind the one in which the gelding was currently housed. Looking at Christopher with dark eyes that seemed infinitely tired, he went on:

"For more generations than I can count, my family has trained horses for the noble house of Falconieri. So when that *facinoroso* came along, boasting of his skills, promising to restore the glory of my lineage, I was weak. I let him in. And you saw what he was like. I *knew* what he was like. There is nothing more to say. I do not know that I will ever forgive myself."

Seeing the old man's pain and remorse, Christopher discovered he no longer had it in him to be angry. He said, "Do the other horses need tending to, then?"

"Yes."

Without another word Christopher went to the other stable, where he fed the six horses he found within—all skittish, all thin—and brushed them, cleaned their hooves, gave them fresh water. He shoveled manure. Used a pitchfork to lay down fresh straw. Finally he put a loose-fitting rope harness over the chestnut gelding and patiently coaxed him to join the others in the main stable, into a freshly cleaned stall.

Then he went to the old man's house—it was a handsome flat-roofed mansion, made of warm yellow brick, but dirty and altogether decayed by years of neglect—and in the vast dilapidated kitchen he managed to prepare a meal of sorts, a simple stew of beef and carrots and onions, a bowl of which he set before the old man, who sat at the head of a table incongruously large for just the two of them; in years past, it would have accommodated a large staff of servants.

"*Grazie*," said the old man. "Sit. Eat." And when Christopher took a chair at his right hand, he added, "I am Mauro della Valle. You are—?"

"Christopher Beck."

"An Englishman, of course. You are far from home."

"Yes."

Mauro della Valle didn't ask why. Instead he said, "You are good with horses, Cristoforo."

Christopher only shrugged and dug his spoon into the stew.

"You are; surely you must see it?" insisted Mauro.

"Perhaps."

"Not perhaps. A certainty. You like animals, I think?"

He thought about it, and finally said, "Animals are honest."

Mauro nodded. "*Sì.* That is true."

They spoke little else during the meal, but Christopher was aware that the old man was observing him closely, and by the time the stew was finished, Mauro asked him if he would stay on and help.

Christopher didn't have to think twice about it.

He said yes.

With Mauro's assistance and advice, born of decades of experience, Christopher cared for the horses, gently, patiently, kindly, and trained them. Without complaint he repaired the weather-beaten stables, fixed broken-down fences, shoveled manure, mopped floors, chopped and stacked wood. He cooked for himself and Mauro— never anything complicated, but simple, hearty meals that suited them both. And when the time was right, he went to the *palazzo* where the present Duke of Falconieri dwelled, just outside Perugia, and persuaded him to come see the della Valle horses once more; in due course the Duke did, and left having gladly purchased four of the horses.

There was money again, and the promise of prosperity once more.

Christopher had never worked so hard in his life.

Never had he been happier.

Too, Mauro wasn't one to heap on superficial compliments, but his occasional and well-chosen words of praise meant more to Christopher than any easy flattery, for he knew he had earned them. *Deserved* them.

Whitehaven, England
Autumn 1817

Home again!

And oh, how wonderful to be back.

Beloved faces, familiar things.

Gwendolyn had been gone for nearly two years—two very interesting and enjoyable years during which, in the delightful company of the Marksons, not a single whiff of danger threatened (slightly to her disappointment), and even the inevitable discomforts of travel were, thanks to Mr. Markson's careful planning, minimal.

She arrived in a joyful flurry of sketchbooks and art prints as well as an avalanche of little, carefully chosen gifts for family, friends, and servants. Goodness, so much had changed since she'd left! She had heard the news through the affectionate correspondence which had been a constant feature of her life while abroad, but it was one thing to read about things in letters, she thought, and quite another to witness them with her own eyes.

Katherine had had her babies—yes, *babies*, and,

moreover, identical twins!—and now, with winter on the way, Cordelia and Rosalind were fast approaching their second birthday. They were both plump and cherubically beautiful, with curly dark hair and big, dark eyes sparkling with fun. They had let Gwendolyn kiss them right away, the darlings. How splendid, how glorious, to be an aunt!

And Katherine had done more than have babies.

Already the author of two successful books, she'd had two more published, one of them a second volume in what had become a series about British maritime history; the other was a bold, spirited defense of the novel as a suitable literary form not just for men but for women, too—both to read and to write—which had sparked a tremendous wave of responses, negative *and* positive. The negative ones, Katherine had wryly written to Gwendolyn, only served as a catalyst to further book-sales, and quite a few fellow authors whom she admired had said nice things about it so, on the whole, she was satisfied with its reception. She was, she added, working on a new book.

A novel.

Percy had at last fulfilled a long-held ambition and with Hugo's assistance had purchased his commission, gaining a coveted spot as a lieutenant in the elite Royal Horse Guards. Despite his disappointment at having missed by months the tail end of the Army's occupation in France, he accepted with reasonable equanimity his less exotic post at Windsor Palace—it providing him, most conveniently, an ample amount of free time in which to enjoy the many and varietous pleasures of London.

His twin Francis, meanwhile, was now happily established at Oxford, while Bertram, likewise sanguine, was in his final year at Eton and looking forward to joining his elder brother at Oxford next year.

It was a bit of a shock, Gwendolyn thought, to peep into their neat, quiet bedrooms at home and to realize that her little brothers were now out in the world, each making his own way.

Next door, there was another sort of shock: the Becks' house was empty, Mr. Beck having moved with Diana to Nottingham where he had a large nexus of business interests. Within months of his arrival, he had married again; with similar speed Diana had gotten married also, to an ambitious young barrister. Diana wrote infrequently, but often enough for Gwendolyn to learn that no word had come from Christopher and that Mr. Beck never even mentioned his son's name. Still, he hadn't sold their Whitehaven house, and left nailed on its front door a placard, his Nottingham address carefully painted on in small neat letters.

Gwendolyn went to look at the placard.

A cold, sharp wind, pungent and damp from the nearby ocean, whipped at the hems of her gown and pelisse, and she crossed her arms tightly against her chest to warm herself. Her eyes were fixed on the neat little letters, but into her mind had come a memory—a painting by Diego Rodríguez de Silva y Velázquez which she had seen in Madrid. Its subject was a striking young nobleman, dark-haired and dark-eyed, very proud and aloof in his black doublet, his neck and face set off by a small white pleated ruff and the strong, rather eerie shaft of light with which the painter had illuminated them. All else was shadows, black and deep, dark blue.

In the silent gallery at the Museo Nacional del Prado she had stood before the portrait, unmoving, until Mrs. Markson, who had unawares come to stand next to her, said in her soft, pleasant way:

"What marvelous technique."

Gwendolyn had jumped. "Yes," she answered, then added, gesturing at the proud young nobleman, "He reminds me of someone I know."

"A friend, my dear?"

"Yes—well—I *think* so. Somebody from back home."

A more forceful person might have commented upon the ambiguity of Gwendolyn's reply, but Mrs. Markson only said mildly, "I see." And together they went on to Bartolomé Esteban Murillo's portrait of Saint Isidore of Sevilla, which, they both agreed, made them think that the famous saint would be a perfectly delightful person with whom to sit at dinner and enjoy a long, confidential chat.

Now, staring at the placard, Gwendolyn's thoughts turned to Christopher's father Mr. Beck. He had always seemed very pleasant, and generous too, yet he was also capable of shouting harshly at his son, according to Diana, and holding on to what struck Gwendolyn as a deep-seated anger.

People were complicated, she thought. How could one get to know another person—*really* know them?

All at once she realized she was shivering in the cold and, still with her arms crossed against her chest, turned away and swiftly went home, glad to step into its familiar light and warmth.

Some two years after Christopher's fateful brawl in the horse-ring, a nephew of Mauro's, having served under Marshal Suchet in Spain and thought to have been killed in the siege of Tarragona, arrived unexpectedly on the doorstep of the della Valle house, thin, careworn, but alive. He was greeted with tears of joy by his uncle, who suddenly looked twenty years younger. Tommaso, Christopher saw, was more than willing to stay on and work with Mauro, and before too many days had passed he went to Mauro who stood on the wide front loggia looking out over the spacious pasture where the horses—including two new ponies—were enclosed.

"*Buongiorno, maestro*," said Christopher, coming to stand next to him.

"*Buongiorno*, Cristoforo. What do you think of our little Frieslands?"

"Very promising."

"*Sì*. I believe so also."

They stood in silence for a few minutes. With a heightened awareness Christopher took in the beauty of the Italian countryside on a crisp cold morning: the rolling green-brown hills, the sleeping orchards, a soft yellow winter sun overhead. Finally he said:

"*Maestro*, it's time for me to go."

Mauro looked at him. "You need not. You know that, don't you?"

He smiled a little. "Thank you for your generosity, but—this is Tommaso's time now."

There was another silence.

Mauro said, "Where will you go, Cristoforo?"

"Back to England."

"And what will you do there?"

"I don't know."

Mauro nodded. "Perhaps you'll marry, and settle down."

"Good Lord, *maestro*, who would have me?"

"You underrate yourself, Cristoforo." Mauro looked at him contemplatively. Then: "You have changed a great deal since we first met."

"God, I hope so." Christopher laughed.

"You were *uno selvaggio*—a wild one. Like that chestnut you saved."

"I think it was the chestnut that saved me, *maestro*."

"Perhaps. You saved *me*, Cristoforo. From despair, and worse."

"And you took me in. Thank you for that. Well—" Christopher felt within himself a sadness, but also, now, a rising eagerness to begin what came next. "I'll go pack."

Within minutes his old valise was filled with his few possessions. He went to see the horses one last time, then he shook hands, heartily, with Tommaso and embraced Mauro, who tried to press on him some money. This Christopher refused without hesitation. "I'll work for my passage. I'll go the same way I came, *maestro*."

And then he was gone.

Whitehaven, England
February 1818

The family was gathered, as it always did after supper, in the library, where a warm fire crackled cheerfully in the big old hearth. On Hugo's lap was little Rosalind, who was examining with intense concentration a small carved wood bear Gwendolyn had given her, and next to them on the sofa, snugged up close, was Katherine, who had leaned her head against Hugo's shoulder and closed her eyes.

Gwendolyn, sitting on the hearthrug with Cordelia and playing pat-a-cakes with her, paused for a moment to look closely at Katherine, noticing—not for the first time— how pale and wan she appeared. Mama did too, Gwendolyn thought, turning her gaze to where her mother sat in her chair sewing a rent in one of Hugo's shirts, though not with her usual energy.

It had been a hard winter for more than one member

of the family. Aunt Claudia and Grandpapa had been laid low with the influenza, as had the maidservant Eliza here at home, and then the little twins had gotten sick too, altogether leading to several weeks of anxious nursing, both at home and at the parsonage where Grandpapa and the aunts lived. Gwendolyn had pitched in heedless of any risk to herself, and so had the kind Mrs. Studdart, but it had clearly taken its toll on both Mama and Katherine.

And here it was, nearly March.

Gwendolyn had something to say on the subject and was dreading it. She hated disappointing people she loved, but she knew it was the right thing to say and do. When should she tell them?

"Pat, pat," demanded little Cordelia, and Gwendolyn, setting aside her pensive thoughts for the moment, at once obliged. And then Cook, immaculate in a neat gray gown and blindingly white ruffled cap, came into the library in her slow magisterial manner, in her hands a large tray.

"Sandwiches, stewed pears, and fresh-made ginger biscuits," she announced, and put the tray down on the low table near the sofa where Hugo, Katherine, and little Rosalind were ensconced. "Do have some, madam, Mrs. Katherine," she added, sternly eyeing them both. "Eliza says neither of you but barely touched your dinners."

"Oh, thank you, Cook," said Mama, looking guilty, "what a delightful-looking tea. Dinner *was* delicious. It's just that I haven't much appetite lately."

"I know that, madam, don't think I haven't seen it. And I won't have you going off into a decline. Mr. Hugo, you see that your good ladies *eat*."

"Don't worry, Cook, I'll bully them into it," promised Hugo, "ruthlessly," and Cook nodded, satisfied.

"Letters came," she said. "They're next to the biscuits."

With the same stately pace Cook departed, and Gwendolyn did the honors of the tea tray, handing round the letters as well. There were several for Katherine, one for Mama, and one for herself. She looked at it, puzzled; she didn't recognize the large looped handwriting. But she put off opening it and instead shared a ham sandwich, some biscuits, and tea with Cordelia who ate and drank with a relish suitable to a person twice her size.

"Mama, what is it?" said Hugo, sharp concern in his voice. "What's wrong? Is it Francis, or Percy? Bertram?"

Quickly Gwendolyn looked up at Mama, who held her letter, opened, in her hand and was silently weeping.

"No, no," she answered shakily, and pulled a little wisp of a handkerchief from her reticule with which she mopped rather ineffectually at her face. "It's not that, Hugo darling. It's just that—I'm so *relieved*!"

"Relieved, Mama?" asked Gwendolyn. "What about?"

"Oh, Gwennie, I'm relieved about you, dearest."

"Me? What do you mean, Mama?"

Her mother wiped her eyes again, and took a long restorative sip of tea. "It's about your Season. I know you've been looking forward to it ever since you came home, and so was I, and dear Katherine as well, but when everybody fell ill . . ."

"I've been wanting to talk with you about my Season, Mama." Gwendolyn took a deep breath, then went on: "I feel dreadful about letting you and Katherine down—and I hope you don't think I'm being impertinent—but I just don't think either of you are quite well enough to go to London this spring. I'm worried it would be, well, exhausting for you. So I propose we postpone it for a year."

"I'd hate for you to have to do that, Gwennie," said Katherine, looking remorseful.

"I don't mind," answered Gwendolyn stoutly. "Truly I don't."

"But that's just it, Gwennie darling," said Mama. "You *can* go. If you like." She held up her letter. "This is from the Duchess of Egremont."

"Cousin Judith? She was in London, you know, when Hugo and I were there, not long after we were married," Katherine said. "She's a good soul."

"Yes, and a better judge of horseflesh I never saw," added Hugo. "What does she say, Mama?"

"She writes to invite Gwennie and me to stay with them in Grosvenor Square for the Season. Isn't that so kind, and so fortuitous? She's bringing her granddaughter Helen, who, she says, is absolutely longing to meet you, Gwennie."

Gwendolyn had been listening wide-eyed. First a letter from their relation Henrietta Penhallow two years ago had brought with it marvelous opportunity, and now this from the Duchess of Egremont. Manna from heaven indeed! She said, buoyant:

"Well, I like this! Helen's a sort of cousin to me, isn't she, Mama?"

"Not strictly by blood, dearest, but through family connection, yes."

"Even after six years, I'm *still* trying to figure out the various Penhallow lines," said Katherine with a laugh. "Cousin Judith had a brother who married Henrietta Penhallow, and Henrietta's a cousin to *you*, Mama, is that right?"

"Through my marriage, yes, Katherine dear."

"I've called her 'Aunt Henrietta' my whole life," said Hugo, "which somehow seems more appropriate given she's so much older than me. She must be nearly eighty, I daresay. And yet Judith, who's just about the same age, is 'Cousin Judith.' I suppose it's because Aunt Henrietta's such a towering figure in the family."

Katherine laughed again. "She certainly is. How badly she frightened me when we first met! Is there more to your letter, Mama?"

"Yes, Judith also says that her grandson Owen has agreed to come to London, to get a little Town polish, and also to support Helen, for at least part of the Season." Mama's eyes were shining as she added, "According to Judith, Owen has persuaded Francis to come too. Isn't it lovely they're at university together, and still just as good friends as ever they were at Eton? Oh, and here's the postscript—it made me feel as if the weight of the world had lifted! Judith says that she herself loathes London, and if I feel the same way, I needn't come—especially as her daughter-in-law Lady Almira, Helen and Owen's mother, will naturally accompany them." Mama looked up and over at Gwendolyn, her brow crinkling again. "Are you absolutely certain you won't mind going without us, Gwennie darling?"

Gwendolyn nodded vigorously. "I'm positive, Mama. It'll be an adventure! I'll miss you, of course, but Francis and Percy will be there."

"That's a comfort, to be sure. I've been so afraid to tell you that I simply wasn't up to going to London."

"I have, too," admitted Katherine. "And I don't care to leave the girls, either. I know they're fine now, and I did so want to be a part of your Season, Gwennie, but I really couldn't enjoy myself, I'm afraid."

"Well, it's all settled then," Gwendolyn said cheerfully, and gave a bit of her sandwich to Señor Rodrigo, who had been staring at her expectantly from where he perched nearby on the arm of a sofa. "Now we can really and truly *plan*! I shall dance every single dance there is to be had, go to all the galleries, and ride every day in the Park. And I *must* visit Carlton House, where I shall be suitably impressed by its staggering magnificence."

Next she gave some of the sandwich to Cordelia, and went on, further illuminating this delightful vision of herself:

"I'll crane upwards at all the ceilings, just like the provincial that I am, and go up and down the main staircase at least twice, pretending I'm a princess in disguise. I daresay I'll bump into the Prince Regent, too. Do you think it's true that he wears a corset, and creaks when he walks about? Oh, goodness, I hope I don't giggle. That would be *fatal*. Also, of course, I'm going to meet my one true love."

"Come about, matey," loudly uttered Señor Rodrigo, and little Cordelia immediately said:

"Comma boot, mitey."

Everyone laughed, Cordelia proudly repeated herself, and suddenly Gwendolyn remembered the mysterious letter which had come for her; she picked it up from the low table where she had left it, opened it, and looked to the signature. "Why, it's from Helen FitzClarence." The letter was brief; the handwriting was poorly formed and there were several misspellings, but the tone was warm and eager. Helen reiterated her grandmother's invitation and begged Gwendolyn to say yes.

Do come, I know we shall be the Best of freinds, Cousin Gwendalynn.

As Gwendolyn looked down at the childish handwriting, a memory flickered. Several years ago, Francis and Percy had gone on school holidays to stay with Owen FitzClarence at his home in Northamptonshire, where they had met Owen's sister Helen.

What had they written home about the visits? Oh yes, horses and riding and steeple-chasing, and Percy saying that Helen was a superb rider, and Francis complaining about Helen hanging about bothering them and trying to pinch him. How long ago that seemed! Gwendolyn wondered if Helen would even remember Percy and Francis after all this time.

"Papa, eat," said Rosalind, generously attempting to insert her little wooden bear into Hugo's mouth. He pretended to chew on it, enchanting his fascinated offspring, and then beguiled her with a ginger biscuit, this simple distraction allowing him to pass round the plate again to both Katherine and Mama, looking at them with such innocent supplication—this being his version of ruthless bullying—that they couldn't help but laugh and each take a biscuit, thus neatly and collectively averting the dread possibility of Cook's wrath.

Chapter 3

London, England
May 1818

It was some two weeks after a notice had appeared in the *Gazette* announcing the betrothal of Miss Gwendolyn Penhallow and the Earl of Westenbury that, on a cloudy spring morning, two men, former neighbors in Whitehaven, met by chance in Hoare's Bank.

Christopher had just stepped into the high vaulted interior but abruptly checked when he was hailed by a friendly voice:

"I say, Christopher! Christopher Beck!"

A very tall young man with bright gold hair and vivid blue eyes, and clad in the distinctive black and scarlet uniform of the Royal Horse Guards, came toward him at a rapid clip and held out his hand.

Christopher stared and shook the hand extended to him, recognition coming after a stunned moment. Good Lord, one of the Penhallow twins! Not Francis—the other, the Army-mad one, of course. He said with a sudden rush of gladness at seeing someone he knew: "Percy! How do you do?"

"Lieutenant Penhallow, at your service," replied Percy, whipping off his tall hat, a dark blue bicorne dashingly embellished with gold ribbon, and gave a deep mock-bow. He straightened, grinning, and with military precision tucked his hat under his arm. "I say, it's been ages since we've seen each other! What the devil happened to you? You look like hell, if you don't mind my saying so."

"Pirates," said Christopher, briefly. "Just off the coast of Portugal." There was no point in mentioning just how bad three of the pirates looked after *he* got through with them. All that brawling at university and elsewhere had, apparently, proved useful.

"Pirates! How *ripping*. Aren't you the lucky one. Well, I daresay those stitches will heal well enough," said Percy cheerfully. "Gives you a wonderfully Gothic appearance. The ladies'll swan over you like anything. Speaking of which, come to a party tonight and liven it up, won't you? Bound to be a dreadfully staid affair, thrown by a relation of mine, the Duchess of Egremont. Frank—my brother Francis, you know—is due to arrive today and show up there as well—he'll be delighted to see you, of course— and my cousin Owen, too. A splendid fellow, I assure you. But bear in mind, if you want something strongish to drink, have it before we get there. That's what I'm doing, at any rate."

Christopher hadn't planned on staying in London. He'd arrived at dawn and thought he'd stay on just long enough to visit his bankers and go . . . somewhere. But now he found himself saying:

"Thanks. I'd like to come. If you're sure the Duchess won't mind?"

"Not a bit of it. She's a brick—not at all high in the instep. Come by the Windsor barracks around seven or so—I'll tell 'em you're expected—we'll have dinner and go on to Grosvenor Square together. Well, must dash—off to White's, to settle a bit of a faro debt, and then over to Berkeley Square, to visit a lady-friend." Percy laughed. "By Jupiter, we've all grown up, haven't we? It's awfully jolly being my own man, I must say. Ah—a word of advice, if you're going on the Town. Stick with the married women, the unmarried ones would as soon clamp the old ball-and-chain on you as look at you. See you later on, then."

He hurried away, and more slowly, Christopher proceeded into Hoare's. When he emerged an hour later, he was considerably plumper in the pocket—pleasant evidence that he had, at long last, come into his fortune. Bless old Uncle Dan, the mysterious, much-maligned eccentric of his mother's family, who had shocked them all by secretly making a great deal of money as a supplier to the British Navy and then leaving it all to his nephew Christopher, then ten years old, following the untimely death of his sister—Christopher's mother—whom he followed to the grave in quick succession.

Bless them both, he thought. Would they be proud of the person he'd become? He hoped so. He was far from perfect, he was still restless, his life's course as yet unknown—but he had come a long way, both literally and figuratively, from the rough-spoken, intractably sullen youth he'd once been.

Christopher paused on the busy sidewalk of Fleet Street. All around him people went to and fro; the street was filled with carts and carriages, riders on horseback, the occasional two-wheeled velocipede barreling past and pedestrians crossing the street whether with reckless speed or due caution. It was noisy and crowded, the air was damp and a little dank, heavy gray rainclouds loomed overhead, and suddenly he broke again into a smile.

Jolly old England.

It was good to be back.

He thought, now, about the evening ahead. A party hosted by a duchess, and no doubt attended by the *crème de la crème* of Society. He pictured himself back at Mauro's only a few months ago, his boots ankle-deep in horse manure and his hair likely strewn with hay. *You're flying high, lad*, he thought to himself, amused, recalling his hostile and unruly schoolboy days among the British elite. *Back among the nobs, eh? Try not to pick any fights or otherwise embarrass yourself.*

Well, if he was going to be traveling in elevated circles again, he'd need some proper clothes. Lodgings, too. But—most pressingly—something to eat. He was hungry. He wanted eggs, kidneys, chops, liver. India tea, scalding hot, pungent and familiar.

Still smiling, Christopher went off in search of breakfast.

Gwendolyn took a last quick look at her reflection in her bedchamber mirror, happy that this new gown—made of simple white crepe over a white satin slip—had arrived in time for the evening-party the Duchess had organized to celebrate her engagement to the Earl. Her hair was gathered high at the back of her head *à la Grecque*, with soft strands let free to fall about her ears and frame her face.

She suddenly remembered the illustration in *La Belle Assemblée* over which Diana had sighed, three years or so ago, and smiled. How shockingly underdressed she was in comparison to that fashionable lady! No gauzy silk headdress or low-set wreath of glittering brilliants on her head; only a simple garland of tiny pink roses. And rather than exposing a good portion of her slip, the hem of her gown lay demurely above her white satin slippers, no ribbons dangled from her bodice, and her only ornament was the beautiful pearl ring the Earl had given her.

"Thank you, Lizzie," she said to her maid, who placed about her shoulders a soft shawl of fine white net silk, and then she went with a light step downstairs—feeling as if she could float with happiness—and into the big drawing-room where their guests would shortly be assembling. Soon she'd be seeing her love! She could hardly wait.

Gwendolyn paused just past the threshold. Helen stood by one of the windows and Gwendolyn was struck by what a delightful picture she made, with her red hair blazing in the bright luminescence of the many candelabra, and her heart-shaped face, with its charming riot of freckles and *retroussé* nose, in stark profile as she gazed out the window.

She said, sincerely, "How pretty you look, Helen!"

Helen started and half-turned away from the window. "Oh! I didn't hear you come in," she said in her gruff little voice. "I was—I was checking—to see if it was raining, you know."

"Is it? I hope not." Gwendolyn went to stand next to Helen, and peered outside.

"No. At least, I don't think so." Suddenly Helen gripped Gwendolyn's hand in hers. "I'm *so* looking forward to the party!"

"Are you? I'm so glad. I don't think I've heard you say that about *any* event we've attended."

"This is different."

"Different how?"

"Because—because—" Helen flushed a vivid scarlet. "Those other events were rubbish. Oh, how pretty *you* look!" She squeezed Gwendolyn's hand. "I say, I'm terribly glad you came to London! I was sure we'd be the best of friends."

Gwendolyn smiled, hoping that would suffice as a cordial, if not entirely reciprocal, response. Even after living under the same roof for several weeks, Helen was rather a puzzle to her. She was relentless in her compliments and listened with an appearance of fascinated attention to whatever Gwendolyn said, even the most banal remarks; when Gwendolyn picked up a book and settled in for an hour's happy diversion, Helen did as well (though it didn't seem as if she were turning any pages). If Gwendolyn didn't care for a particular dish at supper, neither did Helen.

Friends—in Gwendolyn's opinion—ought to be kind to each other, and honest, and *real*. Not behaving as might a courtier to a queen.

So when Helen said, "I do wish I had straight hair like you, yours is so much nicer than mine, Gwendolyn," she suppressed a quick pang of annoyance and only answered lightly:

"Well, I do admire curly hair, like yours. Lizzie keeps wanting to try the hot irons on me, but I've told her it's no use. My hair can't hold a curl for more than an hour."

"Oh, your hair is better. Such a lovely gold color! And I wish I had blue eyes like you, Gwendolyn! You're so tall too. You look just like—I mean—that is, you look so much like your brothers."

"Not *too* much like them, I hope," Gwendolyn replied, heartily disliking Helen's fawning words of comparison and wishing Helen were satisfied with her own very attractive looks, then was annoyed again when Helen nodded.

"Oh yes, you do. When do you suppose—when do you think Percy and Francis will arrive? Won't they be pleased to see what great friends we are?"

Gwendolyn was spared the necessity of thinking up a

tactful response when from behind them came a breath-less voice:

"Girls! Here I am! Right on time!" Lady Almira, Helen's mother, fluttered into the drawing-room, the fringed ends of her India silk shawl dragging on the floor behind her. "Oh, ma'am, don't the girls look *marvelous*?" she exclaimed to her mother-in-law the Duchess, who had followed her in, issuing some last-minute instructions to the butler Tyndale, and Gwendolyn took the opportunity to disengage her hand from Helen's and go toward them.

"Cousin Judith, is there anything I can do to help?"

The Duchess, tall and thin, with a kind, weather-beaten face and a great mass of thick gray hair only partially subdued beneath an unfussy silk *toque*, concluded her remarks to Tyndale with "And do remind the footmen to look after the horses," then turned to Gwendolyn and said in her brisk pleasant way, "Thank you, m'dear, but I believe all is in order. Almira, what's the matter?"

Lady Almira's wide-set brown eyes were brimming with tears. "Oh, ma'am, if only my dear departed Lionel were here! Your precious son, gone from us too soon! How *proud* he would be of his only daughter!"

"Mother, *will* you stop saying that? It's so tedious," said Helen, in her gruff little voice more than a hint of a growl. "I'm sure Gwendolyn is tired of hearing it."

"And if only my dear Philip were here as well," Lady Almira went on, referring to the son of her first marriage who, engulfed in both scandal and debt, had fled the country some five years back. "How proud he would be as well! His beloved half-sister making her London debut! I *know* he would have liked nothing better than to lend his support!" She gave a lingering sob, her shawl slipped from her shoulders and fell unnoticed to the floor, and Helen, from her place by the window, snorted audibly and said:

"Philip lend his support? Ha! He'd be asking all of us for money, Mother, you know he would!"

"Oh, my dear Helen, how *unfeeling* you are," said Lady Almira reproachfully, then, as Gwendolyn picked up her shawl and handed it to her, she brightened. "*Thank* you, Gwendolyn dear! What a lovely gown! Just like Helen's! I declare, you two look just like *twins*!"

Startled, Gwendolyn turned to look again at Helen and now realized that their two gowns were, in fact, so similar in style and fabric as to nearly be identical. Seeing Gwendolyn's eyes upon her, Helen flushed bright red again and said:

"I asked Madame Hébert to make my new gown like yours, Gwendolyn. I—I hope you don't mind?"

"Good heavens, Helen," said the Duchess to her granddaughter, "what on earth were you thinking? This is Gwendolyn's evening, not yours."

Helen hung her head. "I'm sorry," she muttered. "I'll go change."

But before she had taken a few steps, Tyndale announced the presence of the first guests, and so the moment was lost; Helen retreated to her post near the window, by an unfortunate mischance Lady Almira dropped her fan into a large vase of flowers and struggled to extricate it, and then Gwendolyn forgot all about duplicate gowns in the flurry of greeting people and, soon, in came the Earl of Westenbury, serene, unhurried, devastatingly handsome in his elegant dark evening-dress—and a smile just for her in those entrancing, deep-green eyes of his. Gwendolyn watched as from all around came the usual admiring glances sent his way; she heard the little murmurs of appreciation. Which the Earl never seemed to notice. It was another thing she loved about him.

Naturally she and Julian couldn't go a little apart for

an intimate conversation immediately, as that would have been impolite, but it seemed to Gwendolyn like years—decades—*eons* before they were finally seated together on a small sofa toward the distant end of the drawing-room.

Only a few inches separated her from Julian, and Gwendolyn was vividly aware of how much she hated those dreadful, hideous, torturing inches.

She wanted to be closer to him, wanted to slide herself over until they were side by side, body to body.

How warm Julian made her feel, with a sort of lovely tingling heat that surged through her from head to toe, an extremely pleasant sensation unlike anything else she had felt before. She had met some very interesting and attractive men while traveling under the aegis of the Marksons. She had talked and even flirted with some of those men. But none of them had sparked in her a response this powerful. This exciting. Transforming her from the ordinary, everyday Gwendolyn into a new, vibrant version of herself.

And yet . . .

And yet she was hungry for more. For an embrace. A kiss.

She found herself staring at his beautifully molded mouth, and wondered what he tasted like.

A new wave of warmth flooded her. If she were a betting woman, she'd lay odds that he would be . . . *delicious*.

Gwendolyn pulled her fan from the white satin reticule looped around her wrist, snapped it open, and began waving it vigorously in front of her face.

These were, she supposed, highly unladylike thoughts, especially in the context of a crowded drawing-room surrounded by other people. But this was how Julian made her feel, from the very first moment she met him, and why try to deny what she thought and felt?

Suddenly she thought of other places, other rooms in this vast townhouse. Many of them were empty. Why couldn't she and Julian slip away to one of them?

It would be a highly indiscreet thing to do.

Particularly as they were the guests of honor.

Gwendolyn smiled mischievously.

Why not?

Even if only for a little while.

"How beautiful you are, my dear Gwendolyn," said Julian softly. "You quite take my breath away." Leaning just a bit closer, he went on:

> *"Hear my soul speak:*
> *The very instant that I saw you did*
> *My heart fly to your service; there resides*
> *To make me slave to it . . ."*

"*The Tempest,*" said Gwendolyn instantly. Wasn't it splendid that the Earl knew his Shakespeare? And could quote it to her so romantically? She had always hoped her one true love would do that.

"Just so, my Miranda. And I your Ferdinand."

She smiled back at him and said:

> *"What I desire to give, and much less take*
> *What I shall die to want. But this is trifling,*
> *And all the more it seeks to hide itself*
> *The bigger bulk it shows. Hence, bashful cunning,*
> *And prompt me, plain and holy innocence!*
> *I am your wife if you will marry me."*

"'Ay, with a heart as willing,'" Julian answered, "'as bondage e'er of freedom. Here's my hand.'"

Only, of course, he didn't hold out his hand, as that would have been improper.

Bother propriety!

Gwendolyn thought again about an empty room somewhere, where they might do more than clasp hands. "Julian, do you think there's a copy of Shakespeare's plays in the library? Shall we go see? There's probably nobody else there."

His eyebrows went up. "Leave our own party, my darling?"

"Just for a little while," she said coaxingly. "We could be alone. We're engaged. Surely no one would mind."

He smiled. "I wouldn't. But I daresay plenty of sticklers would. And even if we tried to slip away, we couldn't— there's a gauntlet of guests between us and the door."

Gwendolyn gave a little sigh. He was right, of course. But *still*. She wanted to kiss him in the worst way, and right now, and for a long time. She found herself staring again at his mouth, made herself wrench her gaze away, but she couldn't stop looking at his eyes—his nose— his hair—and then back again to his mouth, which she wanted but couldn't have. *Stupid* propriety.

"By the way," Julian said, "I've some delightful news."

She gave herself a mental shake, telling her sulking inner self to stop it, and answered, "Oh? What is it?"

"I've just today heard from m-my mother, who's very anxious to meet you. She'll be arriving here in Town by the end of the week. She'd have come sooner, she said in her letter, had it not been for a sudden illness."

"Poor lady," said Gwendolyn with quick sympathy. "I do hope she's quite recovered."

"Oh, she never complains. Rupert's accompanying her, she says, and will be a great comfort to her on the journey."

At this mention of Julian's younger brother, Gwendolyn nodded and smiled. "I'm sure he will. I look forward to meeting them both. Which of your sisters are coming too?" For the Earl had—almost unbelievably—eight older sisters, and all of them still living at home.

"Oh, none, they're country girls, you know."

"Can't you persuade—well, *some* of them to come, Julian? I should so like to meet my sisters-to-be."

"If you wish it, I'll write to them," he said smilingly.

"Thank you! And please send them my love."

"I will," he said, and then they were interrupted when Étienne de Montmorency came strolling over, saying in his languid way:

"*Ma foi*, how wonderfully *confortable* you appear, *mes chers*. The very picture of affianced bliss. Julian, I felicitate you yet again."

The Earl smiled up at him. "Thank you, Étienne. I'm the luckiest man in England to be marrying this beautiful goddess, and I know it. I was just telling Miss Penhallow that m-my mother and Rupert are coming to Town."

De Montmorency looked at the Earl with brows slightly raised—a slow and penetrating gaze—and then his lips curled in a smile of faint amusement. "The Countess is to grace us with her presence? How delightful." He turned to Gwendolyn and bowed courteously. "A compliment to you, *mademoiselle*, without doubt."

He said it with every appearance of affability, which signified, Gwendolyn hoped, that he bore her no ill will for choosing his friend the Earl over himself: she had, in fact, been dancing with him on that fateful evening at Almack's, and by the time de Montmorency had escorted her back to the Duchess she had frankly forgotten his name. Prior to that he had presented himself, very plainly, as a candidate for her hand with flattering promptitude following her first appearance in Society. A scion of the French aristocracy, a crony of the Prince Regent, and one of the chief arbiters of fashion after Brummel's disgrace and exile, Étienne de

Montmorency traveled in the highest circles of the *ton*; he was famed for his elegance of person, his cultured address and charm. She liked him well enough, but no better than any of the other gentlemen she had met. It was only the Earl who had captured her heart.

"Thank you, *monsieur*," Gwendolyn said, just as a little stir across the room attracted her attention. Two men had entered. One was her brother Percy, she saw with gladness, and the other—

Gwendolyn stared. And gasped.

Christopher Beck paused just past the threshold of the Egremont drawing-room. A huge, elegantly furnished and brightly lit room, crowded and cheerfully noisy. As loud as any busy Greek *taverna* or *osteria* in Italy. A reassuring similarity, he thought, amusement rising in him. Well, should it happen, being cold-shouldered by aristos might be unpleasant, but it would still be better than being kicked by a horse. An experience with which he was all too familiar.

Occupied at first by being introduced to his hostess the Duchess, her daughter-in-law Lady Almira, and some elderly friends of theirs—"I say, do meet this chum of mine from home, Christopher Beck," said Percy breezily—all of whom, rather than looking down their noses at him, instead greeted him cordially, Christopher finally advanced some ten paces into the room and accepted a glass of champagne offered to him by a liveried servant.

He nodded his thanks.

No cuts direct so far, he thought, and smiled a little to himself. He wouldn't have cared if there were. Having lived for years by one's wits, as well as fighting for one's life against a pack of savage freebooters, certainly provided one with a helpful perspective on things. If nothing else, it had given him a self-confidence he had badly lacked as a youth.

Percy said, nudging him, "There's my cousin Helen over there by the window. Not an actual cousin, really, but we've never stood on ceremony. Let's go and talk to her. She's a good fellow, but rather awkward at parties. Doesn't know how to talk to people." Wielding his own glass of champagne, Percy nimbly made his way through the crowd toward a short, round, sturdy-looking girl with bright red hair who stood alone. Christopher, following more slowly in Percy's wake, saw how the girl greeted Percy with obvious relief, then he himself stopped when he heard someone—with a youthful female voice—saying:

"Christopher. *Christopher!*"

He turned and saw a young woman coming toward him.

She was breathtakingly lovely, golden-haired, blue-eyed, slim, dressed all in white and moving with what struck him as unselfconscious grace. She was smiling at him with such evident friendliness that he couldn't help but smile back.

And then it hit him.

Of *course*.

It was Gwendolyn Penhallow.

In his lively careless way Percy had failed to mention that his sister would also be attending the Duchess's party, though he had during their dinner together earlier that evening regaled Christopher with amusing barracks tales along with some suggestions as to where they might go after leaving the Egremont townhouse.

Christopher took another swallow of his champagne and put the glass onto the tray of a passing servant.

The last time he'd seen Gwendolyn, it was back in Whitehaven and he had been little more than a rude, restless, hostile boy—angry and lost. He had left England the very next day and, every once in a while, when his spirits had sunk very low, he'd thought back to that moment, years ago, when she had taken his hand in hers, and with such kind sweetness that he had been rather paralyzed. And here she was, graceful, radiant, coming close, holding out her gloved hands to him, saying warmly:

"Christopher! You're *alive!*"

"As you see," he said, smiling down at her, and, recalling her sweet gesture all over again, he took her hands in his own, as if it were the most natural thing in all the world.

"I'm so glad! How long it's been! But—are you all right? Your cheek—"

"Oh, a few pirates, on the way from Portugal" was all he said, because it was easier to be honest than to make up some story or another, and he was surprised when the poised, elegantly clad young woman before him—rather than recoiling with horror or distaste, as he supposed well-bred ladies might—instantly replied:

"Pirates! How *splendid*, Christopher!"

He laughed. "How bloodthirsty you Penhallows are. Percy said much the same thing."

Gwendolyn laughed too. "When I was fourteen I so much wanted to be a pirate, do you remember? Or at least a sailor. Hugo gave me a hat that looked like an admiral's bicorne and oh, how I swaggered about in it!"

"I remember seeing you in that hat. You looked very dashing in it, as I recall."

"I felt so, at any rate." Then Gwendolyn squeezed his hands, sobering. "But Christopher, are you really all right? Perhaps it was dreadful fighting pirates, and you were badly wounded and nearly made to walk the plank . . . *Was* there a plank? I've always supposed pirates all have planks, but how could one know for sure?"

Christopher laughed again. "No, there wasn't a plank. Not a single peg-leg or eye-patch among the lot, or even a mention of buried treasure. I'm afraid you would have found it an entirely dispiriting affair."

Her vivid blue eyes were fixed on his face. "Dispiriting? It sounds very exciting! Did it hurt a great deal? The wound on your face?"

"It wasn't so bad. The cook, as it turns out, had a little experience as a surgeon during the war, and stitched me up straightaway."

"He did a marvelous job, I think."

"I'm glad you think so. Percy says I look Gothic. Whatever that means."

Gwendolyn giggled, an infectiously charming sound between a chuckle and a laugh. "I suppose he means that with your intriguing wound and your long hair, you look like a character in one of those eerie stories—*you* know, with mysterious castles, ghosts clanking chains about, fog-covered moors, helpless heroines fleeing unutterable evil, enigmatic brooding heroes . . . All you need is a swirling cape, Christopher! *Very* romantic."

He grimaced. "Oh God, no. I'll crop my hair tomorrow, if that will help."

"No, don't. It suits you. Oh, I can't wait till Francis gets here—he'll be so pleased to see you again!"

"Likewise," he said, glad to his soul that the old resentments had faded away over the years. "Are any other of your family here?"

"No, just Percy and Francis," Gwendolyn answered, and began to animatedly tell him about how Hugo and Katherine and everyone else at home was doing, but soon her bright cheerful flow of words was abruptly stemmed by a deep, pleasant voice which said:

"My dear Gwendolyn, introduce me, please, to your friend."

Christopher watched as Gwendolyn's face lit up again, rendering her yet more lovely, and quickly she turned her head to look up into the face of the tall man, whose age he guessed to be thirty-five or so, who had come to join them. Christopher was no judge of masculine good looks, but here was, plainly, a female's *beau ideal*, and, he thought, someone Gwendolyn admired very much. He suddenly realized that he still held her hands in his, and released them. She smiled at him and then at the other man.

"Oh, Julian, I've been prattling on, for here indeed is someone from home, whom I haven't seen in *forever*! May I introduce to you Mr. Christopher Beck? And Christopher, this is the Earl of Westenbury—my fiancé."

Christopher was surprised all over again—Gwendolyn *engaged*?—but it took only the briefest moment of introspection to move beyond his surprise. Why not? She was all grown up and no longer the giddy fourteen-year-old girl who had so audaciously, so fancifully, proposed marriage to him. Her joy was obvious, almost like a visible nimbus around her. Good for her, he thought, to have found someone who makes her so happy. He smiled and held out his hand to the Earl. "How do you do, sir," he said, and then, looking between them: "My congratulations to you both."

He and the Earl shook hands and Gwendolyn said, "Thank you, Christopher," and to the Earl she went on, "Only think, Julian, Christopher's been fighting *pirates*. Isn't that marvelous?"

"Indeed," said the Earl, in that deep pleasant voice. "A particular ambition of mine in my long-ago youth. Alas, I never fulfilled it, and now I indulge in the tamer sport of boxing. Do you box, Mr. Beck?"

Christopher wanted to laugh. Excellent—high-society brawling, even for men long past the university age! But he answered politely, "I have, sir, but only in a manner of speaking."

"Perhaps you'll join me at Jackson's Saloon sometime."

"Thank you, sir, that's kind of you."

Gwendolyn looked pleased. "You'll be in London for a while, Christopher?"

He said, "I believe so," and Gwendolyn said, "I'm so glad," and he was amazed by how glad he felt, too. If he hadn't happened to bump into Percy this morning . . .

"I say, Gwennie, what about a jaunt to Richmond Park tomorrow?" It was Percy himself, with the short red-headed young woman—his sort-of cousin Helen—at his side. "Helen and I are longing for a good gallop somewhere. Oh, hullo, Westenbury." Adroitly Percy plucked from a passing servant's tray a new glass of champagne and deposited his empty one.

"Oh yes, let's," agreed Gwendolyn, "if Cousin Judith will chaperone us," then exclaimed, "Francis is here, and Owen!" She waved, and it wasn't long before Francis— just as tall as his brother, with the same blue eyes and golden hair—joined them, along with Owen FitzClarence, the Marquis of Ellington, who had the same distinctively red hair as that of his sister Helen, as well as a similar riot of freckles upon his long, pale face; where Helen was short and rounded, Owen was taller and skeletally thin.

Amidst the volley of cheerful greetings and introductions, no one noticed that Helen, standing quietly between Percy and Gwendolyn, was looking up at Francis as if he entirely filled her vision. Francis himself was oblivious to this as he was meeting his sister's fiancé for the first time and shaking his hand; when his glance fell upon the red-haired young lady in the pretty white gown he had to be reminded by a waggish Percy as to her identity.

"Of course now I remember you, Lady Helen," said Francis. "From our visits to your estate several years ago." Like Percy, Francis was plainly a schoolboy no longer; he had about him a new air of reserve and gravity. In itself that might suffice for the observant to distinguish him from his livelier twin, but for others it perhaps helped that Francis's hair was longer.

"Oh, don't call me 'Lady,'" said Helen, "it sounds so stuffy," and then flushed very red.

"He's practicing to be one of those elevated scholarly parsons," Percy remarked, "so there you are."

Francis only smiled at his brother, and Gwendolyn said:

"Don't be ridiculous, Percy! Not all parsons are stuffy. And I think it's wonderful that Francis is going to be a vicar like Grandpapa—who's not the tiniest bit stuffy, as you well know!"

Percy laughed and put up a hand. "Cry peace, dear sister! It was said in jest. Although I do think Frank ought to spend a little more time with people, and a little less with his head in a book. It's not healthy."

"*I* think reading is a marvelous thing," said Helen. "I do it as often as I can."

Onto Gwendolyn's face came a brief expression of surprise, but she said nothing. The talk turned to tomorrow's outing, and Percy went over to the Duchess, neatly detached her from the little group of acquaintances with whom she was conversing, and brought her back to their own group as would a triumphant collector present his prize specimen.

"Cousin Judith says yes," he announced, and when a slim pale-haired man of medium height and an appearance of supreme modish elegance joined them, introduced all round by the Earl as his longtime friend Étienne de Montmorency, he was invited also; he graciously accepted, and thus their party for tomorrow was declared complete.

Chapter 4

The sun shone warmly down upon the little expedition to Richmond. There had been, after all, a last-minute addition to their numbers: Lady Almira, scandalized by the idea of the Duchess overseeing such a large group of young people, had insisted on coming along, undeterred by Helen blurting out at the breakfast table:

"Oh, Mother, *don't*! You know you hate riding."

"Nonsense!" said Lady Almira, airily waving her hand in a dismissive gesture and accidentally knocking over the silver toast rack near her plate. "Oh, dear, I *am* so sorry," she said to the footman who had immediately come to set things aright, and to Helen she went on, in a tone of virtuous conviction, "*Nothing* you can say will dissuade me! I know my duty!"

Helen rolled her eyes and said across the table to her brother, "Can't *you* talk some sense into her?"

Owen, having left last night's party with Percy and Christopher and decamped to parts unknown, was this morning decidedly wan and even paler than usual. He was staring down at the plate his mother had filled for him with something that looked like revulsion, and when Helen addressed him he only shrugged, his listless neutrality on the subject making her scowl at him.

The Duchess said, "That's quite enough, Helen. Although," she added fair-mindedly, "it's true, Almira, that you're not much of a rider."

Lady Almira's face drooped as might that of a child being harshly criticized. "Oh, ma'am, I only wished to be a *help*. Do let me join you. Please!"

"Now, now, don't cry," said the Duchess hastily. "There's a pretty little mare in the stables, very docile, just the thing for you."

Instantly Lady Almira brightened, and Helen began to roll her eyes again but checked herself as Francis just then came into the breakfast-room. He apologized to the Duchess for his lateness and explained that he had been deep into Milton's treatise on the Reformation and so had lost track of time.

"How *fascinating*," said Helen in a rather loud voice. "Do try one of those muffins, Gwendolyn and I think they're very good."

Francis nodded and went over to the sideboard, Helen following his tall form with her eyes and Gwendolyn wondering if she wanted to make sure he took a muffin. Which he didn't, and returned to the table to eat his breakfast in peaceful self-contained silence, no doubt with his mind still fixed on the absorbing intricacies of the Reformation.

Now, as the group of riders made its way in a leisurely fashion along the Kingston Road, Gwendolyn, her horse side by side with the Earl's, lifted her face to the sun and wondered if life could possibly be any better than this.

"Julian," she said on a sudden impulse, "let's get married very soon."

He looked over at her and smiled, and her heart gave a huge happy leap within her breast. He answered: "A splendid idea."

"Oh, hurray! I'm so glad you agree."

"I do, my darling. But—can we?"

"Why not? What would stop us?"

"I imagine it takes a while to plan a wedding at St. George's."

"St. George's? Oh, Julian, I was thinking that my grandfather could perform the ceremony in his church back home in Whitehaven."

The Earl looked surprised. "I was assuming you'd prefer a wedding here in Town, with the usual breakfast to follow. Prinny wants to attend, you know, he told me so last week at a *levée*. He's hoping, by the way, you'll attend his next *fête* at Carlton House. He's having the cards of invitation sent to the Duchess."

"Well, that's very nice," said Gwendolyn, thinking suddenly about the fabled creaking corset and repressing an immature impulse to giggle.

"Nice?" He looked at her quizzically. "My darling girl, it's rather in the nature of a signal honor."

"Oh yes, to be sure," Gwendolyn answered, but stuck to her point. "Julian, I care more about Grandpapa than about the Prince Regent. It would mean so much to me to have him perform the ceremony."

"Would it, my darling? Then let's do that, then."

She beamed at him. "Thank you! You've made me very happy."

"That," he said, "is my sole aim in life," and he looked so handsome as he smiled back that Gwendolyn wished they could get married tomorrow.

"Here again," said Étienne de Montmorency, drawing his horse up alongside the Earl's, "the two of you positively radiate *le bonheur*. As the poets say, you shine like candles in a dreary world."

"My dear Étienne," said the Earl, "even after all these years of friendship, I had no idea you were poetical."

Étienne de Montmorency bowed slightly in his saddle.

"You wound me, *mon ami*, as I am, *en fait*, interested in poetry along with a great many other things. By way of example, I wonder with sorrow in my heart why last week I felt obliged to bet a hundred guineas on a horse so plainly afflicted with spavin. I muse to myself, should Weston or Meyer create my next jacket? Too, I observe that some of the young gentlemen of *notre groupe* have on their faces the look of one who has recently consumed *trop d'alcool*, and also that *la chère* Lady Almira may fall off that plodding little mount of hers at any moment. And—" Here he looked directly at Gwendolyn. "I find myself a little curious, *mademoiselle*, about your friend Mr. Beck. He has not, I think, appeared previously in Society?"

"I don't believe so."

Étienne de Montmorency nodded as if in confirmation. "He has, just a trifle, a—how shall I put it?—a raw quality."

"What does *that* mean?" Gwendolyn said, rather sharply.

"I have offended you, I perceive. Do forgive me."

The Earl looked between them. "Come now, don't let's quarrel. Disagreements quite take the zest out of life, don't you think? Mr. Beck is an old friend of Gwendolyn's, that's all there is to it."

"Yes. That's all there is to it." Gwendolyn was emphatic. "Thank you, Julian."

"He is, of course, a gentleman," the Earl went on, now addressing de Montmorency. "He's quite self-assured and speaks so well. Don't you agree?"

"*Mais oui*," answered de Montmorency, with, however, just the faintest edge of cynicism in his voice, and so the Earl turned to Gwendolyn, a hint of doubt now in his gold-flecked eyes, and said:

"He is, isn't he, my darling?"

Gwendolyn felt her fingers tightening on the reins she had, heretofore, been holding loosely. "Oh, Julian, you're not going to be absurdly snobbish, are you? Christopher's father is perfectly respectable, I assure you."

"Not a gentleman, *eh bien*," said de Montmorency softly.

"He's a very successful man of business," Gwendolyn said, annoyed, the more so when de Montmorency lifted his shoulders and murmured:

"Trade."

In that one little word nothing but disdain.

"My brother Hugo," she said pointedly, "engages in trade, in case you weren't aware, *monsieur*. He's a ship-builder. And the whole family couldn't be prouder of him."

"*Oui*, that is so," replied de Montmorency, "but such is the esteem in which your family is held, *mademoiselle*, a Penhallow might be employed as a boot-black and remain firmly on its illustrious pedestal."

"I really don't see the difference, and besides—"

"What about Mr. Beck's mother?" intervened the Earl, looking between them in a rather troubled way.

"I don't know anything about her. She died a long time ago. The only other thing I know about Christopher's family is that his uncle left him a great fortune."

"Well, that's a help then," said the Earl more cheerfully. "Money compensates for a great many sins in this wicked world, doesn't it? And he seems like quite a nice fellow. A bit raffish in his appearance, but perhaps, should the occasion arise, I might drop a hint as to how his man could correct that."

Gwendolyn stared at him. She knew he meant well, but . . .

The Earl went on, "I remember what it was like when I first came to Town—how green I was. Lord, Étienne, but you saved me from many a gaffe."

De Montmorency smiled. "One endeavors to pass on what little wisdom one has acquired. If I can be of any assistance to Mr. Beck, *mademoiselle*, be assured that I would be glad of the opportunity."

Oh, she was just being prickly, Gwendolyn decided. Both Julian and de Montmorency simply wanted to be helpful. She nodded and smiled, and her fingers relaxed again on her reins.

"I daresay Mr. Beck's going on the Town to find himself a wife," said the Earl. "Perhaps we can be of use here. Who do we know, Étienne, who might be suitable? Lady Agatha's oldest, perhaps?"

"A charming *jeune femme*," agreed de Montmorency. "Also, perhaps, Miss Lowry-Corry? A relation of the Earl of Belmore, I believe."

"Irish, isn't she? Yes, I've met her. A very nice girl. From County Kildare. Beautiful country there."

Gwendolyn looked ahead, to where Christopher rode next to Owen. That uneasy, prickly sort of feeling had come rushing back. Christopher was *her* friend, and the Earl and de Montmorency were making assumptions about him; it bothered her. She didn't care for the way they were idly attempting to arrange his fate, almost as would two gods in Olympus play puppet-master to helpless humans below.

Or was she simply being oversensitive? And absurd herself? And . . . possibly even proprietary? Christopher didn't belong to her, after all, and if in fact he was in search of a wife, he was certainly old enough to do that. He was a man now, full-grown, not the boy she had known back in Whitehaven.

Goodness gracious, Gwendolyn, she said firmly to herself, do snap out of it, you *are* being ridiculous. And she looked again at the Earl's handsome face, very serene, very open in its expression; his intentions were, very obviously, good ones, an impression confirmed when he said, smiling at her:

"If I've been lucky enough to find the bride of my dreams, the least I can do is to be of service to your Mr. Beck."

Gwendolyn nodded, smiled, and relaxed again.

The conversation divagated to the more general subject of the Earl of Belmore who, apparently, was renowned throughout County Kildare for his eccentric habit of wearing wigs dating back to the eighteenth century. De Montmorency recalled a memorable wig he had once come across in the attic of his family's Parisian *hôtel*, well over a foot in height, with elaborate rolled curls at the peak meant to evoke waves, and upon which was attached a beautifully crafted miniature frigate, complete with masts, rigging, and sails.

"Wouldn't one's head hurt carrying all that about?" said Gwendolyn, trying to imagine herself so attired.

"My family is, *je crains*, a slave to fashion, and always has been," replied de Montmorency lightly. "Whether it is a curse or a blessing I leave it to you to decide."

"Well, it's certainly been a blessing to me," the Earl said. "I daresay I would have agreed to that puce jacket last week were it not for your timely intervention."

De Montmorency shuddered ever so slightly. "My dear Julian, let us not speak of that ever again. Mademoiselle Penhallow, you laugh, but I assure you, had Julian presented himself to you in that *monstruosité* you may well have reconsidered the wisdom of affiancing yourself to such a man."

Gwendolyn laughed again, and the Earl joined in. De Montmorency smiled, complimented Gwendolyn on the elegance of her riding-habit, wondered again about Weston or Meyer, expressed a hope that the weather would remain fine, and so the talk drifted on to other topics.

Helen FitzClarence drew a deep breath, urged her horse into a brief canter, and brought herself next to Francis, who sat with an easy, if slightly absent grace in his saddle. "Hullo again," she said, trying to keep her voice casual.

He turned his golden head. "Oh, hullo."

His voice was pleasant and polite, but to Helen it was the tone one would use to address anybody. Even a perfect stranger. Her heart sank a little, but she persisted. "I say, it's—it's a lovely day."

"Yes."

"It's—well, it's nice to see you again after all this time."

"Thank you. You as well."

Again that same pleasant civility. Helen's heart sank some more and frantically she cast about for something else to say. "Gwendolyn and I have become great friends, you know. She—she's my *best* friend, really."

"Oh? That's splendid."

"I wouldn't have come for the Season if it weren't for her."

"Indeed? And how are you enjoying your Season, Lady Helen?"

If only he sounded genuinely interested! "*Helen.* Do call me 'Helen.'"

He smiled, very gently but impersonally, and responded, "Helen then. How are you enjoying your Season?"

"Much better now," she answered without thinking, and could have bitten off her own tongue. But Francis only nodded. Oh, how handsome he was, with his golden hair and blue eyes, his tall straight form, those manly shoulders! She went on, laboring: "I've never forgotten your visits to Hathaway Park. I—I escaped my governess whenever I could to follow you—I mean, to follow the three of you about."

He nodded again. "I remember Percy saying what a bruising rider you were."

At last! Francis recalled *something* from that time.

Perhaps she should jog his memory yet further. With what? She blurted out: "Do you remember me trying to pinch you?"

"Did you? Why?"

So much for his recollections. Oh, God, why did she have to bring up that particular anecdote? Was there anyone, ever, in the whole world who was as inept as she was? Time to talk about something else. *Anything* else. Milton's treatise on the Reformation? She didn't know who Milton was, she wasn't even sure what a treatise was, and at breakfast had, nonetheless, said, *How fascinating* and then had broken out in an anguished sweat for fear that Francis would expect her to say something clever on the subject.

Distraught, she groped about in her mind for something else to say—not that Francis even seemed to notice she hadn't responded to his casual questions.

"I—uh—it's a lovely day, isn't it?" she finally managed, before realizing she had already muttered this exact same boring stupid thing approximately two minutes ago.

"Yes," said Francis, and she wondered if he even noticed.

Helen's heart dropped to her toes.

For all she knew, it could just as well have dropped to the dirt roadway and been trampled by the horses' hooves.

Which might, actually, give her some relief from how badly it was hurting.

Helen wondered, for perhaps the thousandth time in all these years, why Francis? He had shown up with Percy and Owen at Hathaway Park for a school holiday—the Lent Half, to be precise, in 1812. She hadn't been looking forward to it at all—certainly not having Owen around, and certainly not friends of his whom she was sure would be just as repugnant. The last thing on her mind had been the idea of liking—in the romantic sense—one of Owen's friends.

And yet, within minutes of meeting Francis she felt as if her entire world had been turned upside down. Her empty heart had been filled to the brim; life suddenly had purpose, meaning, hope. Happiness beckoned. Francis and Percy had, in those days, made a deliberate effort to have the exact same cut to their hair, and loved nothing better than pretending to be the other brother. But she had always known, from the very beginning, which was which. She didn't know how she could. Nor did she know why Francis affected her the way he did.

It was just what had happened.

Love at first sight.

Inexplicable, indefinable, practically indescribable.

And she had never, ever wavered.

Percy rode next to the Duchess, together leading their little cavalcade to Richmond. They had chatted about the cracked heel from which her horse had recently recovered as well as canvassing the latest offerings at Tattersall's, and Percy had inquired after the absent Duke's health, as back in March he had (according to the Duchess in a tone of fond exasperation) attempted a fence too high for one of his superannuated years and been lucky to only break an ankle in his subsequent tumble; thank the heavens, his horse was all right, and in any event the Duke remained home at Hathaway Park recuperating, rejecting the light nourishing dishes suitable for an aged invalid, annoying his doctor by refusing to be bled, and altogether making a great nuisance of himself. She now assured Percy that the Duke was coming along splendidly despite his overall unreasonableness.

Percy smiled and made a suitable reply, though in fact he was at the same time thinking of the luscious Lady

Tarrington whom he hoped to see tonight if her husband was, conveniently, elsewhere.

He hoped to do much more than merely see Wynda, of course.

Although, upon reflection, he *did* derive a great deal of pleasure from looking at her, as she was blessed with a breathtakingly ripe figure which included the most astounding pair of breasts imaginable.

There was less pleasure to be had in conversing with Wynda, as her Scottish brogue was liberally interspersed with mangled French phrases which sometimes made it either difficult to understand what she was saying, or required stern discipline to not burst out laughing. Also, she continually made a great deal out of the fact that she had once been in competition for the hand of the great Highlander chieftain Alasdair Penhallow, but as Percy had never met the man—literally a distant cousin—it was hardly the fascinating anecdote Wynda clearly thought it was.

But despite her shortcomings, Wynda provided, for now, just the sort of amusement he preferred, especially since she was married, had entered into their arrangement with equal enthusiasm, and posed no threat to his happy bachelor state. Had it not been for his sister Gwendolyn's Season, he'd be avoiding the various *ton* events as he found them rather dull and, worse still, heartily disliked navigating his way among the matchmaking mothers and their daughters, who struck him, on the whole, as insipid and overeager.

Someday, he supposed, he'd find someone he liked well enough to marry.

Though it was hard to imagine what sort of girl that might be.

Gwennie, now, had found her match without much

difficulty—said she'd fallen in love with the Earl of West-enbury at first sight, and practically within minutes of ar-riving in London. They seemed awfully happy together. Percy glanced over his shoulder, to where Gwendolyn and the Earl rode side by side, with that French fellow next to the Earl.

It was hard to like de Montmorency: too many years of war between their respective countries, for one thing. For another, Percy didn't care for his manners—he was too suave by half.

As for the Earl, his future brother-in-law, he seemed a decent enough chap. Very pleasant and easygoing, quali-ties ladies liked, Percy supposed. And besides, it didn't matter what *he* thought. What mattered was what his sister thought.

Percy glanced back again. Gwendolyn was smiling up at the Earl. She looked so happy that it was impossible to entertain any doubts on that score. Fancy that! he thought. The second of the five of them getting married: first Hugo, now Gwennie. He wondered who'd be next. Not him, that was for certain. And not Bertram, the youngest of them all—he'd stake his life on that. All Bertie cared about was science. You might even say it was his great love.

Percy looked back a third time, to where Francis was riding next to Helen. She was talking and Francis was lis-tening. He was glad Frank had agreed to come to Town, the dear old boy. It took a lot to tear him away from his precious books. He seemed rather to live in his own head these days. No doubt thinking lofty theological thoughts. Egad! Percy grinned. Give him the carefree life of earthly—earthy—delights instead.

Speaking of which: Wynda tonight, he hoped, and a couple of bottles of champagne. A few hours of snatched pleasure and a quick, discreet exit before the Viscount came home. And then Percy turned his full attention back to the Duchess who, apparently, hadn't noticed his lapse.

Judith, the Duchess of Egremont, had in fact observed that young Percy had fallen silent, but as this little break in their conversation gave her an opportunity to ponder some of the things currently on her mind, she made no objection.

Firstly, it was impossible to deny that so far, Helen's Season had not been going well. And there was no reason why it shouldn't, as Helen possessed all the advantages of breeding, an enormous dowry, and a pleasing appearance. Eligible gentlemen swarmed around her. Yet she responded to them like—well, like a horse being bothered by flies. Why, the Duchess wondered, perplexed, had she agreed to come to London then?

Secondly, she had just received a letter from an acquaintance who was traveling through Austria, and claimed to have seen Almira's scapegrace son, Philip Thane, in Vienna. If true, this was the first sighting of Philip in a long time.

The Duchess repressed a long, deep sigh.

She and the Duke had done their best to help raise Philip when, as a young boy, he had joined the Egremont family upon the marriage of his widowed mother to their only son; however, it had not been an easy task.

Even as a youth Philip had been wild and obstreperous, and in adulthood these unfortunate qualities had not subsided into anything resembling a more sober maturity. Nonetheless, the Duchess's strongly ingrained sense of family responsibility had never faltered; she *did* hope Philip was all right, wherever he was.

Thirdly, she had not failed to notice that both her grandson Owen and Mr. Beck were looking the worse for wear this morning, and it wasn't difficult to guess why. Percy, on the other hand, was evidently unimpaired, which suggested a remarkable capacity for drink. This sort of thing was what young men did, but it wasn't really the Town polish she wanted Owen to acquire, nor did she like the idea of Percy following in Philip's footsteps. Yet what right did she have to interfere in Percy's life?

As for Mr. Beck, she knew nothing of him except for Percy's careless introduction as an old friend. But there was something about him that she quite liked, the way he carried his tall rangy self with a quiet assurance, and the deep intelligence in his dark eyes. Very gentlemanly in his manners, too, not strutting about as so many young men did nowadays. Also, she had noted earlier with approval, he rode his horse well. Altogether, she now thought, a fine addition to their party.

As they rode along side by side, Julian, the Earl of Westenbury, looked at Gwendolyn with a rush of pleasure. He never tired of looking at her—would never tire of it. She evoked for him all the wonder, all the mystery, of womanhood. Aphrodite. Helen of Troy. Cleopatra. Guinevere. Lady Godiva.

Julian gazed at Gwendolyn's shining gold hair and wondered what it would look like, unbound, falling free about her bare shoulders and breasts. It was thick, lustrous, living silk; it was easy to understand why a woman's hair was thought to be her crowning glory.

He wished he could bury his face in it right now— gently wrap a long gleaming length of it about his throat, binding himself to her.

Julian shifted a little in his saddle. It *was* a splendid idea to get married sooner. He wanted to see Gwendolyn like this. He'd been waiting a long, long time for someone who could make him feel this way.

He thought back to the first time he had seen her, when he'd come into Almack's that memorable evening. Her beauty had struck him with almost a physical force and, at the same time, with it was a subtle and wonderful sense of having already known her, of immediate familiarity.

Perhaps this was why he'd rushed off to White-haven, without a word to anybody, to request her hand in marriage. This feeling that they belonged together; had, somehow, already belonged together. He wasn't a believer in the so-called transmigration of souls—the fanciful idea that he and Gwendolyn had been together in a previous life. It was just that he felt so, well, *at home* with her. And what a relief it was, after so many years of being incessantly targeted as a highly eligible prospect on the Marriage Mart.

Speaking of home, wasn't there something in regard to that which Gwendolyn had asked him about?

Oh, yes, she'd asked him to write to his sisters and per-suade some of them to come to London. It had seemed like a good idea at the time, but now, as he tried to envi-sion Agnes, Martha, Sarah, and so on gallivanting about Town, his imagination failed him. Country girls through and through, as he'd tried to explain to Gwendolyn.

No, not a good idea, really.

Still, he'd promised to write to them.

A promise was a promise, wasn't it?

And about the wedding—yes, yes, he was all for ad-vancing the date. Though it would be a bit of a shame to not have Prinny at the wedding. Or a large convivial break-fast afterwards, with all his friends. Still, the planning of weddings was a woman's purview, not a man's. Julian was glad his mother would soon be in Town. She would be a great assist; she'd know exactly what to do. Bless her, she always did.

Christopher rode in companionable silence next to Owen FitzClarence, the thin, pale young Marquis of Ellington. Owen, Christopher had come to learn during last night's revels with Percy, was a pleasant but largely monosyllabic fellow and so this morning, with both of them suffering from the aftereffects, he'd felt no particular urgency to carry on a conversation. Fortunately, the fresh air and warm sun were working wonders, and he felt himself at last to be in good trim again.

He looked to where Percy and the Duchess rode at the head of their group. He was no stranger to spirits, having more than once overindulged while abroad, but Percy's capacity had astonished him. As he'd dragged himself out of bed in his new lodgings this morning, he wondered if Percy would even be able to dress himself, much less ride a horse—and yet Percy had arrived at the Duchess's townhouse clear-eyed and energetic, not a whit the worse for wear.

The resilience of youth, Christopher thought, and grinned to himself. Good God, he must be getting on.

He suddenly remembered Mauro della Valle saying, *Perhaps you'll marry, and settle down.*

He didn't know about the settling-down part, but all at once he remembered the look on Gwendolyn Penhallow's face as she turned last night to greet her fiancé the Earl. The joyful glow. The obvious, nearly palpable sense of connection she felt for him.

That, Christopher thought, must be a splendid thing.

Not that he'd ever experienced it himself, really. Occasionally he'd fancied himself smitten, but in reality those brief amorous interludes in his past, while enjoyable, had been only that—quick, pleasurable moments in time and then done with.

"Owen," he said, "ever been in love?"

Owen looked even paler, if that were possible. "No."

"Do you want to be?"

"No."

"Why not?"

Owen was silent for a while, then finally produced, slowly: "Must marry sometime. For duty. Last of my line, you know. No point thinking about love." He slumped a little in the saddle, as if exhausted by the effort it took to string together so many words.

Well, that was one problem he didn't have to confront, Christopher thought, looking sympathetically at Owen's melancholy face. Marrying for dynastic purposes.

Bloody hell, what a concept. Time-honored among the aristos, of course, with their obsessions about bloodlines and so on. As if they were racehorses. It had been his observation that among dogs, mongrels tended to be healthier, more robust, than purebreds.

It wasn't much of a stretch to apply the same reasoning to humans.

By way of poignant example, you only had to look at the royal house of Hanover. Inbreeding going back centuries, and here they were with poor old incapacitated King George. Mad as a March hare. His ancestor Mary Queen of Scots *and* her father James V suffered similarly, and their country suffered right along with them. There was a lot to be said, Christopher thought, for the radical American experiment in democracy. The odds were good it wouldn't last another decade, of course, but it was certainly interesting to watch from afar.

He grinned again. These were probably not good

topics to introduce while he was traveling in such lofty circles—rubbing elbows, as it were, with a duchess, an earl, a marquis. A French nobleman. And, of course, the Penhallows. As a side note, how pleased Father would be to hear about his son's social ascendancy!

Thinking of his father, Christopher's grin faded.

Father didn't even know he was back in England. Would he care?

Christopher thought about all those letters he had begun and never finished.

What now?

His train of thought was broken when his gaze suddenly focused on Owen's mother, Lady Almira, who was riding ahead of them on a docile little gray mare. He thrust his own horse's reins into a surprised Owen's hands, slid onto the ground, and quickly went to Lady Almira who was listing dangerously far to the left.

"If you'll excuse me, ma'am," he said, and gently propped her upright.

"Oh! Thank you, Mr. Beck!" exclaimed Lady Almira, whose tall feathered hat promptly fell off. "I *thought* something was amiss! It came upon me so gradually I supposed it was my *vision* going awry."

Christopher picked up Lady Almira's hat and handed it to her; then, with a hand to the reins, he brought the compliant mare to a halt. "Ma'am, may I check your billets and girth?"

"My—I *beg* your pardon, Mr. Beck?" Lady Almira looked so taken aback that Christopher, schooling himself not to smile at her confusion, quickly answered:

"The fastenings of your saddle, ma'am."

"Oh! I see! Billets and girths. What *odd* words! They rather remind me of fish. Yes, by all means, Mr. Beck, thank you so much." Smiling gratefully, Lady Almira put her hat back on (backwards), and waited while Christopher checked to see that her mare's saddle was still properly secured.

"All's well, ma'am," he said, and ran a caressing hand along the little horse's velvety muzzle before giving back to Lady Almira the reins she had dropped while replacing her hat on her head.

"Oh, that's comforting to hear, thank you, Mr. Beck." Lady Almira leaned down to whisper confidingly, "I'm not a very good rider, you see. I do *try*, you know, but I never seem to get the hang of it. The truth is, I'm dreadfully frightened of horses. They're quite *large*, aren't they?" She looked so suddenly full of despair, with the tall feathers in her hat now pitifully crumpled, that Christopher said:

"Would you feel better if I rode with you, ma'am?"

Lady Almira lit up at once. "Oh, Mr. Beck, *would* you? But I'm afraid it will be a ghastly bore for you."

"Not at all," he said, and swiftly retrieved his horse from Owen, brought himself back into the saddle, and made his way to Lady Almira's side. She immediately began talking—about her three children (Philip, Helen, and Owen), about her first husband (the late Mr. Thane), her second husband (the late Marquis of Ellington), the book she was reading (*Lucy Dale*, by Gwendolyn's sister-in-law Katherine), her inability to really enjoy opera ("It just sounds like cats *screeching*"), her delicate constitution (which made eating anything cold an unnerving risk to the health of one who so enjoyed ices), and so on.

With a long open road before them, empty of other riders or carriages, most of the members of their party now enjoyed that hearty gallop Percy had suggested last night. Christopher glanced at them, but kept his attention fixed on Lady Almira who only shrank a little in her saddle as she watched the others race along. To be sure, he would have enjoyed a gallop himself, but he'd had plenty of that in his day, and would have further opportunities in the future. In the meantime he only said:

"Don't worry, ma'am, we'll catch up to them soon enough."

"Oh, Mr. Beck, do you think so?" Lady Almira said anxiously. "They won't leave us behind?"

"I'm sure they won't, ma'am."

Lady Almira looked a little less worried, then kept on talking.

And Christopher listened, with a patience that would have astounded his seventeen-year-old self. For he had, he thought, been lucky enough to learn over the years—and most definitely the hard way—that kindness mattered.

Chapter 5

As Christopher had predicted, their party was reunited before too much time had elapsed: those who had embarked on a vigorous gallop turned their horses back and retraced their steps until they came abreast with Christopher and Lady Almira. Percy and Helen, in the lead, raced neck-and-neck, with Owen FitzClarence close behind; hard upon these three came Gwendolyn, the Earl, the Duchess, and, lastly, Étienne de Montmorency.

Helen, flushed and exhilarated, pulled up her horse, looking, Christopher thought, very pretty in her animation, and Percy exclaimed:

"Well done, old girl! You nearly beat me!"

Helen laughed at him. "I could have! You sprang your horse too soon."

"Ho! I don't take kindly to critiques. Race me again, when the horses have rested."

"Maybe," answered Helen, and glanced around. Francis wasn't among the group of returning riders, and then she saw him, ahead in the distance, slowly returning, walking his horse. When everyone caught up with him, he turned his horse about; Helen brought hers alongside and said, anxiety in her voice:

"I say, are you all right?"

Francis blinked and turned his vivid blue eyes to her. "I beg your pardon?"

She repeated her question, and Francis answered, sounding a little baffled, "Why wouldn't I be?"

"You fell behind. I—I thought something was wrong."

"No. I was thinking about Emanuel Swedenborg."

"Who?"

"Swedenborg. He was an eighteenth-century theologian and philosopher who defined 'correspondence' as a series of relationships among the spiritual plane of the mind, the Creator, intention, and so on."

"Oh! How—how interesting."

"Yes, I'm writing an essay about him. Kant, of course, thought he was a fraud, and published a vituperative little book, *Träume eines Geistersehers*, in the hopes of exposing him."

"Oh. Ah. Really?"

"Yes. It was absolutely scathing. Three years prior to that, curiously enough, Kant met Swedenborg and thought him to have what he described as a miraculous gift. And so when Kant published *Träume eines Geistersehers*, his friend Moses Mendelssohn thought he might have actually been joking about the whole thing."

"Oh."

"Yes, it's all very interesting, especially since Kant published it anonymously. I'd like to figure out if he was serious or not. I wish I'd brought along his *Critique of Pure Reason* with me, or at least his *Brief Gesammelt* prior to 1780. I looked in your grandmother's library and there's practically nothing on German theology—only a rather dubious volume of *Der Franckforter*."

"Oh."

Helen had lost her animated look, and onto her face was creeping an expression of despair which, however, Francis didn't seem to notice, for he went on:

"I did find a copy of Ephraim Udall's *Communion Comlinesse*, though, with the original binding. What a remarkable fellow. He broke away from the so-called Great Rebellion in 1641, you know, and announced his support of the established liturgy. The resulting uproar was tremendous."

"Oh. Oh, I say," Helen said, rather tremulously, "we're here."

They had arrived at the entrance to Richmond Park, and everyone made their way between the wide-open iron gates and to the stabling area. Lady Almira gratefully accepted Christopher's help in dismounting.

"Thank you, Mr. Beck! Oh, isn't it lovely here? How *green* everything is! All those beautiful old oak trees. Oh, and just *look* at those bluebells! And daffodils!" she said rapturously, but broke off amidst a sudden torrent of sneezes. A frantic search in her reticule proving useless, Christopher offered her his handkerchief.

"Oh, thank you *again*, Mr. Beck! I can't imagine where my own handkerchief went. I know I had it before we left. Or at least I *think* I did. Dear me, how vexing!" Lady Almira sneezed several more times, blew her nose, and tried to give Christopher back his handkerchief, now rather sodden.

"Keep it, ma'am," he said, which proved to be a useful recommendation as Lady Almira sneezed again.

"I do love spring," she said mournfully, "but it doesn't love *me*."

"What you need, Almira," said the Duchess, "is a cup of tea," and she swept her daughter-in-law away to the big covered pavilion where they were immediately seated and Lady Almira could admire the flowers at a relatively safe distance.

The other members of the party shortly joined them for refreshments. Owen FitzClarence, his earlier malaise at breakfast having resolved itself, proceeded to astound those unfamiliar with his usual capacity for food by methodically consuming four scones lavishly spread with raspberry jam, two muffins, three or four sandwiches, and several small cakes topped with sweet butter icing, all washed down with multiple cups of tea.

"*Just* like his dear father," remarked Lady Almira proudly. "*He* could eat six capons at a stroke and still have room for soup."

"I say, you're disgusting," Helen said to her brother, who, having contemplated a plate heaped high with filbert-studded biscuits, took one, bit into it, and replied:

"Says the girl who keeps having her gowns let out."

"Oh! You—you *beast*! Shut up, won't you?" Helen had gone scarlet.

"Just like old times," said Percy nostalgically. "The two of you, at each other's throats."

"She started it," Owen said, and took another biscuit.

"I hope you *choke* on it," Helen hissed at him.

"That," said the Duchess, "will suffice. Almira, there's no need to cry. Your sleeve is in the jam-pot, by the bye; do remove it. Is everyone finished? Shall we attempt the famous maze?"

"I'm not finished," said Owen.

"Then you may stay here until you are," answered his grandmother, rising. "Come along, Almira."

Lady Almira obediently rose too, clutching Christopher's damp and crumpled handkerchief. "Oh, dear ma'am, I hope we won't get *lost*. Mazes *do* make me nervous. They're rather like a bad dream, aren't they? You know, a nightmare where you're trapped, and you don't know where you are, and can't find your way free?"

"Nonsense," said the Duchess. "We shan't be lost. Who else would like to join us?"

"I would," Gwendolyn said, standing up as well. She

had a plan. Oh yes, a very good plan. A delightful, marvelous, and *brilliant* plan, in fact. She looked at the Earl. "Julian?"

He rose at once to his feet, and offered his arm. "By all means."

She smiled and slid her hand into the crook of his arm, relishing the strong masculine feel of him, the faint musky scent of his cologne, the incredibly pleasurable sensation of being so close. Together they followed the Duchess and Lady Almira—who had begun sneezing again—and then Percy said to Christopher, "I say, shall we go check on the horses?"

His tone was so elaborately casual that Christopher knew at once that Percy was hoping for a private word. He replied, "Yes, I think we should," and off they went to the stabling area.

At the table remained Owen, who had helped himself to another sandwich and was placidly chewing; Francis, who'd taken a pencil and a small notebook from a pocket of his jacket and was now absorbed in writing something in his fine, even hand; Lady Helen, who was staring down at the crumbs on her plate with an open look of misery; and Étienne de Montmorency, very sleek and elegant in neat buckskins, shining dark boots, an exquisitely cut claret-colored jacket, and a crisp white neckcloth tied with the subtle and perfect precision which was the envy of many less skilled in the art. He took a delicate sip of his tea, made a faint moue of distaste, glanced thoughtfully around at his tablemates, and finally said, very gently:

"Lady Helen, do you care for mazes?"

Not lifting her eyes from her plate, violently Helen shook her head, sending her red curls bobbing. "No."

"Then perhaps," he suggested, "you might enjoy a stroll down to the pond? There is, I perceive, a very pretty vista."

At this, Helen did lift her eyes and looked at Monsieur de Montmorency as if seeing him for the first time. She had encountered him on many occasions in recent weeks, especially since Gwendolyn's engagement to the Earl, but she'd been so occupied in waiting for Francis to arrive in London, it was as if she had been wrapped in a kind of all-encompassing blindness.

Now Helen saw that Monsieur de Montmorency was looking back at her in what seemed to be a—an *understanding* way. As if he was peering into her soul, recognizing her anguish and shame, and was offering her the chance to walk away from the table—where Owen's cruel taunt still felt as if it was hanging in the air—with some of her pride intact. He was so old, thirty at least, maybe even forty, and so calm and controlled in his manner that she needn't fear any awkward advances from him either. She hated it when the young men crowded around her, asking her to dance, offering to fetch her a beverage, complimenting her on her appearance, wondering if she would like to go for a carriage ride, when all the while they doubtless were hoping to get their hands on her dowry; it took everything she had not to scream at them to go away, it was Francis, *Francis*, whom she loved.

Quickly she stood up. "Yes. I *would* like to see the pond."

Monsieur de Montmorency stood as well, smiling down at her. *"Allons-nous, alors?"*

She must have looked very blank—not a single one of her governesses had ever managed to instill in her the slightest grasp of the French language—because Monsieur de Montmorency gently said, without missing a beat:

"Shall we, Lady Helen?"

She nodded, and then was glad, as they walked away from the pavilion toward what was, in fact, a charming lake, where many ducks peacefully floated, that Monsieur de Montmorency refrained from holding out his arm to her. Common decency would have compelled her to slide her hand around the extended arm, and she didn't want Francis to think she was attracted to Monsieur de Montmorency.

And suddenly Helen nearly gasped out loud.

Maybe that was exactly what was needed.

What a brilliant idea!

If Francis were to see her—well, there was no reason to cavil at niceties, she was desperate—if he saw her *flirting* with another man, that might well inspire in him an awakening. Such things happened, didn't they? She remembered Gwendolyn talking about a book she had recently finished. What was it called? *Possibilities*? *Pretense*? No—*Persuasion*.

In the story, the heroine had loved a gentleman for a long time (just as she, Helen, had loved Francis for years!), but long ago, in the past, she'd made the mistake of refusing his offer of marriage and now the gentleman was cold and angry toward the heroine. And then, in Weymouth or Lyme or someplace like that, another gentleman paid attention to the heroine and *then* the hero began to change his entire attitude toward the heroine. And eventually everything worked out wonderfully well, and the hero and heroine were going to live happily ever after.

While Gwendolyn had been talking, Helen had pretended to be listening eagerly, but all the while had thought it a very boring, rubbishy story.

But now it just proved her point!

She needed to get another gentleman to pay attention to her, and then Francis would change his attitude.

But who?

She glanced up at her companion.

No, not Monsieur de Montmorency. Nobody would believe that so elegant a gentleman—a close friend of the

Prince Regent's, everybody said, so rich and urbane and always so beautifully turned out!—would be interested in *her*.

Who then?

And then Helen had *another* clever idea.

What about Christopher Beck?

Not that she was drawn to him, of course—it wasn't that he was bad-looking, and she supposed that some young ladies would think him attractive enough, with his rather long dark hair and dark eyes and strongly marked dark brows. It was just that she preferred (naturally!) golden hair and blue eyes.

Besides, it didn't matter, because it was all going to be a pretend flirtation.

Now, how exactly did one go about flirting?

She had absolutely no experience in such matters.

Helen thought hard. She could, she supposed, behave toward Christopher Beck as Gwendolyn did toward the Earl—smiling and putting her arm through his and dancing at balls and all that sort of thing.

A sudden venomous stab of envy pierced her.

The only reason she had pleaded with Grandmother to invite Gwendolyn was so that Francis might agree to come to London, to spend time with his sister. And it had all seemed to be coming together perfectly. And then what had happened? Gwendolyn had waltzed into London and within a few weeks—weeks!—was engaged. Whereas she, Helen, had been waiting for *years* for Francis. And he, all too obviously, wasn't the least bit interested in her. (So far.)

It wasn't fair.

It wasn't fair at all.

Why should Gwendolyn be so happy, when she herself was so miserable?

Well, that was going to change, and right away.

She would flirt as hard as possible with Christopher Beck.

And she would keep on pretending that she actually liked Gwendolyn.

Also, she was going to deliberately ignore Francis, to further inspire in him a burning jealousy of Christopher.

"Shall we sit?" said Monsieur de Montmorency, and Helen, jolted out of her thoughts, gave a little jump, and realized that he was gesturing to a picturesque iron bench placed on a hillock near the pond.

"Yes." She went to it and sat down, but soon fell into another abstraction, staring sightlessly at the ducks.

Love, she realized, certainly made you do strange things.

"The horses seem all right," said Christopher to Percy, who was fidgeting with a halter suspended by a nail on the wooden stabling wall.

Percy nodded, let go of the halter, and turned to Christopher. "Here's the thing," he said, in a burst of confidentiality. "Lured you here on false pretenses, I'm afraid. I'm a trifle under the hatches, you see, and wonder if you might be able to float me a loan? Lost quite a bit at faro last night, to a devilish unpleasant chap I'd just as soon not be under obligation to."

"I did wonder," Christopher said, thinking that Percy suddenly looked very young to him.

"Yes, and I'd rather not turn to Hugo for any more brass. He's helped me out before, but—well—I *do* want to stand on my own feet."

"I understand," said Christopher, refraining from pointing out Percy's somewhat faulty logic about independence. Which was the exact sort of thing Father would instantly have done. "How much do you need?"

Percy disclosed a sum that had Christopher repressing a whistle of amazement. He only said, "Absolutely. I'll go to Hoare's tomorrow and get you a bank note."

Relief broke out on Percy's face and he wrung Christopher's hand in an enthusiastic handshake. "I say, it's awfully good of you. Thanks ever so much. I'll pay you back, of course."

"When you can," answered Christopher in an easy tone, but mentally consigned the money as a gift. Debts were pernicious things. He remembered the time, in Naples, he'd turned off the Piazza Dante into a quiet alleyway and had come across the corpse of a well-dressed man; on his jacket had been pinned a bloodstained scrap of paper which read *Attenzione, qui giace uno sciocco che non è riuscito a rimborsare i suoi prestiti.*

Behold, here lies a fool who failed to repay his loans.

It had been, to say the least, a cautionary tale.

"Care for a drink?" Percy pulled from an inside pocket of his jacket a slender silver flask and offered it to Christopher. "Now that I'm out of the basket and all."

Christopher declined, and Percy took a long pull from the flask. "Well," he said, exuberant, "shall we join the others? I wouldn't mind having a go at that maze."

Together they left the stables and made their way toward the maze which was constructed out of tall, artfully tended hedges, very green and lush. As they reached the entrance, to their ears came the faint but distinctive sound of sneezing.

"Wouldn't be hard to find Lady Almira," remarked Percy with a boyish grin. "But let's go find Gwennie. I want to leap round a corner and startle her, just as I used to do at home. Lord, how she'd screech!"

"I'll leave you to it, my larky friend," said Christopher, "and enjoy a solitary stroll instead."

"As you like," answered Percy cheerfully, and dashed down a twisting gravel path, soon disappearing from sight.

Christopher, more slowly, followed a different path.

Having unobtrusively separated themselves from the Duchess and Lady Almira, Gwendolyn and the Earl had come—just the two of them—to a little private cul-de-sac, where there were only the sweet lilting sounds of birdsong for company. Surrounded by these tall green hedges, it wouldn't be hard to pretend that they were the only two people in the world. Gwendolyn turned to him. "I'm afraid," she said, twinkling up at him, "that we might be lost."

"How dreadful," he answered, smiling. "Shall we shout for help?"

"Not yet." She reached up and slid her fingers slowly down the wide soft lapels of his beautifully cut bottle-green jacket, and took a step closer. "Not just yet." She lifted her face to his. What a lovely place for a first kiss—a kiss for which she had waited for so very, very long. Softly she said, "I do think, Julian, there's something else you ought to do instead."

"I think I might have an idea."

A hot dizzying thrill ran through her, and to her surprise Gwendolyn felt her knees actually go a little weak, just like she had read characters in books doing under similar circumstances. How amazing—life imitating art!—and how delightful. She gripped the Earl's lapels, barely able to focus on his handsome face as he lowered it toward her own.

And then—

Oh, and then—

His mouth was on hers. The first kiss, the first of a

lifetime of kisses . . . and more. A small happy satisfied sound rose in her throat and she brought her arms up and around the Earl's neck, brought herself up close to him, reveling in the feel of his body—masculine and exotic— against her own.

The Earl pressed his mouth against hers a bit harder.

Lovely, *lovely*.

"My darling," he whispered, pulling away. "My beautiful Gwendolyn."

"My love," she whispered back. She could feel her heart hammering excitedly within her, which was *another* thing writers had their characters doing in this situation. Focus, Gwennie, she ordered herself, focus! She murmured, "Don't stop. Kiss me again."

"Shall I?"

"You must. Or I'll die from longing."

"We wouldn't want that, would we."

And he brought his lips against hers again, only this time—oh, goodness, his tongue was in her mouth, against her own tongue, against her teeth, filling her, exploring her, and Gwendolyn received this new intimacy with an electrifying shock, her jaw reflexively going slack which seemed to please him, for he gave a little groan and pressed his mouth more firmly against her own.

Her mind was alive to every movement of his tongue— now against her own tongue again, now sliding slickly across her teeth, and now across her lower lip. Back into her mouth. Gwendolyn found herself considering its wet, lively, muscular texture. Tongues were rather odd, once you started thinking about them. Like eels. Or like the curiously shaped sea-squirts she would come across in the tidal pools back home. How they'd made her laugh! Bertram, of course, had known all about them. Ascidians, he had said, the earliest known versions being the

Shankouclava shankouense found in the Lower Cambrian Maotianshan Shales in China. Her dear, clever, scientific little brother! She owed him a letter. Even though he was dreadful about writing back—or, to be more precise, he would write back and then forget to post the letter—she still wrote him faithfully.

Which reminded her. Yesterday she'd had a nice letter from Mama. How lovely to hear that everyone was doing well. All of little Cordelia's teeth had finally come in, and Rosalind wasn't far behind. Aunt Claudia was busy painting a portrait of them, although of course it was next to impossible to get them to sit still for any length of time.

The Earl groaned again, the low guttural sound very loud in her ears, and Gwendolyn was jerked back into the present moment. He was still kissing her. Ought she to try and kiss him back? That only seemed fair, but she wasn't quite sure how to go about it—his tongue was much bigger than hers and it was rather busy at the moment. She didn't want to make it seem as if hers was fighting against his, struggling for dominance. Into her mind instantly popped an absurd image of two disembodied tongues engaged in a duel and flourishing little swords. *En garde, monsieur! To the death!* And then, of course, she wanted to laugh.

Don't, don't, she urged herself, but still a half-strangled chuckle leapt from her disobedient vocal cords. She did hope it sounded like a noise one would make while in the throes of passion.

Speaking of which, what *was* a "throe"? Or could there only be "throes"? She made a mental note to ask Katherine when next she wrote to her. How splendid it was to have a writer in the family. Hopefully her new novel was coming along well. *Lucy Dale*, her first, was such a wonderful book. Gwendolyn was glad it had done so well.

Suddenly it got very bright out, and abruptly she realized that Julian had pulled away from her. Apparently he'd been blocking out the sun with his head. He was breathing heavily, as if he had been running or otherwise engaged in intense physical activity, and he was smiling down at her.

"My darling Gwendolyn," he said, raggedly. "Thank you."

Gwendolyn was aware of a sudden feeling of conversational awkwardness. Ought one to be thanking one's beloved in this kind of situation? As if one had conferred a favor upon the other? How puzzling. Then again, Julian was so much older than her and doubtless much more experienced. So that must be the correct thing to do. Automatically, she replied, "You're welcome, Julian," even as she was wondering if this was pretty much all that kissing was about.

Surely not . . . ?

Once she had burst into Katherine's study at home, wanting to show her a watercolor she'd just completed, and found her in Hugo's arms. They were kissing each other. They had quickly realized they were alone no longer and had pulled apart. They had both, Gwendolyn recalled, looked extremely happy.

That had obviously been a *good* kiss.

Was what she had just shared with the Earl one, too?

Gwendolyn now recalled something else. Dear Bertram, he of the brilliant analytical mind, had more than once talked about the scientific method, and the value of careful experimentation.

Well, she'd just better try it again.

So Gwendolyn took a firm grip on the Earl's lapels once more, went up on tiptoes, and pressed her mouth against his.

He gave a soft laugh and the next thing she knew, it was the same sort of kiss. His tongue, vigorous, explorative.

She thought of eels again. Dueling eels. She couldn't help it this time and she giggled.

Apparently it must have been an entirely acceptable noise, for when the Earl lifted his head again he was smiling down at her. "Thank you, my darling."

"You're welcome," Gwendolyn answered politely, and released his lapels. Oh dear, she'd crumpled them. In the throes of passion? She brushed her hands against them, trying to smooth out the wrinkles. "Julian, I'm dreadfully sorry, but I think I've ruined your jacket."

He captured her hands and squeezed them. "It was worth it."

There was a sound of crunching gravel and swiftly the Earl squeezed her hands again and released them. Two little boys, aged eight or so, came barreling around a hedge, skidded to a stop some ten feet from where Gwendolyn and the Earl stood, and one said to the other:

"It's a dead end, you sapskull! I *told* you to take a left turn!"

"Ah, go on, shakebag!" retorted the other scornfully. "Follow me!" And he darted away. The other boy, looking harassed, paused for a few moments of painful indecision and then plunged after him, managing at the very last second to avoid cannoning into the Duchess of Egremont who had come around the hedge. Behind her was Lady Almira, who gave a cry of alarm, pressing herself against the shrubbery, and exclaimed:

"*Do* watch where you're going, little boy!"

It was a futile exhortation as the boy was already out of sight. Lady Almira shook her head. "The youth of today," she said dolefully. "I don't know what's to become of them, I truly don't."

"I daresay they'll grow up to become perfectly respectable citizens," said the Earl. "With a very colorful vocabulary."

Further noises of crunching gravel came to their ears, and within a few moments Christopher came strolling around the hedge. He came to a stop, looked at all of them, and laughed. "Fancy meeting you here."

Just then Percy flung himself around that same hedge, giving a loud yell. Lady Almira screeched and shrank back further into the shrubbery, and the Duchess frowned at Percy.

"My dear young man, what on earth are you doing?"

Percy had the grace to look ashamed. "I'm very sorry, ma'am. I heard the Earl's voice, assumed Gwennie was with him, and thought I'd give her a little surprise, that's all." He turned to Lady Almira. "Please forgive me, ma'am. Won't you let me make it up to you? Pray allow me to escort you out of here." He said it with such winning cajolery, and held out his arm with such a charming flourish, that Lady Almira was immediately wreathed in smiles again.

"Oh, *thank* you, Percy dear." She slipped her hand around his extended arm and as they turned about, it became apparent that she was covered in little green leaves from collar to hem.

The Duchess sighed, and the Earl gallantly extended his arm to her. "Your Grace? I fear you're a trifle fatigued."

She did accept the proffered arm but said, "Not a bit of it. But I *am* ready to be out of this maze. Take a left up ahead, then a right, and two lefts after that."

Off they went, leaving the distinct impression that it was the Duchess setting the pace of their brisk departure.

Christopher, amused, watched them go. Then he turned to Gwendolyn and stood for a moment looking down at her. He admired the pretty picture she made, tall and slender in a simply cut riding-habit the exact shade of the Mediterranean Sea in calm weather; it made her big, dark-lashed eyes look even bluer. What he most liked about her eyes, as lovely as they were, was the intelligence that shone from them, very bright and quick.

It was easy to picture Gwendolyn as an older woman, even an old woman, with bright gold hair turned to a soft silver, perhaps, and with laugh-lines around her eyes and framing her mouth, even moving without the easy suppleness of youth, but nonetheless an enduringly beautiful woman, with that same intelligence illuminating her eyes and her face and her whole being, really. Then, as now, she would be a pleasure to know, of that he was sure.

Looking at her a little more closely, however, Christopher saw that she seemed a bit pensive. "All well?" he said, and saw how she jumped a little.

"Oh yes, Christopher, thank you."

He held out his arm to her. "Shall we?"

She smiled, seeming to shake off that pensive mood, and came to him, sliding her hand around his arm. "I'm so glad to have a chance to talk with you. I meant to, on the ride here, but I don't know how it happened, I was with the Earl the whole time."

"It's only natural. He's your fiancé, after all."

They began slowly walking along the gravel path.

"There's another thing, Christopher. I saw how you helped Lady Almira. That was splendid of you."

"I was glad to help."

"Well, somebody had to, or she might have fallen off her horse." Gwendolyn's expression was now troubled. "Monsieur de Montmorency made a flippant remark about it, and neither Julian nor I did a thing about it. He— Monsieur de Montmorency, I mean—was just talking and talking, and then he said something which irritated me and I got distracted. I'm ashamed of myself, Christopher, I truly am. It would have been dreadful if poor Lady Almira *had* fallen."

He was aware of a desire to—what? Reassure her? Comfort her? He said, lightly, "She didn't, Miss Penhallow, so *non ti preoccupare più*."

"Italian? Mine is rudimentary, but I think that meant 'don't worry about it.' *Sì?*"

"Sì, signorina." He smiled down at her, pleased to see her expression brightening again.

"'*Signorina*'! I feel like I'm in Italy again. But also, you can call me 'Gwendolyn' if you like. After all, we're old friends! Or, perhaps, new friends. Oh, Christopher, we had just started to get to know each other when you went away. Where did you go? What did you do?"

"You really want to know?" Christopher said, unable to repress a note of amazement in his voice. His experiences since leaving home felt to him like—well, like chapters in a book he assumed no one would want to read.

"Of course I do! I was so sure you were off on a splendid adventure, and I was quite envious, you know."

"Envious? Really?"

"Oh yes. I don't know what it is, but—well, I do like *doing* things. Won't you tell me all about it?"

So he did tell her about his years abroad. Not in great detail, but enough of a sketch to give her a sense of what it had been like. She heard him without interruption as slowly they paced along the gravel path, turning left and right without really noticing where they were going. And Christopher thought to himself what a good listener Gwendolyn was; he thought to himself, how remarkable it was to feel genuinely heard.

When he had done, Gwendolyn said, "Oh, Christopher, I was right! It *was* a splendid adventure! Your Mauro sounds such an interesting person, and Tommaso too—I feel as if I know them. How curious to think that I might have seen you in Italy, if not for the little quirks of fate." She laughed. "I'm sure I would have asked my kind friends the Marksons to stay on with you so that I could help with the horses! I would have enjoyed that so much."

"How did you like Italy?" he asked. "And where else did you go?" So then it was Gwendolyn's turn to tell him about her time abroad. And when she was done, he said, "It sounds like yours was very much a splendid adventure, *signorina*."

"Oh, it was, it was." She smiled. "Katherine said I should write a book about it all, and use my little drawings to illustrate it."

"Will you?"

"Oh, no, I don't think so. But Katherine's writing career is coming along so beautifully—I didn't get a chance to tell you all about it last night. And about Hugo, and his ships, and—" Gwendolyn broke off and looked up at him with fresh trouble on her lovely face. "Christopher, you do know that your father and Diana moved to Nottingham, don't you? And that your father remarried, and Diana's married too?"

He stopped abruptly. Tried to absorb the shock of the news. "No." He was vaguely aware that a large family—a man and a woman, with four or five chattering children in tow—walked past them, and that a bluebird, with a beautiful sheen to its sleek feathers, had landed on top of the hedge, and that the sky was filled with big, puffy white clouds drifting overhead. "I tried to write, many times," he slowly told Gwendolyn. "But Father—well, before I left, he said not to bother."

"He must have been so angry with you," Gwendolyn said softly. "But to say something like that—oh, Christopher, I can't *imagine* it."

He felt himself smiling wryly. "I'm afraid I'm not the son Father was hoping I would be."

"I think he should be *proud* of you! For how hard you worked, and how you helped all those horses, and saved poor Mauro from destitution!"

She spoke with such passionate zeal that Christopher couldn't doubt her sincerity. "You're a good soul, Gwennie," he said, and, surprising himself, leaned down to lightly kiss her forehead. "Thank you."

A little of the trouble left her face then, and she said, tucking her hand more firmly around his arm, "Oh, I like that you called me that! It's so cozy."

There was more he might have said, how her championing of him helped lighten the sudden sharp ache in his heart, but then Percy came galloping along the path and exclaimed:

"By Jove, *there* you are! We've all been waiting for you. Did you get lost?"

"No, we were talking, and lost track of time," answered Gwendolyn, as she and Christopher joined up with Percy who cheerfully went on as they walked together:

"Well, you missed something capital! Lady Almira dropped her reticule in the pond, and as de Montmorency was standing right there when it happened, of course he had to retrieve it and now his precious boots have lost their shine!" Percy laughed. "He's in a right royal pelt."

And Christopher saw, when they emerged from the maze, that de Montmorency was, in fact, in a very bad mood, and he wondered to himself how anyone could care so much about a pair of boots.

Chapter 6

They were all on their horses again, and Gwendolyn said quietly to the Earl, "Julian, I'm going to ride with Lady Almira."

"Good Lord, must you?"

"I beg your pardon?"

He grimaced good-naturedly. "She *does* talk. Well, I'll keep you company. Besides, I fancy Étienne needs some time alone to nurse his grudge."

So they rode alongside Lady Almira, who did indeed talk all the way from Richmond back to London, but was so volubly grateful for the escort that Gwendolyn couldn't help but feel glad of her decision.

Occasionally she glanced around to see where everybody else was. Owen and Francis were riding together, Percy and the Duchess had once again taken the lead, and Helen was next to Christopher, with Monsieur de Montmorency some distance behind them. Gwendolyn couldn't hear what Helen was saying to Christopher, but she certainly seemed to be enjoying herself.

What a change from earlier in the day!

Gwendolyn was surprised to notice that she wished she knew what the two of them were talking about.

As the afternoon wore on, the bright spring sunlight gave way to thick, pale gray clouds massing overhead. In this softer, more subdued light the auburn of Helen FitzClarence's curls seemed to glow with life, and the green of her eyes made yet more vivid. A striking girl, Christopher thought, if, perhaps, a moody one. She had been hostile and resentful while their party had been seated in the pavilion—reminding him quite a bit of himself a few years back—but when he had emerged from the maze with Gwendolyn and Percy, she had met them with smiling eagerness. And as soon as everyone was mounted again, she had skillfully brought her horse alongside his own.

She talked and talked, the words tumbling from her, about steeple-chasing and riding to the hounds, about tack and saddles and bridles and reins, about hay and oats, about pastures and stables. On and on she went, eager, hurried, and Christopher listened, nodded, wondering at the sparkling glances she gave him, the broad smiles, the way she leaned in her saddle toward him.

He found himself thinking of how Gwendolyn looked at the Earl in the same way. How close they had seemed, walking arm-in-arm from the pavilion into the maze.

It came to him then, slowly, subtly—how agreeable it must be to share that kind of connection. To be so close to another person, emotionally, physically.

Although "agreeable" was far too tame a word.

He looked at Helen, smiled and nodded, inside him a new longing.

A new and powerful longing.

When finally they arrived at the Egremont townhouse, Gwendolyn saw Helen tugging at the Duchess's sleeve, whispering to her; the Duchess nodded, then said to Christopher:

"Would you like to join us for tea tomorrow afternoon, Mr. Beck? There's to be a little practice dance after, so that Owen can reacquaint himself with the various steps, but of course you wouldn't be obliged to participate."

"Thank you, ma'am, I'd like that. And the practice dance as well." He smiled. "I need to more than reacquaint myself with the steps—they're strangers to me, I'm afraid."

"*Un naïf*, Mr. Beck?" said Monsieur de Montmorency. "And you so advanced in age." His voice was pleasant but there was within it—to Gwendolyn's ears at least—the faintest undercurrent of malice.

"Alas, yes," answered Christopher easily. "I had no interest in what you might call proper dancing. On the other hand, I'm not bad at the *pentozali*, though I doubt it's popular in London ballrooms." He laughed.

"The pento—pento *what*, Mr. Beck?" Helen said.

"The *pentozali*. It's a Greek folk dance. It begins slowly and then gets quite energetic."

"How *fascinating*," replied Helen, with rather loud enthusiasm. "Maybe you could show us tomorrow."

"How came you to learn a Greek dance, Mr. Beck?" inquired the Earl. "On your Grand Tour, I suppose?"

Christopher laughed again. "I wouldn't call it that, sir. I lived in Greece for a while, working in the olive groves."

"Indeed? Overseeing some family property?"

"No, sir. Picking olives."

Monsieur de Montmorency murmured, *"Naturellement,"* and Gwendolyn found herself suddenly very glad that his boots had gotten ruined.

"Olives!" said Lady Almira. "Once I nearly choked to death on a pit, and somebody clapped me on the back so hard I'm afraid I quite *spat* it out and it bounced onto someone else's plate, right into their boiled potatoes."

Owen and Percy guffawed, Helen looked mortified, and the Earl said to Christopher, "How very interesting," with such pleasant civility that Gwendolyn's heart swelled with love for him all over again. The Duchess graciously extended the invitation to tea to the Earl and Monsieur de Montmorency, who both accepted; after which the party began to break up—those who were returning to the townhouse, and those who were going their separate ways elsewhere—and Gwendolyn took a moment, as she and the Earl said their goodbyes, to add:

"I'm so looking forward to the Aymesburtons' ball tonight."

"As am I, my love."

Later, preparing for the ball, Gwendolyn said to her maid Lizzie, "I'd like to wear the white net and satin gown, please—the one with the blue trim and the little row of points below the bodice."

Lizzie answered, a little doubtfully, "You wore that just last week, miss. Are you sure?"

"Oh yes, it's one of my favorites." When Lizzie still looked hesitant, Gwendolyn laughed. "I know, it's dreadfully unfashionable to be seen in the same gown! But I don't care."

"As you like, miss." Lizzie went over to the capacious oak armoire and carefully took from it the frock, then laid it on the bed till Gwendolyn was ready to put it on. "It *is* lovely, miss, it's easy to see why you favor it so." She returned to where Gwendolyn sat at her dressing-table, and went on, "How would you like to do your hair, miss?"

Gwendolyn smiled at Lizzie in the mirror's reflection. "You do take such very good care of me, Lizzie. You're right to try and set me straight, you know. I'm afraid I'm a stubborn, troublesome mistress to you."

"Oh, no, not a bit of it, miss," exclaimed Lizzie, her

round, pleasant face flushing up beneath her white ruffled cap. "You're ever so easy and kind, truly you are."

"I'm glad you think so. Now then, what do you propose for my hair?"

"Dressed high up toward the back of your head, miss? With that little pearl band, and some ringlets about your forehead? 'Twould be wondrous cunning."

Gwendolyn laughed. "You know how I feel about the curling-tongs! Well, you'll wear me down eventually, I suppose. But for tonight, perhaps let's just draw back the front hair with some pins—those pretty ones with the little brilliants on them."

"Very well, miss," said Lizzie, and went about her work, and when she was done, Gwendolyn was pleased with the results. Her gown really was lovely, with its short puffed sleeves and rather full skirt; she liked how it swirled about her ankles when she danced. And Lizzie was a marvel with her hair—it looked so sleek and elegant, with just a touch of pomade to give it an added luster. Gwendolyn did want to look nice for the Earl. In fact, she wanted to look *tempting* to him. For she had been thinking hard. She wasn't finished with her scientific experiment.

On the sofa opposite Christopher, Percy lay half-sprawled, holding in one hand a glass full to the brim with brandy. His neckcloth had loosened and his golden hair was rumpled. "This," he said cheerfully to Christopher, "is rather more in my line."

Christopher glanced around the crowded drawing-room. As they'd ridden away from the Egremont town-house, Percy had invited him to an evening-party hosted by the Viscount and Viscountess Tarrington in their pa-latial townhouse in Berkeley Square. Gilding and crystal and mirrors everywhere, the fatty sweet scent of innumerable candles burning, soft rich carpets underfoot, everything suggestive of money liberally spent.

The Viscountess herself—a self-assured woman in her mid-twenties who spoke in a Scottish accent intermingled with some kind of French patois—seemed eminently suited to such an opulent setting: she was dressed in velvet and silks, and jewels sparkled in her earlobes, her befeathered headdress, on her fingers and at her wrists; around her neck and descending into a daringly low décolletage which showcased a monumental embonpoint. (Her husband the Viscount, on the other hand, looked abashed in his expensive-looking evening-clothes, stared around him as if amazed by his luxurious surroundings, spoke in a stammering mutter, and altogether gave the strong impression of being a fish out of water.)

As for the gathering, the atmosphere here was decidedly less formal than that which he'd encountered last night at the Duchess's; it was much noisier. Voices were louder and there was a good deal of raucous laughter. People were drinking, playing cards, helping themselves to a lavish buffet which took up the entire length of a wall; servants circulated busily, replenishing beverages and carrying away empty plates and glasses.

Christopher looked thoughtfully at the champagne flute he held in one hand. So assiduous were the servants that he could have been well on the way toward being entirely drunk by now. But last night had sufficed on that score, and he was content with the one glass he'd had. Owen—seated next to Percy—seemed to have come to the same decision, and was instead happily and methodically plundering the buffet, just now focusing his attention on an enormous lamb cutlet swimming in mushroom sauce.

Francis had declined the invitation, saying he wanted

to work on his essay about Emanuel Swedenborg, which only made Percy roll his eyes and say, *Some dashed dull dog, I've no doubt, quite likely moldering in his grave. Come on and join us, there's a good fellow, Frank!*

Francis had stood his ground, however, and for a minute or two Percy seemed genuinely angry with him. And then Helen had sidled over to where Christopher stood next to his horse and said with what struck him as a kind of nervous intensity, *I say, you will come tomorrow, won't you?*

He had smiled and nodded, and she looked oddly relieved. Disproportionately relieved. For some reason he had felt sorry for her.

It had felt much more natural to hear Gwendolyn say goodbye to him, to hear her say, easily, *Tomorrow then, Christopher*, and to see her friendly smile.

He wondered where she was tonight.

He hoped she was having a good time, wherever she was.

"**T**his is nearly as good as a maze, isn't it?" Gwendolyn said mischievously, provocatively, to the Earl. They had left the Aymesburtons' ballroom through one of the wide-open French doors and onto a broad stone portico; from there they had made their way into a long, deep garden filled with beautifully tended sycamore, elm, and beech trees as well as a dazzling variety of shrubs and flowerbeds, leaving behind them the bright flickering candelabra, the crowded parquet floor, the music of the orchestra. Now they stood in a remote, quiet corner of the garden, shielded from view by two towering marble planters filled with fragrant white Daphne flowers.

The Earl looked down at her in the moonlight, smiling.

"If I didn't know any better, my darling, I'd guess you were trying to lead me astray."

"Can you, Julian?" Gwendolyn stepped closer to him, her heart beating strongly within her, and her breath coming more rapidly. "Be led astray?"

"Lead away," was all he said, before taking her in his arms.

So far so good, she thought, and reached up to cradle his handsome face between her hands. *Here goes.* "Julian," she whispered, "let *me* kiss *you.*"

He gave a soft laugh. "You're full of surprises, my love."

Gwendolyn supposed she was being unmaidenly, or indecorous, or immodest, or brazen, or wanton—or any one of the dozens of words used to describe female behavior in a negative way—but what did she care?

She would not be judged.

The heart wanted what the heart wanted.

And so did the body.

Flowing all throughout her—legs, arms, breasts, between her legs, *everywhere*—was a wonderful, warm, pulsing energy, delicious, fiery, demanding. And *good.* Of that she had no doubt. Goodness incarnate.

She lifted herself up on her toes and brought her mouth onto Julian's. His beautiful warm mouth. She wanted it. Wanted him.

His lips parted, and his tongue was there, wet and eager.

"No," she whispered. "Let me."

Obediently he subsided. But she could hear, feel, *his* breath coming faster, too, and was satisfied.

And now, for the first time, her tongue was tasting, exploring him. A tang of champagne, a hint of chocolate. Yes, delicious.

She kissed him cautiously. Slowly; unsurely. Then with more confidence.

He was lovely, *this* was lovely.

This was what she wanted.

The feel of his tall strong body against hers; the smooth, yet slightly rough texture of his warm skin against the soft flesh of her hands.

Oh, *bliss*.

A little happy breathy sound escaped her and firmly she wound her arms around his neck to bring herself yet closer.

"My love," Julian murmured against her mouth, his deep voice ragged. "Let me now—let me—"

One of his hands was between them and at her chest, searching, searching, till it found the curve of her left breast, cupping it, squeezing in a slow deliberate way that suddenly made Gwendolyn think of how one might test a pear for ripeness. And then it was Julian who was doing the kissing now, filling her mouth fully with his tongue, jerking her out of that sweet trance of pleasure as his hand groped for her other breast, finding it, slowly squeezing it—like a grocer in a shop, she thought, and despite herself the image instantly formed in her mind. A scale and a signboard: FRUIT FOR SALE. Julian the proprietor, enveloped in a big white apron, delicately evaluating the pears while customers stood by, ready with their baskets.

Don't laugh, don't laugh, she sternly warned herself, and tried to focus again on sensation alone, Julian's warm hand against the thin layers of silk and cambric of her bodice, the lingering kiss which had begun to feel rather familiar—so soon?—and now his other hand sliding down along her waist, around the curve of her hip, to the small of her back and down, quickly, to her backside which he clenched so enthusiastically that she let out a shrill yawp of surprise.

Oh dear, she sounded exactly like Señor Rodrigo whenever someone surprised him in a nap. He'd bolt awake clutching his perch and make *just* that sound, glaring so comically that it was impossible not to laugh.

"My darling, my precious darling, I'm so very sorry." Julian was peering anxiously into her face. "I'm afraid I got carried away—the throes of passion, you know. I'm dreadfully sorry."

With supreme effort Gwendolyn banished the memories of Señor Rodrigo looking both deeply offended and extremely indignant, and managed likewise to repress the fit of giggles bubbling inside her. It would be terrible to laugh at such a moment. "No, no, Julian, you didn't hurt me," she said, glad that she sounded reasonably composed. "You only—you only surprised me, that's all."

"It's just that—" He drew her into his arms again. "It's just that you're so beautiful, so lovely, and I want you so much, my darling."

"I want you too."

"My love, my love," he whispered, and began to kiss her all over her upturned face—quick, light touches of his lips upon her forehead, cheeks, chin, mouth—and next he bent his head to nuzzle at the side of her face, to nibble at her earlobe, to draw his tongue around the perimeter of her ear.

"Oh my," murmured Gwendolyn, feeling her body react with a jolt of warm sinuous pleasure. "Do that again, Julian."

He did, and Gwendolyn forgot all about pears and giggling and Señor Rodrigo. That warm pleasure within her bloomed and spread, all throughout her, everywhere, till there was nothing but this moment, this man, this *goodness*—

"You're so beautiful, so very beautiful," Julian said softly into her ear, and she shivered deliciously. "Can you feel how much I want you?"

Could she? Gwendolyn found herself puzzling over the question. Because he was giving her pleasure, did that mean she could assume he desired her? Also, even though she was inexperienced in these matters, it did sound like one of those questions which presumed an affirmative sort of response. Should she lie and say yes, despite not being really sure? She hated lying. Honesty was something that was so very important to her. On the other hand, she didn't want to hurt Julian's feelings. Was this a situation in which a small falsehood would serve the greater good?

Apparently it was all right not to say anything, as Julian was taking her hand and smiling at her.

"Let me show you," he said softly. "Let me show you how much I want you, my love."

He brought her hand to the front of his black silk breeches, and gently pressed it to the—well, there was a hard cylindrical sort of thing underneath the silk. It had to be an actual part of his anatomy. What a curious shape, all tube-like. And then it made sense.

Once, at home, back when she and her brothers had been little and they would take their baths in the kitchen, she had just come into the entry hall and the door to the kitchen passageway was flung open. Out hurtled Francis, stark naked and wet, followed by Percy, also naked and wet, brandishing a piece of toweling which he was flicking at Francis's bottom, both of them howling with laughter. This was how she'd learned a little bit about the male body and its appendages. Oh, how scandalized Cook had been by the boys' behavior! Even so, Gwendolyn, Percy, and Francis had laughed about it for months afterwards.

"You can squeeze it," Julian whispered encouragingly.

"What?"

His hand closed over hers a little more firmly, to dem-

onstrate what he meant. "Go ahead, my love, you won't
hurt me."

Squeeze it?

And right away, there it was in her hideously unruly
imagination: the scale and the signboard, only now it read
VEGETABLES FOR SALE, Julian in the big white apron, encouraging a customer to test a—a *cucumber* for firmness.

Gwendolyn bit her lip, hard. She would not laugh. But
neither was she going to squeeze Julian's body part. Even if
it meant she was being ungenerous after he had licked her
ear and made her feel so good. Besides, surely that wasn't
the way things were supposed to go? Surely she wasn't
obligated to do things, just because he'd done things to her?

Suddenly Gwendolyn felt very confused. And tired—
not physically, but mentally. Her *brain* was exhausted.
How had life gotten so complicated, and so quickly? She
pulled her hand free and stepped back. "Julian, I think
I hear someone coming." Which was a lame, stupid lie.
And irrationally, she blamed him for it. She was glad
when they began walking back to the ballroom. He was
thanking her, thanking her over and over again with sweet
earnestness, and she was ashamed by how relieved she
was to go on to her next partner, for a quadrille, and to
make a little light chitchat with him, and let her mind rest
for a while.

When she was back in her bedroom in the Egremont
townhouse, in her nightgown and with her hair plaited by
Lizzie into a single long braid down her back, she still
didn't feel physically tired, even though it was very late
in the evening.

"Leave those candles, Lizzie. I'll blow them out myself."

"Are you sure, miss?"

"Yes indeed. Thank you—and goodnight."

When Lizzie had left, closing the door carefully

behind her, Gwendolyn wondered what she should do now. Thanks to Lizzie, her room was immaculate and orderly, so there was nothing to tidy up.

Gwendolyn went to the fireplace and picked up one of the iron pokers with which she idly and unnecessarily jabbed at the cheerily burning logs. The warmth from the fire felt good on her bare toes, but she couldn't stand here all night poking logs. Maybe she could read for a while?

She went to the table next to her bed and looked at the volumes there.

Endymion. History of a Six Weeks' Tour. Frankenstein. Rob Roy. Emma. Characters of Shakespeare's Plays. And Katherine's *English Ships Out of Portsmouth: A National Heritage*, which Aunt Claudia had illustrated so wonderfully, just as she had for Katherine's first book, about Liverpool ships. Gwendolyn was nearly finished with *English Ships Out of Portsmouth*, admiring Katherine's writing so much, and Aunt Claudia's drawings, too, but she just wasn't in the mood to read right now.

Her eye fell upon the table's drawer.

Of course!

She pulled open the drawer. There was her sketchbook and a variety of pencils as well as Conté crayons in black, white, gray, reddish brown. It was always soothing to draw when she felt restless or troubled.

Gwendolyn got into bed, propped up her pillows, tugged the covers up around her waist, and opened her sketchbook to a blank page.

What should she draw?

A sparkle of crimson abruptly drew her attention to her left hand, to the lovely antique ring Julian had given her; the way the rubies glittered in the candlelight was almost mesmerizing.

Imagine—Queen Elizabeth herself had held this ring in her hand so many years ago. Julian's ancestress had worn it, as had so many others in the Westenbury line. Beyond its monetary value, the historical and sentimental heritage of this ring was quite literally priceless. That Julian had given it to *her* was a clear symbol of his love—his devotion—his trust.

Julian. Soon to be her husband.

Gwendolyn used a plain graphite pencil to begin creating a sketch of his beautifully molded head, his hair so fashionably cropped *à la Brutus*, and strong wide shoulders. When at length she got to his mouth—its firm and shapely lines straight out of classical antiquity—she paused.

What had she learned so far in her scientific experiment?

She thought about what had happened today between the Earl and herself, at Richmond and at the ball.

A little chill went through her, and she pulled the covers a bit higher.

It certainly seemed as if she didn't enjoy kissing as much as she'd thought she would.

There had been moments when she did, but overall today's experiences hadn't gone as she'd hoped.

This was a disturbing conclusion.

She had tried hard to enjoy it all. And Julian had been very eager. Flatteringly so, in fact.

What had gone wrong?

Perhaps this was a time for brutal honesty. After all, she did value honesty so deeply.

And maybe the truth was that there was something wrong with her.

Gwendolyn recalled again the time she had interrupted Katherine and Hugo in Katherine's study—how happy they looked emerging from the kiss they'd been sharing. And she suddenly remembered her friend Diana,

Christopher's sister, telling her, back in Whitehaven when they were both about fifteen, that she'd let the butcher's son—a bold, good-looking lad much admired by the town's girls—kiss her behind the shop. *Oh, it was marvelous, Gwennie, and so romantic, I felt as if I was floating,* Diana had said. *I could have let him kiss me forever if his mother hadn't come out and found us. I wonder how she knew we were there?*

Gwendolyn remembered being amazed that Diana had thought being kissed behind the butcher's shop romantic. The smell certainly wasn't. But evidently kissing was so delightful that one could overlook such sordid surroundings.

Oh dear, there *had* to be something wrong with her.

Gwendolyn blinked and realized that she'd left off Julian's portrait and had instead drawn a little pear on a scale.

She looked down at her chest.

Was the problem that she wasn't—well, made for desire?

Her breasts were quite small, nor did she have much in the way of hips. Maybe she wasn't womanly enough.

She drew another pear.

Or maybe she was just bad at kissing.

She drew two little disembodied tongues holding tiny swords. She gave them fierce faces. And had one of them say, in a stream of words in all-capital letters issuing from its disproportionately large mouth, *En garde!*

It didn't seem as humorous as it had earlier on.

She wished there were someone she could ask about kissing and so on. If she were at home, she could probably talk to Katherine, who was so kind and clever, and as dear to her as any sister-by-birth could be. But she wasn't at home, and it wasn't the sort of thing one could write about in a letter. Besides, this was *urgent*.

Gwendolyn cast about in her mind for someone else in whom she could confide such a very unsettling question.

The Duchess was very nice, but it would still feel awkward introducing an extremely delicate topic like this.

Lady Almira? Also very nice, but apt to blurt things out.

What about Helen, someone her own age?

No—she didn't feel close enough to Helen. The same was true for the young ladies among her acquaintance here in London. She had made some nice new friends, but still would hesitate to divulge something so personal.

Francis or Percy? Goodness, no.

All at once Gwendolyn felt very alone.

She had begun this day with such high hopes, and now that it was coming to an end, she felt sad, confused, worried, and very, very alone.

She gave a deep sigh, sinking a little lower on her pillows.

And she saw, looking at her sketchbook, that she had been, all unknowingly, drawing Christopher.

What a very interesting face he had. Not handsome in the way the Earl was, but there was something so compelling about Christopher's eyes—the strong line of his jaw—the unfussy way he wore his long dark hair. And there was a quickness about him, an easy sort of alertness, a confidence in the way he held his body, which she had, she thought, looking critically at her sketch, managed to convey pretty well.

It was strange to think that it was only last night that their lives had intersected again. And yet how easy it had been to talk together. He was a good listener, too.

Gwendolyn was glad Christopher would be coming over tomorrow. Here at least was something she didn't have to be confused or worried about.

Tomorrow she would see Christopher, her friend.

She finished his portrait by adding a few more details— some quick lines to his neckcloth, the suggestion of a smile dancing in his eyes, some shading about his boots to make it clear he wasn't floating in space but, rather, had his feet firmly on the ground.

There. Done.

Gwendolyn found herself thinking of what Christopher had told her about his time in Italy. About staying at Mauro's. She drew a horse, with its head lifted proudly, and then another one, this one in motion with its mane flying. She wondered what Mauro looked like, and what his old yellow-brick house looked like, too.

She made a little sketch from pure fancy, but it wasn't satisfying. What she liked best was drawing things from life.

A yawn suddenly overtook her.

Thank goodness, she was getting sleepy at last.

Gwendolyn put her sketchbook and pencil next to her stack of books, got up, and blew out the candles which Lizzie had set on a tall bureau on the other side of the bed. Then she slid underneath the covers and yawned again, feeling somehow better about life, and fell fast asleep.

Chapter 7

❧

Christopher walked along Brook Street on his way to the Egremont townhouse. It was another mild afternoon and he was glad to be outdoors enjoying it. He could have called a hack from his lodgings in Piccadilly, but he wanted the exercise.

He turned onto Davies Street, then went on to Grosvenor Street and toward the large green garden square around which several magnificent townhouses clustered. The vista before him was vibrant with life: children played on the green, with their governesses attendant, carriages rolled to and fro, there were riders and pedestrians all about. He came around the green and was just about to cross the street to the Egremont townhouse when there came an anguished scream.

"*Purkoy!* Oh, my Purkoy! Come *back*!"

Two elegantly dressed women stood on the pavement near a stylish carriage stopped in front of the Duchess's—the one who had screamed was gesturing toward a fat little King Charles spaniel which at present was careening around the street, ignoring her and in imminent risk of being trampled by a horse.

A footman leaped off the back of the carriage and tried

in vain to capture the little dog, who clearly thought this a delightful game and one which it intended to continue for as long as possible. It dashed toward an oncoming carriage, yapped with absurd braggadocio at the horses, and, as the woman screamed again, veered away from the deadly hooves at the very last second.

Well, there was nothing for it, thought Christopher. The footman wasn't having much luck, so he'd try and help that idiotic little dog, too.

He looked around and saw a boy of about five or six staring at the melee through the widely spaced iron pickets of the square's fence. In one hand was a large piece of bread-and-butter which he had perhaps forgotten in all the excitement. Christopher went over to the fence, crouched down on his heels, and said to the little boy who was now more or less at his eye-level:

"May I have that slice of bread?"

The boy looked at him suspiciously. "It's mine."

"I know that. But it would be a great help if you gave it to me."

"Why?"

"So I can try to catch that dog."

"Do dogs like bread-and-butter? Ours only get meat."

"I think that little dog eats whatever it can get."

The boy looked at the slice in his hand, and then at Christopher. "You'll not run away and eat it all yourself?"

"I promise," he said gravely.

"Very well," said the little boy, just as gravely, and reached through the pickets to hold out the bread-and-butter to Christopher.

He took it. "Thank you very much," he said to the little boy, who solemnly nodded, as one man to another, and as it was obvious to Christopher that smiling at him might possibly be an affront to the boy's dignity, he nodded back, then straightened up and went with swift steps to the street, where he saw the dog Purkoy standing as if frozen, eyeing the footman who was slowly approaching and saying in an appeasing tone:

"That's right, that's right, stay where you are, there's a good doggie."

The footman got within arm's length and made a desperate grab for Purkoy, who nimbly shot between his legs with a visibly merry look on his face, showing his teeth in what Christopher had no doubt was an actual grin.

The woman on the pavement screamed *"Purkoy!"* again and in her voice was also desperation.

Blithely oblivious, Purkoy shot past Christopher and dodged an oncoming horse and rider, then looked as if he were about to make friends with a large pile of horse-droppings. Christopher said in a friendly but firm voice, "Purkoy. Come."

Perhaps the little dog registered the easy authority in the stranger's tone, for it stopped, turned, its ears pricked high as it looked at Christopher. Skittish. Ready to bolt. Another one of those mad dashes might very well lead the dog to an ugly death. He repeated "Purkoy, come," crouched down again on his heels, and held out the bread-and-butter temptingly low.

The little dog cocked its head and Christopher could almost hear the tiny, tiny gears in its equally tiny brain turning as it weighed the advantages of food versus running about playing games with the amusingly slow and clumsy humans.

Finally, the demands of the stomach seemed to win out, for slowly Purkoy approached Christopher, his little brown eyes darting back and forth from the bread to Christopher's face. Christopher, meanwhile, remained still, completely still, as if he had nothing better to do, and when Purkoy came close enough to snatch a bite of the bread, he only waited. Waited until the dog had taken a few more bites and was engrossed in the act of eating. Then he dropped the remaining bread on the ground and as Purkoy rushed at it, picked him up and stood.

"You," he said pleasantly, "are a fool." And Purkoy, as if he had not just disrupted an entire street of Grosvenor Square and imperiled his very existence, wagged his curly tail and tried to lick Christopher's chin. "I think not," he said, still pleasantly, to Purkoy and then went to the pavement where the two fashionable ladies stood.

One of them, with dark curly hair and bright dark eyes brimming with tears, hurried over to him and held out her arms. He passed Purkoy over to her and she said lovingly, "Oh, *here* you are, you dreadful, nasty, impertinent little beast," and permitted the joyfully wiggling Purkoy to lick her chin with servile enthusiasm. Then she looked up at Christopher. "Thank you *so* much, I really don't even know how to thank you properly."

He watched with some amusement as her dark eyes assessed him, knowing that she was wondering if she ought to press on him a gratuity. His clothing, he assumed, persuaded her otherwise for she went on, delicately, inquiringly, "Mr.—?"

"Christopher Beck, ma'am," he said, in his voice the same gravity with which he had conducted a solemn conversation with the little boy in the green. "Delighted to be of help."

She gave a gracious little bow, then handed Purkoy over to her footman, who carried Purkoy over to the carriage and shut him in with careful punctiliousness, then stood by the door as if there was even a remote possibility that Purkoy would figure out how to turn the handle and escape again.

The door to the Egremont townhouse opened and Gwendolyn came hurrying out and down the steps, the skirts of her pretty white gown fluttering and at the same time revealing, to all who cared to notice, a charming pair of ankles. "I saw it all," she said, smiling and breathless. "Oh, well *done*, Christopher!" She turned to the elegant woman and went on, "Lady Jersey, I'm so glad you got your little dog back safely! My heart was in my throat the whole time!"

"As was mine, Miss Penhallow, I do assure you," said the elegantly dressed lady—Lady Jersey, evidently. "You are acquainted with Mr. Beck, I see."

"Oh yes, ma'am. Christopher's a friend of mine from back home."

"Indeed," said Lady Jersey, and Christopher saw the same assessing expression in her dark eyes as she looked at him again. Clearly she was wondering how to categorize him. Was he on equal par with the Penhallows? Or a *parvenu*—a social upstart who ought to be discreetly quashed? Luckily, that was her problem and not his. He smiled pleasantly at her. For just the tiniest second she seemed surprised by his smile, and then she returned it. "Mr. Beck, may I introduce you to the Honorable Mrs. Drummond-Burrell? My dear Clementina, do come and meet Mr. Beck."

At this, the other fashionable lady slowly came forward, moving with such deliberate precision that she gave the impression of gliding on wheels instead of actually walking. She looked at Christopher as she might eye a small repugnant insect which had had the temerity to climb onto her exquisite nankeen half-boot.

He wanted to laugh, but only said, politely, "How do you do, ma'am."

She gave a small, chilly bow. "Mr. Beck." And then, thawing slightly: "Good afternoon, Miss Penhallow."

"Good afternoon, ma'am. How kind of you to call on us. Won't you all please come in?"

Lady Jersey and Mrs. Drummond-Burrell stayed only long enough for a cup of tea each. Mrs. Drummond-Burrell unbent sufficiently to talk a little with the Duchess, whereas Lady Jersey—who seemed to have a lively, amiable disposition—managed to chat with not only the Duchess, but also Lady Almira, Gwendolyn, and, finally, himself. She warmly repeated her thanks for his rescue of Purkoy, then surprised him when she said:

"Where are you staying here in London, Mr. Beck?"

"At the Albany, ma'am."

"Indeed?" That assessing look again. "A delightful residence. I understand the rents there are exorbitant."

He repressed a grin. It wouldn't do to say *Fishing, eh?* "I'm comfortable there, ma'am."

A little smile curved her mouth, as if acknowledging his civil evasion. But she wasn't done. "You're quite tanned, Mr. Beck. You're an outdoorsman?"

"I've spent the past few years working outside, ma'am, so yes, I suppose that makes me one."

Her delicate eyebrows rose. "Working at what?"

"Picking olives, ma'am, and training horses."

"I see."

Christopher could only imagine her ladyship's mental processes of trying to align olive-picking, his friendship with Gwendolyn Penhallow as well as with the Duchess, and being able to afford rent at the Albany. Telling her about pirates, he thought, or about shipping out with rum smugglers might undo her completely.

Lady Jersey surprised him again by smiling yet more broadly. "I think, Mr. Beck, that you are—to employ a modern colloquialism—quite the deep one."

He smiled back. "Is that a compliment, ma'am, or an aspersion?"

"I think—" She looked at him consideringly. "I think perhaps the former." She rose to her feet in a rustle of silk and taffeta. "It was a pleasure to meet you, Mr. Beck."

He stood up as well, and bowed. "Likewise, ma'am."

Lady Jersey and Mrs. Drummond-Burrell left just as the Earl of Westenbury and Étienne de Montmorency arrived. Greetings were exchanged, and Christopher watched with amusement as Mrs. Drummond-Burrell favored both gentlemen with a gloved hand over which they might bow. Quite the mark of her approbation apparently. And then she glided away.

Gwendolyn had come to stand next to him, and all at once she giggled. "Oh, Christopher," she whispered, her blue eyes alight with humor, "don't you wonder how she does that?"

"Once, in Rome," he said, "I saw a man wearing a sort of skating-shoe. They were made out of foot-shaped wooden boards, with four metal wheels attached underneath, and had leather straps fastened around his shoes. He was rolling along the Via la Spezia, as fine as fivepence. Until—alas—he came upon a little spray of pebbles on the roadway."

"Oh dear," said Gwendolyn. Then she giggled again. "Let's hope Mrs. Drummond-Burrell doesn't meet the same fate. It would quite undo all her dignity. She's such a dreadful snob! Oh, Christopher, I'm *awful*, aren't I?"

He smiled down at her. "Well, *signorina,* if you are, I am too."

"**G**ood heavens, Sally, what mad spirit has possessed you?" Clementina Drummond-Burrell looked across the carriage at Lady Jersey, in her voice both astonishment and dismay. "Vouchers for Almack's for that odd young man? To be sure, it was commendable of him to catch

Purkoy, but you needn't bestow *vouchers* as a token of your gratitude."

"Oh, I'm not, I'm not." Lady Jersey was holding Purkoy in her arms, and now pressed a kiss upon his silken little head. She looked back at Mrs. Drummond-Burrell, a distinctly mischievous expression in her lively dark eyes. "I like Mr. Beck. He's quite interesting, don't you think? And the latest crop of young men are, by and large, so *dull*."

"We know nothing about him."

"I do. He's picked olives and trained horses."

Mrs. Drummond-Burrell looked alarmed. "What?"

"I daresay that accounts for how robust he looks. He's good-looking, too, isn't he? And not just in the common way. If I were a trifle younger . . . Well, that's neither here nor there. I'm going to send him vouchers, Clementina, and I'm going to invite him to my evening-party on Friday."

"Sally . . ."

Lady Jersey chuckled. "You'll be needing smelling-salts when I tell you what else I'm going to do."

"What is it?" said Mrs. Drummond-Burrell, the very picture of dread.

"You know Prinny's hosting a *fête* at Carlton House on the fourteenth. I'm having a little private supper with him tonight, and I think I'll suggest—"

"Sally, you *wouldn't*."

Lady Jersey chuckled again. "Oh yes, I would."

Gwendolyn and Christopher were seated together on a sofa, holding their teacups and laughing. She said, "You were *so* furious with me, do you remember?"

"Only because you had climbed the tallest tree behind my house."

"Oh, that lovely beech! Well, I had to, of course. Percy said I couldn't do it."

"More fool he."

"That's what I thought! And I had to climb that particular tree, because ours weren't as tall."

"I suppose I should apologize for shouting at you like that. In retrospect, I was more worried than angry."

"Were you? That's very sweet. At the time I thought you were upset because I was trespassing."

"God, no. You had climbed up to the top—very nearly at the level of our roof. I was afraid you'd be stuck up there."

She laughed. "Not a bit of it! Although I *will* concede that it was harder coming down than it was going up. Do you remember how covered in scratches I was?"

Christopher laughed as well. "Yes. You were very gleeful, too. You said the breeches and shirt you stole from Percy were ruined, which would serve him right."

"Well, the joke was on me. Mama made me mend them, and it took *hours*."

"Worth it anyway?"

"Yes." Gwendolyn laughed again. She did like the way Christopher's eyes crinkled up at the corners when he was smiling like that.

"What are you two laughing about?" It was Helen, who had come to stand next to Christopher.

"Oh, about old times," Gwendolyn answered.

"Oh. Can I join you?"

Gwendolyn paused, suddenly feeling very awkward. The sofa wasn't really made for three people. She supposed she should give her place away to Helen. But—strangely, stubbornly—she didn't want to. Christopher said:

"You can have my seat, Miss FitzClarence."

"You don't need to go," Helen quickly replied, and lowered herself onto the sofa next to him. He slid over, which brought him rather close to Gwendolyn, and she considered squeezing herself against the sofa's armrest to make more room for him, but decided she wouldn't, torn between annoyance at Helen and wanting to laugh at how silly the three of them probably looked, crowded together like this. Also, she noticed, she was enjoying sitting right next to Christopher. He exuded a kind of—of *solidness* that was very appealing. An easiness in himself. And she liked how he smelled, too. A hint of soap, really, that's all it was, but it was subtle and clean and masculine.

Gwendolyn took a deep appreciative breath.

And then another scent teased her nostrils. It was rather familiar somehow, wasn't it? Like . . . a garden or something like that?

She sniffed again.

And frowned.

Why, it smelled exactly like her own perfume, a light rosewater scent she occasionally used.

But she wasn't wearing it today, so . . .

Gwendolyn leaned forward and looked past Christopher to Helen. She breathed in deeply, and there was her confirmation: Helen smelled like a giant bouquet of roses, in fact.

How very irritating.

Also, how odd.

Helen never wore scent of any kind. Not only that, she had a green silk ribbon woven among her red curls today—usually she scoffed at such things as being stupid furbelows. And she was wearing jewelry as well! A pair of pretty emerald ear-bobs, and a matching emerald necklace, very dainty and fine.

What was Helen up to?

Just at the moment, Gwendolyn saw, she was gazing at Christopher, with an expression Gwendolyn couldn't decipher. Was it admiration, or something else?

"Are you going to show us that—that pento dance after tea, Mr. Beck?" Helen asked.

Her voice was sweet. Noticeably sweet. As if she was making an effort to subdue the gruffness that was usually there.

"The *pentozali*?" Christopher laughed. "I'd prefer to embarrass myself in other ways. Like learning how to waltz."

"I'll show you," Helen said quickly, "it's a very jolly dance."

Gwendolyn stared at her in astonishment. Helen hated to dance. What was going on here?

She stared at Helen staring at Christopher.

And then it came to her.

Goodness gracious, was Helen actually setting her cap at Christopher?

Gwendolyn leaned back and took a long sip of her tea. A curious jumble of thoughts and emotions roiled within her, chief among them a feeling of distaste. She didn't like the idea of Helen and Christopher together. On the other hand, what business was it of hers? Was she—again—being proprietary simply because Christopher was *her* friend? That wouldn't make her much of a friend, would it?

She searched inside herself and what rang true, very deeply, was a sincere—genuine—*strong* desire for Christopher to be happy.

Well then. That would guide her actions.

If Helen liked him, and he liked her, she certainly wouldn't stand in their way.

Even if, a tiny secret part of her whispered stubbornly, she still didn't like the idea of it.

"Is everyone ready for our little practice dance?" inquired the Duchess. "That is, those who wish to participate?"

Owen groaned, sliding down low in his armchair, and Helen said mockingly:

"Scared, brother dear?"

"Not *scared*," muttered Owen resentfully. "Not *interested*."

"Easiest thing in the world," declared Percy, jumping to his feet. "Come on, Helen, old girl, let's show him how it's done."

"But I—I was—" Helen glanced at Christopher, visibly upset.

"I'm sure we'll have a chance later, Miss FitzClarence," he said kindly. "That is, if you're brave enough to risk dancing with my ignorant self."

"Of course I am!" she answered loudly, standing up, and Gwendolyn saw her glance around the drawing-room, taking in the Earl and Étienne de Montmorency, Lady Almira and the Duchess, Percy and Christopher, and, finally, Francis, who still sat in his armchair, his tea untouched, gazing out the window.

As everyone else got up and began making their way to the ballroom, Francis remained in his chair, unmoving, and Gwendolyn went to him.

"Francis."

He turned and looked up at her. "Oh, hullo, Gwennie," he said, sounding as if he'd just returned from a journey. Which, she supposed, he probably had, in the intellectual sense. She smiled down at him.

"Our practice dance is starting."

"Oh, is it? Have a nice time."

"Aren't you joining us?"

"No. I know all the dances. Besides, I had the most interesting idea about Kant and Swedenborg, and I was just thinking about the implications for the essay I'm writing."

"You know the dances?"

"Yes. There's a book with all the steps. I read it before coming to London. It all seems very straightforward. Though why people make such a fuss about it I can't understand."

"Well, I suppose because it's fun for some people."

"Is it? Do you enjoy it?"

"I do. But I don't insist that everyone ought to feel the same way."

Francis nodded. *"Nosce te ipsum."*

"Know thyself," she said softly, and he nodded again.

The Earl called from the doorway, where he stood waiting: "Anything wrong?"

"No, Julian, not at all." Gwendolyn put her hand on Francis's shoulder. "Will you tell me more about your idea later?"

"If you like."

"I'll look forward to it." Gwendolyn went to the Earl, who looked so stunningly handsome and serene in his beautifully tailored bottle-green jacket and buff pantaloons that it was hard to remember exactly why she had been so unhappy last night. She'd probably just been tired—it had been a very long and busy day. One's spirits did tend to sink when one was fatigued. She smiled up at him as they turned into the long high-ceilinged hallway that led to the ballroom.

"Are you going to dance with me, Julian?"

"Of course I am, my darling. Francis isn't coming?"

"No, apparently he knows all the steps."

"Ought he to join us anyway? Being a guest of the Duchess and so on."

"Oh, I'm sure Cousin Judith won't mind."

"You don't think she might consider it a trifle rude of Francis?"

"No, I'm certain of it. She's so lovely and easygoing. Besides, she did say the practice dance was optional, you know."

"Still, perhaps Francis ought to bestir himself. Shall I go back and talk to him?"

"I really don't think that's necessary."

"I'm happy to do it. As his future brother-in-law, it's perfectly appropriate."

"I don't think it is, Julian."

They came to a halt and looked at each other, both of them, Gwendolyn thought, in perplexity. For an instant she felt the heavy weight of politeness bear down upon her—*don't make a fuss, don't make a scene, smooth over the troubled waters, let it go, it's not that important really, be nice, above all be nice*—and she pressed her lips together, as if to hold back the soothing words of apology, of retreat.

"Very well then, my dear," Julian said. "Shall we go on? I hear the piano."

"Yes, by all means."

They began walking again, and Gwendolyn glanced up at his face. His brow, which had been slightly wrinkled, was smooth once more, and his expression was benignant. She wondered, had this been their first quarrel?

The thought made Gwendolyn feel suddenly panicky. She didn't want to fight with him. She clutched at his hand and brought them to a halt again. "Julian," she whispered, "Julian, I love you." Quickly she looked left and right; the long hallway was, for the moment, empty but for themselves. She lifted herself up on her tiptoes and brought her mouth to his.

Very gently, he stepped away. "Not here, my darling." He disengaged his hand and smiled down at her. "I love you too. What we need is a garden or a maze right now, don't we?"

Panic had ebbed away, to be replaced by an acrid sense of humiliation. "Yes," she said, rather stonily. "That's what we need. Shall we go on?"

"Left foot here," said the Duchess to Christopher, "then step back and do a half-turn before returning to the center."

He did as she instructed. "How was that, ma'am?"

"Very good. Now we clasp hands and take three steps forward before parting, turning in a circle, and meeting again."

Christopher complied, and the Duchess said:

"You're getting the hang of it nicely, Mr. Beck. Now we wait while the others move down the line. If there *were* any others."

They were standing, just the two of them, in the center of the big ballroom. Lady Almira sat at a piano which a footman had rolled out of a corner and was playing a pretty, stately tune with, Christopher noticed with pleasure, remarkable skill and sensitivity. She even managed to turn the pages of her music-sheets without incident. *Sotto voce*, the Duchess added, "I *am* so sorry about Helen and Owen, Mr. Beck. Sometimes they act just like children."

Christopher glanced over to the long row of gilded chairs, set against a wall, which the footman had uncovered. Owen sat on one, arms crossed over his chest, and scowling; he had flatly refused to dance with his grandmother. Several seats away from him was Helen, *her* arms over her chest. She was scowling at Percy, who sat next to her.

"You said you'd dance with me, old girl," he was saying. "Come on then."

"I changed my mind."

"Don't be a bore! Keep to your word!"

"Go dance with Gwendolyn! Everyone knows she's a better dancer than I am!"

"Maybe because she's practiced! I say, what's gotten into you all of a sudden? In the drawing-room you were perfectly all right."

"I'm *fine*," Helen said between gritted teeth.

"The devil you are!" Percy jumped to his feet and went over to sit next to Owen.

Étienne de Montmorency, Christopher saw, stood at one of the windows, his expression inscrutable save for the thoughtful look in his pale-blue eyes. The light streaming in through the window made his pale hair look almost white, and lent his face a startling pallor.

The Duchess gave a little sigh. "And now we clasp hands again, take three steps forward, three steps back; finally, at the same time I curtsy—like so—you bow. Well done, Mr. Beck." The music had stopped and she called, "That's splendid, Almira, thank you so much."

Lady Almira beamed. "Shall I play another, dear ma'am?"

"Yes, do, here are Gwendolyn and Westenbury." In the Duchess's tone was relief, and she added in an undertone to Christopher, "We can count on *them*, at least."

But when Christopher looked at Gwendolyn, he saw that her earlier, cheerful mood had changed into something else. The Earl seemed untroubled, however. Odd. Especially as Gwendolyn seemed . . . deflated somehow. Sad; unhappy.

Christopher noticed in himself a quick, savage reaction and it took him a moment to figure out what it was.

Not anger, but something else.

Fierce and primitive and urgent.

Protectiveness.

If the Earl had hurt Gwendolyn—been unkind or cruel to her—

His hands, Christopher realized, had doubled into fists.

Steady, he warned himself. *Don't overreact. Just— observe.*

Carefully, deliberately, he relaxed his hands.

"Gwendolyn, m'dear, would you mind very much dancing with Owen?" said the Duchess.

"Not at all, ma'am," answered Gwendolyn, adding with what seemed to Christopher an unusual soberness, "If he doesn't mind dancing with me."

"*You're* all right," Owen said, unfolding his long skinny self from his chair. "I don't mind."

"You might," said the Duchess, "try for just a bit more finesse."

"I say, where's Francis?" demanded Helen.

"He's not coming." Gwendolyn turned back to the Duchess. "If that's all right with you, ma'am?"

"Of course it is," said the Duchess, and Christopher watched as Gwendolyn shot a look at the Earl, who didn't seem to notice.

"What do you mean, he's not coming?" Helen said, scowling at Gwendolyn. "Whyever not? What did you say to him? Did you upset him?"

"Helen," said the Duchess, "you might also try for a little more finesse. Almira, if you're ready?"

"Yes indeed, ma'am," responded Almira, and launched into another song.

Christopher danced with the Duchess, learning as he went, while Gwendolyn and Owen danced. Owen was not a good dancer, but Gwendolyn was kind, and patient, and tactful, and by the dance's end he seemed to have gained some confidence. The Duchess complimented him on his improvement, and Owen actually smiled.

The next dance was a quadrille, announced the Duchess.

Christopher thanked the Duchess for all her help, and then went to where Helen sat, still with her arms crossed over her chest and a sullen look on her face.

"If you're still feeling brave enough to let me partner you, Miss FitzClarence, may I have this dance?"

"No, I don't want to," she answered gruffly.

He tried a joking tone. "Is it because you're unimpressed by my progress? I promise to do my best to not step on your toes."

"I said, I don't *want* to."

He stood there rather nonplussed, then turned away. Lady Almira had begun to play the opening measures. And Gwendolyn was coming to him, moving with that easy, unselfconscious grace he'd come to associate with her alone. She said:

"Christopher, will you dance with me?"

"Gladly, Gwennie." And he meant it.

Together they went to the center of the shining parquet floor where Percy had already gone and, with a humorously elaborate bow, asked the Duchess for the favor of this dance. He had, knowingly or not, nipped in ahead of the Earl, who then went to stand next to de Montmorency at the window.

Christopher looked down into Gwendolyn's lovely face. She had brightened, but still he had the sense that something was troubling her. Now was not the time to ask. He only said, lightly, "You'll have to talk me through this, Gwennie."

She said, "I will, Christopher," and somehow, it seemed to him like a larger promise than that of merely describing the steps of a quadrille.

"Owen, where are you going?" called the Duchess.

Owen stopped at the ballroom's doorway. "To see if there's any tea left."

"You've only had the one dance."

"But Grandmother, you said I did well."

"You did. But you ought to try some more dancing."

Owen looked over at Helen scornfully. "There's nobody to dance with."

She shot him an equally venomous glance. "I'd die before dancing with *you*."

"Oh, Christopher, I really ought to be dancing with Owen again," Gwendolyn whispered. "Would you mind very much?"

He smiled at her. "You truly are a good soul, *signorina*. Of course I don't mind."

And so Gwendolyn went to Owen, and persuaded him to come back with her onto the dance floor, which earned her a very grateful look from the Duchess. Lady Almira began the song all over again.

Christopher went to lean against a wall. He watched the dancers for a while, admiring Gwendolyn's skillful execution of the complicated steps. He also watched as de Montmorency went to sit next to Helen and how, in the space of just a few minutes, he seemed to have talked her out of her sulks.

A memory came to Christopher then—he'd been lounging around a piazza in Rome, all lit up with hanging lanterns; a band had been playing, and people were dancing. Nearby, a dapper, jaded-looking man of about forty was doing his best to cajole a pretty young girl to join him in the *tarantella*, and when before too long he succeeded, next to Christopher an old woman shook her head and muttered:

"Il diavolo dalla lingua argentata."

The silver-tongued devil.

There was no question about it, Christopher thought, watching de Montmorency and Helen: the Frenchman certainly had a way with words. And even though Helen was smiling, her arms uncrossed from her chest, Christopher was aware again that for some reason he couldn't fathom, he felt sorry for her.

"The quadrille's not difficult once you grasp the pattern." It was the Earl of Westenbury, who had come to stand next to him. "The couples move in a square formation. One couple dances while the others wait their turn. Percy and the Duchess have taken on the role of the head couple, and the others—in this case only Gwendolyn and

Owen—are thus the side couples. Right now they're doing the *chassé*, the gliding 'step—feet together—step again' movement. Do you see?"

Christopher nodded, noticing that within him was a distinct animosity toward the Earl. But he tamped it down and replied in a pleasant tone, "I suppose I'll figure it out eventually."

"To be sure you will. How are you liking London, Mr. Beck?"

"Very much, sir."

"Getting on all right? You've found lodgings, a man-servant, and all that? I'd be glad to help if I can."

"Yes, I'm settling in nicely, sir, thank you."

"You'll be wanting up-to-the-minute clothes, I expect. Bond Street is where you ought to go—you'll find all the best tailors, boot-makers, and hatters there, though you might care to stop by Weston's on Old Bond Street. And if you're looking for jewelry, seals, snuff-boxes, that sort of thing, Rundell and Bridge, on Ludgate Hill, is the place to go."

"Thank you, sir, I'll keep it in mind."

"One other thing, Mr. Beck," said the Earl, then paused. And went on, with a careful delicacy: "You may not, perhaps, be familiar with all the little nuances of etiquette among the Upper Ten Thousand. Here among our small, intimate circle, addressing the Duchess as 'ma'am,' myself as 'sir,' and Owen without any honorific is, of course, entirely suitable. But when in company, you may want to address the Duchess more formally as 'Your Grace,' and Owen as 'my lord' or 'Your Lordship.' And Helen as 'Lady Helen.' For the sake of appearance, if you catch my meaning? So that no one need disparage you for your manners."

"I see. And how ought I to address you, sir?" Christopher hoped he'd managed to keep his voice flat, polite, neutral.

Apparently he succeeded, for the Earl smiled at him with undimmed affability. "Oh, you needn't change your ways for me, Mr. Beck. But if you should encounter another earl, you ought to initially address him as 'my lord' or 'Your Lordship,' just as you would a marquis as Owen is, or a viscount. Later, if your acquaintance advances, 'sir' is perfectly suitable."

Still with the same neutrality Christopher replied, "There's a great deal to learn, isn't there, sir?"

"I fear there is." And the Earl, evidently taking Christopher's comment as an invitation to be relieved of burdensome social ignorance, proceeded to further enlighten him as to the various forms of proper aristocratic address, starting with a baron and progressing all the way up to a member of the Royal Family. "Now, if you ever were to meet Prinny—the Prince of Wales, I mean—you'd first address him as 'Your Royal Highness,' and after that, 'sir.' Of course," the Earl added, laughing, "few people outside his intimate circle encounter Prinny face-to-face, but I did want to be thorough."

"It's very good of you, sir."

"Think nothing of it, Mr. Beck. I'm delighted to provide any assistance that I can—a friend of Gwendolyn's is a friend of mine. Do you know how long you plan to remain in London?"

"I'm not sure."

"Well, if you do stay on, I hope you'll come to the wedding. I'm sure Gwendolyn would be delighted to have you there, as would I. It's to be at St. George's, in Hanover Square, you know, with a breakfast after."

"Thank you, sir." Christopher was aware that his animosity toward the Earl, rather than subsiding, was

intensifying. He wondered about that. It wasn't as if the
Earl had been haughty, or bellicose, or malicious. No, he
seemed utterly sincere in his desire to be helpful. Still,
Christopher wasn't sorry when the quadrille was over and
the Earl moved away.

"Shall we try a cotillion next?" said the Duchess.

Étienne de Montmorency stood and expressed a wish
to be allowed to supplant Lady Almira at the piano, so
that she might dance too.

"How *kind*," exclaimed Lady Almira, looking hopefully about her, and Christopher went to her and asked if
she would care to dance with him. She agreed with flattering alacrity and he caught Gwendolyn's smile of approval before she turned to the Earl and took his hand.

Percy went again to Helen, who refused, saying, in the
prideful manner of a child who has been given an important task, that Monsieur de Montmorency had asked her
to turn the pages of the sheet-music for him, and so Percy
returned to the Duchess, who said with a smile and a look
of fond remembrance in her eyes:

"My first dance with the Duke was a cotillion. How
long ago that was, to be sure." So deep was her drop into
happy recollection that she failed to notice that Owen,
with cunning unobtrusiveness, slipped out of the ballroom in search of much-needed replenishment—even
Helen, on the alert for any opportunity to publicly mortify
her brother, unaware of this, since she couldn't read music
and had to rely on Monsieur de Montmorency nodding his
sleek head to notify her as to when she should turn a page.

How kind he was, Helen thought with a sudden rush
of gratitude, how nonjudgmental. He hadn't said, *You are
unable to read music? Why, what a dunce!* No, he had
merely suggested (without any confusing French phrases)
that a simple nod would do the trick nicely.

She stared at the indecipherable black squiggles on the sheet music and abruptly had to fight back tears. This practice dance had turned out to be an utter failure. The stupid ribbon in her hair, the stupid perfume she'd had her maid run out and buy (just like Gwendolyn's stupid perfume, along with the large bag of stupid sweets she told the maid to get), the stupid jewelry she'd put on.

All useless.

Francis hadn't come, so what would have been the point of continuing to flirt with Christopher Beck? (If riding next to him on the way back from Richmond and squeezing up next to him on a sofa really *had* constituted flirting.) Luckily, Monsieur de Montmorency had come to her rescue yet again.

Chapter 8

Christopher stood in Hatchard's bookshop and looked at the little stack of books he'd amassed and set on a table. Four of the five were volumes on contemporary theories of horse-rearing and breeding, which he thought Mauro della Valle would find of interest, if only to dispute their methods and ideas entirely. He smiled, picturing Mauro's vehement and joyful denunciations. The fifth book was a new translation of Marco Polo's *Book of the Marvels of the World*, a history of his colorful adventures in the Orient—a little gift for Gwendolyn.

"Is your purchase complete, sir?" asked a clerk. "May I wrap these up for you?"

Christopher thought for a moment. "Not just yet, thank you." And he went to a section where fiction was housed. After looking at the various titles, he picked up Mrs. Stanhope's *The Bandit's Bride*.

"An exciting new romance, just published," said the clerk, who had come trailing up behind him. "Very popular with the young ladies, sir."

Just the sort of thing Diana enjoyed. Or used to. It would be a gesture, at any rate; it would be something. "I'll take it. Thanks."

Inevitably he thought about Father. He hadn't been one for pleasure-reading—too busy poring over newspapers and journals and the endless reports and correspondence he brought home with him. He did like birds, though, and had made sure the servants put out seeds and watering pans all year round. Maybe a book of illustrated plates?

The obliging clerk found just such a volume for him. *Birds of the British Isles and Their Ancient Domains.*

Christopher thanked him. His pleasure in the acquisition was brief, as it next occurred to him: what about Father's new wife? What about Diana's new husband? He ought to be looking for wedding-gifts. (*And something for Gwendolyn, too*, flashed the thought in his mind. A thought he found he didn't particularly like.)

Ought to.

Ought to.

He stood staring unseeingly at the stack of his books, wrestling with different imperatives, conflicting emotions.

What should he do?

He suddenly remembered a conversation he'd had years ago with Gwendolyn's brother Hugo, when he'd been working for him in his shipbuilding business. Hugo had assigned him to the sawpit for the day—no doubt seeing in him the rage threatening to boil over after enduring another of Father's protracted homilies.

It had been a wise assignment. Six or seven hours toiling with saws and long, heavy wood planks had helped him calm down, and after, Hugo had taken him off to the Blue Dolphin and ordered large meals for them both. He'd confided in Hugo his deep ambivalence about going back to university, and finally—won over by Hugo's easy, friendly kindness—had asked for his advice.

I can't tell you what to do, Hugo had said. *It's not my place. But—if it's of any value to you, lad—my father*

*used to say, Do what brings you the most peace. As a
young man he'd been pressured to not pursue a career
in science, and he said it was a tormenting time for him.
But once he realized that doing anything else would have
been the wrong choice for him, he said it was as if a
stormy sky cleared away into bright sunshine.*

"Do what brings you the most peace," murmured Christopher out loud, and then a little smile twisted his mouth. He didn't know exactly what that was, but nonetheless he bought all the books and carried them back to the Albany. He'd have just enough time to change his clothing into something a little more formal and make his way to the Egremont townhouse. Yesterday, after the practice dance was over, Percy had galvanized everyone into forming a party to go to Vauxhall Gardens—where they could have supper *en plein air* and listen to an orchestra, stroll about, watch fireworks, and so on—and the Duchess had suggested they all meet early in the evening for a quick sherry before departing.

In the entry-hall the porter gave him some letters and when Christopher got to his rooms he opened them and swiftly scanned their contents.

A note from a Mrs. St. Pelham, who ran a charity to help impoverished former sailors and their families, thanking him for his recent and generous donation on behalf of his relation the late Dan Allum.

A similar letter from the Reverend Arthur Broome, thanking him for his financial support of his nascent Society for the benefit of animals of all kinds.

A card of invitation from Lady Jersey, to an evening-party on Friday. Included were vouchers to Almack's, with his name written neatly at the top, and a warm little note from Lady Jersey. (Purkoy, she added in a postscript, sent his regards.)

Also, an invitation to join the Prince Regent at a *fête* at Carlton House, inscribed on a card so thick it was actually difficult to bend. Christopher looked again at the address: yes, there was his name, and correctly spelled. Not some curious mix-up evidently.

Well, thanks to the Earl of Westenbury, Christopher thought wryly, if he went he would know how to properly address his host.

Gwendolyn was the first one into the drawing-room. She settled into a comfortable armchair and smoothed down the soft white silk of her skirts. What a nice day it had been! The Earl had escorted her, and the Duchess of course, to the Royal Academy of Arts where there was an exhibition of the recent works of J. M. W. Turner that she'd been keen to see. (Lady Almira had a headache and had stayed behind, Francis was holed up in his room writing, and Helen, indifferent to art in any form, declared she would attend to her ailing mother.)

The Duchess, whose own interest in art was limited to anything portraying a horse or the countryside, soon tired of promenading along the gallery and found a little knot of acquaintances with whom to converse, and so Gwendolyn and the Earl were able to wander along at their own pace. It had felt so much to Gwendolyn like that exciting time before they'd become engaged, when every meeting felt like the first one all over again, when the whole world seemed to stop when he smiled at her and she felt she could fall into his deep-green eyes and happily drown in their magical depths.

They amiably debated the merits of Mr. Turner's work—Gwendolyn plumping for his moody atmospheric style while the Earl found it a trifle overdramatic, but ultimately yielded to Gwendolyn's arguments—and spent a merry hour or so playfully deciding which of his paintings they would like to have hanging in their drawing-room. Here again he gracefully gave way, leaving Gwendolyn to decide in favor of *Crossing the Brook*, *Dort or Dordrecht: The Dort packet-boat from Rotterdam becalmed*, and *High Street, Oxford*—this last because of its brilliant use of perspective.

Altogether it had been a very enjoyable interlude and Gwendolyn found herself looking forward to the evening at Vauxhall with nothing but happy anticipation.

Francis came in, very handsome and distinguished in his dark blue jacket, neatly tied neckcloth, and fawn-colored pantaloons. His expression was absorbed, ruminative, a little beatific. She said:

"You look as if your essay's coming along well."

He sat in a chair next to hers and stretched out his long legs. "It is. I've finished the first draft. Not half-bad, I think. Your suggestion about incorporating Kant's theory of perception was very helpful. But I also got a letter today from Schlegel—he's my philosophy tutor, you know. He's asked me to help him organize this year's colloquium on the latest thinking in science and religion. He doesn't usually invite students, so it's rather an honor."

"Oh, that's lovely. I'm so pleased for you, Francis."

"Thanks."

Tyndale entered the drawing-room and announced the arrival of Mr. Christopher Beck. Christopher too looked very distinguished, Gwendolyn thought, dressed similarly to Francis in a dark jacket and pale breeches. She was glad he hadn't cropped his hair as he'd jokingly threatened to do. Long hair suited him so well. And she liked how the candlelight picked out just a bit of midnight blue in its dark sheen. He said:

"I'm early. I think I scandalized Tyndale. Shall I apologize for barging in on you like this, or brazen it out?"

She laughed. "Brazen it out, by all means."

"Then that's what I'll do. Hullo, Francis."

Francis blinked and came out of his happy dream of colloquiums. "Hullo, Christopher. What's that you're reading?"

"It's for Gwennie." He held out a slim volume to her, its binding a rich burgundy leather embossed with raised gilt letters.

"Marco Polo's *Book of the Marvels*!" she exclaimed, opening it and glancing at some of the pages. "And how beautifully illustrated it is. Thank you, Christopher!"

"I'm glad you like it. I hoped you would."

"Oh, I do! I've just finished reading Katherine's latest book and it's had me longing to hop on a ship and go adventuring somewhere, so this is perfect!"

"Hop on a ship? Really?" It was Helen, whose tone was so odd that for a crazy instant Gwendolyn suspected her of *wanting* her to do just that, and disappear from London. Then Helen strode right past Francis, as if unaware of his very presence, and went up to Christopher. "Hullo, Mr. Beck. I say, how fine you look."

He gave a courtly little bow. "Thank you, Lady Helen. Are you looking forward to tonight's expedition?"

"Oh yes, now that *you're* here. And do call me 'Helen.'" Her voice had once again been softened, sweetened, through deliberate effort.

Gwendolyn found herself staring at Christopher. How would he respond to such a coquettish reply? His pleasant expression didn't change; he merely said in that same civil way:

"I've never been to Vauxhall, so you and the others will have to be my guides."

"*I'll* be your guide," Helen answered loudly, and went a step closer to Christopher, putting her hand on the arm of his sleeve and gripping the fabric hard, as if to prevent his escape.

Barely a foot of space lay between them.

Gwendolyn saw on Christopher's face a new expression, one she couldn't entirely read. He was looking down at Helen with a strange kind of—it struck her as—almost—well, *tenderness*. It reminded her of the time Katherine had found an abandoned kitten and brought it home, cradling the poor little thing in her arms with that same look on her face.

She caught her breath. Was Christopher coming to care for Helen?

"I say, what's going on? You two look like a pair of wax dummies." Percy came briskly into the drawing-room, Tyndale trailing behind him with the subtly pained look of a conscientious butler whose quarry has outmaneuvered him.

"Lieutenant Percy Penhallow," Tyndale said sonorously.

"No need to shout, man," said Percy over his shoulder. "Everyone already knew I was here. Wasn't there going to be sherry?"

"At once, sir."

Percy came to a stop next to Helen. "Why the devil are you hanging on to Christopher like that? It's dashed rude. You'll wreck his sleeve."

Flushing red, Helen released her grip on Christopher and stepped away, just in time for a footman to come in with a tray, and the Duchess and Lady Almira to arrive in his wake.

"I'm feeling *vastly* better, thank you, ma'am," Lady Almira was saying, then added wistfully, "Though I *should* have liked a little company from time to time. It gets rather lonely being by yourself all day."

So much, Gwendolyn thought, for Helen taking care

of her mother. She was surprised to observe in herself an impulse to say this sarcastic comment out loud, but firmly quashed it. What was the *matter* with her? She had been in such a good mood, and now this . . .

She accepted from the footman a little crystal glass of sherry and felt like swallowing it all at once. She took a little sip and grimaced. She didn't care for sherry in the first place. Why had she taken a glass? Wonderingly she watched as Percy tilted his own glass, drank it all down, and hailed the footman for another.

Tyndale said, "The Earl of Westenbury, the Countess of Westenbury, and the Honorable Rupert Durant."

Gwendolyn jerked her gaze toward the entrance to the drawing-room. Good heavens, it was Julian and his mother! And his brother! She saw at once that Rupert's hair was lighter than Julian's, and that his eyes tended toward blue rather than green; he was handsome, but not as stunningly so as Julian was. Rupert's features were by comparison a tiny bit coarse, his physique not quite as powerful. Standing next to his older brother, he gave the impression of being the product of a mold that, used a second time, hadn't worked quite as well.

As for the Countess, she was a slender, fragile-looking, middle-aged lady, whose elegant gown of dazzling white satin was draped in fine white lace and embellished with whisper-soft ruffles from neck to hem; on her head was a gorgeously crafted turban made of shining white silk festooned with a full plume of curling white ostrich feathers, and she wore a lacy white shawl of so delicate a weave that it resembled a dainty spider's web.

She looks like a snow queen, thought Gwendolyn, *like a beautiful snow queen out of a fairy tale*, and without knowing why she turned her eyes to Christopher. He was also looking at the Countess. And on his face was an expression of unguarded surprise.

As if involuntarily, Christopher half-turned to look at *her*.

What? she wanted to ask him. *What is it?* But there was no time; the Countess was saying in a soft, sweet voice:

"My dear Duchess, such a joy to make your acquaintance! I do hope you don't mind that Rupert and I have ventured to join your party? We've just this afternoon arrived, and though I really ought to be resting after our long journey, I simply couldn't wait to meet you all." She swept the room with her gaze, pausing when her eyes fell on Gwendolyn. "And you must be my soon-to-be daughter! Julian has said many times how beautiful you are! I couldn't mistake the gold of your pretty hair, or the lovely blue of your eyes. Indeed, I quite feel as if I know you already! Come and give me a kiss, my dear child!"

Her voice was warm, she was smiling broadly. Oh, she was *nice*. A friendly, beautiful snow queen. Smiling too, Gwendolyn set her sherry glass aside, rose to her feet, and went quickly to the Countess, who presented a soft white cheek which Gwendolyn gently kissed.

"How do you do, ma'am? I'm so pleased to meet you at last!"

"As am I, my dear. Charming! Charming! We must have a long chat very soon, but first, I want you to meet my Rupert—and we must be introduced to these other delightful young people—"

Between them, the Duchess and Julian made sure that everyone was soon introduced to everyone else. There was a cheerful hum of voices, and the footman circulated with his tray; Étienne de Montmorency arrived, greeting the Countess and Rupert with the cordiality of long acquaintance; Lady Almira, as she was talking animatedly to Percy, knocked over a potted plant and sent dirt scattering all over de Montmorency's beautiful dark evening-shoes, which made Owen, coming in just then, snicker uncontrollably. The Duchess gave him a warning glance, and while Lady Almira, very flustered, was apologizing to de Montmorency, and the footman was rushing to clean up the mess, and Julian was tenderly escorting his mother to a comfortable chair, Gwendolyn paused in the midst of all this and looked for Christopher.

There he was: standing apart, by one of the windows, looking so much like the Christopher of old—stormy and wild—that her heart gave a great anxious thump within her breast.

Swiftly Gwendolyn went to him. "Christopher," she said, searching his face, "what's wrong?"

His eyes were deep and dark, mysterious, smoldering with an emotion she couldn't decipher. He only gave a slight shrug, and she persisted:

"You were looking at the Countess as if you were— were astonished, or shocked. Christopher, have you met her before? Do you know her?"

He was silent for a little while. Finally: "No. I've never met her."

"Why did you look that way, then?"

"Gwennie." His voice was low and harsh. "Don't ask me. Just don't."

She stared up at him. "I'm worried for you."

"You needn't be."

"But I am. Oh, Christopher, I want so much to help you if I can."

His face twisted; there was a kind of agony in it. "I know you do. I'm all right. It's nothing to do with me."

She wasn't convinced. But she only said, "Will you tell me if there's anything I can do?"

"Yes."

"Do you promise?"

"Yes."

With that, Gwendolyn supposed, she had to be satisfied. But the truth was, she *wasn't* satisfied, not at all. She still didn't know what was wrong, and Christopher still looked so troubled. A little chill shivered through her and she found herself thinking back to that time in Whitehaven, when they had both stood before her drawing-room window, looking out at the cold, black, snowy night. He had left the very next morning, gone from her life like a leaf blown away by the wind, never, perhaps, to be seen again.

Without hesitation she reached for his hand, just as she had done that other time. And she clasped it in hers. His skin was warm against her own. "Christopher, I'm *so* glad you came back."

He looked at her, his dark eyes still fiery and depthless. "What would you like for a wedding-gift, Gwennie?"

"What?"

"A wedding-gift. What would you like?"

Thrown by the change of subject, Gwendolyn gave her head a little shake, as if to clear it. "Why are you asking me that now?"

"The Earl's invited me to your wedding."

"He has? Oh! Well, of course you're invited. Do you mind traveling all the way to Whitehaven?"

"What?"

"Going to Whitehaven. That's where the wedding's to be. In Grandpapa's church."

"He told me it's going to be here in London, at St. George's."

"You—you must be mistaken, Christopher."

"No. That's what he said, during the practice dance. At St. George's with a breakfast after."

Gwendolyn believed him. But confusion was roaring

through her. It was only the day before yesterday—the day *before* the practice dance—that she and Julian had talked about the wedding, on the ride to Richmond. And he had agreed to her plan, to have it take place in Whitehaven. Had Julian somehow forgotten? Or had she misconstrued what he'd said? She felt herself holding on harder to Christopher's hand, as if for ballast on a stormy sea. Clinging to his reassuring strength.

"You shouldn't be doing that, Gwendolyn." Helen had come to where they stood by the windows.

Startled, Gwendolyn twisted about and, reflexively, let go of Christopher. "Doing what?"

"Holding hands with someone you're not engaged to." Helen's voice was like spun sugar, her vivid green eyes glinting in the candlelight. "That's very bad form, you know."

A ribbon of anger flickered through Gwendolyn. "I haven't done anything wrong."

"If you say so."

"I do say so."

"Well, maybe you shouldn't."

"I just did." All at once Gwendolyn felt a strange desire to laugh. Possibly a slightly hysterical laugh. She and Helen sounded like silly little girls. In another minute they'd be pulling at each other's hair and calling each other names. It was with real relief that she saw Lady Almira fluttering toward them.

"My dears, are you ready? Tyndale says the carriages are outside. And you *know* how the dear Duchess hates making the horses wait. Girls, don't forget your shawls. Helen, *pray* don't dawdle—Mr. Beck will follow shortly, I'm sure."

Gwendolyn gave Christopher a last lingering glance, hating how closed-off his face looked, how remote, and as reluctantly she walked away she saw the Countess, still in her chair, pulling from underneath her a burgundy-colored book, which apparently she had sat on. She looked at it, puzzled, and Gwendolyn hurried to her.

"Oh, ma'am, that's mine."

"*Book of the Marvels of the World*?" said the Countess, looking at the gilt letters of the title, and then up at Gwendolyn. "What sort of book is it?"

"It's a memoir, ma'am."

"I see. And who is this author—Marco Polo? He sounds like a foreigner."

For a moment Gwendolyn wondered if the Countess was joking, but there was nothing in her placid voice or gently inquiring expression to support that suspicion. So Gwendolyn answered, "He was an Italian explorer, ma'am."

"Indeed? I don't care to read books by foreigners. I don't know why it is, but somehow I don't trust them. My dear late husband Edmond always said what a loyal Englishwoman I am. I would have had Julian and Rupert go fight against those dreadful—what do they call themselves? Americans?—those dreadful traitors, but of course I couldn't let them risk their lives. And Julian particularly, as the heir. Not that they wanted to, which I think very wise of them. Now, I understand your brother's wife writes books?"

"Yes, ma'am. My sister-in-law, Katherine."

"It would be so interesting to see a female author," remarked the Countess, in the exact manner of one hoping to catch a glimpse of a freakish curiosity at a fair.

"She's a wonderful writer," Gwendolyn said, trying to keep a defensive tartness out of her tone. "In fact, I have one of her books upstairs. I'd be glad to lend it to you, ma'am."

"Do you indeed? What is it about? A romance, I daresay? With castles, and ghosts, and a horrid villain?"

"No, it's called *English Ships Out of Portsmouth: A National Heritage*."

"Oh, ships," said the Countess, visibly losing interest. "What an odd thing for a female to be writing about."

"I," said Gwendolyn, "like ships."

"Do you, my dear? Dear Julian told me what a lively mind you have."

"My brother Hugo builds ships. I've gone on many of them. I know a little about celestial navigation and Hugo's shown me how to steer a ship." Gwendolyn had a vague feeling that she probably should stop, but she felt like a tea-kettle coming to a boil. "I can raise a sail by myself, if the wind's not too strong. I know how to tie knots and climb a rigging, too."

"Climb a rigging?" Rupert Durant said. "In a *gown*, Miss Penhallow?"

On Rupert's face was a look she didn't like—a gleam of lascivious interest—and she heard the definite snap in her voice as she answered, "In sailor's trousers."

"Trousers," repeated Rupert, still with that same gleam. "Did you hear that, Mummie?" he said to the Countess. "Miss Penhallow's worn trousers. Gad, how *dashing*."

"We really ought to go," said the Earl, "the Duchess is waiting for us." He held out his hand to his mother, to assist her to rise, which she did with slow gracefulness, and as together they made their way out of the drawing-room the Countess could be heard asking him, "Julian dear, what is celestial navigation? Is it one of those odd spiritual fancies so prevalent nowadays? Dear Gwendolyn isn't a *Dissenter*, is she? I thought you said her grandfather is a perfectly respectable clergyman."

In the bustle of their party dispersing into the various carriages, Percy murmured into Gwendolyn's ear:

"You're in the basket now, Gwennie! Lord, the look on

Westenbury's face when you said 'trousers'! Luckily for
you, the Countess was so stumped by 'celestial navigation' that I don't think she even noticed!" He laughed.

Gwendolyn hunched a shoulder. "I don't care."

"In a bad skin, are you? Regretting your outburst already? I say, do cheer up! Vauxhall will be jolly, you
know. I'd take you round myself, but after supper I'm slip-
ping away to meet someone."

"Percy, you *instigated* this outing."

He grinned. "Clever of me, don't you think?"

"You're awful," Gwendolyn said, but without heat.
He looked so mischievous that it was impossible to be
really angry with him. Curiously she asked, "Who are you
meeting?"

"Oh, a friend."

He said it with such casualness that Gwendolyn's curiosity was only heightened. "Who is it? Is it anyone I
know?"

"I doubt it. I say, why is Helen crowding into that seat
with Christopher? Doesn't the old girl know there's not
enough room? She ought to sit on the opposite seat with
Frank."

Gwendolyn said with sudden vehemence, "I wish I
could stay home."

"You could cry off. Now's the time."

She thought about it. She could get into her nightgown,
have supper brought to her on a tray, lie in bed devouring
Marvels of the World. It was tempting. *Too* tempting. "I'd
feel like a coward."

"That," Percy said, wrapping his arm around her shoulders in a brief but affectionate hug, "you are not. Trousers!" He laughed again and went loping away toward the
Duchess's carriage.

More slowly, Gwendolyn went to the Westenbury

carriage, a vast and elegant barouche with the family's crest—depicting a ferocious black bear, a medieval castle with red pennants flying, and an extremely sharp halberd—emblazoned on the door. The Earl stood waiting for her. If he had been shocked by her earlier disclosures, he certainly didn't seem to be now. He smiled down at her and took her hand to help her up the steps. "There's no need to look so worried, my darling," he said softly. "I told m-my mother that your little—ah—larks occurred in your youth. She understands completely."

Gwendolyn hesitated with her foot on the bottom step, not at all sure that she wanted or needed Julian to be apologizing on her behalf. "Little larks"—wasn't that a rather patronizing way to put it? Or was it, rather, a soothing euphemism? Also, how on earth could one man be so incredibly handsome? She wanted to kiss him or, possibly, snap at him for being condescending. Maybe both. Gwendolyn felt very confused all of a sudden, and at that moment she would have sworn that her cozy, quiet, peaceful bed upstairs in the townhouse was calling out to her. A siren's song, seductive, trying to lure her away—

"Gwendolyn, dear child, do come inside and sit next to me," said the Countess warmly, patting the empty space beside her. "We have so much to talk about."

I am not a coward, Gwendolyn told herself, then stepped inside the carriage and took her place next to the Countess.

Their party was so numerous that they needed two supper-boxes to accommodate them all. There was a sort of mad scramble among some of the younger members for places, and so it fell out that at one table sat the Duchess,

Lady Almira, the Earl of Westenbury and his mother the Countess, and Monsieur de Montmorency.

Christopher came last of all. He observed at once that the group had divided into the classic configuration of older adults separated from the younger people, and would have grinned to himself had his mood been lighter. He took a moment to acknowledge that he was, in his current state of mind, creating his own kind of configuration: people he would have liked to sit with, and others he would just as soon avoid.

For example, it would be a special ring of hell to be forced to stare at the Countess of Westenbury for the entire duration of a meal. Did no one else notice? he wondered. God in heaven, *he* certainly did, and it was tearing him apart.

And speaking of Westenburys, he didn't particularly want to sit with the Earl, no matter how affable and helpful, nor did he like the look of the Earl's brother. A shifty lot if he ever saw one. The Honorable Rupert could well have been a pickpocket, or worse, save for the lucky accident of his birth; as it was, he had the look of a man who enjoyed cornering maidservants in stairwells.

And who did that leave him with?

He looked at Gwendolyn. He'd have sat next to her in a heartbeat, but she was already seated between Owen and Percy. She was talking and smiling; however, there was a subtle grimness to her jaw, a set to her slender shoulders, that had his own shoulders tightening.

He'd watched her talk with the Countess, defending Katherine, proudly mentioning Hugo and his ships, defiantly tossing in the detail about wearing trousers. He'd wanted to cheer her on from the sidelines—*Brava, signorina, molto bene!*—but it was clear she needed help from no one.

Her blue eyes had been blazing, her voice clear and steady, and she stood very straight.

She was, he had thought, the most beautiful woman he'd ever seen.

Looking at her now, he thought it again.

"Mr. Beck! I say, Mr. Beck!"

Christopher dragged his gaze away from Gwendolyn to where Helen sat next to the Honorable Rupert. She was waving vigorously. "Do sit with us!"

"Thank you, but there's no room."

"Owen, *move*," Helen hissed across the table at her brother.

"You move," answered Owen.

She glared at him so ferociously that a lesser man might have quailed, but Owen merely smiled in a superior way and tried to flag down one of the waiters rushing to and fro.

"Percy, will you please move?" asked Helen, injecting a softer note into her voice.

"Damned if I will."

"Never mind, Lady Helen," Christopher said, and caught a look from Gwendolyn—wistful? Forlorn?—before finding an empty place at the other table, between Lady Almira and—of course—the Earl, and—*of course*—directly opposite the Countess.

The only bright spot was that he could keep an eye on Gwendolyn as the plates of ham and chicken arrived, the custards and salads set before them, the platters of plump half-moon tarts; the wine dispensed. He did see, three times by his count, Gwendolyn give a little start and glance across at the Honorable Rupert, and knew, with black rage in his heart, that Rupert was playing sly games with his feet underneath the table.

The fourth time he saw Gwendolyn jump he was just

about to get up and throttle the Honorable Rupert—yes, let everyone (to quote the Earl) *disparage him for his manners* and the hell with it—throttle that damned toad until he squeaked for mercy, but then Rupert gave a yelp and pushed back from the table as if involuntarily.

And Gwendolyn looked Rupert right in the eye. Said nothing. Smiled ever so slightly. Then calmly cut a little slice of ham and proceeded to eat it.

Christopher nearly burst out laughing. She'd kicked him, and with any luck right in the sensitive part of the shin where it would hurt the most. He thought again, *Brava, signorina!* He would have liked to hug her to him then and there.

Chapter 9

❧❧❧

Supper had wound down, dessert had been eaten, Rupert Durant had been keeping his feet to himself, and now the orchestra was playing a waltz so enticing that many people from the dozens of supper-boxes all around them were making their way to the large open area around which the boxes had been built, and joining in the dance.

Various members of their own party were rising from the tables amidst a buzz of conversation and laughter. Gwendolyn remained sitting, and considered what she wanted to do next.

She looked over to where the Earl was helping his mother to rise. He was, she thought, very tender, very solicitous of her. Clearly, he loved her very much.

Clucking a little, Lady Almira was brushing crumbs from the front of her gown and giving the strong impression that quite a few of them had descended into her bodice; Étienne de Montmorency was watching sardonically.

And there was Christopher.

He was—why, he was looking at *her*.

She looked back. How dark his eyes appeared from here, yet lit with fierce, fiery intelligence. A long shaggy lock of hair had fallen over his forehead. It occurred to her that he had the sort of face which one could easily look at for a very long time.

Then, to her annoyance, someone blocked her view. It was the Honorable Rupert, who, having stood up, put his hands on the tablecloth and leaned toward her. Goodness, how strange it was to see in him a slightly off-kilter version of the Earl.

Rupert said, "You won't—ah—tell Mummie or Julian about—about our little—ah—our little disagreement?"

"You mean about your wandering feet?" she answered coolly, at the same time wondering how a man well into his twenties could so easily give the appearance of a five-year-old caught doing something naughty.

"Yes, that. It was only a bit of harmless fun, you know."

"And the table's so narrow that it was practically unavoidable."

"Yes, exactly!" he said, and Gwendolyn felt like she might kick him again if he kept on. She stood up and moved away. And where to?

Helen had already gotten up and was headed toward Christopher. For a crazy moment Gwendolyn wanted to take hold of the satin ribbons at the back of Helen's gown and bring her to a skidding halt.

And in realizing this, she wondered if maybe she really *should* have stayed behind at the townhouse. What other dreadful thing would she contemplate doing tonight? Or *actually* do?

Percy swung in front of her and took hold of Helen's upper arm. "I say, old girl, let's dance! You owe me one from yesterday."

He was, Gwendolyn saw, in very high spirits and also, perhaps, a little drunk. He had at supper partaken liberally of wine. Helen was shaking her bright head. "No, I was—

that is, I'm going to—" she began, but Percy, undeterred, swept her off toward the dancing area, and Helen cast a last helpless look over her shoulder before she and Percy joined the other dancers. Seeing it, Gwendolyn wondered with whom Helen was trying to connect.

Christopher?

Because Helen liked Christopher, and Christopher liked Helen—was that what was happening?

Gwendolyn had to sternly remind herself that she wasn't going to stand in their way.

"May I have the honor of this dance?"

Rupert had come up alongside her, and Gwendolyn stared at him, amazed at his—effrontery? Resilience? Arrogance? Pointedly she said, "Aren't you worried I might step on your feet?"

"Step away," he said breezily, and leaned in close. "Besides, I want to hear all about those trousers."

And now Gwendolyn had to sternly instruct herself not to really and truly kick him again. Hard. She set her jaw.

"Excuse me," she said to Rupert with all the civility she could muster, and moved away. She went straight up to where Christopher was standing against the back wall of the supper-box. He didn't smile at her, but neither did she think he was sorry she was there.

"Christopher."

"Signorina."

"Will you tell me something?"

He gave her a long look. "If I can."

"Do you want to dance with Helen?"

"She's dancing with Percy."

"I know that. But are you waiting for the next dance so you can ask her?"

"Are you hinting that it would be the polite thing to do?"

"No, I'm not hinting. I'm asking you a question."

He was silent. Finally: "No," he said, as if the word was being dragged from him. "I don't particularly want to dance with Lady Helen, lout that I am."

"You're not a lout. Thank you for your honesty. What *do* you want to do, then?"

"I'd like to get out of this damned supper-box."

"That's what I'd like too."

"Shouldn't you be dancing with the Earl?"

"He's busy taking care of his mother."

Christopher looked over her shoulder. "In fact, they're dancing."

Gwendolyn turned to look also. "She's a good dancer, isn't she? So lively. I expect she's refreshed from her nap in the carriage."

"Ah."

"Yes, as soon as the carriage started to roll she fell asleep. Which means Julian and Rupert and I sat there like—what was Percy's expression earlier?—yes, we sat there like wax dummies the whole time, not daring to utter a word."

"Sounds jolly."

"Oddly enough," Gwendolyn said, "it was a relief to not have to talk. Can we get out of this box now?"

"By all means."

On their way out Gwendolyn stopped to say to the Duchess, who was patiently waiting for Lady Almira to find her reticule: "Cousin Judith, Christopher and I are going for a walk."

"Enjoy yourselves," answered the Duchess in her kind, brisk way. "Do come back in time for the fireworks."

"We will," Gwendolyn promised, and then she and Christopher were walking away from the supper-boxes and the dancing, past the gilded life-sized statues from Roman antiquity, the Turkish tent from which wafted a delicious odor of freshly prepared coffee, a grove in which acrobatic dancers capered high on a rope, a lavish artificial castle, several bowling greens, and finally into the famed gardens through which many people strolled, talked, sought solitude along the pathways which were not as brightly illuminated by the colorful glass lanterns as elsewhere.

Gwendolyn slid her arm through Christopher's. "It feels like we're escaping."

"Yes."

In a little while they paused by a waterfall which emptied, splashing and burbling, into a large fenced pond. Next to them a man gave his companion a coin and said, "Make a wish, Nell," and she squeezed her eyes shut, opened them again, then tossed the coin into the pond.

"What'd you wish for, love?" said the man.

"I can't *tell*, looby, it'd spoil the wish!"

They moved away, arm-in-arm and laughing, and Christopher said, "Would you like a coin, Gwennie?"

She thought about it. In other circumstances—say, when she was feeling less oppressed—she would have instantly said yes. For example, when she and the Marksons were in Paris, they had stopped at the Desaix fountain and gaily she had tossed in a *sou* and made a wish as she watched the little coin sink swiftly to the bottom.

I wish for happiness.

How young she'd been!

I wish for happiness.

How long ago that seemed.

Well, Gwennie, she thought to herself, *how's that wish working out for you?*

Just at the moment, she had to admit, she wasn't too sure.

"*Signorina?* A coin?"

Christopher was looking at her. His expression remained serious. But she still had the same impression that he wasn't sorry she was with him.

"No, thank you, Christopher," she finally answered.

Slowly. Pensively. "I'm getting the feeling that—that I need to make my own luck. Shall we go on?"

"Yes. Where to?"

"Let's go that way."

This was her third time at Vauxhall. Twice before she'd been here with the Earl as part of festive groups which had joined up together. Both times she and Julian had stuck to the brightly lit areas, surrounded by other people; not once had Julian suggested they slip away to the so-called Dark Paths where, Gwendolyn knew from what the other young ladies had confided to her, there was considerably less interest in propriety. Of course, he had been all that was proper.

So—rather defiantly—she took Christopher with her along one of the Dark Paths. As they walked they passed fewer and fewer lanterns. Fewer and fewer people. There was silence between them, but it didn't feel like it had in the Westenbury carriage. *That* had been an enforced muteness, broken only by an occasional soft snore from the Countess.

No, this felt easy.

It was *inside* her that there was turmoil.

She glanced up at Christopher's profile in the dimness. If she had to guess, there was turmoil inside him too.

After a while they came to a little iron bench which had been placed in a kind of alcove formed by a curved trellis of luxuriant ivy, its lush, abundant leaves rippling gently in a light and pleasant breeze.

"Christopher, shall we sit?"

"Yes."

The bench wasn't much wider than the sofa on which they had sat yesterday afternoon, before the practice dance. The sofa which had become quite crowded when Helen had joined them.

She said, "Should I feel guilty for taking you away from Helen?"

"Should I feel guilty for taking you away from the Earl?"

"You didn't take me away. I'm my own person. I can decide what I want to do."

"Then you don't need to feel guilty. I made my own decision as well."

Gwendolyn nodded. She and Christopher were so close together that her skirts lay in a long pleated bunch next to his thigh. She could smell that lovely hint of soap about him. The breeze stirred the shaggy dark lock of hair which still lay low across his forehead, nearly reaching his nicely defined cheekbone. She would like to have drawn him like this, with quick pencil-strokes that could capture the unique details of eyes, nose, hair, jaw, mouth . . .

"Your wound is healing nicely, Christopher."

"A shame."

"A shame? Why?"

"Because soon I won't look Gothic at all. Like a villain in the romance the Countess hoped Katherine had written."

Gwendolyn turned a little on the bench, so that she could see him more clearly in the dimness. "I'm afraid without that swirling cape you'll never look Gothic. Or even Byronesque."

"Are you disappointed?"

"Why would I be? You look exactly like yourself."

"Is that a good thing?"

"Yes, of course it is. I'm not expressing myself very well. What I mean is—well, you're—you're *congruent*, Christopher."

"Are you describing me in mathematical terms, *signorina*?"

"No, not really. How can I put it? It seems to me that you're—you're in *agreement* with yourself."

"Not right now."

"No," she said softly. "Nor am I."

They were quiet for a while.

Gwendolyn sat very still, but her mind felt like a beehive. Swirling with questions, doubts, fears. Did she dare . . . ? She looked at Christopher next to her; he also sat very still. From him emanated that same quiet, steady strength, which seemed to give her the courage she needed to say:

"Christopher, can I talk to you about—about a problem I have?"

He looked at her. "Is it the Dishonorable Rupert? Say the word and I'll do more than kick him underneath the table."

"You saw that?"

"Yes. I was about to take him by the throat and rattle him about, but I saw that you had the situation well in hand."

"Would you really have taken him by the throat?"

"And more. Are you worried he'll keep on bothering you? Is that the problem you mean?"

"Rupert? Oh, no, that's not what's troubling me."

"What is it, then?" His face was grave.

Impulsively she reached for his hand where it lay on his thigh. "Oh, Christopher, my friend—my dear friend—I feel as if I could tell you *anything*. And yet—"

His fingers closed around hers. Easily. Reassuringly. "And yet what, Gwennie?"

"I'm worried you'll think badly of me."

"Nothing you can say would make me think badly of you."

"Really?"

"Yes."

Gwendolyn gripped his hand a little harder. She was right, she *could* talk to him freely, he truly *was* her friend. She thought back to the night before last, when she'd returned to the townhouse after the Aymesburtons' ball, when she'd gotten into bed and sketched, feeling sad, unhappy, alone. How wonderful, now, to not feel alone. To have a friend she could trust. Gwendolyn took a deep breath of relief, feeling a little of that oppressive weight lifting from her. Then:

"Christopher, have you—have you kissed a lot of women?"

He looked surprised. Clearly this wasn't the direction he was expecting their conversation to take. But calmly he replied, "I'm not sure what a lot is, *signorina*. But have I kissed some women? Yes. Why?"

"Well—did you like it?"

"Yes."

"A lot?"

"Yes."

"Are you—are you *good* at it, do you suppose?"

His dark brows went up. But he only said, "I hope so."

"Would you mind—well, would you mind telling me how to kiss well?"

Christopher didn't say anything and anxiously Gwendolyn said, "Are you thinking badly of me now?"

"No, not at all. I'm just trying to figure out how to answer you. It's about paying attention to the person you're kissing, I suppose."

"Yes, but that's an abstract explanation, Christopher. I'm not sure it really helps me."

"You're interested in the mechanics?"

She nodded eagerly. "Yes, exactly."

"It's probably even less helpful to try and talk about lips and mouths and . . ."

"Tongues."

"You know about tongues, then."

"Yes."

"Gwennie," Christopher said, "what's going on?"

She hesitated, but not for long. The words tumbled out,

as if wanting, *needing*, to be said. "It's just that I'm worried. I'm—I'm afraid that I'm dreadful at kissing, you see, and that I'm—underdeveloped, or—or *cold*."

He didn't laugh, or draw back, or seem shocked. Not Christopher. He just kept on looking at her, calmly, thoughtfully, with concern in his dark eyes. It was frightening to voice her fears out loud, but at the same time she felt—oh, she felt *safe* with him. He said:

"You're the least cold person I've ever met."

"Really, Christopher?"

"Yes. What do you mean by underdeveloped?"

"Oh, my figure. Do you see? I'm not very—very *womanly*."

"You're beautifully made, *signorina*. Every inch a woman."

There was a certain tension in the hand holding her own, she could feel it, like lightning running from him to her. Doggedly she went on:

"So you don't think it means I'm not capable of—you know—kissing well, and enjoying it?"

"No, I don't."

"Oh, Christopher, would you show me?"

"What?"

"Show me."

"Show you?" Now he did look taken aback. "Gwennie, I—"

Gwendolyn rushed on. "It would help me so much, Christopher, truly it would. Please won't you help me?"

"I want to, Gwennie, of course I do, but—"

"But you won't?" she said, very sadly. "Oh, Christopher, why not?"

"Don't you see why not?"

He meant the Earl, of course. Julian, her fiancé. But that was *exactly* why she needed his—Christopher's—help. Even as this thought streaked through her brain Gwendolyn knew her logic was more than a little convoluted. But she didn't care. Here was Christopher, mere inches away—Christopher her friend, who cared for her and wanted to help her—but who wouldn't—who couldn't—

Oh, she was confused again, muddled, and sad, so very sad—

To her horror Gwendolyn realized that her eyes had filled with tears, and that they had spilled down her cheeks. She pulled her hand from Christopher's and swiped them away.

"Gwennie, Gwennie, don't cry, please don't cry." His voice was low and rough. And then his arms were around her, pulling her close to him. Gwendolyn couldn't help it, she sobbed out loud. Maybe she'd been holding in these tears for a couple of days now. She brought her hands up and around Christopher's neck and clung to him. How solid he was, how *real*. Already she was feeling better. He was *such* a comfort to her—

"Gwennie," Christopher said softly. He put a hand underneath her chin, gently tilted it up. *"Signorina, signorina,"* he went on, very softly, and then he lowered his head and brought his mouth near hers. Not *on* her mouth, but leaving just the slightest distance between them. Her tears stilled—were vanquished—and Gwendolyn breathed in sharply. It was like tasting him, feeling him, smelling him all at once, her senses mingled into a single, unified, dazzling experience of pure sensation . . .

A kiss but not a kiss but a kiss nonetheless.

She could almost feel her soul rushing out to bridge the gap between them, to connect them, and with it came a welcome warmth. A fire, roaring all throughout her body. Burning her up. It was all so simple. And so good—

Oh, she *wasn't* cold, she was warm, she was *hot*, and cracklingly alive, and—yes—*womanly*—and *happy*—

She heard herself making a little soft breathy noise.

Happy, happy.

And then Christopher abruptly drew back.

He too was breathing rather heavily, his dark brows drawn together. He definitely didn't look happy.

"Gwennie, I—I can't."

She brought her hands from around his neck and onto his shoulders, clutching at him as if to save herself from falling. "Why not? Oh, Christopher, why not?"

"You know why," he said quietly. "I haven't the right."

"But don't you want to?"

"More than anything in the world."

"I want it too! Then—why don't you—go on?"

His mouth twisted in a half-smile, with a kind of bitter amusement. "If I did, how would that make me any different from the Dishonorable Rupert?"

Gwendolyn gripped his shoulders harder. Almost wanting to shake him in her bewilderment and frustration. Wanting to shake him because she knew that what he said was—

Well, it was true, wasn't it?

And—this time—painfully simple.

An honorable man didn't kiss a woman who was engaged to another man.

So what did that make *her*—a woman engaged to one man trying to kiss another man?

She didn't want to think about that.

What madness had possessed her?

Just a little while ago she'd been wondering about what dreadful thing she'd contemplate doing tonight—or actually do—

Here, she supposed, was the ignominious answer.

Happiness had vanished and in its place came sadness again, heavy and leaden. Her eyes filled again with tears; she took her hands from him and wound them together in her lap, tightly interlacing her fingers as if to prevent them from doing something they shouldn't.

"I'm hurting you," he said. "Oh, God, I'd do anything rather than hurt you."

At the self-loathing in his voice Gwendolyn quickly shook her head. Blinked away the tears. "No. You're not. I swear it. Oh, Christopher, you're right. I—I just didn't want you to be right."

His dark eyes searched her face. "I'm sorry, *signorina*."

"I know you are." She tried to smile at him, but wasn't quite sure how well she was succeeding. "*Now* do you think badly of me?"

"No."

"Truly?"

"*Sì, signorina.*"

"We're still friends?"

"Always."

She felt her smile strengthening. "You mean it?"

"Yes."

"Can we—can we go on as before? Without any stupid awkwardness between us?"

"Yes."

"I'm so glad." And she was. She *was*. Not happy, but relieved and grateful. How terrible it would have been to lose Christopher's friendship over an illicit kiss. She unlaced her fingers, let them relax in her lap. "You're still coming over tomorrow night for supper, to celebrate Helen's birthday? Cousin Judith told me she invited you."

"Yes."

"Oh, good! I hear there'll be cake."

"I like cake."

"I do too." She smiled at him, and was thankful that it felt more natural again. There was a noise high overhead, a distant explosion, and quickly she looked up to see a burst of white light in the black sky, an evanescent flower whose petals flew free, sizzled, fell back to earth. "The fireworks are beginning. We ought to go."

"Whenever you're ready."

Gwendolyn stood up, and he did as well.

"You're all right, Gwennie?"

"Yes, Christopher."

He nodded. And they began to retrace their steps. She told him about a lecture she was hoping to see, on the subject of Renaissance art, and they soon fell back into their easy way of talking. He told her about the books he was sending to Mauro della Valle, and his probable reaction to them, which made Gwendolyn laugh.

They had just passed the waterfall and pond again when from around it, coming from the opposite direction, appeared Percy and a voluptuous, richly dressed woman of about Christopher's age. She was just a trifle rumpled—as was, Gwendolyn saw, Percy too. He came to an abrupt halt when he saw her and Christopher and looked rather discomfited,

"I say, what the devil are you two doing here?"

"We've been for a walk." Gwendolyn was trying not to stare at Percy's companion who had pulled from her reticule a pair of luxurious, pale violet gloves which she was putting on, though not before Gwendolyn noticed on her left hand a gold wedding-band. The woman said to Percy:

"You brought this gentleman to my house the other night, *ma sherry moo*, but there was such a squeeze I've forgotten his name. *Ma foy*, my parties are always so crowded! And who is this *juhn fame*? You resemble her exceedingly."

Percy looked as if he didn't know whether to laugh or to try and hustle his companion away and out of sight. Gwendolyn got the distinct feeling that even if Percy himself fled, the woman would stay on and perform the introductions herself; she gave the impression of supreme self-confidence. Perhaps Percy knew it too, for he said, resignation in his tone:

"Gwennie, may I introduce to you the Viscountess of Tarrington? Ma'am, this is my sister, Miss Gwendolyn Penhallow, and Mr. Christopher Beck, whom you've already met."

The Viscountess sailed forward, skirts rippling and the curling downy plumes in her high-crowned satin bonnet fluttering as if in a strong wind. *"Awnshantee!* How delightful this is! *Juh soo submerjee doo jwah."*

Rapidly Gwendolyn translated in her mind as best she could. The Viscountess was, evidently, enchanted and also submerged—overwhelmed?—with joy. "I too, ma'am."

"You're betrothed to the Earl of Westenbury, *nit vooze peas*? I read the announcement in the *Times. Toots noo* felicitations, Miss Penhallow. And where is *luh sherry* Earl? I should so like to meet him and wish him very happy *oo sow."*

What a curious accent, Gwendolyn thought. Was it a Scottish brogue mixed in with all those contorted French phrases?

"Another time, hey?" Percy said to Lady Tarrington, rather hastily. "I'll take you back to your box, shall I?"

The Viscountess didn't move. To Gwendolyn she said complacently, "I am, *voo set*, very well acquainted with your relation Laird Alasdair Penhallow."

"Oh! Are you indeed, ma'am? I've never met him."

Lady Tarrington nodded benignly, which made the plumes in her bonnet nod also, as if a small sycophantic Greek chorus was perched on her head, ready at all times to agree with her. *"Oui*, it's true. *En fett*, he nearly married me."

"Indeed, ma'am?" Gwendolyn was sure it would be tactless to mention the fact that her sister-in-law Katherine had been corresponding with the laird's wife Fiona for some time now.

"*Oui*. But I rejected him, *poove hahm*. And now here I am, a viscountess, one of the Upper Ten Thousand! So you see, *moo sherry* Miss Penhallow, things work out for the best. We must always follow our dreams."

"Yes, yes, very true, and now we must be off," said Percy, "I'm sure your party is missing you, ma'am," and he bore Lady Tarrington away with an air of great determination.

"Goodbye," Lady Tarrington called over her shoulder. "*Oh voor*! Till we meet again!"

Christopher and Gwendolyn followed more slowly behind Percy and the Viscountess. Overhead, a few more fireworks exploded, fizzled, and faded away.

"Christopher, did you see Lady Tarrington's wedding-band?"

He nodded. "Are you shocked?"

"Should I be?"

"You're asking the wrong person, *signorina*."

"In other words, you're suggesting that I make up my own mind." Gwendolyn smiled up at him, and he treasured that singularly sweet smile of hers, immeasurably thankful to see those heartrending tears gone. She went on, thoughtfully:

"It's difficult, isn't it? I mean, one is *supposed* to be shocked. But what if the Viscountess is married to a wicked, awful, cruel man who makes her wish she'd never been born? Would that be a justification?"

"If it's any help, I've met her husband, and he seems very mild-mannered."

"Oh, is he? But what if he doesn't love her at all and she's miserable and lonely? Would that make it all right?"

"Or what if *she* doesn't love *him*?"

"Yes, that's a possibility too. Or what if Percy and the Viscountess are so madly in love that they simply can't resist each other? Love that o'erthrows empires, as Shakespeare might say."

"Having spent five minutes in their company, do you think that's so?"

They were passing the artificial castle and Gwendolyn glanced at it. "Every time I see that I want to laugh. It reminds me of the Hansel and Gretel story—do you know that one? I always want to go over and break off a piece to see if it's actually made of gingerbread."

"If you do, keep an eye out for the witch."

"I shan't be bamboozled, I assure you! Unlike those poor lost children. What a dreadful story, don't you think? The moral escapes me, but I do love the idea of an edible house. I remember, years ago, telling Cook all about the witch's delicious abode and she became absolutely livid. A waste of good ingredients, she said." Gwendolyn smiled, then continued:

"As for Percy and Lady Tarrington—well, no, I must admit they didn't seem to me like people who are madly in love. Perhaps it's just a casual thing between them. I'm very naïve, I suppose—I don't understand it at all. But who am I to judge? And yet—I couldn't possibly imagine my parents being unfaithful to each other, or—or Hugo and Katherine, for example. *That's* love to o'erthrow empires, I think. Christopher, do *you* believe that fidelity in marriage is important?"

He was silent for a little while. Then: "I can only speak for myself, Gwennie, but yes, I do. I think if a person intends to marry, he or she ought to be as sure as anybody in this life can be about it. And that promise should be kept.

But again—and like you—I'm not here to judge anyone else. Only to live my life in the best way I can."

Gwendolyn nodded. "That makes sense to me. Oh, what a highly indelicate subject I've raised! But I know you're not shocked, are you?"

"No."

"Of course you're not, my dear friend—or, as Lady Tarrington might say, *ma sherry moo.* I quite like how she speaks French, don't you? It's very piquant, and it makes one really pay attention to what she's saying. Oh, Christopher, isn't it curious that she knows my relation Alasdair Penhallow? Sometimes the world is so delightfully small. I wish I'd had the presence of mind to ask her if he wears kilts all the time."

He smiled. "I remember your mentioning him, that time you came to me when I was chopping wood."

"Yes, when I proposed to you! What a madcap child I was! Sometimes I think I still am. Christopher, there's something I want to know. Diana told me how much you hated university. Do you mind if I ask you why?"

"No, I don't mind." He shared with her a little about his experiences there and Gwendolyn listened with a sorrowful look on her face. When he was done she said:

"I don't blame you for hating it! How awful some people can be. Why did your father make you go?"

"Advancement, I suppose. He never had a chance to go to university. His own father died when he was very young, and he began working when he wasn't much more than a child. In a warehouse of some kind, I think." Christopher stopped for a moment and Gwendolyn paused with him, her lovely face lifted to his. Slowly he went on, "He wanted something better for me. My God, I've never thought of it that way before. At the time it just seemed that he was pushing and pushing me against my will. It felt as if he was pushing me to a breaking point. That's why I left."

"I think I know what you mean, Christopher. Katherine's parents were like that too. She's talked a little bit about it—how they kept trying to make her into something she wasn't. I could see how hard that was for her."

He nodded. "I saw her father once, by the way. He came to the house, wanting to persuade Father to invest in one of his business deals."

"Isn't he one of the *oiliest* people you've ever met? I only saw him twice but I used to check if he left greasy footprints behind him when he walked."

Christopher laughed. "That, *signorina*, is a perfect description."

Gwendolyn twinkled up at him. "Thank you! Maybe I *should* become a writer, like Katherine! Did your father invest in the deal after all?"

"No, he said it stank to high heaven."

"Good for him."

"Yes," said Christopher thoughtfully, "good for him."

High above their heads, the fireworks began in earnest, filling the night sky with sound and light, and together they went back to the supper-boxes where they joined their party once more. Gauging by the various expressions on people's faces, Christopher thought, overall the expedition had been a mixed success. Francis and Owen were bored, Helen was sulking, Lady Almira and the Countess were dozing in their seats despite the loud percussive noises of the fireworks. On the other hand, the Earl was serene, the Duchess as vigorously unflappable as ever, and Rupert was jovial, making Christopher wonder if he'd managed to jockey some poor unfortunate woman into an obscure corner somewhere. De Montmorency had apparently recovered from the insult to his evening-shoes, courtesy of

Lady Almira's flying elbow and the potted plant; he now had about him the anticipatory air of a cat with a plump mouse in sight. And Percy, who came hurrying up, the last to arrive, was positively glowing with good cheer.

As for Gwendolyn, he was glad to see her looking tranquil again, though he watched with foreboding as she went to the Earl. Watched him smile at her. Smile and smile, like a man utterly besotted . . .

And so what about himself?

What sort of evening had *he* had?

For one thing, he had seen something which he couldn't unsee. A tiny little secret, a worm in a beautiful apple. Gnawing, gnawing insatiably.

What else?

Well, he'd almost throttled a man. In public.

Also, he'd nearly kissed Gwendolyn.

Too, they'd talked about things both amusing and deeply felt.

She had cried and he had comforted her.

He'd had, thanks to her, some new and unexpected insights about his father.

Yes, altogether quite the evening.

So how *was* he?

He hardly knew.

Chapter 10

❧⟨∾∾⟩❧

Helen's birthday celebration started off well enough, but went rapidly downhill during dinner when Owen stood, held up his wineglass, and called for a toast.

"Happy birthday," he said to his sister. "How does it feel to be an old maid?"

Helen went very red. "I'm twenty-one, not a hundred and one."

"Might as well be." Owen sat down and returned to his third serving of broiled chicken.

She glared at him, muttering, "You're an *ass*."

"That's enough, both of you," said the Duchess. "Almira, you needn't cry. It's merely a silly squabble."

Lady Almira was dabbing at her eyes. "Oh, dear ma'am, I did so want for this to be a *happy* dinner."

"Apparently," the Duchess said, "with Owen and Helen present, that may be too much to ask. As there are only three gentlemen with us tonight, we ladies won't withdraw. Shall we proceed directly to the drawing-room?"

"I'm not done," protested Owen.

"I think you are," said his grandmother, with a hint of steel in her voice.

Sullenly Owen laid down his knife and fork, and everyone made their way to the drawing-room. It was a small party this evening, with Christopher their only guest from outside the townhouse. Military duties had Percy elsewhere, but he had sent a large bouquet of daisies for Helen which she received indifferently and passed over to Lady Almira who had alternately admired them and sneezed while arranging them in a vase.

Gifts were tendered. The Duchess gave Helen a new pair of riding gloves; Lady Almira, a pretty set of lovingly embroidered handkerchiefs which had Helen rolling her eyes. "*You* need them more than I do," she said to her mother, which made her look as if she was going to cry again.

Quickly Gwendolyn leapt into the breach. "Happy birthday, Helen," she said, and gave her a flat oblong package wrapped in a length of printed cotton and neatly tied up with yarn.

Helen undid the bow and pulled off the cotton to reveal a framed portrait of herself which Gwendolyn had done in watercolor. It showed Helen in profile, in her favorite green riding-dress which buttoned up high around her throat, and such was the effect of light which Gwendolyn had delicately captured, Helen's freckles looked as if she'd been dusted with fairy gold.

"Oh, how *charming*!" exclaimed Lady Almira, and the Duchess said, "Very pretty indeed, Gwendolyn, and what a thoughtful gift."

Helen set the watercolor aside without comment and picked up Christopher's gift. "Thank you *so* much, Mr. Beck," she said, tearing away the paper to reveal three slim books. "Oh!" she said blankly. "*Guy Mannering*."

"A clerk at Hatchard's told me it was very entertaining," Christopher said.

"Oh."

"You mentioned you enjoyed reading, so I thought—"

"I do! Very much! What a wonderful gift, Mr. Beck, thank you! I shall *treasure* it always!" Helen's voice seemed unnecessarily loud and she pressed the books to her chest as if embracing them. And then she glanced over at Francis—a darting sideways look which made Gwendolyn wonder why she'd done that. Was she hinting that it was time for Francis to give her the present he had in his hand? But he was staring at the flames in the fireplace, a distracted, dreamy look on his face.

"I say, *Francis*," Owen shouted, and Francis gave a start.

"What?"

"Give the old girl your gift."

Helen scowled at her brother. "Don't call me that."

"It's just an expression."

"Well, stop it."

"Oh yes," said Francis. "I forgot." He stood and went over to Helen, holding out a small rectangular package.

"Happy birthday, Lady Helen."

Helen pulled off the paper. It was another book. "*A Practical View of the Prevailing Religious System of Professed Christians,*" she read out loud, "*in the Higher and Middle Classes in This Country, Contrasted with Real Christianity.*"

"It's one of Wilberforce's finest works," said Francis. "A first edition. There's an index as well, which I think a particularly nice touch."

"Oh."

Owen guffawed. "Lord, Francis, you're a corker!" He stood up and thrust a large package at Helen. "Here you are, old girl."

"Stop calling me that, you ass."

"Open your gift."

She did, but cautiously, as if it might contain something dangerous. It was a box from Fortnum & Mason, and inside was a lavish array of chocolates, taffy, sugared almonds, marzipan, and licorice.

"In case you didn't have enough on hand," said Owen.

As if involuntarily, one of Helen's hands went to the waist of her gown and she tugged at it, as if it were too tight on her. Her face was scarlet again. "You're a *monster*," she burst out, and with a sweep of that same hand she shoved the box onto the floor, its contents scattering everywhere.

A footman came at once, but the Duchess waved him away. "Thank you, but Lady Helen and the Marquis are going to pick all those up."

"*Me?*" said Owen. "*She* did it."

"Yes, you. And Helen. No, Almira, get up, you're not to help them. Nor you, Gwendolyn."

Reluctantly Owen sank onto his knees and began gathering up sweets and putting them back in the box, but Helen stayed where she was, hands clenched in her lap and her face the color of a perfectly ripe tomato.

"Helen," said the Duchess, a warning note in her voice.

"I *won't*! And you can't *make* me!"

The Duchess merely looked at her, very calm and stern. Christopher stood up. "Ma'am, Lady Almira, I'll be on my way."

"Oh, *don't!*" Helen exclaimed. "Do stay, Mr. Beck! Look, I'm cleaning up! See?" She dropped onto her knees and grabbed a handful of almonds.

But Christopher only looked over her head to the Duchess. "If you'll excuse me, ma'am?"

"Of course, Mr. Beck. Goodnight."

Gwendolyn walked to the drawing-room doors with him. At the threshold she said, very quietly, "I'm so sorry, Christopher."

"Why should you be? It's not your fault."

"I know, but . . ."

"Just save me a piece of cake."

"I will."

"Shall I come by tomorrow afternoon?"

"Yes, that would be—no, wait, I won't be here, the Countess has invited me to tea. But if you still want to call, I'll tell Tyndale to set it aside for you."

"Will the Honorable Rupert be there?"

"I don't know."

"Don't let him get you alone."

His voice was serious, and Gwendolyn looked up at him curiously. "Are you worried about me?"

"I worry about you being alone with him."

"I'll be careful. Besides, he can't very well carry me off with his mother right there." She kept her tone light, but there was no answering smile from Christopher.

"Will you remember what I said?"

"Yes, Christopher."

"*Grazie, signorina*," he said, "goodnight," and for a moment Gwendolyn thought he might take her hand—might hold it in his own—but he didn't.

"Goodnight, Christopher." She was unaccountably disappointed, and watched him leave the drawing-room and go toward the stairs. From behind her she could hear sounds of sweets being dumped back into the Fortnum & Mason box, and then the footman, standing next to the doorway, sneezed.

"Bless you, Sam."

"Thank you, miss," the footman said, and sneezed again.

Gwendolyn slowly retraced her steps into the drawing-room but stayed standing, feeling very awkward.

Helen paused for a moment to glare up at her. "You ought to have made Mr. Beck stay."

"I don't see how."

"Well, you're *useless* then, aren't you?"

Her tone was angry and vindictive. So much for their being the best of friends, Gwendolyn thought. Had she

failed Helen in some unknown fashion? She had tried,
over these past weeks while living under the same roof, to
be pleasant, attentive, courteous. But somehow it wasn't
enough. Helen was looking at her as if—why, as if she
loathed her. And even as Gwendolyn thought this, Helen
grabbed the watercolor portrait of herself and flung it into
the fireplace.

"Helen!" gasped Lady Almira, and Owen scrambled
to the hearth and snatched the portrait out of the flames.
But it was too late. It was already ruined. He blew out
the flames that licked along one side of the frame, then
looked rather helplessly at Gwendolyn.

"I say, I *am* sorry."

"Thank you for trying." Never mind that she had spent
hours creating the portrait, and after that, searching for
just the right frame. Never mind.

Owen said to his sister, "You know, *you're* the monster."

"Shut *up!*"

"Helen," said the Duchess, "your behavior is absolutely
shocking. What have you to say for yourself?"

Helen was standing on the hearthrug with her hands
clenched into fists and her mouth working. Lady Almira
was quietly weeping, but other than that a heavy silence
had descended. It was finally broken when the Duchess
spoke again, her voice very stern.

"Well, Helen?"

"I don't have anything to say! Except—" Helen paused,
then kicked the Fortnum & Mason box, sending it peril-
ously close to the fireplace, and said with a snarl in her
gruff little voice, "Except that I hate you! I hate *all* of
you!" She whirled and ran out of the drawing-room, her
slippered feet pounding on the floor.

The Duchess sighed. "Gwendolyn, m'dear, I'm sorrier
than I can say."

"It's all right, Cousin Judith."

"I really don't think it is. Thank you, Owen."

Owen had pulled the box away from the fireplace and was back on his knees, gathering up the sweets. He stopped for a moment and said to her, "Grandmother, I'm sorry too."

"I know you are. Your gift was thoughtless, and unkind, but Helen had no business behaving as she did. Almira, let's go upstairs, and I'll have my maid make a nice tisane. Hawkins will know precisely the sort you need."

"Thank you, ma'am," tremulously answered Lady Almira, rising to her feet with her shawl hanging precariously by one shoulder, and so the two ladies left the drawing-room. Owen doggedly kept to his task, and Gwendolyn went to sit next to Francis, sharing the sofa.

Pensively, she pulled her feet free from her white slippers, drew her knees up to her chin, and hugged them to her. There was an acrid smell in the air from the burnt paper and wood that had been Helen's portrait.

"Quite the birthday celebration," she said to Francis.

"Was it really? It seemed to lack a certain *joi de vivre*, but perhaps that's just me."

Gwendolyn nudged him with her toe. "Oh, Francis, were you even paying attention?"

"Well, I *was* thinking about a conversation I had last year with Grandpapa, about the tensions between conservative theologians and what might be called progressive theologians, or even radicals, depending on one's perspective. He mentioned the Elizabethan Settlement as a foundational effort to resolve these tensions—it's only ever been moderately successful, you know, and just last month the Archbishop of York gave a speech about communion practices that nearly set off a riot among the deans."

Owen laughed and popped a chocolate into his mouth. "My God, Francis, but you *are* a corker."

Francis only smiled, and Gwendolyn said, "May I have one of those chocolates?"

"Not worried about dirt?" Owen said.

"It's the least of my worries."

"Here." Owen handed her a chocolate, and thoughtfully Gwendolyn nibbled on it. It was delicious, even if not entirely pristine. Yes indeed, it had been quite a birthday celebration. She wished Christopher had stayed.

Gwendolyn's note was brought up by a porter.

Dear Christopher,

I would have had a slice of cake sent on to you, but after last night's fiasco, Cousin Judith told Tyndale to share all of it with the staff. Which I think was a very good idea, don't you? Breakfast was very uncomfortable. Cousin Judith forced Helen to apologize to Francis (who at first had no idea what she meant, having forgotten all about it) and then to me (she had thrown the portrait into the fire, you see, after you left), and I didn't really know what to say except to try and be gracious about it—though, honestly, I'm not sure just how well I succeeded. And then half an hour later, Owen and Helen quarreled about who would have the last sausage. Poor Cousin Judith. Poor Lady Almira! I must say, I was glad when breakfast was over.

So, no cake for you, I'm afraid, ma sherry moo.

Would you like to go for a ride in Hyde Park tomorrow, around five? If so, let's meet at the top of Rotten Row.

G.

Christopher set aside the note, then went restlessly to the wide bay windows of his front room. He looked out onto the courtyard below. It was raining heavily today, and he watched as half a dozen people emerged from the Albany's main entrance with umbrellas which they opened against the downpour. For a moment he knew a powerful longing for the countryside—for the sea—for open spaces. He thought about Mauro and those expansive pastures on his estate, the gently rolling hills which would be vividly green this time of year, and the orchards come to life again after their winter sleep.

Christopher turned from the window and looked at the books he'd gotten from Hatchard's, which lay on a side-table. He'd already sent Mauro's on their way to Italy. What remained was *The Bandit's Bride* and *Birds of the British Isles and Their Ancient Domains*. He went over and looked at them for a long time. An idea had come to him—or, rather, renewed itself—and he was weighing it in his mind.

Hugo Penhallow had told him: *Do what brings you the most peace.*

So Christopher got his jacket, and went out into the rain.

Under the shelter of Sam the footman's umbrella, Gwendolyn went down the townhouse steps and into the Westenbury barouche. "Thank you, Sam."

"You're welcome, miss," Sam answered, and sneezed. His face was a little flushed, and, leaning forward, Gwendolyn said:

"Sam, are you all right?"

"Oh yes, miss, right as a trivet."

"If you're sure?"

"Certainly, miss, thank you," and Sam shut the door to the barouche. Gwendolyn settled the skirts of her gown and pelisse, and the Earl, across from her, banged on the roof with his walking-stick, the signal for the carriage to move, and so they began their journey to the Westenbury townhouse.

"Hullo," he said, smiling at her.

It had been two days since she had seen Julian, and for some reason it felt like years. Looking at him was almost like looking at a stranger—like the entrancing stranger he had been, that unforgettable night at Almack's—oh, how very like a prince he was in the fairy tales, the embodiment of a girl's romantic dream . . . but *real*. Living, breathing, *alive*. His hair as tawny as a lion's, his eyes as green as the forest, with those fascinating flecks in them that reminded her of the gold bits floating in the sea at home.

A memory came to her then, from years ago. Hugo, having just gotten home from the wars, asking his younger siblings what they'd like to be when they grew up. She had been fourteen, a giddy, dreamy girl, and had said:

On the one hand, I want to do something useful and important. But on the other hand, I'd like to have some adventures. And I'd want so much to have a London Season and go to a different ball every night and have a beautiful wardrobe with all the latest fashions and meet my one true love.

And here she was—lucky, lucky her—having her London Season at last. She'd been to many balls. She had a beautiful wardrobe. *And* she had found her one true love. Who was sitting right across from her. Sometimes, Gwendolyn knew, people scoffed at the idea of love at first sight. But what did *they* know? Besides, it happened all the time in books. Which had to tell you something, didn't it?

Gwendolyn smiled back at the Earl. "Thank you for

coming to get me. I could have walked, though—your townhouse is only ten minutes from here."

"You'd have gotten soaked."

"It's only a drizzle right now. Why didn't you bring your curricle?"

"M-my mother thought the barouche would be more suitable."

"Well, it's certainly capacious. What have you been doing since last we met?"

"Mostly spending time with family, of course, but I did manage to slip away with Étienne to the docks."

"The docks? Why?"

"There's a sailmaker there—he's commissioning a new mainsail for his racing yacht."

"He has a racing yacht? Here in London?"

"No, in Bournemouth. We used to go every summer, for the races, and then we'd sail to Le Havre and from there go to Rennes—his family's country estate is not far from there, you know. We haven't gone in a couple of years, however. Pity. It's tremendous fun."

"It does sound like fun. But somehow Monsieur de Montmorency doesn't quite strike me as the sailing type. I can't picture him hauling up an anchor, say, or furling the jib."

Julian laughed. "He has a crew to do that for him. He's the captain, you see."

"Hugo always says that a captain has to be able to do everything his crew does. He says it helps keep both the crew and the ship safe."

"That makes sense. Still, good luck persuading Étienne to change his mind! He's not what I would call a very biddable fellow."

Gwendolyn nodded. But she didn't really want to be chatting about de Montmorency. Something had been tugging at her, and now was the time, while they had a few minutes of privacy, to talk about it. She said, "Julian, Christopher Beck told me that you'd invited him to our wedding."

"Yes, I thought you'd like that."

"He also told me you said the wedding was going to be here in London, at St. George's."

"Yes, I did."

"I thought—we were riding to Richmond, don't you remember?—I thought we'd agreed to have it in White-haven."

Julian looked a little uncomfortable. "Do you know, my love, I'm afraid it had simply slipped my mind. It was terribly careless of me. Do forgive me. Of course it can be in Whitehaven."

"You mean that?"

"Absolutely." He smiled at her, and Gwendolyn felt the constriction in her heart begin to unravel itself. "Some-times," Julian went on, "when I'm looking at you, my darling—well, all I can do is think about how beautiful you are, how you're the woman of my dreams—how lucky I am to have you. How much I want you. Honestly, there are times I feel a little deranged. In a good way. Didn't Shakespeare say that love is a kind of madness?"

Gwendolyn thought about it. "I believe he did. In *As You Like It*."

"Well, there you are."

It occurred to Gwendolyn that she wasn't sure if she quite agreed with Julian's line of thinking on this point, but there wasn't much time left for private conversation and there was something else she wanted to discuss with him.

"Julian, if you knew that a married woman was having an affair with a man other than her husband—an unmarried man—what would you think about it?"

His eyebrows went up. "My darling girl, what a question! Why do you ask?"

"I'm just curious."

"Is this someone you know?"

"It doesn't matter. What would you think, Julian?"

He was looking uncomfortable again. "I daresay it would—well, it would depend."

"On what?"

"Well, I suppose—that is, if it were happening among my staff, for example—I'd—I suppose, really, the best thing to do would be to have the woman let go. To set the right tone. Her husband would have to go as well."

"And the unmarried man?"

Julian paused, his brow furrowed. "As for him—well—I daresay he'd be given a warning to not repeat his behavior."

"Wouldn't that be treating the woman and her husband unfairly?"

"Unfairly?"

"If you believe the woman's behavior to be questionable, wouldn't her—her paramour's be as well? That's what I mean about unfairness."

"Well—well, perhaps so. It's complicated, really."

"Yes, it is. And what about the husband? Is he in any way responsible, or is he merely a victim?"

"I suppose—I suppose it depends."

"Yes. And what if this affair was being conducted amongst the *ton*?"

"Well, I daresay—Gwendolyn, my dear, I—I'm wondering—may I ask why you're concerning yourself with this subject?"

"Is it indelicate of me?"

"I'm rather surprised, that's all."

"Have I shocked you, Julian?"

"As I told m-my mother, you certainly have a lively mind."

"So what if it *was* happening amongst some members of the *ton*?"

"Standards are, perhaps, a trifle different in the Upper Ten Thousand."

"Why would they be? Shouldn't the same morality apply universally? Assuming it's a morality worth embracing. That's what my grandfather would say."

"It's just the way things are, my darling."

"Does that make it right?"

"I see your point, but I'm still not sure exactly why we're having this discussion. When we're married, you must certainly deal with the domestic staff as you see fit. Honestly, I'd rather talk about how beautiful you are. And how much I adore you." He leaned forward to take hold of one of her hands.

Gwendolyn almost wanted to pull it away from him. But at the same time she could feel herself staring at his handsome face, studying him, drinking him in with her eyes, his broad shoulders, his powerful legs, the exotic and enticing manliness of him—could feel herself wanting to sway toward him, irresistibly, like one magnet to another. Her body overcoming her busy brain. Oh, she felt so unclear—frustrated—miserably ineffectual.

What was right and what was wrong? What had happened to her—to her life? She had met a wonderful man and they had fallen in love and they were going to be married. It had all seemed so easy—so simple—so straightforward. Oh, goodness, maybe love *was* a kind of madness. Because suddenly she wanted to grab his face and kiss him fiercely. *Yes, just like you wanted to do with Christopher the other night*, said a tiny little voice within, and immediately a wave of guilt rose up, massive and ominous, and swamped her. Was she a bad person? A bad, defective person? She had opened her mouth to reply to Julian and, feeling foolish, promptly closed it.

The carriage came to a stop and Julian glanced out the window. "We're here," he said, and the faint note of relief in his voice didn't escape Gwendolyn. Perhaps *she* was relieved, too. Maybe she was not only a bad, defective person but really also a coward.

It was, to say the least, a very lowering thought.

"And," Julian went on, his voice cheerful now, "it's stopped raining. Excellent."

A footman came to open the door and help her out of the carriage, and shortly, she and Julian were entering a large, richly furnished drawing-room where the Countess—resplendent from head to toe in white satin and silk, a beautiful and regal snow queen—sat waiting to receive them, her blue eyes warm and glowing with friendliness and approval.

Chapter 11

***

"**G**wendolyn, my dear, dear child!" Smiling, the Countess held out her hands, and Gwendolyn moved quickly to take them in her own.

"How do you do, ma'am?"

"I'm so happy to see you. Please do sit down, and we can have a cozy chat." She released Gwendolyn's hands to gesture toward a chair next to her own, and obediently Gwendolyn sank down into it. The Earl had just sat on a chair next to Gwendolyn's when his brother Rupert came strolling into the drawing-room.

"Hullo, it's my magnificent sister-to-be," he said, just as if he had never engaged in secret little games with his feet, and hers, underneath a table. "Miss Penhallow, I do believe you get more beautiful every time I see you."

As this was only the second time they had met, this seemed to Gwendolyn an annoyingly fulsome compliment, but she let it pass, and only said, politely, "How do you do, Mr. Durant?"

"Rupert," said the Countess, "I don't care for your waistcoat. It's positively *loud*. Go and change it at once."

Gwendolyn looked at Rupert's waistcoat. It was made

of pale green silk and embroidered in a subtle paisley pattern with violet thread, and featured two columns of small, embossed brass buttons.

Was it, she thought, loud? That was certainly a subjective term, especially since she had seen plenty of men wearing waistcoats that were considerably more vibrant in color and eye-catching in design. For example, there was that gentleman at the Aymesburtons' ball whose waistcoat was fashioned out of shiny gold fabric, with buttons that flashed and sparkled like diamonds. At any rate, Rupert was a grown man, and—

"Very well, Mummie," said Rupert, and turned around and left the room.

Oh dear, how awkward. Gwendolyn glanced at Julian, who seemed unperturbed, however, and then of course she *had* to look more closely at *his* waistcoat, which was made of cream-colored linen embroidered in horizontal stripes of plum thread. Was it less loud? Would the Countess ask him to go change it? Surely not—

"Julian dear," said the Countess, "do go see that Rupert selects a more genteel waistcoat."

"Of course," answered the Earl, rising at once, and with a little smile at Gwendolyn he also turned and left the room.

There was a silence. The Countess smiled benignly at her. A clock ticked from somewhere in the room. Outside, in the street, a dog barked. Oh dear, oh *dear*, thought Gwendolyn. Say something. But not about waistcoats. She cleared her throat. "I understand, ma'am, that you were taken ill not long before your journey here to London. I do hope it was nothing serious."

"How kind of you to ask, my dear child! Female troubles, I'm sorry to say. I've never been quite right after Julian was born. Really, it was Amelia's birth which started it all—a breech birth, you know, *most* uncomfortable. The doctors quite feared for my life."

"How—how dreadful, ma'am." Amelia, Gwendolyn remembered, was the fourth child, after Agnes, Martha, and Sarah. Then there was Mariah, Fanny, Georgiana, and Mary (as if, with the arrival of the eighth girl, ingenuity in naming her had been exhausted).

"Yes, it was rather harrowing," said the Countess, with a kind of proud relish in her voice. "Blood everywhere, quite a lot of screaming, and an entire set of bed linens ruined. Afterwards I was told to refrain from having any more children, but of course I *had* to have more. I knew my duty! We had only girls. Besides, my dear late husband Edmond was a man of great appetite, you see, so thankfully it all worked out very well, because by and by we were blessed with Julian. And then Rupert. It wasn't long after Rupert was born that poor dear Edmond died in a hunting accident, else we might have had more children."

"Would you—would you have wanted more, ma'am?"

"Why, of course! Anything could have happened to Julian, or Rupert, and then where would we be? Point *non plus*! The Westenbury line stretches back unbroken to the arrival of the Conqueror, and I certainly wasn't going to be the first Countess to fail in my maternal obligations! Dear Edmond always said I was the most determined woman he had ever met. So, as you can imagine, I watched over Julian and Rupert most carefully. They were the first children to be inoculated in Gloucestershire. Poor little boys! How they *did* cry."

Gwendolyn wanted to ask if her daughters were inoculated too, but then she saw that the Countess was looking her up and down, as one might eye a horse whose paces were a little off.

"You have four brothers, my dear child, is that right?"

"Yes, ma'am."

"All healthy?"

"Yes, ma'am."

The Countess nodded. "That's reassuring, to be sure. You *are* a trifle thin, my dear, and your hips—well—they're a bit narrow, aren't they? Is your mother of the same build?"

In her mind's eye Gwendolyn saw herself telling Christopher about this rather odd conversation, envisioning the gleam of laughter in his eyes, and bit her lip to repress a giggle. As she did so, the butler came into the drawing-room, heralding the arrival of the tea tray, and Gwendolyn was so happy to have a diversion that she could have hugged him, the footmen that followed behind, *and* the tea tray.

"Those macaroons look marvelous," she said to the Countess. "And the tarts as well. I'm famished, really—it feels like years since nuncheon. And those cakes, how delightful. I'm very fond of cakes, especially if they've got icing on them, and . . ." She rambled on in this vein for what really did feel like years, wondering if it were possible to bore oneself to death with one's own speech, but would have kept on till the bitter end to avoid further discussion of hips, childbirth, and the late Earl's appetites.

"Oh, tea's here already?" It was Rupert, reentering the room in a sober waistcoat in shades of beige and gray. "Excellent."

The Earl followed behind, and Gwendolyn saw at once that he had changed his waistcoat, too. Its colors were equally drab—brown and ecru.

"We were just talking about your sisters," Gwendolyn said, making her voice bright, as they sat on the sofa set at a perpendicular angle to the Countess's chair. She turned again to the Countess. "Julian's written to them, ma'am—I would so like for them to come here, so that we can get to know each other."

The Countess's blue eyes opened wide. "Come here? Oh no, my dear, they're needed at home."

"But surely—"

"Macaroons!" Rupert said. "My favorite."

"They're terribly busy getting ready to oversee the refurbishment of the Dower House, which has been empty for decades," said the Countess. "You and Julian will naturally occupy the State Bedchamber, which I shared with my dear Edmond for so many happy, happy years. And I will retreat, as is only proper, to a mother-in-law's domain. It's nearly a quarter-mile from the main house, but I shan't mind that at all. Although in spring, when it gets muddy, that *will* present a problem. I wonder if I can manage to stagger along in pattens? A trifle dangerous, at my age, but what a small price to pay for doing what is right. And in winter I shall snuggle up all alone, as cozy as any dormouse, patiently sleeping the long gray months away."

Gwendolyn, through a supreme act of will, tamped down any images of the State Bedchamber and what may or may not have transpired within it. If she never set foot in there, it would be fine with her. "Please don't give up your bedroom on our behalf, ma'am. I'm sure Julian and I can find very comfortable accommodations elsewhere in the house. Isn't that right, Julian?"

He nodded. "Yes indeed."

"Of course you'll have the State Bedchamber," the Countess said. "It's a Westenbury tradition."

"It really doesn't matter to me," said the Earl. "Whatever is best for everyone."

"I shouldn't dream of supplanting you, ma'am," said Gwendolyn. "All that fuss and bother. I'm sure you'll be happiest where you've been for all these years. Don't you agree, Julian?"

"I do know what you mean about avoiding unnecessary fuss, my love. Still, if she really doesn't mind," said the Earl, "the Dower House will be very nice once it's refurbished. Or—" He turned to his mother, as though he'd just been struck by a particularly clever idea. "Or perhaps the Blue Suite would suit you very well indeed. It's very spacious, and you'd have a wonderful view of the knot garden. You wouldn't have to leave the main house."

"The Blue Suite is one of my favorites, Julian dear, but you must realize that it's too far from the stairs, and dreadfully inconvenient for the servants."

"Oh, do you think so? Well, what about the Rose Rooms?"

"Yes, they're certainly pretty, but I've quite made up my mind about the Dower House."

"I wouldn't mind a change of rooms," said Rupert. "I'll just take Julian's, shall I, after he and Miss Penhallow move into the State Bedchamber."

"No, dear, you're to stay where you are," said his mother. "More tea, Gwendolyn, my dear child? Do have another cake."

"Well," said the Earl cheerfully, "it does seem that all roads lead to the State Bedchamber. You'll love it, my dear Gwendolyn."

"But Julian," Gwendolyn began, and then the Countess said, smiling:

"Don't be silly, Julian darling. There aren't any roads *inside* the house. Only hallways, of course. Now, if you two dear children are going to keep on insisting that I remain in the State Bedchamber, then it would be positively *mulish* of me to relinquish it. I have many faults, I daresay, but mulishness isn't one of them." She reached over to pat Gwendolyn's hand, and brightly went on: "I'm delighted that it's all settled. I don't care in the least for disagreements and quarreling. They quite take the zest out of life. Do let's talk about the wedding. I've been simply wild with excitement to put our heads together and firm up the plans. I've had the rector of St. George's over, and he's given me a list of several possible dates."

Gwendolyn looked at the Earl. He, in turn, shifted in his seat and then looked at his mother. "As to that, we're thinking of having the wedding in Whitehaven."

He might as well have announced the site of their wedding as being the moon. So high did the Countess's eyebrows go up, they briefly disappeared underneath the bit of golden fringe displayed beneath her white satin turban.

"Whitehaven? Oh no, my dears, that would never do. The rector told me that yours is already being described as the wedding of the year, and how he's been putting off several important couples until you've decided on the date you like the best. And Étienne de Montmorency mentioned that the Prince Regent is eager to attend—you certainly wouldn't wish to incur dear Prinny's displeasure by having the wedding elsewhere."

"Gwendolyn would like to have her grandfather perform the ceremony," said the Earl, "at his church in Whitehaven."

"Prinny ain't going to Whitehaven, wherever that is," put in Rupert, and took another macaroon.

The Countess smiled warmly at Gwendolyn. "It's a lovely idea, my dear child, and very commendable in you. Family loyalty is everything! But I'm afraid it's just not practicable, and I know you wouldn't want to deprive Julian of the chance to have the Prince Regent attend, as well as all his many, many friends who are here for the Season. Would the very end of June suit you both? It doesn't give us a great deal of time, but if we all work very hard, I'm sure we can pull it off. Oh, what fun this is! I've always longed to plan a wedding. My own dear mother, God rest her soul, wouldn't permit me to lift a finger to help with *my* wedding, so here at last is my opportunity to be of service. I'll do everything in my power to make this not just the wedding of the year, my dear ones, but the wedding of the *century*." She beamed at her listeners, her face aglow with pleasure and anticipation.

"Am I to be married too, Mummie?" asked Rupert.

"Of course you will, dear, once Julian is. What do you think of Lady Helen? Her lineage isn't fully what I would like—Lady Almira having been married previously to a commoner—but her grandfather is a duke, after all, and I understand the dowry is substantial."

Rupert grimaced. "She's fat."

"Nonsense. A little high in the flesh, perhaps, but she looks to be an excellent breeder."

"Too many freckles. Reminds me of a speckled toad."

"My dear Rupert, we can't all have the ideal complexion. Like Gwendolyn's, for example. Or mine, perhaps, when I was younger. Lady Helen can always try Gowland's Lotion, you know."

"Yes, that's true," said Rupert.

Gwendolyn sat very still in her chair. She did want to ask the Countess why, with eight daughters well into adulthood, none of them were married, and also, if the Countess wasn't going to be taking possession of the Dower House after all, why couldn't at least some of those daughters come to London, *and*, incidentally, she didn't like in the least how they were talking about Helen (who was a very attractive young lady, no matter *what* the Westenbury might think and say). There was too much coming at her, and she was struggling to process it. The eight daughters. Why did Rupert have to wait for Julian to get married first? And speaking of which—the wedding. Here in London. *Not* in Whitehaven. Was she being stubborn and selfish? *Mulish?* Only thinking about what *she* wanted?

She didn't know. She hoped not. But she didn't know. All she *did* know was that she felt like a whirligig, spinning in a dangerously high wind. She looked over at Julian again. He gave her a little smile, a slight shrug of the shoulders.

She had no idea what he was hoping to convey.

The clock chimed and the Countess jumped. "Only look at the time! I've been so engrossed in our delightful conversation that I didn't realize how late it's become." She rose to her feet, adding, "Come along, Rupert."

Rupert stood up and the Earl, standing also, said:

"Where are you going?"

"I'm off to see Lady Hertford, and Rupert is to escort me. You're to join us after you've taken Gwendolyn home. Do excuse my mad dash, my dear child—I look forward to seeing you again very soon."

Gwendolyn got up and kissed the soft white cheek presented to her. The Countess bustled away, calling for her pelisse and gloves, and Rupert followed close behind. When they were gone the Earl said:

"If you're quite finished with your tea, my love, would you care for a quick tour of the townhouse? It will be your home soon—one of them, I mean."

Did she want a tour? Did she want more tea? Was she glad or sorry the Countess was going to keep the State Bedchamber? Did she really even like cakes, with or without icing? She wasn't sure about anything anymore. Rather numbly Gwendolyn replied, "If you like, Julian."

He showed her the other drawing-rooms, various saloons, the library, an enormous ballroom, the equally vast dining-room, then they went up a flight of stairs to the next level where the bedchambers were. They glanced into a few of them, but when they came to a room at the end of the hallway, the Earl pushed open the door and drew her inside.

"This is mine. Soon to be ours, my darling."

It was a very large, handsomely furnished bedchamber, with a massive four-poster bed, two fireplaces, three or four sofas, a similar number of chairs, and quite a few paintings. Gwendolyn caught a glimpse of several life-sized portraits in ornate old-fashioned frames, including one of a man whom Julian and Rupert greatly resembled, and took a step to look at it more closely, but paused when Julian said:

"Wait, please."

She did, and watched as he shut the door and locked it. Surely not very proper behavior? Or was this different from being reluctant to slip away from their engagement party? Was it like being in the Richmond maze? It took all of Gwendolyn's self-control to not clutch at her own head, to try and slow down the confusion whirling about inside her brain. "What is it, Julian?" she asked, hearing in her voice a new kind of coolness.

He came to her and took her hand. "About the wedding. I *am* sorry. I'll talk to her again."

"Did you write to your sisters, by the way? About coming to London?"

He paused, and Gwendolyn had her answer. "I suppose," she said, "it wouldn't have mattered if you did."

"My dear love, they wouldn't have come. Please don't take it personally."

Was that what she was doing? Or was it about Julian saying he would do something and not doing it? Why did she care so much? It was only a letter. A small, tiny, insignificant little letter, that wouldn't have changed anything anyway. Wasn't she foolishly making a mountain out of a molehill? All at once Gwendolyn remembered Lady Almira saying, that afternoon at Richmond: *Mazes do make me nervous. They're rather like a bad dream, aren't they? You know, a nightmare where you're trapped, and you don't know where you are, and can't find your way free?*

"Never mind," she said, and pulled her hand away.

Julian stood for a long moment looking down at her. "Are you upset with me?"

Yes—no—maybe. Gwendolyn shrugged.

"Please don't be angry," he said.

Still she said nothing.

A silence descended between them, heavy, all-encompassing, like a blanket made out of lead. It would take superhuman effort to even open one's mouth, Gwendolyn thought, let alone have the strength to form words.

And then Julian sank to his knees.

How gracefully he did it—how very like a hero in a romantic story. He hadn't gotten onto one knee proposing to her, as first he'd gone to see Hugo, and then Hugo had come to talk with her privately, and then the Earl had come into the room with Hugo still there, and that was when he had given her the ancient Westenbury ring. She looked from Julian's tawny head to her left hand, to the ring; the little perfect rubies around the beautiful pearl seemed to wink and shimmer at her. She remembered, suddenly, Diana once saying dreamily about the butcher's boy, *I do wish he would go down on his knee and pledge his troth, whatever that is. Wouldn't that be the most romantic thing in all the world? I vow I'd die on the spot, wouldn't you?*

Julian slid his hands around her legs, embracing her tightly. "I love you," he said. "I love you so much. Please don't be angry with me—please don't withdraw. You're my whole world, don't you know that? I live for you—for our love—for our lives together. You're my *everything*."

In his deep voice was nothing but humble sincerity.

And fear.

And pain.

Gwendolyn didn't know what to say. Was she some kind of horrible beast, to hurt him so badly?

That lead blanket pressed down upon her, inexorable, irresistible; and silently, giving way to it like a drowning person going under, she sank down onto her knees as well. Julian brought her to him and began to kiss her, murmuring feverishly, "I love you, I love you," and then he was pulling off her bonnet and tugging her hair free from its pins. "Glorious," he breathed, "so glorious," and took great handfuls of it in his fingers, as would a man clutch precious jewels, and then, the next thing she knew, they were lying together on the gleaming wood floor, and Julian had moved so that one of his legs, very solid and heavy, straddled one of hers, and one of his hands was tugging up the hem of her skirts. My goodness, here on the floor, Gwendolyn thought, and with a bed right over there. Not ideal, really: it was hurting the back of her head. She was looking up at the ceiling, but by craning her neck a little, she could see some of the portraits again, though, of course, upside down. How very odd people looked when seen from this perspective—

A hand slid up her leg, wresting Gwendolyn's attention away from the wall behind her and to what Julian was doing. Here she was again, thinking about other things. Christopher had said, *It's about paying attention to the person you're kissing.* She obviously wasn't succeeding.

Gwendolyn wondered, with a kind of distant curiosity, what would happen if she let the Earl do whatever he wanted, here on this uncomfortable wood floor. For all she knew he'd end up—what was the expression in those novels she and Diana used to gasp over?—yes, he'd end up having his way with her.

Was this what it was all about? Groping, and panting? Hands here and there, tongues darting in and out? Goodness, how *grubby*. Especially with all those people in the portraits. It felt like they were staring. Avidly.

Julian brought his groin up hard against her hip and thumped himself against it. Not only was it an odd, unpleasant sensation, it also made the back of her head drag to and fro on the floor.

Speaking of grubby, wasn't "groin" a hideous word? It sounded like a cross between "groan" and "oily."

She found herself thinking of Katherine's oleaginous father Mr. Brooke, and the Countess's remark about her late husband's carnal appetites, and the State Bedchamber, and its blood-soaked bed, and suddenly she felt her gorge rising. For an uneasy minute or so she thought she might actually throw up all over Julian. All those cakes she'd eaten, given fresh purpose. It was such a strangely energizing thought that with it Gwendolyn felt her will springing back to life.

"Stop," she said, and pushed at him with all her might.

He did, and slid away from her, and quickly Gwendolyn got to her feet.

Well, she thought, she'd just saved herself from a fate worse than death (another delightful phrase from those books—how excitedly she and Diana had whispered it out loud!). What to do now? If she were a proper heroine, she ought to wilt, or cry, or flee, or spout some exquisitely phrased recriminations that would have Julian on his knees again, hands clasped at his chest and begging for her forgiveness.

Oh, bother it all.

She wasn't in the mood for histrionics.

Gwendolyn picked up her bonnet and the pins which had scattered about. There was a tall pier-glass next to an armoire and briskly she went to it. Her skirts weren't badly crumpled, at least not in front, and she definitely wasn't going to twist around to see what she might look like from the back. She formed her hair into a simple coil, sliding the pins in to secure it, and put her bonnet back on, firmly tying the ribbons underneath her chin. In the pier-glass's reflection she saw Julian, behind her, tugging his waistcoat—his drab brown and ecru waistcoat—back into place.

If he said anything about the throes of passion, Gwendolyn thought, she would—she would—well, she didn't know what she might do. Kick him? *Throttle* him?

Anything seemed possible.

She turned away from the mirror and he said:

"Are you angry with me still?"

"No," she lied, and, simultaneously, both hated herself for lying and felt absurdly grateful she hadn't vomited.

A look of relief came over his handsome face. "I'm so glad, my darling."

So, he was glad and she was pretending not to be angry, and beyond that, there didn't seem to be much else to talk about. She said, "I'm going back to the townhouse."

"I'll call for the barouche."

"No, I'm going to walk."

"I'd rather take you in the barouche."

"You'd better hurry on over to Lady Hertford's, or your mother will worry about you."

In her voice there was a faint note of sarcasm she hadn't quite been able to repress, but Julian nodded. "I daresay you're right. I'll have a footman go with you."

"Fine."

He unlocked the door and held it open for her with such courtesy that for a disconcerting instant she wanted to giggle. How grubby and how absurd. They walked along the hallway and down the stairs, side by side and as decorous as could be, just as if they hadn't been lying on a cold wood floor a few minutes ago, with him thrusting himself at her and his hand sliding up her skirts.

In the large high-ceilinged entry-hall Julian told one of the footmen to escort her home. He said to her, "Thank you for coming to tea."

"Thank you for having me." Infelicitous words, she realized too late, and had to suppress another inappropriate giggle, conscious of an audience in the entry-hall—the impassive butler and several of his equally wooden footmen.

"When may I see you again?"

"Are you going to Lady Jersey's evening-party tomorrow?"

"Yes."

"I'll see you there, then."

"Have you any other free time tomorrow?"

Gwendolyn thought about it. In the morning she had planned to read *Marvels of the World* and write some letters; after that, Lady Almira wanted to visit some shops, and she had offered to go with her; and then she was meeting Christopher later in the afternoon. She said, "I'm afraid not."

"I'll see you at Lady Jersey's then. Shall I . . ."

"Shall you what?"

"Shall I discuss that—ah—matter with m-my mother?"

"Whatever you like," Gwendolyn said, surprised to notice that she didn't care if the wedding was to be in London, in Whitehaven, or on the moon (where they could all eat cheese, and save the trouble of menu-planning). "Goodbye."

In ten minutes she was back at the townhouse. It had begun to drizzle again, but she had declined the footman's offer to shield her with the umbrella he carried. At the top of the steps she thanked him and gave him a *douceur*, then thanked the Egremont footman who held open the front door to her.

Tyndale was in the entry-hall, sorting through some correspondence, and she said:

"Is Sam all right, Tyndale? He looked a little unwell earlier in the afternoon."

Tyndale set aside the letters and circulars on a salver and advanced to meet her. "A trifling cold, Miss Gwendolyn, that's all. Still, I've sent him off to bed so that he can rest."

Gwendolyn nodded. "I think that's a very wise idea. Where is everyone?"

"I believe the family's still at tea, miss. However—"

He broke off and Gwendolyn said, "What is it?"

The slightest flicker of unease passed across his face. "I beg your pardon, Miss Gwendolyn, I'm sure it's none of my concern."

"Oh, Tyndale, are they fighting again?"

He hesitated. Quickly Gwendolyn went on, "I shan't put you on the spot, Tyndale, do forgive me. I'll go up directly." Shaking out her damp skirts, she went up the stairs and onto the landing, where she could hear through the closed door of the drawing-room Helen's voice, very loud, and then Owen's.

Good heavens, she thought, now what?

The door opened and Francis emerged. He shut the door behind him and came toward her, looking untroubled and, in fact, rather happy.

"Hullo, Gwennie."

"Hullo, Francis. What's going on? What are Owen and Helen fighting about?"

"It appears to be something I said."

"Really? How so?"

"It's because I told Cousin Judith that I'm going back to Oxford. I've got more papers to write, and the colloquium to help plan, and—well, I didn't say this to her, but I find I'm dreadfully bored here. It's splendid to see you and Percy, of course, but this Society thing isn't my cup of tea." He looked a little worriedly at her. "You're not offended, Gwennie, are you?"

She smiled up at him. "No, of course not, Francis. I'll miss you, but I completely understand."

His brow cleared. "I hoped you would."

"How did Cousin Judith take the news?"

"She couldn't have been nicer about it."

Gwendolyn nodded. "She's lovely, isn't she? But why are Owen and Helen fighting?"

"Because now Owen's going too. He asked Cousin Judith for her permission, which she gave at once, saying she was tired of all the fighting, and then Helen simply exploded—blaming Owen for *my* going. Entirely illogical. Rather an odd girl, isn't she? Well, I'm off to pack. Are you going in?"

"No. I want a bath before dinner. Hopefully Helen will have calmed down by then."

They went upstairs together, and met again a few hours later for dinner, which proved to be a highly uncomfortable experience, as Helen was openly upset, Owen uproariously cheerful, Lady Almira melancholy, Francis wrapped in beatific silence, and even the usually unflappable Duchess was a trifle subdued. The upside for Gwendolyn, who was herself in a deeply pensive mood, was that nobody expected her to try and make conversation. Still, she was glad when she could go back to her bedchamber, where Lizzie helped her out of her dress and into a nightgown. She was just about to plait Gwendolyn's hair when she quickly stepped aside to give a loud sneeze.

"Bless you, Lizzie! I hope you're not getting Sam's cold."

"I'm sure it's nothing, miss, thank you."

"Well, you do look a little tired, Lizzie. I'll do my hair. Why don't you go on to bed?"

"If you're sure, miss?"

"Absolutely. Goodnight, Lizzie, and thank you."

When Lizzie was gone, Gwendolyn settled herself in bed with her sketchbook and opened it to a blank page. She stared at it for a while, her pencil held poised over the paper. Sometimes it was hard to know where to begin. She thought about the day—about the afternoon. By no stretch of the imagination could it be said that tea had gone well. She found herself wondering, idly, how long it had taken the Earl to get to Lady Hertford's. She was said to be the Prince Regent's mistress. Had Julian, or his mother, told Lady Hertford all about the upcoming wedding at St. George's, and invited her? Maybe, Gwendolyn thought sardonically, they could have the Hertfords seated next to the Prince Regent. And if Lord Hertford had a mistress, she could sit with them, too.

What a merry little group it would be. With all their careless, sophisticated infidelities.

Gwendolyn remembered the Countess saying, *I'll do everything in my power to make this not just the wedding of the year, my dear ones, but the wedding of the century.*

So she sketched a strange, knobbly sort of surface. The moon. She drew a large wedge of cheese, and gave it legs, arms, hands, feet. Then a face. The man on the moon. Facing him she drew, in a long column of human figures, the Earl, Rupert, and eight women who all looked alike. The Westenbury sisters. All very pretty, all rather dolorous. And middle-aged. Then she drew the Countess, wrapped in fluffy furs and a great enveloping turban— the beautiful, smiling snow queen.

She paused to look at her tableau.

Then she gave Rupert a big rectangular block of a hat, made of cheese. Herve cheese, to be specific, the nastiest-smelling cheese in all the world. She drew some wavy lines emanating from the Herve hat to show the terrible smell.

Also, she gave the man on the moon a clergyman's surplice and a little flapping stock around what might have been a neck. He was going to perform the marriage service.

The wedding of the century.

Next she drew an enormous round wedding cake, placed on a table next to the moon-minister. It was made of Herve cheese too, and she gave it very long wavy lines to indicate that it smelled just as bad as Rupert's hat.

Gwendolyn looked again at her drawing.

Something was missing.

But what?

She drew a very small round object in a corner of the paper. It was the earth, impossibly distant. How would one get back to it, she wondered.

Well, a flying horse would do. She drew a handsome stallion with great powerful wings. Then she gave it a horn growing out of its forehead. A unicorn. Why not?

She looked once more at the drawing.

It felt as if she was finished with it.

Yet at the same time, she still had a nagging feeling that it was missing something.

It took her a long time to figure out what it was.

And once she had, with lightning quickness she closed her sketchbook and shoved it back into its drawer.

Chapter 12

Christopher sat on his horse at the top of Rotten Row and looked around for Gwendolyn. The wide graveled path was crowded with other riders and carriages too, all very fashionable and stylish. Yesterday's rain had cleared away and now, in late afternoon, sunlight glimmered through the trees, their green leaves stirring gently in a soft, mild breeze.

It was pleasant and cheerful, but he was aware that within him was—conversely—painful tension and unease.

He caught a flash of gold and there was Gwendolyn, coming toward him on her neat bay, a groom following discreetly behind her. She was wearing the same simply cut blue riding habit which she'd had on the day they'd gone to Richmond Park, and the same close-fitting blue hat with her bright golden hair showing beneath.

His breath hitched in his throat, just a little, with the knowledge that lay heavy in his heart.

She rode close and he saw, now, that she was pale. There were dark circles beneath her eyes, and her jaw was set tight. Altogether a very different look from the easy, glowing radiance with which she had greeted him that first evening at the Egremont townhouse. If it was because of that damned Earl, or his damned brother, or that mother of theirs—

Christopher let the anger, the contempt, the violence of his emotions flow through him and away. Remaining was his concern, and his other feelings—barely articulated, not to be explored, or, worse, encouraged—for Gwendolyn. Nonetheless, shining like a beacon on a dark night. He said:

"Ciao, bella. Come va?"

"I'm glad to see you, Christopher."

Her smile, he thought, was a tired one. He nudged his horse around, so that they were facing in the same direction. "Shall we?"

"Yes."

They began walking their horses side by side. Gwendolyn nodded to several people hailing her from open carriages but didn't stop to engage in conversation. She said, "Francis and Owen are gone."

"Back to Oxford?"

"Yes, they left this morning. They both wanted me to send you their warmest regards."

"That's kind. Is the Duchess upset? Or relieved?"

"A little of both, I'd say, but probably more relieved. Helen smashed a teacup at breakfast, then cried so hard she had a nosebleed, and when Lady Almira tried to comfort her, she pushed at her so roughly that she fell over."

"Good God. Was Lady Almira injured?"

"Fortunately, no—although it was very painful to hear her claiming it was all her fault for taking a tumble. Owen gave Helen *such* a look, and then he went to help Lady Almira back to her seat, which made me so glad to see how tender he could be."

Christopher nodded. "And Lady Helen? The nosebleed resolved itself?" He saw that Gwendolyn was looking at him closely, as if assessing his reaction. It was the same look she'd had that night at Vauxhall when she had asked, *Do you want to dance with Helen?*

He thought to himself, What the hell?

"Yes, it did resolve quite quickly," Gwendolyn said. "But Cousin Judith sent for the doctor, to check on both Helen and Lady Almira, and also on a handful of the servants who've come down with bad colds."

"It does seem to be making the rounds. Are you all right, *signorina*?"

"Oh yes, I'm perfectly well, Christopher."

He didn't fully believe her, but he only nodded again. She added:

"And you?"

"I'm fine."

"Are you? Truly?"

Now *he* was looking closely at her. "What do you mean, Gwennie?"

"I don't know precisely. You seem—you seem troubled."

He had hoped he was concealing it, but Gwendolyn seemed attuned to his moods, able to sense when things weren't right with him. A desire to tell her—tell her what was in his head and in his heart—rose up, powerful and urgent. But he resisted it. Not for him to indulge in the brief, selfish pleasure of unburdening himself. Her happiness was all that mattered. And so he said:

"I'm all right. Care for a canter? To blow away the cobwebs?"

Her smile was a little brighter. "I would."

They urged their horses along and for some twenty minutes they swiftly wove their way among the other riders and carriages. It felt good, Christopher thought. Movement—speed—bodies in easy harmony with their horses. Minds slowing, relaxing. He could have gone on like this for much longer—maybe forever—but as they were approaching

a section of the path next to which stood a wide, open grove
where several riders clustered, Gwendolyn said:

"We must stop. There's Julian and Rupert, and Monsieur de Montmorency."

They pulled up their horses, waiting until the others,
coming from the opposite direction, reached them. Greetings were exchanged, and commonplace small-talk
ensued. Christopher saw that the Earl was his usual serene,
affable self. He wondered, and not for the first time, how
tea had gone yesterday.

"What a delightful surprise," said the Earl, and added,
looking smilingly at Gwendolyn, "I didn't think to see
you till this evening."

"Yes, what a surprise," Gwendolyn said. "I trust you
had a pleasant visit with Lady Hertford?"

"To be sure we did."

"Ha," said Rupert. "If you like being shown acres of
porcelain, Egyptian furniture, and silver plate."

"The Hertfords," the Earl said to his brother, a faint
note of reproof in his voice, "are widely acknowledged as
connoisseurs of the *beaux arts*."

"Yes, but why must they drag one about? We've got
plenty of that stuff ourselves. And the way Lady Hertford *looks* at you, as if expecting a comment upon each
and every item. Good gad! When you've seen one Roman
platter, you've seen 'em all."

"It's said to be the finest private collection of Roman
dinnerware anywhere in Europe," the Earl responded,
and Rupert grimaced rudely at him.

"I didn't come to London to look at damned *plates*."

"Where, one wonders, are the other members of your
party?" said Étienne de Montmorency to Gwendolyn. "You
seem, *d'habitude*, to travel about *dans un groupe*."

"My brother and the Marquis have returned to Oxford,"

Gwendolyn answered. "And Lady Helen's at home, a little under the weather."

"Nothing serious, *j'espère*? Lamenting, perhaps, the loss of her so-lively companions?"

Gwendolyn looked at de Montmorency a little fixedly, as if suspecting him of irony.

Rupert said, "Will she be at Lady Jersey's tonight? Thought I might have a go at her, you know."

Christopher watched as Gwendolyn gave Rupert that same fixed look. Coolly she said, "I don't know if she's going or not."

"Do have her come, won't you?"

"Lady Helen will do as she likes."

"Strong-willed, is she? Well, I do enjoy a challenge."

"Do you?" murmured Étienne de Montmorency, very softly. "I wish you luck, *mon jeune ami*."

Christopher's eye was abruptly drawn to the nearby grove, where a beautiful gray horse was tossing its head back and forth, and shifting so restlessly, so uncomfortably, on its hooves that it nearly unseated its rider, a well-dressed, middle-aged man with a distinctively large head and whose expression, he noted, was one of complete bafflement.

He couldn't stop himself, of course, and he slid off his horse. "Gwennie, can you hold the reins for me?" His own horse was so well-behaved he had no fears that she couldn't safely do so.

"Of course," she said, and took them into her gloved hands. "What's wrong?"

He jerked his head toward the gray horse, and had taken a few steps toward it when the Earl said, rather sharply:

"Mr. Beck—wait—you really oughtn't—"

He paused. "Why not?"

"Don't you know who that is?"

"I couldn't care less," said Christopher, and went swiftly

to where the man was struggling to keep his seat. The other riders—the man's companions—were looking worriedly at the gray horse but seemed hesitant to do anything, and so Christopher went between them and to the horse where he saw at once that the bearing rein was forcing its head too high, causing considerable strain to its neck.

He took hold of the rein, saying to the rider, "If you'll permit me, sir," then quickly he unbuckled the strap which had been holding the rein too tightly.

The horse immediately calmed, lowered its head, shook it, as if happy to have free movement again, and gave Christopher a rough but friendly nudge with its great head.

"There, that's better, isn't it," Christopher said to the horse, running a hand along its muzzle, and rebuckled the strap, but this time with appropriate looseness. He looked up at the man who now sat much more comfortably in the saddle and was smiling broadly at him.

"Thank you, young man! Nearly came a cropper just now. Didn't know why she was so gingery today."

"It was the bearing rein, sir. Too tight."

"I'll tell that groom of mine."

"Do, sir. Horses don't like it."

"Well, well, I daresay I'd dislike it if *my* head was confined. Could hardly look about, could I?"

"Just so."

The man leaned down a little to say in a confidential tone, "Never been much of a rider, you know. I'm best on the deck of a ship. Sea-legs! But speaking of heads, you've got a good one on your shoulders, young man. What's your name?"

"Christopher Beck."

The man held out his hand and Christopher shook it.

"A pleasure to meet you, Mr. Beck. Come by Bushy House sometime and take a little pot-luck with us. The place is overrun with children, but you won't mind that, will you?"

"Not at all," said Christopher politely, mystified. "Good day."

"Good day, good day. Nice to know there are still some promising young men about. Most of 'em are rotters, like that Durant fellow over there, or that damned Frenchman next to him. Although he's hardly a *young* man, hey? A great favorite of m'brother. Can't abide him myself." He nodded pleasantly at Christopher and rode on, his companions nodding with equal courtesy (and, perhaps, more than a little surprise) before they too went on their way.

Christopher went back to his own horse, took the reins from Gwendolyn with a word of thanks, and brought himself up into the saddle again. He noticed that the Earl and Rupert were staring at him goggle-eyed, and that de Montmorency had on his face a faint, amused smile.

Gwendolyn said, "You *do* have a knack with animals, don't you, Christopher? Bravo!"

"Indeed, *tout à fait le magicien*," murmured de Montmorency.

"Hardly a magician," said Christopher. "Shall we ride on?"

"Mr. Beck," the Earl said, "don't you want to know who that was?"

Christopher looked at him. "Feel free to enlighten me, sir."

"It's the Duke of Clarence."

"Ah."

Rupert put in: "That's all you can say? 'Ah'? You just barged over, without so much as a by-your-leave, and spoke to the *Duke of Clarence*. Royalty. *Royalty!* The Prince Regent's brother, and very probably the heir to the throne."

"That's why I attempted to dissuade you, Mr. Beck," the Earl said, "from making a terrible gaffe."

They were both so serious, so earnest, that Christopher wanted to laugh. But he only said, "What is Bushy House, and why is it overrun with children?"

"It's his home, and where he lives with the ten children from his—ah—" The Earl glanced cautiously at Gwendolyn. "His—ah—shall we say, previous affiliation—"

"With the beauteous Mrs. Jordan," said Rupert. "An *actress*, don't you know."

The Earl frowned at him, and Gwendolyn remarked:

"Ten children! Just like *your* family, Julian."

"It's not at all the same, my dear. One involves the sanctity of marriage, and the other, well—"

"Oh, are we going to talk about morality again? Do let's do that. Such a fascinating topic."

Her tone was a little pointed, and Christopher saw the sudden glitter in her eyes. He also saw that the Earl was looking rather taken aback. There was a silence, abrupt and awkward, and then de Montmorency intervened in his soft voice:

"*Mes amies*, we are blocking the path. Mr. Beck is quite right to suggest we ride on."

They all began to walk their horses, and Gwendolyn brought her mare alongside Christopher's. She said:

"I wish *I'd* gone over to say hullo to the Duke. Hugo and Katherine met him several years ago, at the Queen's Drawing-room. Katherine says they had an interesting conversation about his happy years in the Royal Navy. He has a nice face, I thought."

Christopher nodded. "Why is he considered the probable heir to the throne?"

"Well, as the Prince Regent is unlikely to have any more children with Princess Caroline, given that she's living abroad, it means that when the Regent eventually becomes King, all his brothers become *his* heirs. And the Duke of Clarence—according to the reports in the newspapers—is healthier than his older brothers, suggesting that the odds are in his favor. But if the newspapers are correct, *all* the brothers are scrambling to produce their own heirs and so solidify their claims."

"Sounds like an unholy mess to me."

"Doesn't it? It makes me glad for my insignificant little life."

"Not insignificant," he said quietly.

She flashed a grateful look at him. "Thank you for that! Christopher, I—"

"So, about tonight." Rupert brought his horse jostling up against Gwendolyn's and very quickly Christopher reached for a strap of the bay's bridle, to urge it toward him; a single side-step brought Gwendolyn away from Rupert's horse and out of danger.

"Watch where you're going, Mr. Durant." He didn't bother to soften his tone, and coolly he watched as Rupert sat up straight in his saddle, bristling.

"I say, what cheek!"

"You nearly crushed Miss Penhallow's legs."

"Well—what?—surely not—it's this damned horse of mine, anyway, a stupid disobedient creature—"

"It's not your horse's fault, and you know it."

Rupert's handsome face was very red. "The devil it is! And you're not to talk to me like that."

"What, as one man to another?" Christopher said, very cool.

"That's where you're wrong. You're not an *honorable*, are you? You're not descended from an *ancient* lineage! You're nothing but a—a jumped-up *commoner*!"

Rupert ferociously hurled these words with the air of

one uttering the most devastating barb possible. In response Christopher gave him a very slight, mocking bow. "Too true. Are you sure you ought to be seen speaking to me, sir?"

"How dare you! You—you *varlet*!" Rupert hissed. He dug his heels into his horse's sides and cantered angrily ahead of them, to where the Earl rode with de Montmorency.

Christopher, watching him go, laughed. "Varlet." He looked at Gwendolyn, whose expression was grave. "Do laugh, *signorina*. It's very funny, you know."

"Well, I would, Christopher, but I must say I didn't like how—how *hateful* he was to you."

"Don't let it bother you. It certainly doesn't bother me. Come now, admit it—have you ever heard anyone outside a theater actually say the word 'varlet' before?"

Her lovely smile dawned, and he was glad to see the humor leap into her eyes. "I haven't! It's quite medieval of Rupert, isn't it?"

"Very."

"Or Shakespearean," Gwendolyn added, warming to the topic. "In fact, there's a scene in *King Lear* where Kent calls Oswald a 'brazen-faced varlet.'"

He laughed again. "*Much* more insulting."

"I agree! Shakespeare's very good with insults, isn't he? When I was traveling with the Marksons I learned that Mr. Markson—he's a Shakespeare enthusiast—knows quite a few of them. His favorite is 'More of your conversation would infect my brain.' It's from *Coriolanus*."

"That's a good one. You should make a list and give it to the Honorable Rupert. So that he could study it, and make reference to it as needed."

Gwendolyn giggled. "He could keep it in a pocket of his waistcoat."

"Because you never know, in these parlous times, when you might need to dampen someone else's pretentions."

She giggled again, and as they continued walking their horses side by side, she regaled him with some more choice Shakespearean insults; together they ultimately decided that "Thou art a boil, a plague-sore" was one of the most delightfully withering, along with "Would thou wert clean enough to spit upon" and "There's no more faith in thee than in a stewed prune."

They were still laughing when they came to the bottom of Rotten Row.

"Oh, Christopher, I enjoyed this so much! Thank you. But I'm afraid I must go now."

"Yes, it's getting late. Are you going to Lady Jersey's evening-party?"

She hesitated, and he added:

"I was invited too."

She brightened right away. "You were? I'm so glad. I didn't want to talk about it, in case you hadn't been. Will you go?"

"I believe so."

"Oh, good!" Then she hesitated again. "Shall I—shall I make sure Helen knows you're going?"

He remembered Percy saying about Lady Helen, that first night at the Egremont townhouse: *She's a good fellow, but rather awkward at parties. Doesn't know how to talk to people.* Well, if he could help Helen along a little, he wouldn't mind that. What he *did* mind was how Gwendolyn had lost her brightness again. It puzzled him—worried him.

"If you like," he answered, wondering at the sudden reluctance he felt, especially when she nodded with what looked like a kind of—

It looked like a kind of *resignation*.

Why would that be? he wondered.

Their little party broke apart, the Earl and Rupert (who merely dipped his head coldly at him in parting) to accompany Gwendolyn, with her groom in tow, back to Grosvenor Square, and de Montmorency, who gave him a surprisingly civil bow, going off to talk to some acquaintances in a dashing high-perch phaeton.

Thoughtfully, Christopher made his own way back to the Albany. When he got there, he looked for a long time at the parcels he'd set on a side-table.

Do what brings you the most peace.

He was sure, now, about his decision. He just wished it wasn't so damned hard.

The party at Lady Jersey's was crowded and lively, filled with a great press of people milling about, standing in groups, leaving and arriving. Lady Jersey hailed him as Purkoy's savior, and had a footman bring him into the drawing-room so that he could meet his benefactor again. Christopher crouched down to greet Purkoy properly, and when he rose again to his feet he saw one of the Duke of Clarence's companions from Rotten Row approaching, a tall, balding, affable-looking man, whom Lady Jersey introduced as Admiral Sir Charles Poole. He complimented Christopher on his deft handling of the Duke's gray, and they fell into easy conversation which produced the remarkable discovery that Sir Charles had known Christopher's uncle, the late Dan Allum, quite well.

"Never knew anyone who kept the fleet as well-fed and well-supplied with armament," said Sir Charles. "Dan could find gunpowder when nobody else could. And lemons! He made us take lemons long before it was a widely accepted practice. Our mortality rates dropped like—well, like an anchor into deep sea."

"I'm happy to hear this, sir. I never knew him myself. Apparently, he was thought by my mother's family to have been rather an odd fellow."

Sir Charles laughed. "He *was* that. He kept a pet mouse in his jacket pocket, and stopped shaving when he was twenty—had the most tremendous beard you ever saw. Never ate meat. Never married. And he could do the most complicated sums in his head like a mathematician. Didn't need pencil and paper. Yes, quite an unusual fellow."

Sir Charles introduced him to some of his friends, and after that Christopher talked with some acquaintances he had made at the Duchess of Egremont's party, parting from them with a smile and a bow when he saw Gwendolyn coming into the drawing-room, accompanied by the Duchess and Lady Almira.

Gwendolyn wore a simple, elegant white gown that swirled about her ankles as she walked, and had her bright gold hair in an unfussy coil high at the back of her head. He could never imagine Gwendolyn swathed in ruffles and bows, draped all over in ribbons and flounces and bunches of lace—styles, he had observed, favored by so many other women. She was, he now thought, uniquely herself. He looked hard at her, committing to his memory this dazzling image of her: all white and gold, shining blue eyes and tender smiling mouth, grace and intelligence personified . . .

"Good evening, Mr. Beck, how lovely to see you again," said Lady Almira warmly, and sneezed. "Oh, do excuse me!" She searched in her reticule and triumphantly pulled from it a handkerchief as one might, with a flourish, produce a rabbit from a hat. "*Voilà!* Oh my goodness, Mr. Beck, this is *your* handkerchief. Shall I give it back to you?"

"Keep it, ma'am. Really."

He had only a brief opportunity to talk privately with

Gwendolyn, when the Duchess and Lady Almira had turned away to greet some new arrivals. She said:

"Why were you staring at me when I came in, Christopher? Is something wrong? Did you spot a ghastly rent in my gown, or a spider in my hair?"

He smiled a little. "No." He wanted to tell her why he was emblazoning in his memory the image of her, but now wasn't the time or place. Most likely it would never be.

"Well, that's a relief. I do take a quick look in the mirror before going out, but I don't *study* myself. Christopher, I'm very sorry, but Helen refused to come with us."

"That's bad news for Rupert, isn't it."

She didn't reply, and he saw that she was looking at him as if confused by his answer. He went on, "Gwennie, may I come by tomorrow, unfashionably early? Perhaps around breakfast?"

She paused. Drew in her breath. Nodded. "Of course. I'll—I'll make sure Helen is up."

Damn it, he wanted to talk with Gwendolyn alone, but he supposed it would be rude, and possibly hurtful, to exclude Helen. He gave a mental shrug. He'd just have to make the best of things. Then he heard familiar voices from behind Gwendolyn and saw the Westenbury party coming into the drawing-room—heard, too, the admiring whispers:

"Oh, isn't the Earl the handsomest man in London."

"The handsomest man in England, *I* think."

"Lucky, *lucky* Miss Penhallow."

Christopher could barely bring himself to look at the Countess, but he did his best as she swept near, resplendent in a gown of striped silver and white gauze, with its shimmering silver-edged hem drawn up to the knee, revealing the white satin slip beneath it and festooned with a big cluster of artificial flowers. On her head was a gauzy silk headdress, wreathed with sparkling brilliants, and from her low bodice dangled a knotted bunch of wide silver ribbons. She wore long ruby ear-bobs and several jangling bracelets over her white satin gloves.

Next to him he heard Gwendolyn murmuring, "Oh my, that *gown*," and then the Westenburys were upon them. The Countess had completely forgotten him—despite having spent three excruciatingly long hours sitting across from him at Vauxhall—and the Honorable Rupert looked as if he'd like to pretend he'd never met Christopher either. The Earl, after a civil greeting, had eyes only for Gwendolyn, and despite the sardonic promptings of Christopher's evil genius to prolong this extremely awkward encounter with the Westenbury clan, he knew it would only distress Gwendolyn; and so, with a polite general bow—and a last quick look at her—he withdrew, only to be swiftly drawn into Lady Jersey's circle where he passed a pleasant half hour and then excused himself, glancing around the crowded room.

He saw Gwendolyn with the Earl. Next to him was the Countess, nodding and smiling, and next to her stood Rupert, looking very sulky indeed. Somehow he reminded Christopher of a tethered animal, and he found it within himself, despite his dislike, to feel a kind of pity for Rupert Durant. Then he realized, suddenly, that Gwendolyn was looking at him, and he made himself smile at her before turning away; and not long after that he left, already dreading tomorrow.

The morning.

And what he had to say.

Chapter 13

Gwendolyn stared down at her empty plate. She didn't feel like eating, and had only managed to drink a little chocolate. The breakfast-room, normally a cheerful parlor, felt too big somehow, almost cavernous, and it didn't help that the sun was hiding behind great, heavy-looking clouds; the light from outside was dull and gray. Ponderous. Bleak. Matching her mood, Gwendolyn thought.

Only the Duchess and Helen had come down for breakfast. Lady Almira wasn't feeling quite well and was going to rest today, explained the Duchess. Helen, her face like a thundercloud, spoke to no one and steadily made her way through a plate heaped high with eggs, bacon, scones, and spiced deviled kidneys.

Gwendolyn and the Duchess talked in a desultory fashion; Gwendolyn could see that she was distracted this morning. A little worried about Lady Almira, perhaps, or troubled about Helen. When Tyndale announced the arrival of Christopher Beck, it was at once a relief to Gwendolyn and a sharp renewal of the dread she'd been feeling since Christopher had asked to come over unusually early. Was today the day he was going to propose to Helen?

No matter what, she was going to be unselfish. A good friend to Christopher, who had become, in these past days, so very, very important to her.

Christopher came into the breakfast-room dressed for riding in breeches, tall boots, and a plainly cut jacket. How well such apparel suited him, Gwendolyn thought, how very distinguished he looked. Although he also looked—

She stared at him.

He looked tense. Unhappy. Was it because he wanted to be alone with Helen—and she and Cousin Judith were making that difficult? It was a nasty, troubling feeling to be an encumbrance. Getting in someone else's way. Could she make up some kind of pretext to leave?

Christopher stopped at the foot of the table. "Good morning."

"Good morning, Mr. Beck," said the Duchess. "Gwendolyn mentioned that you might be coming by. Won't you join us for breakfast?"

"Thank you, ma'am, but no. I'm leaving town in a little while and I wanted to come by in person and say goodbye— and to thank you for your kind hospitality to me."

"Leaving?" Gwendolyn echoed. Inside her chest was a sinking feeling—as if her heart was literally dropping down and away. Suddenly the whole world, not just this room, seemed bleak. *Get ahold of yourself, Gwendolyn,* she told herself sternly. *Think about Christopher and Helen.*

She glanced over at Helen, whose gaze was fixed upon her plate as she stolidly continued eating. She didn't seem the least concerned that Christopher was going away. Was she trying to hurt Christopher by pretending to be indifferent to him? Gwendolyn turned her eyes to Christopher, and saw that he was looking at *her*, his face set and tense. What could she do to help him? Was he signaling for her to leave, so that he could talk to Helen alone?

"I shall be sorry to see you go, Mr. Beck," said the Duchess. "We've all enjoyed your company so much."

Sometimes, Gwendolyn thought miserably, it was very difficult to be good. But for Christopher's sake she would try. She took her napkin from her lap and set it next to her plate, then got up. Maybe if *she* left the breakfast-room, the Duchess would follow suit.

"I hope—I hope you have a safe journey, Christopher," she said, hating how small and shaky her voice sounded, and wishing her stomach wasn't clenched so tightly. She turned to the Duchess. "Will you excuse me, Cousin Judith?"

"Of course, m'dear," answered the Duchess, then added rather tartly, "Helen, if you can be bothered for five seconds, do say goodbye to Mr. Beck."

"G'bye," Helen mumbled through a mouthful of egg, sounding not at all like a person sorrowing over the imminent departure of someone for whom she deeply cared, and cheerfully could Gwendolyn have flung away Helen's plate, lifted her up by the scruff of her neck, and forced her to be *nice* to Christopher whom she no doubt was wounding very painfully.

But this being, unfortunately, an impossible course of action, Gwendolyn did the only thing she could do, which was to make herself go over to Christopher and lift her eyes up to his. "Goodbye," she said shakily.

"Walk me to the door?"

A few more seconds together! Had he given up on trying to be alone with Helen? He looked *so* unhappy. Gwendolyn was startled to realize that at this moment she rather hated Helen, but she pushed aside such violent feelings as best she could—her time with Christopher was so short. "I'd be glad to."

"Goodbye, ma'am, Lady Helen," Christopher said, and then they were making their way to the entry-hall where

Tyndale and a couple of footmen stood. Oh, she didn't want to say her farewells so closely observed!

"Let's go onto the porch," she said, and, having refused with thanks Tyndale's offer to dispatch a footman to fetch a shawl, she and Christopher went onto the wide stone porch. His horse stood waiting for him at the bottom of the steps, with full-looking leather saddlebags fastened behind the saddle.

"It may rain," she said, more or less at random.

"I won't melt."

"I'm so sorry about Helen."

"Why would you be? You're not responsible for her behavior."

"I know, but . . ." *Damn* Helen for being so rude and hurtful! "Christopher, where are you going?"

"To Nottingham."

"Nottingham? To see your father, and Diana?"

"Yes." His dark eyes were somber, intense. "Gwennie, I must try. To try and reconcile with Father. He may turn me away—but I've got to make the attempt."

She put a hand on his arm, gripping it tightly. "I understand. Oh, Christopher, I wish you well!"

"Grazie, signorina."

"I know where your father lives. He never sold your house next to ours—and he left a placard on it with his new address. It's 14 Primrose Lane, in the Rushcliffe district."

"He left a placard?"

"Yes. I always thought it was because he really did hope you would come back—that you'd be able to find him and Diana again."

Christopher shrugged. "More likely it was to have stray correspondence sent on. Very practical, is Father."

"I hope—I believe—you're wrong."

"I'll find out soon enough."

"Yes. I'm glad you're going. That sounds awful, but you know what I mean, don't you? I'll miss you terribly, but—oh, I'll be thinking of you, so very hard!"

He put his hand over hers. "Likewise," he said quietly.

"Will you let me know how it goes? You could write to me, of course, or—or do you think you'll be coming back? I've no right to ask you, Christopher, but I would like it so much if you did."

"Would you, Gwennie?"

"Yes." She took a deep, deep breath. "Well—*au revoir, ma sherry moo.*"

His smile was a little twisted. "Goodbye, *signorina,*" he said, very low, and they let go of each other, and she stood on the townhouse porch and watched as he got onto his horse and rode away. It was only when Christopher was out of sight that she went back inside, and stood in the entry-hall looking rather blankly around her.

Christopher had only been gone a few minutes and already she felt so lonely without her dear friend that she could hardly bear it.

What to do now?

Last night, at Lady Jersey's party, the Countess had asked her to come over after breakfast today, to talk over wedding plans and share a nuncheon together. Afterwards, Julian wanted to take her and Rupert to St. James's Park, where a balloon ascension was scheduled, and then to Gunter's for ices. Altogether, a full day of the Westenburys.

Her attention was abruptly caught by a maidservant walking past, and carrying a tray which held a teapot, a cup, and a plate of dry toast.

"Is that for Lady Almira?" Gwendolyn asked.

"Yes, miss."

Gwendolyn remembered the day Lady Almira had been

unwell, finally emerging from her room to say, wistfully, *I should have liked a little company from time to time.*

She said to the maidservant, "I'll take it up to Lady Almira. Her Grace is in the breakfast-room—will you tell her where I've gone?"

"Of course, miss."

Gwendolyn took the tray and went up the two flights of stairs and along the hallway to Lady Almira's room. She tapped on the door, and when she heard Lady Almira say "Come in," went inside and found her still in bed, a large ruffled nightcap on her head, and looking quite woebegone, with watery eyes and reddened nose. She struggled to sit up when she saw Gwendolyn.

"My *dear*! How kind of you to bring my breakfast! Completely unnecessary, of course, but I'm *most* appreciative. My throat feels so dry."

"I'm very sorry to hear that, ma'am." Gwendolyn put the tray on a table next to Lady Almira's bed, helped her to sit up, fluffed the pillows, and pulled the blankets up higher when Lady Almira leaned back against her pillows. "Do you think a cup of tea might help?"

"I do *hope* so. I don't know how it is, but somehow life never seems as dark when one is drinking tea. Won't you ring for another cup, my dear?"

"Thank you, ma'am, but I don't want any." Gwendolyn poured tea into the delicate china cup and handed it to her, then brought a chair over next to the bed. Looking more cheerful, Lady Almira alternately talked, sipped at her tea, and nibbled on a piece of toast.

"Wasn't that a lovely party at Lady Jersey's last night? I do think she's the nicest of the Patronesses, don't you? And her gown was so *cunning*—those half-sleeves all set about with puffs and jet beads—simply delightful! It's not something I've seen before. I daresay she's setting a new fashion. I must admit, however, I didn't care at all for the Countess of Westenbury's gown—such a *busy* look, and I'm quite baffled as to why she wears so much white. It's hardly suitable for a woman of her age, and the color quite *washes* out one's complexion. Why, I haven't worn white in *decades*. But oh, how thoughtless of me to criticize your future mother-in-law, my dear Gwendolyn! *Do* forgive me! But you're smiling—which means you're not offended, I hope?"

"Not at all, ma'am." Gwendolyn poured more tea into Lady Almira's cup. "I was only thinking that I had seen a version of that gown in *La Belle Assemblée*."

"Oh, did you, my dear? Well, that makes it all right, I suppose. But still—white is a young woman's color, and nothing *anyone* can say will dissuade me from my opinion! Now! Have you given any thought to your wedding gown? The cloth-of-silver that the poor Princess Charlotte wore at her wedding is still, I believe, very popular, and would become *you* admirably. With some Brussels lace, perhaps?"

Gwendolyn paused before replying.

Everyone, it seemed, wanted to talk about her wedding.

Everyone except her.

Inside her was confusion and loneliness, bleakness and uncertainty. But—also—a stubborn defiance. For today, at least, she *wasn't* going to talk about it. She was going to be like one of those characters in novels who were being cruelly interrogated but who, through incredible determination, refused to reveal the secrets they were carrying.

Gwendolyn would have laughed at this ludicrous vision of herself on the rack. *If* she was in the mood to laugh.

So she said, "I'd love to hear about *your* wedding gown, ma'am. Or gowns?"

And Lady Almira was off, animatedly describing the gown she had worn at her wedding to the dear late Mr.

Thane, a fashionable silk *robe à la française*, very wide, as dresses were back then, with loose box-pleats, and elaborate embroidery at the neck, hem, and cuffs, and also—

Gwendolyn listened and nodded and handed her another piece of toast and poured more tea. When the Duchess stopped by to see how Lady Almira was feeling, she excused herself to go and write brief notes to the Countess and Julian. She was, she told them, in attendance on Lady Almira, who wasn't well, and would see them another time.

Then she had the notes sent on, and went back to Lady Almira's bedchamber.

14 Primrose Lane.

A large, attractive, many-windowed house made of white stucco and with a gray-green slate roof, three stories high with a wide front porch, the overhang of which was supported by Doric columns; there was a basement below which also had plenty of windows. The house looked fairly new and was immaculately maintained—suggesting that Father was prospering here in Nottingham, just as he had in Whitehaven.

Christopher had left his horse at the stables of an inn not far away and walked to Primrose Lane with his saddlebags flung over his shoulder. He paused at the front gate, black iron decorated with elaborate curlicues. It was late afternoon on a Sunday, and unless Father had radically changed his habits, he was likely to be at home.

He put a hand on the gate, and paused again.

Preparing himself mentally to have the door slammed in his face, not just metaphorically but, quite possibly, also literally.

He was also remembering what Gwendolyn had said. About the placard.

I always thought it was because he really did hope

you would come back—that you'd be able to find him and Diana again.

Well, he'd found them at last. A boy no longer, but a man. He would face whatever came. If he was to be rejected, it would be very painful indeed, but somehow he'd get through it.

Christopher could feel the tension tightening his muscles, threatening to keep him frozen in place, and deliberately he made his hands loose, his breathing relaxed. Into his mind came an image of Gwendolyn as they had stood together on the porch of the Egremont townhouse.

Her blue eyes filled with light and warmth, hope and compassion.

I'm glad you're going. That sounds awful, but you know what I mean, don't you? I'll miss you terribly, but— oh, I'll be thinking of you, so very hard!

It helped, knowing that Gwendolyn was there in the world. Thinking about him. Caring about him.

It enabled him to push open the gate, walk up the path and onto the wide front porch.

And lightly bang the knocker on the door.

Easy, easy, he said to himself, almost as he would calm a restless horse. *Easy now.*

He heard footsteps from within, hurried and quick.

Easy, easy—

The door opened, only partially, and a pale anxious face peered out.

"Nan!" said Christopher, recognizing a maidservant from the Whitehaven house.

"Sir?" she replied doubtfully, and then her eyes widened and she gasped. "Mr. *Christopher*! After all these years! Is it really you, sir?"

"It is, Nan. Is Father home?"

"Yes, to be sure, Mr. Christopher, but—but we're all at

sixes and sevens—Mrs. Cora's—oh, she's worse, sir, and as for the baby—we just don't know—it's right dreadful—"

Mrs. Cora? "Father's wife, Nan? And she has a baby?"

Nan nodded. "She's in childbed, sir—has been for two full days. We're waiting and waiting for that baby, but . . ."

He knew essentially nothing about such matters—for horses, yes; humans, no—except that two days seemed like too long. "Father's brought in a doctor?"

"Oh yes, the very best in Nottingham, sir, but—that is—it's not going so well at all—"

Christopher now heard from inside the house heavy footsteps, sounding as if someone was descending a flight of stairs. Then a voice came from behind Nan. A man's. Achingly familiar, but hoarse and ragged, sounding fatigued beyond human endurance. "Who is it, Nan? We're not seeing anyone—send them away."

Quickly Nan turned. "Sir, it's Mr. Christopher! He's back!"

"What?"

Footsteps again, quicker now. The door was flung wide. And there was Father, a little grayer than Christopher remembered, a little stooped, and deathly pale. His eyes, dark like Christopher's own, were wide with shock.

"Christopher," he said, sounding dazed. "My son. My boy."

"Yes, Father."

"You've come."

"Yes."

"Thank *God*." And Father opened his arms wide, and Christopher went into them, and they embraced.

At first Christopher felt like the little boy he'd once been. Long ago, when his mother had been alive and they'd all been happy together. How very long ago that was . . .

Father gave a racking sob, and almost seemed to crumple. Christopher tightened his arms around him. And now he was the strong one, the sturdy one, able to not just receive but also to give.

More footsteps, coming swiftly down the stairs. A young woman's voice—familiar—sounding very frightened.

"Father, Dr. Baynes is asking for you—"

It was his sister Diana, all grown up with her dark hair piled high on her head, and dressed in the rich burgundy colors of a married woman.

Father pulled away, but still gripped one of Christopher's arms as if for support. "Look who's here."

"Christopher!" Diana exclaimed. "I can't believe it!" She ran to him and he used his free arm to hug her tightly to him.

And so they stood, the three of them.

Reunited.

Connected.

A family.

Diana was crying, and Father, his mouth working, seemed as if he might start again. They both looked at him rather helplessly. So he said:

"The doctor wants you, Father. Shall I come up, too?"

"Would you, my son? If you think you can bear it—"

"Yes. Of course. Come on, Father, let's go up."

He set aside the saddlebags and they went up the stairs, with Father still gripping his arm and Diana at his side, weeping. He caught glimpses of handsome furniture, luxurious carpets, light-filled rooms, and everything clean and harmonious and well-kept. And clearly loved. So unlike the old house in Whitehaven, which had come to feel sad and neglected despite the small army of servants Father employed. This house was obviously very different; it was a home. Presided over by his stepmother.

Who was now, it seemed, fighting for her life, and that of her unborn child.

The three of them went down a hallway and came to a room where the door had been left half-open. Together, softly, they went in.

A big, elegant, comfortably furnished bedchamber, curtains drawn against the sun. A large bed, and within it a still figure. His stepmother. Hair of light brown and lank beneath a little cap. Eyes sunken, and a face that looked as if all color, all life, had been washed away. And a large bulge at her midsection. Her hands, above the covers, upon that bulge, with such protective tenderness that it almost broke Christopher's heart with pity to see it. Slowly she turned her head and looked at Father.

"Jonathan," she whispered, her voice a mere thread.

Father went to the bed, bringing Christopher with him.

"Cora, here is my son. Here is my Christopher."

Those sunken, tired eyes went to Christopher's face, and a faint smile curved her bloodless lips. "My son too," whispered Cora Beck. "If that's all right, Christopher?"

On an impulse Christopher sat on the edge of the bed. And he reached out to put his hand atop hers, gently, gently, as light as a feather. "It's more than all right, ma'am. And you're my mother now." Deep inside, he knew that his own kind mother, so long gone, wouldn't mind; he knew, somehow, that she would approve.

That faint smile on Cora Beck's white, haggard face widened just a little bit, and in that moment he loved her already.

Then he heard a new voice and turned his head. A gloomy-looking man in an old-fashioned tailcoat—he assumed it was Dr. Baynes—was saying to Father and Diana, "There's no hope. For either of them. Have you made arrangements for—after?"

Christ in heaven, Christopher thought, furious, the man

didn't even bother lowering his voice. If *he* was hearing this dire prognosis, so was Cora Beck. He remembered Mauro della Valle telling him during a difficult foaling, *You must never let your fears show, you must always be confident—be brave in the face of despair—so that the mare will draw from you your strength.*

All too audibly Diana burst into fresh tears, and Father turned to look at his wife, his mouth opened in what was plainly a silent scream.

Christopher said to Cora Beck, "Excuse me, *Madre*," and she gave a very small weak nod. He got up and went to where the doctor stood with Father and Diana. "Come into the hallway," he told them quietly, and when they were gathered there, with the bedchamber door closed, he said, "What exactly is Mrs. Beck's condition? What's wrong?"

Dr. Baynes looked at him rather haughtily. "You are, I believe, Mr. Beck's son?"

"Yes."

"Have you any particular medical knowledge?"

"I'm asking you what her condition is," replied Christopher impatiently. "Just tell me."

"In layman's terms," said Dr. Baynes, very frosty, "she's simply worn out. *Vetus mulier gravidam, primum infantem*—it's not unexpected in such cases."

"As it happens, I know some Latin. You mean she's rather old for a first baby."

"Yes."

"She's only thirty-five," put in Father.

Dr. Baynes shrugged. "Further to her condition, the contractions stopped a few hours ago. A very unfortunate sign."

Recalling how white and weak Mrs. Beck looked, Christopher said, "Has she eaten anything since the contractions first began?"

"I don't allow laboring women any food or drink. It interferes with the process of expulsion."

Christopher scowled. "Process of expulsion? That's what you call it?"

"It is," responded Dr. Baynes, with lofty superiority, "a medical description. *Processus ab urbe regnoque tarquinios.*"

What an ass. Or, in terms the good doctor might prefer, *Qualem blennum.* Christopher looked to Father. "It's been forty-eight hours, hasn't it, since her contractions started? That's what Nan told me."

Father nodded wearily. "Yes."

"That's too long without food, or at least something to drink. Diana, is there any broth? Or beef jelly?"

"Yes, I believe so—fresh broth, at least—"

"Go get some and bring it up."

"I beg your pardon," said Dr. Baynes coldly, as Diana hurried away, "but what right have you to interfere?"

Christopher ignored him. "Father, did you bring Mrs. Cranford with you from Whitehaven?"

"Our laundress?" Father sounded dazed again. "Yes, I brought all the servants who wished to come. Why do you ask?"

"She was a midwife. Don't you remember? Where is she?"

"In the basement, I suppose."

"Good. I'll go find her." He took hold of Father's shoulder and gently shook it. "Go back to Cora. Tell her she'll be all right, tell her the baby will be all right."

"I can't, Christopher, I *can't.* My God, I'm losing her . . ."

He tightened his grip on Father's shoulder. "You *must.* If you love her, you've got to try."

"I do love her," said Father, his voice cracking.

"Then go in there and show her how strong you are—how much you believe in her. I'll be right back."

"And what," said Dr. Baynes, "am I to do, pray tell?"

"Oh, for Christ's sake, stand by, man, stand by," said Christopher, and waited only long enough to see Father going back into the bedchamber before he bolted down the stairs and into the basement rooms where, sure enough, Mrs. Cranford stood by a window, wielding her irons on a white bedsheet with the large capable-looking hands he remembered. Sunlight poured over her, enveloping her stout form in what struck him as an actual blaze of glory, and for just a second he found himself thinking of angels descending from on high.

They spoke for a few minutes, and finally Mrs. Cranford said, shaking her head, "These doctors, Mr. Christopher, these *men*! They lay a woman flat on her back and expect the baby to pop right out! Aye, let the poor lady have the broth if she will, and have her sit up, or stand if she can, and walk about."

"Will you come, Mrs. Cranford, and help us?"

"If you like, Mr. Christopher. Will your father allow it?"

"Yes. Can you come now?"

"To be sure. I'll set these irons to cool, and wash my hands first—"

"Thank you, Mrs. Cranford," he said, "I'll see you there," and he ran up the steps three at a time and returned to the bedchamber, where Mrs. Beck was now sitting limply against a bank of pillows, with Father, next to her on the bed, holding her securely while Diana, trembling, offered her a spoonful of broth. Dr. Baynes stood in a corner looking so entirely the picture of offended disapproval that, under other circumstances, Christopher would have laughed and been tempted to tweak his carefully shaped mustachios. As it was, he came to the bedside and smiled down at Mrs. Beck.

"How's that broth, *Madre*?"

"Oh, it's good," she said in that little thread of a voice. "It's very refreshing."

He nodded. "Diana, let me help." He took the bowl and spoon from her unsteady hands, and gratefully she went to sink into a chair. He sat on the bed, close to Father, dipped the spoon into the bowl, and offered it to Mrs. Beck. She sipped at the broth, swallowed, smiled feebly at him.

"Thank you, Christopher."

"You're welcome, *Madre*. More?"

"Yes, please."

She took a few more spoonfuls, and he was glad to see that a bit of color was returning to her face. Father said, "Well done, Cora my love," his voice heartier now, and Christopher was glad to hear that too.

A few minutes later, in came Mrs. Cranford, very brisk, very sure, her hands and forearms red from the scrubbing she'd given them, and Christopher would have sworn he could feel the energy in the room changing—as if she was, in a very real way, a breath of fresh air. She came to the foot of the bed and said with quiet dignity:

"Madam, you'll not know this about me, but I was a midwife in Hensingham for many years, till the doctors came and chased me away, and Mr. Beck took me in. Will you let me help you?"

Mrs. Beck looked at Father. He said, "She's a good woman, our Mrs. Cranford," and so Mrs. Beck answered softly, desperately:

"Yes. Oh, please, if you can."

Mrs. Cranford nodded. "Let's bring your baby into the world then, madam."

She had Christopher give Mrs. Beck more broth, till half the bowl was gone; then she had him and Father, with enormous care, help Mrs. Beck out of bed, help her take feeble steps back and forth across the room. She had

Diana summon a maid, to bring in fresh bed-linens and make the bed clean and comfortable again.

More than once did Father falter, and Christopher would send him an encouraging look, hoping to communicate to him: *You can do this.* And Father would nod, and straighten just a bit, keeping firm hold on Mrs. Beck, and murmur, "Well done, my love, well done."

Finally she gave a little cry. "A contraction," she whispered, and the relief in the room was palpable.

"Good, madam, good, keep walking if you can," said Mrs. Cranford, and so the weary, anxious minutes passed, as slowly, it seemed, as if each one was a year. But more contractions did come, each one something to welcome, something to celebrate. Christopher and his father continued to support Mrs. Beck, who bravely kept at her faltering perambulations until, finally, not long after midnight, Mrs. Cranford had her kneel on an old soft length of carpet she'd had Nan fetch; had Christopher and Father, on either side of her, hold her up. At this the doctor gave a puff of outrage, exclaiming:

"What are you doing? Put her in the bed!"

"No, sir," said Mrs. Cranford, "it's better this way," and he rolled right over her, raising his voice to say:

"And men at the birthing? Unseemly! Get them out at once!"

"*You're* a man, ain't you?" retorted Mrs. Cranford. "I need them here."

"Now see here, my good woman—"

"Doctor," said Christopher, "if you don't shut up, and right away, I'll silence you myself."

Dr. Baynes snapped his mouth closed with an audible click, Diana gave a slightly hysterical laugh, and Mrs. Beck surprised them all by giving a little ghost of a laugh herself.

"Christopher," she murmured, "you're quite wonderful, you know."

He grinned. "Just a brute, *Madre*, that's all."

"My kind of brute," she murmured back, and after that she bent with renewed determination to her work, with Mrs. Cranford right there to advise and reassure her, and Christopher and his father supporting her—Father grayfaced with fatigue, but stalwart.

And just after two in the morning, the baby arrived, a little on the small side, but otherwise pink and healthy and with, as Mrs. Cranford said approvingly, a fine set of lungs.

Jasper Tobias Beck.

Dr. Baynes, in the end, made himself useful by managing to catch Diana just as she toppled over from the aftereffects of fright and sheer exhaustion, and even carried her to a settee in a corner of the room. Still, no one was sorry when, having made a great show of assuring himself that both mother and child were in a satisfactory condition (Mrs. Cranford having already done so fully half an hour previously), he went away.

Mrs. Beck was comfortably tucked up in bed, holding a well-wrapped Jasper at her breast, and Father, his shoes set aside, was next to her, his legs stretched out and a blanket over him. They both looked very, very tired but also extremely happy. Nan had come in, bringing tea for those who wanted it, and stayed to tidy things up and stoke the fire in the hearth. Diana, much recovered, was sitting up and drinking tea; and Mrs. Cranford, at Father's hearty invitation, was sitting in a chair drinking her own cup of tea.

Christopher, looking at all of them, felt a massive wave of contentment sweeping over him. This was, he thought, a perfect moment in time. Well, nearly perfect. It lacked only—

It lacked only Gwendolyn.

He wished she were here with him. With all of them.

Would she have cowered before Dr. Baynes, or refused to help Cora Beck?

No, not his Gwendolyn. Brave, kind, wonderful Gwendolyn—

But not, he corrected himself, *his.*

It hurt to acknowledge the truth of this.

Still, there was no use in dodging reality. She was engaged to another man. He would have preferred it weren't so—but there it was, and with all his heart he longed for her happiness.

"Christopher," said Cora, "would you like to hold your brother?"

With effort he set aside his private pain, and smiled at her. "Yes, *Madre,* very much."

He went to her, and sat down next to her on the bed, and with infinite tenderness he took hold of the little bundle she held out to him. He stared down at Jasper's perfect, peaceful face, with his tiny button nose, rosebud mouth, and absurd wisps of dark hair.

"Ciao, fratellino," he murmured. *"Benvenuto in famiglia."*

Hullo, little brother. Welcome to the family.

"Is that Italian, Christopher?" asked Cora.

He smiled at her. *"Sì, Madre."*

"I didn't know you spoke Italian," Father said.

"Well, I was in Italy for a while."

"Were you? I'd like to hear all about it. Tomorrow?"

Christopher nodded, and Cora said:

"You'll stay with us, Christopher, won't you? We've guest rooms aplenty, and all made up."

"Thank you, *Madre,* I'd like that."

Mrs. Cranford set aside her teacup and rose from her

chair. "Madam, it's time you got some sleep." She went to Christopher and added, "I'll hold him, sir, shall I?"

Carefully Christopher handed Jasper over to her and she said, "You did very well tonight, Mr. Christopher, very well indeed."

He grinned. "As did you, Mrs. Cranford."

Half an hour later, he was in bed and sound asleep. He dreamed of Italy—of Mauro's estate, of horses, green hills, lush orchards, and of Gwendolyn, who perched on the top rail of the horse-pasture fence, eating an apple, jauntily swinging one booted leg back and forth, and smiling at him.

But on her left hand was a beautiful ring made of rubies and a single, glowing pearl.

Chapter 14

What seemed at first to be only a late-spring cold afflicting Lady Almira rapidly devolved into a severe attack of influenza. Several of the servants, including the footman Sam, had also succumbed. Then the Duchess and Helen fell ill as well, though, fortunately, neither one was in bed for longer than a week. Gwendolyn was busy from dawn till late into the night overseeing their care as well as that of all else who were sick under the Egremont roof, and was very thankful for Tyndale's unflagging assistance and that of the Duchess's very competent doctor.

Percy, blithely oblivious to any risks to himself, came by whenever his duties permitted, and proved himself valuable entertaining both Helen and the Duchess when the doctor had given them permission to venture downstairs. He read out loud to them, cajoled them into eating, played cards with them, and in general helped alleviate some of Gwendolyn's caregiving burden.

The Earl sent flowers every day, accompanied by affectionate notes for Gwendolyn expressing his concern for the sufferers as well as his love for her, describing his various activities, and assuring her that he was counting the hours till they could meet again. His mother, fearful of contagion, had forbidden him to call at the Egremont townhouse—a dictum which, he wrote, given her frail state of health at all times, he felt honor-bound to respect.

Gwendolyn would stop whatever she was doing to quickly read Julian's letters and then, without comment, give the flowers to Tyndale to share with the various invalids among the staff. Once or twice she scrawled a hasty note in return, thanking Julian for his kindness. In her few spare moments she would catch herself staring thoughtfully into space. Beyond the immediate preoccupations of caregiving, she could feel her brain working, working, at something—as one would turn a challenging puzzle over and over in one's hands, studying it, looking at it from different angles, trying to figure it out.

It was nearly two weeks after Christopher had gone away that she sat one afternoon in the drawing-room with Percy, the Duchess, and Helen. Tea had been served, with Percy courteously handing round the cups and plates. She'd been doing it again—gazing unseeingly at nothing—but broke out of her reverie when Percy said:

"Gwennie! I say, *Gwennie!*"

She blinked and looked over at him. "I'm sorry, Percy, I was woolgathering. What is it?"

"It's taken me a full quarter-hour to persuade Helen to go to Carlton House tonight, and—"

"Persuade?" said Helen. "Riding roughshod over me, you mean. Easier to say yes than to have you go on nagging me."

Percy laughed. "It worked, didn't it? But for God's sake, Gwennie, don't tell me I've got to chivvy *you* along as well."

"It's well worth going," said the Duchess, "if only to marvel at the Prince Regent's girth. Do you know, if he wishes to ride, he's lowered into the saddle by means of a specially constructed mechanical device. Dreadful! One can't but feel sorry for the horse."

"If it makes you feel better, ma'am," said Percy, "we've brought in a Belgian draft horse. Incredibly strong, and wonderfully good-natured, too. And poor old Prinny rarely calls for him these days—says that as he can't fit into his uniforms anymore, there's no point in going riding. So you'll come, Gwennie?"

Gwendolyn was remembering how, back in February, back in Whitehaven, she had said to her family:

And I must visit Carlton House, where I shall be suitably impressed by its staggering magnificence. I'll crane upwards at all the ceilings and go up and down the main staircase at least twice, pretending I'm a princess in disguise. I daresay I'll bump into the Prince Regent, too. Do you think it's true that he wears a corset, and creaks when he walks about? Oh, goodness, I hope I don't giggle. That would be fatal. Also, of course, I'm going to meet my one true love.

"Look, she's gone off again," said Helen, with a little dig in her voice. "Sleeping with her eyes open. Just like a horse."

Gwendolyn looked at Helen. "It's called thinking."

Helen snickered. "Indeed."

"Yes. *Indeed.*"

"If you don't want to go to Carlton House, just say so. I'm sure we'll manage to get by without you somehow."

"Helen," said the Duchess warningly.

"What? It's true. We'll be fine by ourselves. Maybe even better."

"I say, old girl, that's rather mean-spirited," said Percy. "Carlton House is awfully jolly, and I do want Gwennie to see it."

Helen lifted her shoulders in an ostentatious shrug, and

Gwendolyn held onto her temper with an effort. After an arduous week of helping to nurse Helen, an unpleasant and recalcitrant patient at best, she had yet to receive a single word of thanks. Not that she'd done it for the sake of being thanked, of course—but still, even a brief acknowledgement would have been the civil thing to do. The truth was, she would just as soon go to Carlton House without Helen there, sneering and sniping at her. But she wasn't going to let that stop her. "I *would* like to go, Percy."

"Splendid!" said Percy, and Gwendolyn smiled at him, ignoring the loud extended sigh from Helen.

Étienne de Montmorency stood in the front room of his elegant lodgings on Clarges Street, looking at the stack of correspondence on his writing-desk. Such a very, very large stack. How clamorous his creditors had become, how impertinent. What dreadfully low, vulgar people; it was distasteful, for one so fastidious as himself, to be forced to even acknowledge their existence.

But the conclusion was, unfortunately, inescapable: his debts were many and pressing, and time was growing short.

His eye fell on a folded document next to that unpleasant stack. He gave a little grimace. The proverbial lifeline. Not necessarily how he would have preferred to resolve his difficulties, but—to employ another cliché—beggars couldn't be choosers.

His man Pierre-Édouard came to brush at his blue long-tailed coat, then knelt to smooth out a small wrinkle in one of his expensive striped stockings. As he did so, de Montmorency felt in his right coat pocket for the little, deadly Châtellerault folding-knife he always carried with him. One could not, he thought, be too careful, especially when one was not, alas, universally liked. *Tant pis; c'est la vie.*

Pierre-Édouard was now fussing with the other stocking and de Montmorency, with a sudden rush of irritation, lifted his foot in its shining black shoe and gently pushed Pierre-Édouard aside.

"Enough, fool."

"Oui, monsieur," replied Pierre-Édouard humbly, getting to his feet and bowing very low. He was not, after all, unused to such treatment from his master. *"Pardonnez-moi, monsieur, s'il vous plaît."*

"A suitably moving display of contrition, which I receive with appreciation. I think—yes, I think we may be going on a journey soon. Make all necessary preparations."

"Are we to leave tonight, *monsieur*, when you return from Carlton House?"

"Not as soon as that. But you must be ready at a moment's notice."

"Oui, monsieur. Of a certainty I shall." Pierre-Édouard bowed again, even lower.

As the enormous black carriage slowly made its way along the crowded Pall Mall, Julian, the Earl of Westenbury, realized that he was tapping his fingers on the knees of his black satin knee-breeches. He was anxious to arrive at Carlton House. Hopefully Gwendolyn would be there. He hadn't seen her in nearly a fortnight, and it felt as if the sun had gone out of his existence, as if he was suffering in one of the lowest, darkest rings of Dante's notorious inferno, as if he were Romeo without his Juliet. He loved her so much. So very, very much.

"Julian dear," said his mother, resplendent in white silk and satin, "do stop tapping, it's very *déclassé*."

He stopped.

"I say, do you think Lady Helen will be there?" asked Rupert, for what was possibly the hundredth time that day.

"How lucky she is," said the Countess, "to be held so high in your esteem, Rupert dear."

Rupert nodded, smiling. What was a duke's granddaughter, after all, to a Westenbury? He wondered if she would weep with gratitude when he proposed, or faint in his arms with pleasure. Maybe both.

Lady Helen FitzClarence, walking into the high-ceilinged entrance hall to Carlton House and from there into an immense and brightly lit octagonal chamber, was unmoved by the massive yellow marble columns, the monumental curving staircase ahead, the artwork everywhere. What did she care? Francis was gone, she had failed, and her life was over.

Before they'd left the townhouse, Grandmother had made her go upstairs to say goodnight to her mother, who, although over the worst of the influenza, was still weak and feverish; one of a rotating shift of hired nurses had been there. It was embarrassing how Mother clung to them. Just like a little baby.

Mother had said from her sickbed, *How lovely you look, my dear Helen! I do hope you have a marvelous time tonight.*

What a perfectly foul and idiotic thing to say. As if she would ever again have a good time, let alone a marvelous one.

A few steps behind, Percy burst out laughing and she turned reflexively at the sound. He resembled Francis so closely that it nearly killed her just to look at him. He and Gwendolyn were standing side by side; Gwendolyn was saying with a smile:

"I know it's a silly ambition, but I promised myself that I'd go up and down that staircase at least twice. I'll be right back."

Off she went, lightly and easily up the stairs, and Helen watched her with bitter venom in her heart. Dashing away without a care in the world. *Her* life was perfect, it was all rainbows and unicorns, she had a fiancé who'd been sending her flowers every single day. And she, Helen, had nothing. Oh, she *hated* Gwendolyn—hated *everyone*. She wished she could disappear somewhere. Disappear forever.

Suddenly Helen noticed that Grandmother had been drawn into a little knot of chattering acquaintances, and that Percy was moving toward some ghastly-looking woman with the largest bosom she had ever seen and wearing an extraordinary quantity of jewels.

Now was her chance to disappear—if only for a little while.

She drifted toward the next chamber, moving slowly because of the dense mass of people surrounding her. She would have liked to shove them all aside. Because she hated them too.

Bored, the Honorable Rupert Durant fidgeted, yawned, tapped his shoe on the marble floor, and idly glanced around while his mother and Julian blathered on to some people they had come across. What a stupid room this was. Why an octagon? Was the Prince Regent so high and mighty that a respectable *four* walls wasn't enough, he had to have eight of them? Damned pretentious foolishness, if you asked *him*.

His eye caught a flash of red—of bright red hair, in fact—and all at once his gaze sharpened. Damn if it wasn't Lady Helen there ahead of him. Hey ho, he thought, time to bag his prey.

Rupert took a little crablike step sideways, and glanced slyly about to see if Mummie and Julian noticed. No, they were busy rattling on to their friends.

He took another surreptitious step, and another, and so managed to slip away.

Well, it really was quite a staircase, with its broad, shallow marble steps that curved up and around, the intricately designed balustrade, the classical statues in the enormous wall-niches. It would not, Gwendolyn thought, be difficult in the least to pretend one was a princess in disguise. Cinderella, say, making a grand entrance, with the handsome prince below, staring up at her with his heart in his eyes.

She was coming down the staircase on her second lap, thinking about glass slippers and wondering just how comfortable they really would be to wear, when, halfway down, she spotted Rupert Durant amidst the crowd below. How *intent* he looked, how purposeful, thought Gwendolyn, pausing as she followed his line of sight. She saw that he was staring at Helen—the back of her, at least—as she moved away.

It occurred to Gwendolyn that she didn't like Rupert's expression at all. It was nothing less than predatory. Suddenly she remembered Christopher saying to her, as he was leaving Helen's disastrous birthday party:

Don't let him get you alone.

Very serious he had been, too.

Gwendolyn also remembered Helen throwing the portrait she had made for her—the portrait over which she had labored so painstakingly—into the fire. She remembered the slights and the insults Helen had been lobbing her way, the incessant unkindness and complete lack of civility.

Why should she care if Rupert got Helen alone?

She considered it.

There was no reason in the world to trouble herself.

No reason in the world, except for the fact that she *did*

care. She certainly hoped that if Rupert was stalking her, someone would worry about her, too.

Which meant that there was no time to lose.

Already Rupert was moving past her view.

Gwendolyn hurried down the rest of the staircase and around the newel-post and barreled into someone—a great round person—a middle-aged man, richly dressed, smelling pungently of pomade, cologne, and brandy—and hastily Gwendolyn said, "I *do* beg your pardon, sir, please forgive me," stopping only long enough to see him smile and bow. *Humpty Dumpty!* she thought, and as she rushed away she wondered if she really had heard a faint creaking sound when he bowed.

She made her way down a hallway crowded with fellow guests. Several times did people she knew try to engage her in conversation, which to her frustration slowed her progress considerably, but didn't stop her from peeking into the various rooms she passed. Drawing-rooms. A music room. *More* drawing-rooms. Red velvet, blue velvet, gold leaf everywhere. Sculptures and paintings in abundance. The extravagance of it all was rather stunning, and Gwendolyn would have liked to linger before some of the artworks, but hurried on to the next closed door.

She pushed it open and peeped inside.

A magnificent library.

Hundreds, maybe thousands of books.

Such a room would, quite possibly, be Helen's least favorite room in Carlton House. So, of course, there she was—and in Rupert's arms.

Gwendolyn paused, not wanting to intrude if this was, in fact, a mutually pleasant *tête-à-tête*. But then she saw that Helen was struggling—then Helen exclaimed, "*Stop* it, let *go* of me!"—and Rupert only laughed, then hooked a leg around the back of Helen's knees and brought her roughly down onto the carpet on which they had been standing. Helen gave a muffled scream as Rupert brought himself on top of her, and Gwendolyn, appalled, frightened, furious, said in as loud a voice as she could muster:

"Stop it! Rupert, *stop*!"

He lifted his head, saw her, laughed again. "My beautiful sister-to-be! I do like an audience. Maybe you'll let me watch you and Julian." And then he turned his head back to Helen and forced his mouth on hers.

Fury now replaced every other emotion in Gwendolyn and quickly she looked around the library. On a marble-inlaid side-table stood a tall, exquisite crystal vase. She hurried to the side-table, snatched up the vase—hoping it wasn't some priceless antique—and went to where Rupert was grappling with Helen, then smashed it against the back of his head.

This precipitous act produced exactly the desired result.

Rupert, groaning, went limp, and Helen was able to push him off her. She scrambled to her feet, shivering, and retreated like a scared animal to a corner of the room.

"Are you all right?" Gwendolyn asked her, and Helen, her golden freckles standing out in sharp relief against her white face, only pointed at Rupert with a shaking hand.

He was rolling over. Groggily shaking his head. Then his eyes focused on Gwendolyn where she stood over him, and into them came such a virulent look of rage that involuntarily she took a step back.

"You—you—" he choked out, and for a crazy second Gwendolyn found herself wondering if he was going to call her a varlet. Or even a brazen-faced varlet. She might have giggled wildly, but just then Rupert hauled himself to his feet and began moving toward her, black murder in his eyes.

Gwendolyn backed away. She could easily turn and run for the door, but she didn't want to leave Helen alone

with Rupert again. So she retreated, step by step, until
she bumped up against a bookcase. He was still coming
toward her, and swiftly she reached behind her, feeling for
a volume she could pull out, something large and heavy,
and wouldn't it be satisfying to clout him with a book—an
object, she was sure, entirely repellent to him.

"*Mon cher* Rupert, I suggest you stop where you are,"
said a languid voice, very gently.

They all looked to the doorway.

Étienne de Montmorency had come into the library and
shut the door behind him. He looked so calm, so unperturbed, that Gwendolyn felt again that nearly irrepressible
desire to giggle.

"Stay out of this, Étienne, it's none of your concern,"
growled Rupert, and took another step toward Gwendolyn.

"There, *mon ami*, I fear you are mistaken," answered
de Montmorency in that same gentle voice, and strolled
forward until he stood between Gwendolyn and Rupert.
Angrily Rupert brought up balled fists, as if to strike
out, and with complete *sang-froid* de Montmorency, half
a foot shorter than Rupert and considerably slighter in
build, drew from the pocket of his jacket a small object.
Casually he pressed an indentation in its carved silver
haft and a blade whipped out.

A sharp and extremely lethal-looking blade.

"It would be discomfiting, *mon cher* Rupert, to be
obliged to sink this into you, as you are, *bien sûr*, a very
old friend of mine. But if you persist in your attempt to per-
petrate violence against Mademoiselle Penhallow, having
already, I am deeply sorry to see, troubled Lady Helen, be
assured that I will not hesitate."

Rupert stood very still, then slowly lowered his fists. All
the anger was draining out of him, and Gwendolyn watched
as onto his handsome face came a look of great fear.

"I—I say, Étienne," he stammered, "you won't tell Mummie, will you, or—or Julian? It was just a—a bit of fun, you know. Why, I want Helen to *marry* me."

De Montmorency looked pensively at him, then at the knife he was holding. "Do you know, Rupert, there's really no telling what I might do if sufficiently annoyed. *Eh bien*, you may wish to find a quiet withdrawing-room where you might repair the ravages to your person. You look—if you will forgive my bluntness—quite plebian."

Here again Gwendolyn wanted to laugh. De Montmorency could have delivered no greater insult to the Honorable Rupert.

"I suppose—yes, I suppose you're right. Well—well—goodbye then," said Rupert lamely, and without looking at either Gwendolyn or Helen, left the library in a way that, Gwendolyn thought, could only be described as skulking. When the door closed behind him, Étienne de Montmorency folded his knife and in a leisurely manner returned it to his pocket.

"Thank you for your timely arrival, *monsieur*," Gwendolyn said to him.

He gave a small, graceful bow. "I have no doubt, *mademoiselle*, that left to your own devices you would have very capably—what is the word in English?—yes, you would have coshed *cher* Rupert with that book I saw you reaching for."

"How kind of you to say," answered Gwendolyn, hearing in her voice the slightest tremble of laughter.

"Not at all. *Mademoiselle*, may I trouble you to fetch for Lady Helen a glass of water? I shall stay with her until she regains her composure, and to guard against any unwise return on Rupert's part—unlikely as I believe that to be."

Gwendolyn looked to where Helen had gone to a chair and now sat rather limply. "Is that all right with you, Helen?"

"Yes," Helen replied without hesitation, and so Gwendolyn left the library and went back into the hallway toward the octagonal room where footmen had been circulating with their trays. When she got there she saw Percy coming toward her, a champagne flute in one hand and looking very merry.

"I say, Gwennie, do you realize you nearly knocked Prinny over a little while ago?"

"What?" She looked at him rather blankly, then comprehension came to her in a flash. "Oh, my goodness, when I was coming round the stairs! That was him? I was in a dreadful rush, you see, and—oh, Percy, I think I heard his corset creaking when he bowed!"

He laughed. "Just so."

A footman went by and Gwendolyn said to him, "Could you bring me a glass of water, please?"

"Of course, miss."

"Water?" said Percy. "Whatever for? Have some champagne instead."

"It's not for me, it's for—" Gwendolyn broke off. What had happened in the library was Helen's business, and not for her to broadcast. Hastily she went on, "How did you know I—ah—bumped into the Prince Regent? Did you see me doing it?"

"No, I was talking with Prinny just now, and he wondered if the mysterious young lady who looked so much like me was any relation."

"Is he very much upset with me?"

"Not a bit of it. He said he wished you'd do it again."

"Ugh."

Percy laughed again. "You needn't worry. Prinny likes his women on the plump side."

"It's still a repulsive remark. Why, he's old enough to be my father."

"In a way, it's a compliment, you know."

"Not one I care for."

"Which shows how unusual you are. Most women would trample their grandmother underfoot just to have Prinny flirt with them." He smiled at her in his charming way. "I'm awfully glad you came tonight, Gwennie, as we won't be seeing each other for a while."

"What? Oh, Percy, why not?"

"Prinny's decided to go to Brighton tomorrow, to see how the work's coming along with his Pavilion. They've started on the Banquet Room—he says he wants to make sure they're putting in the right chandeliers."

"The right chandeliers? Doesn't he have anything better to do? Like running the kingdom, for example?"

"Evidently not."

"Goodness me. Honestly, I think *I* could do a better job than he does."

"I quite believe you could, dear sister."

"Thank you for your faith in me, dear brother. Oh, I'm going to miss you! How long will you be gone?"

"According to Prinny, we'll be in Brighton for about a week. Maybe longer."

"And what will you be doing while he's inspecting chandeliers?"

"Oh, the usual. Wine, women, and song. And the occasional parade."

"Percy," Gwendolyn said, "is this how you envisioned your life as a soldier?"

He shrugged. "Sometimes I'd like to see some real action, I'll admit, but this suits me for now. I say, here comes Helen with that damned French fellow. Why is he holding on to her elbow like that?"

Gwendolyn turned. She wasn't surprised that Monsieur de Montmorency was still very composed, very urbane, but she *was* rather startled to see that Helen seemed to have not only fully recovered from her ordeal but was also looking quite cheerful. What remarkable powers of persuasion Monsieur de Montmorency must have, she thought. Just at that moment the footman reappeared with the glass of water she'd requested, and so she went forward to meet Helen and Monsieur de Montmorency, then held out the glass.

"Here's your water, Helen."

"I don't want it."

"Oh." Gwendolyn stood holding the glass and feeling rather foolish.

"Perhaps," said Monsieur de Montmorency to Helen, very gently, "you ought to accept the water as a courtesy to Mademoiselle Penhallow, who has made the effort to procure it on your behalf."

Helen looked up at him. "Do you think so? All right, I will." She took the glass.

"You can let go of her now," said Percy to de Montmorency, who calmly returned Percy's rather belligerent gaze, then with a small, pleasant, entirely affable smile he released Helen's arm.

It was late in the evening when Christopher arrived at the Albany. He looked through his correspondence, feeling absurdly—painfully—grateful not to find any wedding invitations amongst the notes, circulars, and newspapers. There was, however, another sort of invitation from the Earl of Westenbury: an offer to come join him, as he had mentioned on the day they first had met, at Jackson's Saloon for a few rounds of boxing; he was, he said, to be found there most mornings around eleven.

Christopher looked at the Earl's note for a few moments, then carelessly tossed it on top of the Almack's vouchers and also a notecard which was, he realized, his invitation to the Prince Regent's Carlton House *fête*. Which was, he further realized, tonight. He'd forgotten all about it.

How shocked the Earl would be at such a cavalier attitude, he thought with a wry smile.

A lowly commoner disregarding a royal invitation.

Shocking indeed.

Of course, if he had left Nottingham sooner, he might have arrived in time for the *fête*. But there had been so much to do, so much he *wanted* to do there—spend time with Father and Cora, hold little Jasper in his arms, explore Nottingham with Father, visit with Diana and her husband, a rather serious young barrister who adored his lively, chattery wife, who, in turn, was devoted to her very different husband.

Christopher was glad he had arrived with gifts, which had been received with pleasing acclaim. Father liked his book and Cora the pretty pearl necklace he'd gotten for her at Rundell and Bridge, and the silver wedding-goblets as well. For Diana and her husband, similar goblets, the book he'd purchased for her, and also a trio of slender gold bracelets which she had at once put on and declared her intention never to remove.

His conversations with Father—of which there were many—had been so different from the way they used to talk with each other. It took effort to break their old patterns, but, grateful for this second chance, they each of them tried very hard to listen and not judge; to accept and admire the other for who they really were. And by the time Christopher left, new patterns had begun to form— the promise of a new relationship that was healthy, resilient, affectionate.

He hadn't forgotten about Gwendolyn, or about writing to her. There was a great deal he wanted to say to her, so much news to share with her about his family and about Nottingham, and other things, too.

The sheer quantity of it all wasn't what stopped him from writing, though.

He hadn't written because he wanted to see her again, one last time. That was why, without pushing himself to think too hard about it, he had kept his lodgings at the Albany.

Father had asked him if he'd like to stay in Nottingham with them. For a while, or maybe forever.

It warmed him so much to hear Father say that, and to have Cora eagerly add her entreaties as well.

Christopher didn't know what, precisely, he wanted to do.

Except that—

He looked at a package from Rundell and Bridge which he'd left here on the desk. Inside it was a third pair of silver goblets, as expensive and elegant as those he'd gotten for his father and Cora, for Diana and her husband.

It was a wedding present for Gwendolyn and the Earl.

Not very imaginative, but at the very least, appropriate.

He had come back to London to give Gwendolyn her gift, and say goodbye to her in person—goodbye again, and this time, in a final way. Having no better idea just now, he *was* going back to Nottingham. He hoped she wouldn't mind that he didn't attend her wedding, but in point of fact he would rather be torn apart by wild horses—and have his mangled body parts thrown to wolves—than have to sit in St. George's watching the woman he loved marry the Earl.

Yes, he loved Gwendolyn.

He knew this now.

It had come on rather gradually, moment by moment, conversation by conversation, day by day.

But it wasn't till Cora had said to him during a quiet, private talk together, *Is there anyone special in your life, Christopher?*—it wasn't till then that it hit him with all the force of a runaway carriage that the answer was yes, a thousand times yes.

Gwendolyn *was* special.

Special, wonderful, spectacularly so.

He liked her, he respected her, he valued her intelligence, and he enjoyed her sense of humor. He found her intensely desirable. He wanted to be with her—for all his days and all his nights—and he wanted to grow old with her.

Yes, he loved her.

Through thick and thin, trouble and joy, come what may, his heart belonged to her.

But she was going to marry the Earl, and that was that.

Christopher sat at the desk and wrote Gwendolyn a note. He had returned to London, and could he call upon her at her convenience?

A few simple words which conveyed nothing that he felt, nothing that he longed for. But it would be selfish to say more, and he was determined—above all—to do nothing to bring her distress.

He folded the note, went downstairs, and gave it to the night porter to pass along to his colleague in the morning, who would have it delivered to the Egremont townhouse.

Then he went back upstairs and looked around the front room. He'd start packing tomorrow. It wouldn't take him long. He glanced again at the package from Rundell and Bridge. In his mind's eye he saw Gwendolyn and the Earl, drinking from the silver goblets. Happy and smiling. Clinking the rims in a toast. Married. Gwendolyn, lost to him forever.

For a few agonized moments Christopher wanted to take the package and throw it out the window. Toss it in a fire. Let wild horses tear *it* apart. Instead, slowly he went back to the desk, and looked again at the Earl's cordial note. Inside him he could feel the promptings of what was decidedly not his better self.

Bitter and black they were, too.

And already he felt himself yielding to them.

Chapter 15

❧⟨ೞ⟩❧

The carriage had brought them home from Carlton House well after midnight, and when Gwendolyn, the Duchess, and Helen came into the entry-hall they found Tyndale waiting for them, with two footmen standing nearby.

"Your Grace, an express has arrived for you." He came forward, a single letter placed with meticulous precision in the exact center of the silver salver he carried.

"From Hathaway Park?" said the Duchess, moving quickly to meet him. "Is it from the Duke?"

"No, Your Grace. The messenger has come from Great Yarmouth, and his directions are, apparently, to await your reply. Also, he's expecting payment. I thought it best to pay him from my purse, Your Grace, and send him to the kitchen for a meal."

"Yes, yes, quite right, thank you, Tyndale," said the Duchess, rather absently, as she opened the letter and scanned it. "Good God!" she exclaimed, and Gwendolyn came near, saying anxiously:

"Cousin Judith, what is it?"

"It's from Philip. My grandson. He's—"

"From Philip?" interrupted Helen, her tone contemptuous. "Well, that explains why the messenger wasn't paid. So he's washed up in Great Yarmouth? How much money is he asking for, Grandmother?"

The Duchess glanced up from the letter. "Be quiet," she said, with so much sternness that Helen's scornful expression gave way, briefly, to a look of abashment. "Philip is very ill—in a hospital there with a bullet in his chest. It's very close to his heart, he says, and they won't perform the surgery unless they know they'll get paid. He used the last of his money to flee Vienna after being shot by—oh, Philip, how sadly typical!—after being shot by a jealous husband. He had seen the English newspapers from time to time, he says, and knew to find me here, rather than sending the express to Hathaway Park. Well! We must be grateful for small favors! The news might well have sent the Duke into an apoplexy."

"Oh, Cousin Judith, I'm so sorry to hear this," said Gwendolyn, hating to see how distraught the Duchess looked. "What are you going to do?"

"I'll leave for Great Yarmouth at first light. This is all most unfortunate, but you and Helen must remain quietly at home till I return. And under no circumstance are either of you to tell Almira where I've gone, or why. She's far from well, and I'm absolutely in earnest when I say that her fear and anxiety for Philip could easily set her back, and quite possibly put her in very deep peril. Do you both understand me?"

"Of course, Cousin Judith," answered Gwendolyn at once, and Helen said:

"Yes, but Grandmother, what if Philip's made all this up just to get money out of you? I wouldn't put it past him. Why not just send the messenger back with a cheque?"

The Duchess looked at Helen, in her kind, weather-beaten face not just sternness but also a painful sorrow. "You're not wrong, Helen, that Philip could be capable of such duplicity. But that you would risk his life on the chance that he is, this time, telling the truth, speaks to some kind of—some kind of lack in you. You may not be close to each other, but he is, after all, family."

Helen flushed, then shot a resentful glance at the Duchess, but made no reply.

"Have the messenger come here, Tyndale, please," the Duchess went on. "I should like to hear his report as to Philip's health."

"Immediately, Your Grace," and Tyndale dispatched one of the footmen, who shortly returned with the messenger, a laconic but amiable man in a long mud-splashed greatcoat. In response to the Duchess's questions he confirmed the truth of Philip Thane's letter, having received it from Philip's own hand, and made no objection to accompanying the Duchess on her journey within just a few brief hours.

After he had returned to the kitchen to finish his meal, Gwendolyn said, "Shall we tell Lady Almira that you've had a slight relapse, Cousin Judith, and don't want to risk the possibility of reinfecting her?"

"Yes, that's fine. Tyndale, I'll want our fastest curricle and team ready to depart at dawn. You do, I am sure, grasp the complexities of this difficult situation."

Tyndale nodded. "Yes, Your Grace. You may be assured of my discretion, and I will instruct the staff accordingly. I'll send a message to the stables right away."

The Duchess gave him a slight smile. "Thank you, Tyndale. I really don't know what we'd do without you."

"Think nothing of it, Your Grace. I know I speak for the entire staff when I say that we're anxious to do whatever we can."

"I am too," said Gwendolyn. "How can I help? Would you like it if I came with you, Cousin Judith?"

"It's very kind of you to offer, m'dear, but I shouldn't dream of dragging you along. I'll bring my maid Hawkins with me. She's a very capable nurse and has known Philip since he was a boy—knows his constitution and, moreover, is entirely resistant to his wheedling ways. I'm going to try and get a little sleep now. You and Helen ought to go to bed as well."

Everyone dispersed. Gwendolyn managed to doze for a few hours but was up again and downstairs in time to see the Duchess off. Helen was nowhere in sight. "Just as well," sighed the Duchess, and then she and Gwendolyn hugged, and Gwendolyn said, "I'll be thinking of you both, Cousin Judith," and shortly after that, the Duchess climbed briskly into the waiting curricle, a grim-faced Hawkins at her heels, and was gone and on her way to Great Yarmouth.

"**A** few words, gentlemen, as to the rules of sparring," said John Jackson, the tall, strapping proprietor of Jackson's Saloon, in a pleasant voice. "No kicking, biting, gouging of the eyes, pulling of the hair, grabbing below the waist, ripping of the clothing, or spitting."

Christopher stood on the sanded plank floor facing the Earl of Westenbury. They both wore the knee-breeches and white high-collared shirt which were, apparently, *de rigueur* for a nice high-society fistfight—and which Mr. Jackson kindly had provided for him, the Earl, of course, having brought his own, including a dazzlingly white shirt which was monogrammed with his crest and initials. The Earl was nodding, smiling, comfortable and confident, so utterly at peace with himself and the world that Christopher found himself regretting these various prohibitions against the lower forms of violence. He wondered if the Earl would look less at peace with a black eye or a bloody nose.

"Would either of you care for mufflers?" asked Mr. Jackson.

Christopher tried to shake himself free from his dark thoughts. The bitter promptings from last night had returned, it seemed, and in full force. What the hell had he been thinking, to come here this morning? Was he here to prove something? And if so—no matter how bad an idea—*could* he? The Earl was taller, broader, and had, he'd casually mentioned not five minutes ago, been training with Gentleman Jackson for over a decade.

Christopher said, "Mufflers?"

"Padded gloves, sir, to protect the knuckles."

"Ah." Christopher looked to the Earl. "I defer to you, sir."

"Well, there's something more pristine without them, I've always thought. But only if that suits you as well, Mr. Beck."

"I'm fine without them."

"Very well then," said Mr. Jackson. "Fists up, gentlemen, head and shoulders forward, and bend your knees just a bit. Excellent. Begin!"

The Earl danced forward, his fists held high, and when he got close he gracefully threw some jabs, landing two or three hits to Christopher's chest and shoulders. "You can retreat, Mr. Beck, there's no shame in that," he said, and landed another hit to Christopher's shoulder.

Christopher tried not to laugh—laugh in an ugly way. He had deliberately kept his guard down, wanting to assess the Earl's fighting style and ability. The Earl was certainly light on his feet, but these were the jabs of a butterfly. Or maybe he was just testing *him*. He tightened his fists, shifted on his feet, but let the Earl land another light punch near his collarbone. And another. Christopher could almost feel the Earl relaxing, maybe even anticipating the easy win. So casually he shot his left fist out, right against the Earl's jaw.

The Earl wasn't expecting it and staggered back, looking surprised.

"Well done, Mr. Beck," remarked Mr. Jackson from the sidelines. "Very cunning."

The Earl came at him again, hitting out with more force, but Christopher easily evaded the blows, ducking and sidestepping. The Earl wasn't quick; his movements were fluid, but too studied. As if he were an actor playing at fighting. Lightning-fast, Christopher broke through his guard, hit him again, on one of those broad shoulders, and the Earl's body twisted back, leaving the other shoulder open and defenseless. Christopher punched it too—not too hard, but just enough to effectively disorient.

The Earl swayed backwards. It took him a few moments to recover his balance, and then he came back toward Christopher, swinging his heavily muscled arms a little less carefully. Christopher stood his ground, parrying the blows, watching as the Earl got rather winded, his perfect face turning extremely red. It would be easy, Christopher thought, to deliver a stunning blow to the Earl's solar plexus which would hurt a great deal and also send him reeling to the floor. Did he want to do that?

Well, he rather did, to be honest. Within him was dislike—an utter lack of respect—revulsion—and a savage, tormenting fear for Gwendolyn's happiness. Altogether a nasty, vigorously boiling cauldron of black emotion.

But—

What good would it do? Aside from the brief satisfaction of seeing the Earl lying at his feet, would it change anything?

No.

The Earl would get up, he'd get his wind back, he'd soon

be his affable smiling self again, and Gwendolyn would still be engaged to him.

Damn it to *hell*.

Christopher dodged several more jabs—aggressive but ineffectual—from the Earl. Well, he could at least have a *bit* of satisfaction. So he went in fast, purposefully, toward the Earl. Who, red-faced, perspiring, rattled, promptly backed away. Which didn't surprise Christopher at all. He stopped and lowered his fists. "No shame in retreating, sir," he said politely. His breathing was normal, easy, he hadn't even broken out in a sweat. "I'm done here. Thanks for the match." He nodded at the Earl, and at Mr. Jackson, who was regarding him with a distinct twinkle in his eye, and walked away.

Wrapped in a cozy flannel robe, Gwendolyn sat at her dressing-table, drowsily watching Lizzie in the mirror's reflection as she brushed out her hair with long strokes. After the Duchess had left this morning, she had gone back to bed but couldn't sleep, so she'd read for an hour or so, then finally had resigned herself to sentience and gone downstairs for breakfast. Helen had come in not long after and announced her intention to shortly go riding—with a groom in attendance, she had pointedly added.

Gwendolyn had been uneasy about the plan, but what could she do? Lock Helen in her bedchamber? Hardly. Hopefully the presence of a groom would allay any potential objections the Duchess might have had. So she had only nodded, and Helen had sat down and proceeded to eat a hearty breakfast, and nothing further had been said between them.

Afterwards, she had gone upstairs and peeked in on Lady Almira, who was awake, still rather weak and feverish, but glad of the company, and so Gwendolyn had sat with her for a while, chatting about inconsequential things, and then left her with the day-nurse and gone back to her room where she'd asked Lizzie to have a bath prepared. It had felt very nice to soak for a while and to wash her hair, then sit before the fire, doodling in her sketchbook, while it had dried. And then to go to her dressing-table and have Lizzie brush out her hair. Soothing . . . soporific. Fatigue from lack of sleep drifted over Gwendolyn like a ponderous fog and her eyelids felt heavy, so heavy . . .

Lizzie once again drew the brush from the crown of Gwendolyn's head all the way to the ends of her hair, which lay below her shoulder blades. "There now—all nice and smooth. Are you going out tonight, miss, or in a hurry to go somewhere?"

"No, not at all, Lizzie, I've nothing planned. Why?"

"I did think, miss, that we might try the curling-tongs at last," said Lizzie coaxingly. "There's a new style I've seen, with long curls brought together at the back of the head. Very pretty, miss, and you've just the hair for it."

Ordinarily Gwendolyn would have refused, but in fact she had nothing to do, really, and she was so tired and sleepy . . . "Why not, Lizzie? Have at it."

"Wonderful, miss!" said Lizzie, and went off to heat the tongs. Gwendolyn closed her eyes, murmuring once or twice, "Bless you," when she heard Lizzie sneezing, and felt herself slip into a passive, dreamy state somewhere between sleep and wakefulness.

When Lizzie returned with the heated tongs, she looked at her again in the mirror. "Lizzie, you're very flushed. Are you all right?"

"Oh yes, miss, it's just the heat of the fire, that's all. Now—let's set this first curl." Carefully Lizzie wrapped a length of Gwendolyn's hair around the tong, then looked critically at her work. "Your hair's so fine and smooth, miss, I can add more of it, it'll make it go faster." She wrapped another chunk of hair around the tong.

Drowsily Gwendolyn watched in the reflection as after a little while Lizzie pulled free the length of her hair, revealing a single long curl which she brought forward alongside Gwendolyn's neck. "There, miss, isn't that nice?"

"Yes, very," said Gwendolyn, though in all honesty she doubted the curl would hold for very long.

"I told you, miss, didn't I? I'll go heat the tongs again."

Gwendolyn closed her eyes and just barely registered Lizzie's return sometime later; in that sudden way that one occasionally fell asleep, it felt like she'd stepped off a cliff and dropped into instant oblivion—and then, a heartbeat later, as if pushed by invisible hands, she was dreaming, somewhere in a maze, surrounded by tall green hedges stretching up to the sky. Oh, she was lost, lost, never to be found again. She heard, from somewhere far across the hedges, Lady Almira saying anxiously:

"Mazes do make me nervous. They make me feel that I'm trapped, and I don't know where I am, and I can't find my way free."

And then the Duchess's voice in the distance, very firm and sure:

"You shan't be lost. Do stop dropping coins in the fountain, m'dear, and standing about wishing for happiness. You must make your own luck."

In the dream Gwendolyn saw a bluebird, with a beautiful sheen to its sleek feathers, flying overhead. She stretched out her left hand and the bluebird swooped down and landed on her fourth finger. It cackled and said, sounding exactly like Señor Rodrigo:

"Kiss me, you saucy wench."

And then it flew away.

In the sudden silence Gwendolyn thought to herself, *I'm tired of being lost. I'll make my own luck, I shall find my way free.*

She hurried along the gravel path, which lay in deep, dark shadow. The hedges were high, so high, blocking out the sun. Which way to go?

Ahead, she spotted a little sign dangling from a twig in the hedge.

FRUIT FOR SALE.

And then, suddenly, there was Julian, tall and handsome, enveloped in a big white apron, holding out a pear, smiling. His teeth were so white and perfect they nearly blinded her. *"Kiss me, my darling Gwendolyn,"* he said.

But she only hurried past him, turned a corner, and saw another little sign:

VEGETABLES FOR SALE.

Then it was the Countess standing there, dazzling in white from head to toe, smiling, smiling. *"Come and give me a kiss, my dear child."*

Gwendolyn ran past her, turned another corner, and came to yet another sign:

NOSCE TE IPSUM.

She stood before it, puzzled. It was important—more important than anything in the world—that she figure out what it meant.

Understanding it would set her free.

She stared and stared.

She had to hurry.

Danger was all around.

There was an acrid smell in the air, unpleasant in her nostrils, and rather frightening.

Hurry, hurry, there's no time to lose—

Wait. She *had* the understanding, it was deep within her, had been there all along—

Hurry, the maze is on fire!

Not only that, the sign in front of her burst into flames. But it didn't matter, because she *knew*. It meant—

Know thyself.

Yes, yes! She knew, and she was free! Gwendolyn began to run. There was light ahead, the exit to the maze—glorious freedom lay ahead, and happiness!

Suddenly she was jerked to a stop.

Someone behind her was yanking at her hair with vicious force. And then she clapped a hand to her cheek. Oh, it was on fire, too! Then there was a tremendous *thump*—

Gwendolyn jerked awake.

A nasty burning smell filled the air, and her cheek stung. She spun around on her chair. Lizzie had fallen—passed out?—and the tongs were on the carpet, smoldering. And—clamped around them was a great bunch of her own hair. Burnt to a crisp.

Gwendolyn leaped up, grabbed the tongs, stamped on the carpet to put out any little flames there, hastily set the tongs on the hearth, and hurried back to Lizzie, whose eyes were open now although she looked dazed. Her round, pleasant face was very flushed, and she was shivering so badly she was shaking.

"Miss," she murmured, "oh, miss, what happened? I'd just finished with your second curl, and then . . ."

Gwendolyn knelt beside her. "You fainted, Lizzie. I think you may have the influenza."

"Do you think so, miss? Oh, I'm so cold . . ." Lizzie's eyes widened and she gaped up at Gwendolyn. "Miss! Your *hair*! And your cheek! The tongs must've gone against your face just before I fell. Oh, *miss*! I'm so sorry, so sorry!" She began to cry.

Gwendolyn patted her shoulder. "Don't worry, Lizzie.

It doesn't matter. Truly it doesn't. Now, please just stay there—I'm going to ring for help."

"Yes, miss," said Lizzie in a weak, trembling voice, and closed her eyes.

Gwendolyn got up and went to go tug vigorously at the bell-pull, then pulled a blanket from her bed to lay atop the shivering Lizzie, and scrambled out of her robe and into a day-dress, taking a brief moment to glance at herself in her mirror. Her cheek was rather red and raw, and a giant clump of her hair—a full third of it from the nape down, she guessed—was gone. Quickly she dabbed some salve on her face and then, resolutely, she took a pair of scissors and cut off the rest of her hair till it was moderately even all round. It fell just to her jaw now.

It was a shock to see how different she looked.

She ran a hand along the short, blunted ends.

Actually, she rather liked it.

In fact, she looked quite jaunty, really.

After that there was no time to think about her hair, in the flurry of servants arriving, getting Lizzie conveyed to her room and a doctor summoned, and seeing that Lizzie was made comfortable, and then, as she came down the flight of stairs onto the landing which led to the family's bedchambers, she saw someone coming out of Helen's room—her maid, Belinda, who looked around the hallway in a panicked way and then hurried toward Gwendolyn.

"Oh, miss! Miss! Please can you come?"

"What's wrong? Has Lady Helen come home ill, or injured?"

"It's not that, miss. Come and see for yourself, please!"

Helen's room was very clean and tidy. But there was no Helen. Belinda gestured toward the dresser, and Gwendolyn went over to it. On top of the dresser was a letter, and with a sudden feeling of unreality, Gwendolyn picked it up, a memory flashing into her mind. Herself, years ago, saying fancifully to Christopher after suggesting they run away together:

I'd have to leave a note, of course. The heroine usually does. She leaves it on her dresser, and sometimes it's all splotched with her tears. Although you'd think the ink would run and make the note difficult to read, wouldn't you?

And sure enough, Helen's childish, looping handwriting was blurry and hard to make out in places, as if she had been crying while she wrote it.

I am going away, with Monsiuer de Montmorecy, to someplace far away which will be Better than here which is all a lot of rubbish. I don't care that I don't speak the langwidge over there and that I don't like all the sauces they put on their Food and also that Percy Thinks that as a Nation they are not to be trusted, I will be gone and finished with this stupid Season which has been so foul and stuppid. I Have to Go—I MUST go—and I will never, ever see any of you ever again. Good bye.

Helen FitzClarence

PS. Dont let them give my horse too much oats, it gives him Colick.

It took a little effort to decode it all, but having read the letter twice, it seemed fairly clear to Gwendolyn that Helen had fled under the aegis of Étienne de Montmorency, whether willingly or not.

I Have to Go—I MUST go.

Was he forcing Helen into this? Had he threatened her? Compromised her? Manipulated her into this rash act?

Recalling de Montmorency's demeanor last night at Carlton House, and the deadly cold way he'd pulled a knife on Rupert, it would not be hard to believe.

So what about their destination? Gwendolyn's mind moved rapidly across the possibilities. It had to be France, de Montmorency's homeland. And how would they get there? Suddenly she remembered the Earl telling her about de Montmorency's racing yacht—the new mainsail he had commissioned—docked in Bournemouth—the trips to Le Havre and thence to his family's country estate—

What if, even now, Helen was being held captive in a carriage, barreling toward Bournemouth? Was desperately vulnerable, helpless, terrified?

Well, there was nothing for it.

She was going after them.

Furthermore, she'd need some help. It was entirely impracticable to go on her own, especially if a cornered de Montmorency were to lash out. She might be able to smash a vase over somebody prone on the floor, but she certainly couldn't defend herself against a knife attack. She needed someone smart and strong and capable. Someone she could count on. Oh, if only Christopher were here!

But he wasn't, and Percy was away, and so was Francis, and so that left only Julian. Which made sense, because he was de Montmorency's friend—surely he'd want to stop him from doing something so dreadful.

Swiftly Gwendolyn went to her own bedchamber, shrugged herself into a pelisse, and jammed a hat onto her head. She snatched up her reticule and a pair of gloves which she tugged on as she rushed downstairs to the entry-hall. Tyndale was there, sorting through the morning's mail, and Gwendolyn took him aside to quietly share the news about Helen's disappearance.

Tyndale looked grave, but remained as calm as ever.

He sent a footman to the stables who returned with the further news that Helen *had* taken along a groom, but when she had met Monsieur de Montmorency in Hyde Park, she had gotten into his curricle and sent him home with her horse.

"Well, that's confirmation, at least," said Gwendolyn. "Tyndale, I'll try and find them, but first I need to see the Earl of Westenbury. Can you have a hack summoned, please? In the meantime, here's something else we'll need the staff to keep quiet about—Lady Almira mustn't know anything for now, nor should anyone outside this house. Can you talk with everyone while I'm gone?"

"Yes, Miss Gwendolyn. Do you think we should inform Her Grace?"

Gwendolyn thought. "No. Not yet. She's got enough on her hands."

"Very well. What else can I do to be of assistance?"

"I'll let you know when I get back from the Earl's."

He gave a slight bow. "I'll be waiting, Miss Gwendolyn."

They conferred in low, urgent tones for a few more minutes, and when a footman came to escort her to the hack that was waiting out front, Tyndale said:

"I nearly forgot, Miss Gwendolyn. A note came for you."

He held it out to her and hastily she crammed it into her reticule. "Thank you, Tyndale, I'll read it later." She hurried into the hack, and a few minutes later she was at the doorstep of the Westenbury townhouse, being ushered inside by their visibly disapproving butler and into a saloon to await the Earl's arrival.

Restlessly she paced back and forth. It seemed like years—decades—*eons*, but was in all likelihood only a few minutes till the Earl came in, shutting the door behind him.

"My dear Gwendolyn!" he said, smiling. "What an

unexpected pleasure! But—no footman or maid to accompany you?"

"No."

"Let's hope there won't be any talk." As he came closer his smile disappeared. "Your cheek—good God—"

"It's nothing. Julian, I—"

"Have you seen a doctor? You may well be permanently disfigured."

"I won't be."

"But what if you *are*? It would be a tragedy."

"Truly, it's only a small wound. Julian—"

And then his jaw dropped. "My darling, what's happened to your hair?"

"Oh, it's shorter. Julian, listen—"

"Shorter all the way round?"

"Yes, but—"

"But why, my dear Gwendolyn? What did you do to it?"

"There was a little accident. At any rate—"

"It was so beautiful before," he said, sounding so mournful, even devastated, that Gwendolyn, with a rush of impatience, ripped her bonnet off her head and spun around in a full circle.

"There," she said. "That's what it looks like now."

"So short. My God, so very short."

"It's just *hair*. I'm still me."

"But it's hardly a flattering style, my love. I wonder—perhaps a hairpiece, until your own grows longer again?"

"I beg your pardon?"

"A hairpiece, you know. Or a wig. That way no one would know."

Gwendolyn stared at him, aware that within her was a sudden desire to violently bat him about his head and face with her bonnet. Then she gathered herself. "Believe it or not, Julian, I didn't come here to talk about hair. I have reason to think that Lady Helen's been taken away by Monsieur de Montmorency."

His tawny eyebrows went up. "Taken away?"

"Yes, I believe they've run away together, and very likely are on their way to Bournemouth and from there to France."

"Oh, you mean they're eloping."

He said it so casually that Gwendolyn felt *her* jaw dropping. "I'm not sure that Helen's gone willingly."

"You think Étienne's kidnapped her?"

"Maybe."

The Earl shook his head. "No, I doubt it. Hardly seems his style. Well, this will certainly be a blow to Rupert. Poor fellow, he'd quite set his heart on Lady Helen."

Gwendolyn brought her jaw up so hard that her teeth clicked together. "Julian, I'm going after them. And I need your help. Will you come with me?"

"What Étienne does is his own business."

"He's your *friend*."

"Not after what he did to Rupert last night at Carlton House. Threatening him with a knife—and for nothing, really, simply a small misunderstanding. I hadn't thought Étienne could be so common."

"Is that what Rupert told you?"

"Yes. Shall I ring for tea?"

"I don't want any tea. You believed Rupert?"

"Of course. He's family, after all."

"Did he tell you I was there, and that I saw everything?"

"No, but—"

"Will you come with me, Julian? If not to prevent a friend—a former friend—from doing something reprehensible, at least for Helen's sake?"

"I'm very sorry, my dear Gwendolyn, but I won't. And I think you'd be making a great mistake by flying after them in this hey-go-mad way. I shouldn't like you to be involved in a scandal, especially one that's really none of your business."

Gwendolyn stood very still, her hands gripping the ribbons of her hat with unnecessary force. She looked at Julian, so tall and handsome, so calm and unconcerned. Into her mind came swirling bits and pieces from the dream she'd had earlier:

Julian. His mother, the beautiful snow queen with the golden fringe and smiling blue eyes. *Kiss me. Kiss me, my dear child.* NOSCE TE IPSUM. Know thyself. *"You shan't be lost. Do stop dropping coins in the fountain, m'dear, and standing about wishing for happiness. You must make your own luck."* A bluebird, flying free—

All at once something seemed to coalesce inside her brain.

Everything came together, after days and days of thinking, wondering, pondering.

The puzzle solved at last.

And with it, a sharp sense of satisfaction—a brief pang of loss—and a vast, reassuring, overwhelming relief.

Know thyself.

Gwendolyn put her hat back on, said, "Excuse me, please," and went past him toward the door.

"Are you leaving, my darling? So soon?"

"I'm going upstairs first."

"What? Why?"

She didn't answer, only opened the door, went to the stairs and quickly up them, down the hallway, and to Julian's bedchamber. Julian followed behind her, saying in bewilderment, "What's going on? What are you doing?"

Gwendolyn flung open the door and went inside. There, hanging above one of the fireplaces, was a large portrait of the Countess. She had seen it two weeks ago—upside down—

while lying on the floor. And just a few moments ago, her brain had, as it were, put it upright for her to see at last.

To see it, *perceive* it, and, finally, understand.

The portrait of the Countess had clearly been done some years ago, when she had been a much younger woman. Wearing a frilly, panniered white gown and white slippers, she was sitting on a garden bench, with a view behind her of trees, flowers, a placid pond, an idyllic blue sky. At her feet stood a handsome little boy—Julian, clearly—who was looking up at her adoringly. The Countess wore no turban, only a pretty white bandeau in her long golden-blonde hair. Her blue eyes were smiling as she looked down at the little boy.

Gwendolyn stood before the portrait for a minute or two, then turned to the Earl. "Did you know that I look rather like your mother?" she said, and watched as onto his face came a faint flush of red.

"No, not at all—well, I daresay just a trifle—not at first, you see—it rather crept up on me—but I soon forgot all about it—not a *strong* resemblance, surely, I do think you're exaggerating—and if there is, it's really quite a coincidence, don't you think? Besides, your nose is very different, you know, my darling. Frankly, it's much nicer than Mummie's. Don't tell her I said so, of course."

What a perfectly ambiguous answer.

If she were to marry the Earl, she would never, in her whole life to come, be able to trust that what he said was true. Whether it was over a matter trivial, or important. Whether he had written a letter he had promised to write, or if he had knowingly been going to marry a woman who looked a lot like his own mother.

She looked up into his handsome face. There were so many things she could say to him.

You're a wobbly sort of person, Julian.

You're not congruent in who you are and how you present yourself to the world.

You slip and slide about, like blancmange on a plate.

You're complacent and snobbish, and I'm afraid you're rather weak.

You're a little boy who's never really grown up.

Also, I'm not at all sure that you're a good kisser.

You're not a bad person, or a villain, or anything like that. I don't hate you. I don't even dislike you. Actually, when I think about it, I feel sorry for you.

And I don't love you anymore.

If I ever really did.

Yes, she could say any and all of these things. But what purpose would it serve? She had no interest in trying to hurt him, enlighten him, or change him. Besides, she wasn't perfect, she had made mistakes too, she had willingly entered into their arrangement. She had been rash and impulsive and rather blinded by her own illusions. And so their lives had come together for a while; but now it was all over.

So she took off the glove on her left hand, and pulled from her fourth finger the beautiful Westenbury ring.

It was a little surprising how easily it came off.

Gwendolyn held it out to the Earl. "Julian, I'm afraid our betrothal is at an end. I'm very sorry, but I don't believe that we should suit each other after all."

"*What?*" He had gone chalk-white. "My love, my darling child, what are you saying?"

"I'm not your child. Our betrothal is over. Do take back your ring."

But he didn't take it. He only stood staring at her, the very picture of a man dealt a stunning and incomprehensible blow. "You—surely you don't mean it."

"Yes, I do."

"You're upset about Lady Helen, that's all. You're

upset, but it will pass. Surely you're not going to throw away everything we have over something so trivial?"

"It's not trivial to me."

"Is it about the wedding? We can have it in White-haven, I swear to it."

"It's not about the wedding."

His eyes were filling with tears. "Oh God, Gwendolyn, don't do this—don't leave me—I love you so very, very much." Urgently he reached toward her, to try and take her hands, perhaps, or clasp her in his arms. But she was still holding out the ring, which he didn't take, which seemed to stop him from coming closer, and it started to feel as if the ring was a magic talisman keeping him at bay. In other circumstances Gwendolyn might have laughed at her own fancy, but what was pulling at her now was chiefly impatience. She wanted to be gone from here and on her way to Bournemouth.

The Earl was openly crying now.

Gently she said, "Oh, Julian, I know *you're* upset, but please believe me when I say that this is all for the best. You're not right for me, and I'm not right for you. We'd make each other miserable, sooner or later, and I suspect it would be sooner. I'm sure you'll find some nice young lady who will make you very happy." She thought but didn't say aloud, *Perhaps even some nice young lady with blonde hair and blue eyes.* "And whom you'll make very happy, too. Now—I must go. Goodbye."

He didn't say anything, only sank into a chair and put his tawny head into his hands. Next to the chair was a little side-table, and so she went to the table and carefully, gently, put the ring on it. And then she turned and left the room, walking down the hallway and skimming down the stairs feeling as light, as free, as a bird.

Engaged to the Earl no more.

Chapter 16

Christopher had packed, and stood looking restlessly around his bedchamber. No traces remained of his habitation here. He was ready to go, but he hadn't yet heard back from Gwendolyn. She was the only thing keeping him here. Where was she, *how* was she, was she all right?

A sudden tapping sound quickly brought him out into his front room and to the door. It was the porter.

"Young lady downstairs to see you, sir. Name of Miss Sherry Moo."

"Who—" Christopher broke off and grinned. He knew exactly who it was. Relief, and anticipation, and longing, and pain—all washed over him. "Thanks."

He went rapidly down the stairs, through the entry, and into the courtyard below. Gwendolyn stood near one of the railings. She was wearing a soft pink pelisse, the color of spring roses, with the embroidered hem of her white gown showing beneath, and a simple straw hat with bright green ribbons; her gloved hands were linked together at her waist and a reticule dangled from one slim wrist. He caught his breath. God, she was lovely. And God, how he'd missed her.

Gwendolyn smiled as she caught sight of him walking

to her and he felt his heart kick hard in his chest. She came forward to meet him halfway and he smiled back, saying, "Hullo, Miss Moo."

Gwendolyn laughed. "I couldn't resist. The porter was so shocked that I wanted to come up. No women allowed, evidently."

"Well, I've heard a few rumors about women dressing as men and sneaking in."

"Good for them! What a silly rule. Oh, Christopher, I'm so happy to see you!"

"Likewise, *signorina*. Is your cheek all right? It looks a little—singed."

"Oh yes, I've put some salve on."

He looked at it consideringly. "It should heal up nicely."

"I think so too. In the meantime, I'll just tell everyone I got into a fight with pirates."

He laughed. "Do." Then, as he continued to look at her, with wonder and a kind of painful pleasure: "Is your hair different? It looks very fetching."

Her blue eyes went wide and rapidly she undid the ribbons of her straw bonnet and pulled it off, then did a little pirouette so that he could see her hair from all angles. "Yes," she said, "it's quite different."

"Very fetching indeed."

"Do you mean it?"

"Yes. It suits you."

She laughed again, and put her hat back on. "I'm glad you think so. Oh, how I've missed you! We have *so* much to talk about, my dear friend, but first—can you tell me— how did things go in Nottingham?"

"Better than I could have hoped."

"I'm so, so glad! I want to hear all about it, but the thing of it is, I've come to you on a matter of urgency."

Quickly he said, "What's wrong? Are you in difficulties?"

"Oh no, it's not me. It's—you see, I really didn't know what to do after I'd left—well, I was in a hack going back to the Egremont townhouse and I suddenly remembered that Tyndale had given me a note—I was in a bit of a hurry, you see, when he first gave it to me—and it was from you! I was never so glad to hear from anyone in my life!" Gwendolyn took a deep breath, her eyes searching his face. "Oh, Christopher, I hate to tell you this, but Helen's run off with de Montmorency."

"Has she? Why?"

"Well, I think it's possible he's coerced her into it."

"I wouldn't put it past him."

"No, nor would I. I don't really know for certain, but I still feel I ought to go after them, just in case Helen needs help. The Duchess has gone out of town, and so has Percy, and Lady Almira's sick in bed—it's all rather complicated, and it might be just a wild-goose chase, but—Christopher, would you come with me?"

"Of course."

"Oh, I *knew* you'd say yes!" Gwendolyn flung her arms around him and hugged him tightly. "*Thank* you!"

Christopher received her embrace with a shock of pleasure, wrapping his arms around her and wishing they could stay like this forever. The instant he felt her pull back he released her, relieved and glad to see her beaming up into his face. Still, he *had* to say, though he hated to:

"The Earl?"

Gwendolyn merely shook her head. "Just you and me, *ma sherry moo*."

She was very composed, very sure of herself, and so he didn't waste time arguing the point. "Just you and me," he repeated, and he couldn't help but like the sound of it.

She smiled. "How long will it take us to get to Bournemouth, do you suppose?"

"Six or seven hours, I suppose. We could go by carriage, or we could each ride a horse—but that might be rather arduous for you, *signorina*."

"Not a bit of it! Hugo and I used to go for very long rides out into the countryside and I enjoyed every minute. Hmmm." Gwendolyn paused, looking thoughtful. One of her gloved hands came up to toy with a lock of her newly short hair. And then onto her lovely face came a look of playful mischief. "I have an idea."

She told it to him, and he laughed. "Why not?"

A scant two hours later, Gwendolyn and Christopher, each on their own horse, had finally left London behind and were on the dusty Fulham Road, heading southwest in the bright warm light of a sunny afternoon. Christopher wore breeches, boots, and a dark blue, plainly cut jacket, and as for herself—

Why, she was wearing breeches, boots, and a deep red jacket, all of which belonged to one of the Egremont grooms. On her head was a tall black hat, and her hair was pulled back and pinned into a tiny, jaunty queue. She rode astride and sat in her saddle as naturally as if this was something she did every day, her hands in leather riding-gloves holding the reins loosely and comfortably. She looked over at Christopher, admiring the easy skill with which he rode—as he did always.

"Well," she said cheerfully, "we got out of London without my being unmasked. Oh, Christopher, isn't this fun? I mean, except for the worry about Helen, of course, but there's no use worrying just at the moment—we're doing the absolute best that we can. Unless you think we should be galloping?"

"No. They won't sail out today, it'll be too late by the

time they get to Bournemouth. And it would only exhaust the horses."

"Then I'm just going to enjoy the afternoon. Or is that horribly insensitive of me?" She looked at him a little anxiously. He certainly was handling the news about Helen's bolt with de Montmorency quite calmly. She saw that he was looking back at her with his dark brows drawn together a little, as if puzzled. He answered:

"Until we find them, we don't know what's really going on. So—as you've said—worrying isn't going to help."

Gwendolyn nodded. In that case, she was going to treasure every minute of this time with Christopher. "I feel very dashing dressed like this. Tall boots do make one want to swagger about, don't they?"

He smiled, and she was glad to see his frown fade away. She went on:

"Isn't Tyndale a gem? Not even a flicker of an eyelash when I asked him to find me some men's clothing."

"It *was* impressive. Do you suppose butlers practice being so impassive, or do you think it comes naturally?"

Gwendolyn giggled. "Maybe we can ask Tyndale sometime. I must say, it's a great deal easier riding this way, rather than having one's leg hooked over a pommel. I thought it would be! I've always longed to try it, especially after Diana and I read the most *riveting* novel which had the heroine dressing like a man, running away in the middle of the night, and stealing a horse from the nearest inn."

"Why was she running away?"

"Oh, her parents, who were dreadfully poor because the father had gambled away all their money, were going to force her to marry a rich old man. He had absolutely no hair, and he never changed his clothing and he stank of turnips, and also he had no teeth, *plus* he was a ghastly drunkard who had been married four times previously, and all of his wives had died under mysterious circumstances."

"He stank of turnips?"

"Yes, I daresay the author wanted to make completely sure her audience found the old man to be an undesirable suitor."

"I'd say she succeeded. You seem to remember him very well."

"Oh yes! He quite horrified us. Diana and I swore *we'd* run away too, if we ever found ourselves in a similar situation. Unlikely as that might be." Gwendolyn laughed. "And I remember the title page as if it were yesterday! *Escape from Castle Killarney.* In a very gloomy, medieval sort of typeface. I forgot to tell you that the heroine and her parents lived in a horrid old castle which was practically falling down from neglect—it was very damp and cold, there were cobwebs everywhere, the most awful draughts, and it even had an old moat which was swarming to the brim with rats."

"I hope there was a ghost."

"That *would* have been a nice touch. Unfortunately there wasn't a ghost, or even any old bones moldering in a forgotten cupboard. Maybe the author saved them for the next book. Christopher, tell me about Nottingham! I want to hear about Diana, and your father, and your stepmother, and—oh, *everything.*"

So as they rode he told her about his journey to Nottingham and what had transpired there. She listened joyfully, only intervening once to say, "That Dr. Baynes sounds so infuriating! I wonder you didn't kick him downstairs! But then, he was there to catch Diana, so I suppose it all worked out for the best. What happened after that?"

He went on, and when he was done, Gwendolyn gave a deep sigh of satisfaction. "I'm so very, very pleased, Christopher! And I'm so proud of you for going, especially when you couldn't know what would happen when you got there. How does it feel to have a brother?"

"I quite like it. I've never really known any babies before, but Jasper seems to me a splendid little man. Yells like anything when he's hungry. Cora says he's a perfect trencherman."

Gwendolyn laughed. "Good for him! Oh, Cora sounds so nice. I'm so happy for your father."

"As am I. And what about you, *signorina*? What's happened since I went away?"

There was so much to tell Christopher. The best of friends, who would listen to anything she could possibly say, without judgment or censure. "Quite a lot has happened, *ma sherry moo*," she said, and started with the influenza that had been afflicting so many in the Egremont townhouse, then went on to the evening at Carlton House last night, and quite literally running into the Prince Regent (which made Christopher laugh), and finding Helen and Rupert, and hitting Rupert with a vase (to which he emphatically said *Bravo*), and Monsieur de Montmorency arriving in a very timely fashion (he gave a low whistle when she told him about the knife), and then the express from poor Philip Thane in Great Yarmouth, and the Duchess hurrying to him, and the accident with Lizzie and the curling-tongs, and then finding the note Helen had left behind, and after that . . .

She stopped.

Christopher said, "Is there more?"

"Oh yes." Gwendolyn hardly knew how to begin this next part of the story, so she pulled off the riding-glove on her left hand and held it out for him to see, watching the swift gravity come into Christopher's expression, the look of astonishment and deep concern.

He looked at her hand and then into her face.

Slowly he said, "If he's hurt you, I swear to God I'll—"

"No," she quickly broke in. "No, it's not like that at all. I'm the one who's ended it."

"You," he said, still in that slow, careful voice. "*You* ended your engagement?"

"Yes."

"Why?"

Gwendolyn put her glove back on, and looked again at him, into that interesting, delightful, unforgettable face which had become as familiar to her as her own. Many, many times had she drawn it in her sketchbook while he had been gone. How much comfort she'd gotten from that! "Christopher, you knew, didn't you—about the Countess. That evening she came to the townhouse for the first time, and you looked so—so stunned and unhappy. You realized that I look a great deal like her. *Too* much like her."

"Yes," he answered quietly. "Are you angry with me for not saying anything? Did I do wrong?"

"To own the truth, I'm not sure I *could* have seen it, even if you'd told me. I wouldn't have wanted to see it! I was so wrapped up in what I *thought* the Earl was like, and in what *he* thought of *me*, that it was like living in a very odd fairy tale—quite disconnected from the real world. It took me a while to figure it all out, to see things clearly. So no, I'm not at all angry with you, *ma sherry moo*, and moreover, I'm so grateful for you. You reminded me how much I value honesty—because of *your* honesty."

"I'm glad to hear you say that, *signorina*. It nearly killed me, keeping silent. Are you . . ."

He hesitated, and Gwendolyn said:

"Am I what?"

"Are you very sad?"

She thought about it. "Well, for just a tiny bit I was—I think it was the relinquishing of a bright, shiny, foolish little dream. If that makes sense? Seeing the Earl at Almack's for the very first time, and seeing him looking at me so glowingly—I believe we each of us fell in love with appearances—or with an *idea* of what love is—not with an actual person. It's rather embarrassing to admit, but looking back, I—well—I fell for a pretty face. And I think he did, too. Perhaps that might sustain him for a lifetime—that kind of superficial adoration—but it wouldn't me. It had already begun to pall, in fact, though I hardly realized it."

"When did you get your first inkling?"

"I think it must have been the day I had tea with the Westenburys. Oh, Christopher, it was so awful, and in so many ways! I'll laugh about it someday, but for right now I'm just so thankful for my narrow escape. At any rate, that evening I was in my room, drawing—doodling, really, without really noticing what I was doing—and when I looked at my drawing, I saw that I'd drawn a rather odd wedding scene."

"Why was it odd?"

"Because I created a scene with the Earl, the Countess, Rupert, all the Westenbury sisters, and a minister—even a flying unicorn!—but somehow I'd left myself out of the drawing. A wedding without a bride. Deep down, I think I already knew that something was very wrong."

Christopher nodded, looking thoughtful, and after that they fell into an easy, companionable silence alternating with idle talk of this and that, the hours seeming to swiftly go by as they passed through Camberley, Hartley Wintney, East Stratton, Eastleigh, and Totton, and then into a forest through which the road twisted and turned, as sinuous as a snake. They met few travelers now.

"Once we're out of these woods," said Christopher, "we'll nearly be there. How are you holding up, *signorina*?"

"Oh, I'm fine. It really is so much easier riding astride. Very unfair to women to be consigned to the sidesaddle! After today, I'll always want to ride this way. But actually, there *is* one thing . . ."

"Yes?"

"Well, it's—in *Escape from Castle Killarney*, the heroine rides from midnight till evening the next day to get away from her horrid parents and equally horrid suitor. She gallops the whole time, which, now that I think of it, doesn't make any sense at all, because no horse can do that, but also, she never stops once to—ah—relieve herself, which no woman would do! It's curious how I never thought about it at the time, but, of course, when you're completely caught up in the story, you just don't. So, *ma sherry moo*, what would a man do in this situation?"

"Go behind a tree."

"That's what I'll do, then. Hold my reins, will you, please?" She slid off her horse.

He grinned at her and took the reins. "Gwennie, you're pluck to the backbone."

Playfully Gwendolyn lifted up her tall black hat and swept him a bow. "Thank you, kind sir! And now, if you'll excuse me—"

She turned away and went some little distance into the woods, grateful for all those marvelously tall concealing trees.

Christopher waited for Gwendolyn. Within him reverberated the incredible news of her broken engagement, like a drumbeat, over and over again.

I'm the one who's ended it.

I'm the one who's ended it.

A wild surge of happiness rolled through him.

He didn't know what would happen next.

All he knew was that life had changed—suddenly and unexpectedly, and, from his perspective, infinitely for the better.

As he waited, it came to him that the afternoon was waning, and that here, in this dense woodland, dusk came early. Everything seemed to have gone still and silent, and a creeping gray-green shadow had fallen upon them, blurring the demarcation between road and forest, trees and sky.

Tra cane e lupo, he thought. *Between dog and wolf.* Mauro's expression for this eerie time bridging day and night, when an inability to distinguish between the two could be not only dangerous, but fatal.

Just then, from behind him, came the sound of horses, and men's voices—raised, laughing, with the kind of rollicking, sloppy good cheer that could rapidly turn bellicose, a tenor with which he was all too familiar from his experiences in various *osterias* and *tavernas*. Drunk, he thought, quickly turning the horses around to face them, and perhaps three or four in number.

They came around the bend, their horses cantering, and he saw that he was right.

Four men, laborers and townsmen by their dress, all broad and brawny, and plainly inebriated.

Christopher felt himself tensing, his every sense on the alert, but kept his breathing relaxed and steady. He resisted the urge to turn his head to where Gwendolyn had gone among the trees, very glad that she was nowhere in sight, and through sheer force of his will tried to tell her to remain so.

The men pulled up, eyeing him with a kind of riotous, greedy speculation.

"Ooh, a *nob*," one said, slurring, and another chimed in: "Extra horse, eh? Nice little mare, that."

The third one said, "You don't need it, do you, guv?"

"You don't need *two*, m'lord, you can walk, can'tcha?"

The first one said, as if struck by a bright idea: "Ooh, we can sell 'em in Bournemouth, then."

"Split the money three ways."

"Oi! There's four of us, jingle-brains!"

"Who're you calling a jingle-brains, you climp!"

"*I* am. Want to make something of it?"

"Aye, by crikey, I do!"

"Shut up, you lot!" roared the first man. "Let's take the horses and be on our way."

He'd be damned if he let their horses be stolen, Christopher thought. Four against one: not his favorite odds, but so be it. He'd fight if he had to, but first . . . He said, injecting into his voice an obvious nervousness, "Going to Bournemouth, are you? I wouldn't go that way, if I were you."

"Why not?" demanded the first man. "Got every right to go there!"

"Yes, of course, but—I've just come that way—oh well, never mind," said Christopher, looking behind him as if highly uneasy. "It's just that—no, I'm sure I was wrong."

"What? What is it? Tell us, damn it, or we'll beat it out of you!"

"Robbers?" chimed in another one of the men, oblivious to the irony of his question.

Christopher gestured at the riderless horse next to him. In a low, nervous tone he said, "It's like this. My friend Gwyn—he'd fallen a little behind, you see. I didn't think anything of it, because he's not a very good rider, not like you lads—"

A couple of the men nodded proudly. "Well, go on, what happened?" said one.

"I heard a strange noise coming from the woods. At first I thought it was just an owl, but then Gwyn—he gave a terrible shriek—I turned around, quick as anything, and he was *gone*." Christopher closed his eyes as if in horrified anguish. *"Gone,"* he repeated shakily, opening his eyes again to find his audience listening with pleasing attentiveness.

"Couldn't have been an owl," said one of the men. "An owl couldn't carry off a man."

"Might've been a *big* owl," put in another, looking a little worriedly around him.

"No owl's big enough for that, you lobcock."

"You sure it was an owl you heard, guv?" said one, trying to focus his rather blurry gaze on Christopher.

"It *sounded* like it," he replied, keeping his voice nervous, tremulous, "but I suppose it couldn't have been, really, because as soon as I heard it, lads, I felt a dreadful prickling at the back of my neck—"

"Old Blue Alvin!" exclaimed one of the men, and the others murmured uneasily, starting to look around them too.

Christopher gave a theatrical start and clapped a hand to his nape. "Old Blue Alvin—who on God's earth is that?"

"He's feeling it again! The prickles!"

"Old Blue Alvin, guv—ain't you never heard of him? The meanest, ugliest boggart in all of Hampshire!"

"Took three of my sister's best chickens, he did, and just two days ago!"

"Aye, and a goat went missing from Jud Clark's *last night*."

Earnestly another man put in, "Did you happen to see the blue smoke, guv, when you turned about?"

"My God, I did," said Christopher in a horrified way. "Rising straight up from Gwyn's empty saddle!"

The men all exchanged nervous glances.

"Old Blue Alvin can take the shape of any animal he likes," said one man, rather apprehensively. "Everybody knows that."

"You mean," Christopher responded very loudly, "like a giant owl with deadly claws?"

"Aye," whispered another of the men, putting a hand to the back of *his* neck, and just then, floating through the air, as if from high above them, came a long, low, hooting sound.

"It's *him*!" hissed the man, his hand flying to his mouth, his eyes going round with terror. *"Old Blue Alvin!"*

"Surely—surely not," stammered Christopher, by now enjoying himself very much. "It's just—just a regular owl, lads, isn't it?"

"Whoo hoo," came the disembodied sound again. *"Hoo . . . hoo . . . hoo."*

"That ain't no regular owl!" exclaimed one of the men, horrified. "It sounds almost like a person, by crikey!"

"Oh my *God*," said Christopher. "Old Blue Alvin's finished with Gwyn, and now he's hungry again!"

"Well, he ain't getting *me*! I'm going back to Totton, and double-quick!"

"I am too!" declared another of the men, and wheeled his horse about.

"Wait!" Christopher said in an anguished voice. "Don't leave me behind, lads! Wait for me!"

From above them came the eerie disembodied sound, noticeably shaky this time: *"Hoo . . . hoo . . . hoo."*

"Old Blue Alvin's getting *mad*!" shrieked one of the men, and another one added shrilly, "Sorry, guv, you're on your own!"

Then they were all galloping away, back toward Totton, and in very short order had disappeared from sight.

Christopher, his shoulders shaking with laughter, rode his horse, with Gwendolyn's alongside, into the woods where he'd last seen her.

"Oi!" said Gwendolyn, from high above his head. "So I'm a bad rider, am I?"

He looked up. There she was in a tree, standing on a limb and one arm curled firmly around the trunk.

"I had to set the scene," he explained, grinning. "By the way, your hooting was getting shaky toward the end."

"It's hard to hoot convincingly when you're trying not to laugh."

"By crikey, it is."

Then she did laugh, and began to climb down.

"Need any help?" he said.

"I'll let you know." Nimbly she descended, branch by branch, limb by limb, and finally jumped the last five or six feet, landing lightly on the ground. Dusting off her palms with a satisfied air, she said, "Well, I must say, it's reassuring to know that I can still climb trees. And my hat didn't even come off! I'm quite pleased with myself."

"As well you should be, *signorina*. And thank you for pitching in at just the right moment."

"You gave me the perfect cue. Oh, Christopher, you were marvelous! I was so frightened at first, but then I saw how splendidly you alarmed them!"

"You can never be too cautious when Old Blue Alvin's around."

She giggled and got back onto her horse. They made their way onto the road again, and resumed their journey to Bournemouth. And Christopher saw how the levity left Gwendolyn the closer they got, to be replaced with concern, anxiety, and that puzzling look of resignation.

Chapter 17

───────❦───────

They arrived in Bournemouth just as full darkness was beginning to descend. The town was extraordinarily crowded with people, horses, carriages everywhere. An inquiry at the first inn to which they came elicited the news from an ostler that a countrywide nautical festival was in full swing.

To Christopher, Gwendolyn said in a low voice, "The Earl told me that de Montmorency's been here many times before. Wouldn't he want to stay at the finest inn?"

He nodded. "I can't imagine him going anywhere else."

Gwendolyn said to the ostler: "Could you tell us, please, where we can find the best inn in Bournemouth?"

"This here's the best one, sir. Practically no fleas in the beds, and the sheets aired once a month, see?"

"It does sound very nice," she said tactfully, "but the thing is, we're looking for one of those stiff-rumped, prinked-up nobs—the sort who carries around his own bed-sheets and demands a private parlor because the common room's beneath his touch."

"Ah! One of them gorgers! *They* all stay at the Lion's Head, sir, and a pretty penny they pay for it, too."

He obligingly gave them directions, Christopher tossed him a coin, and they continued on their way.

"Stiff-rumped, prinked-up nobs?" he said to her with a grin. "That's a fine vocabulary you've got there, lad."

"Whenever Percy and Francis would come home on holiday, they trotted out all sorts of interesting terms they'd picked up at school," she said, smiling back at him, but all too soon felt her smile fade. How *could* Christopher be so calm, so lighthearted, when Helen was—perhaps even at this moment—in de Montmorency's arms? She went on, trying to match him for calmness, "What if they're not at the Lion's Head?"

"We can only do our best, *signorina*, as you pointed out. Let's take it one step at a time."

Shortly they came to a large, handsome inn fronting the harbor, which itself was crowded with cutters, ketches, yachts, and dinghies of all makes and sizes. They went into the capacious yard, leaving their horses with an ostler who agreed to feed and care for them, but warned:

"You'll not find a room here, gents, nor likely anywhere else. The town's full up this week with the festival and all."

Christopher nodded, gave him a coin, and together he and Gwendolyn passed into the inn's front room which—not unexpectedly—was crowded too. A neatly dressed, middle-aged man bustled up to greet them and introduce himself as the proprietor, and Christopher said:

"We're looking for a friend of ours. A Monsieur de Montmorency, who'd have arrived within the past few hours."

"Aye, sir, he's been here—insisted on his favorite room, too. I had to remove a gentleman from Shropshire, and he was none too pleased about it, neither! But as I said to him, private-like, the *m'soo*'s not somebody to cross, not if you value your own peace of mind, and he took my meaning right away, sir, and went away meek as a lamb."

Gwendolyn's heart was beating hard in her chest. "Was there a lady with Monsieur de Montmorency?"

"Not that I saw, sir."

She shot a troubled, anxious look at Christopher, who calmly said to the proprietor:

"Where is Monsieur de Montmorency? We'd like to see him."

"Not here, sir, at the moment. But he bespoke a private parlor for nine o'clock, and dinner, too."

"We'll wait."

"It's past eight, sir, so you've not long to cool your heels. Drink?"

"Can you bring it to us here? We'd like to see him as soon as he arrives."

"To be sure, sir, what would you like?"

"Ale for me. Gwyn?" He turned to her inquiringly.

"The same."

The proprietor nodded, and hurried off, soon to return bearing two tankards filled to the brim. With a word of thanks Gwendolyn took the tankard he held out to her, as did Christopher, who lightly clinked his tankard against hers.

"Alla vostra salute, signorina."

"To your health as well, *ma sherry moo.*" Cautiously Gwendolyn sipped at her ale. A bittersweet tang, a hint of malt and caramel, and very refreshing. "It's good," she said, surprised, and had a few more sips, realizing only now just how thirsty she'd been.

She watched as Christopher nodded and took a long swallow from his own tankard.

How easy and confident he was, how solid and capable. And what a wonderful companion. Had he been appalled when she proposed they travel with her clad in men's clothing? Did he make a great silly fuss about her climbing a tree, or insist that he help her down, as if she were nothing more than a piece of delicate china about to break? Did he protest, shocked, when she wanted a glass of ale, too?

No, not Christopher.

She wished, suddenly and with all her heart, that this splendid adventure need never end.

But it must and it would, she thought with a deep, deep sigh.

"What's wrong, *signorina*?"

"I—oh—" How selfish of her to be feeling sorry for herself, and at such a time! Quickly she went on, "Where do you think Helen is?"

"We'll find out soon enough."

"I suppose, but—oh, Christopher, what if—what if de Montmorency comes at you with that knife of his?"

"Don't worry, I'll hit him with the nearest vase," he said, and she could only wonder all over again at his cheerfulness.

She put a hand on his arm. "Promise me you'll be careful."

He smiled at her. "I will."

"All right then," she said, and reluctantly took her hand away, then sipped again at her tankard. A small bench near them came empty, and they took it, each of them turned to face the entrance. It was comforting to sit so close to Christopher, with her leg pressed up against his, their shoulders touching, but as the minutes ticked by Gwendolyn felt her nerves tightening, recalling Helen's blotchy note all over again:

I Have to Go—I MUST go.

People came in, people went out.

None of them anybody they knew.

She drank her ale, she fidgeted, jiggled her booted feet, plucked at her neckcloth, readjusted the tall black hat.

I Have to Go—I MUST go.

Finally, just when Gwendolyn's restlessness, her fear, was getting to the point where she might just have gotten up to go blindly searching for them through the town, the bells of a church clock somewhere began to peal, and two familiar people came into the front room.

One was Helen, in her favorite green riding-dress with the long train looped up behind, and the other was Étienne de Montmorency in exquisitely tailored buff pantaloons and a dark jacket, his white neckcloth as crisp, as artfully formed, as if he had recently risen from his dressing-table. He had no hand at Helen's elbow, forcing her inside, but her face was set and pale. On *his* face was a look of subtle satisfaction.

Gwendolyn registered all this in a flash, then jumped to her feet and went to meet them, with Christopher at her side. She watched as Helen's vivid green eyes came to her. They went wide, wide, her jaw fell slack, and she choked out in her gruff little voice:

"Francis!"

And then she swayed on her feet, her eyes closed, and she went limp.

De Montmorency managed to grab her by the armpits before she hit the floor, and stood there looking both awkward and annoyed. As he made no move to do anything further, Christopher went to them and said:

"Can I help?"

Coolly de Montmorency replied, as if it was no surprise at all to encounter Christopher and herself in a Bournemouth inn quite a long way from London, "By all means, Mr. Beck, *merci*. My wife's proportions, being noble, hinder me from lifting her wholesale."

"Wife?" gasped Gwendolyn.

"Indeed yes, Mademoiselle Penhallow—for I perceive

it is you, not one of your brothers—we have just this minute come from the church. Mr. Beck, may I suggest that you convey Madame de Montmorency to my private parlor? I fear we are too much a vulgar object of interest to the *hoi polloi*."

Christopher lifted Helen into his arms and followed de Montmorency down a passageway leading from the front room. Gwendolyn, stunned, trailed behind them. They all went inside and carefully Christopher placed Helen onto a long bench near the fire. She was already coming round; her eyes fluttered open and she glanced in confusion at the three of them, her gaze coming to fix on Gwendolyn with something that looked like horror.

Coolly de Montmorency said, from the chair into which he had lowered himself and now sat with one leg elegantly crossed over the other:

"Not Francis, my dear Helen, but Mademoiselle Penhallow. Certainly a striking resemblance, *n'est-ce pas?*"

"Not—*not* Francis?" muttered Helen, struggling to sit up. "I thought—"

Quickly Gwendolyn went to her to help, but in a spasmodic gesture Helen pushed at her shoulder, with the very hand upon whose fourth finger glimmered a wide gold band. "Get away from me!"

Gwendolyn took several steps backwards, as much from the sudden hatred in Helen's voice as from her roughness in pushing her away. As she did a waiter came into the room and bowed toward de Montmorency.

"Ready for your dinner, *m'soo*? And for four now, is it?"

"No, you had best put it off. You may instead bring us some brandy."

"Certainly, *m'soo*," said the waiter, and withdrew.

De Montmorency glanced at Gwendolyn and Christopher. "Deeply does it pain me to be inhospitable, but I do not believe that among the four of us it would be—shall we say—a convivial meal. Under no circumstances do I dine where there is discord. It is, *vous voyez*, repugnant to a true gastronome such as myself."

Helen had by now sat up. To Gwendolyn she said, with a snarl in her voice, "What do you mean by dressing in that foul way? And what have you done to your hair? You look *ghastly*."

"I believe," intervened Monsieur de Montmorency in that same cool manner, "it seemed an expeditious strategy by which to pursue us. Is that not so, Mademoiselle Penhallow?"

"More or less," she answered, rather blankly.

He nodded. "Do sit down," he said to her and to Christopher, as civilly as might any host in his own drawing-room, and when they did, he went on, looking at Helen, "Am I correct in now assuming that you left behind a note?"

"Yes," she answered sullenly, as might a recalcitrant child admit to wrongdoing.

"I could wish you had a trifle more diligently followed my instructions, my dear Helen, but it hardly matters now."

De Montmorency reached into an inside pocket of his jacket and Gwendolyn tensed, afraid that he was reaching for that deadly little knife of his. But he only produced from the pocket a neatly folded, sealed paper which he set on the table next to his chair. "A letter for the Duchess. Perhaps the two of you might take it with you upon your return to London, and save me the trouble of posting it?"

Gwendolyn looked over at Christopher. His expression was entirely inscrutable; it was impossible to tell how he was taking the news of Helen's marriage. He said calmly to de Montmorency:

"Yes. We can do that."

"Thank you. Mademoiselle Penhallow, did you think I meant to do you or Mr. Beck violence just now?"

"What a perfectly splendid idea," put in Helen, with a certain vicious enthusiasm, and de Montmorency said to her:

"How savage you are, my dear Helen, in your speech. I do hope that—in time—you will learn to refrain from issuing boorish remarks such as this."

A silence descended. De Montmorency sat swinging one of his feet gently back and forth, his expression now rather amused; Helen, huddled into a corner of the bench, eyes downcast and her face very red, turned the gold ring on her finger round and round; Christopher, Gwendolyn saw, was looking at *her*, and finally, spurred on by a kind of righteous indignation on his behalf, she burst out:

"How did you persuade a vicar to marry you, and at this time of night? Is it even legal?"

"A lavish donation to the parish fund helped greatly to ease Mr. Biddlecombe's natural reluctance at being roused so late," said de Montmorency, "and as for the legality of our union, I had, of course, in my possession a special license."

Gwendolyn was a little daunted, but stuck to her guns. "You certainly didn't have the Duke's permission."

"If you will but search your memory a trifle, Mademoiselle Penhallow, you will thus recall that Helen is twenty-one, and requires no such permission in order to wed."

He was right. All too right. Finally, clutching at straws, Gwendolyn said, "But I thought—I thought you had . . ."

De Montmorency laughed softly. "Carried Helen off against her will?"

"Well—yes."

"Really, *mademoiselle*, I am almost—almost!—insulted that you would believe me capable of such crass methods.

No, when last night I suggested to Helen that we might find it to our mutual benefit to join ourselves in marriage, and as soon as possible, she responded with what I can only describe as flattering agreement."

"But the note!" Gwendolyn persisted. "Helen, you cried over it!"

At this Helen looked up and scowled. "I was crying about having to leave my horse behind. And those stupid grooms *will* give him more oats than is good for him!"

It was so plausible an explanation that Gwendolyn found herself wanting to crazily laugh, but instead said, as steadily as she could, "I'll—I'll talk to them myself if you like."

Helen only shrugged coldly.

"So, as you must have already concluded, my friends," said de Montmorency, "your precipitous journey here was, alas, all for nothing. Ah! Here is our brandy. I would infinitely have preferred to call for champagne, so that you might join us in a toast to celebrate our newfound felicity, but a chivalrous impulse made brandy seem more suitable. It would hardly be appropriate to drink champagne in the aftermath of an hysterical collapse, however brief."

But it was only de Montmorency who accepted from the waiter anything to drink, and when the waiter had again left the parlor, he sat very calmly sipping his brandy. Another silence fell, broken at last when he said in a meditative way:

"An inferior beverage, this, and very possibly doctored to produce the amber color that is, *bien sûr*, so desirable in a quality product. How pleasing it will be to return home and restock my cellars with true Armagnac brandy."

She had been correct, Gwendolyn thought, that their destination was France. Well, it was impossible to deny that de Montmorency was right; their journey *had* been in vain. Resignedly she said, "When do you leave?"

"Let's go *now*," said Helen to de Montmorency. "I'm sick of this foul inn, and everyone in it." She shot a malevolent look at Gwendolyn as she spoke.

"While I applaud your gratifying expeditiousness, I fear we cannot sail at this hour," de Montmorency replied. "But you have, I think, made a worthwhile suggestion which would benefit us all. Mademoiselle Penhallow, as you obviously cannot return to London tonight, I propose that you take the room which Madame de Montmorency and I were to share. You will doubtless find no other accommodations in Bournemouth and I can, at least, assure you that the sheets will not be unduly damp. Furthermore, I consign to you and Mr. Beck our dinner. My wife and I shall immediately decamp to my yacht where we will find ourselves ensconced in the utmost comfort, and my chef shall prepare for us a meal which, I may say with confidence, will likely surpass your own. *En fait*, I wonder I didn't think of it myself," he went on, still in that thoughtful manner. "My yacht in all respects will be preferable. Still, one cannot, under these unusual circumstances, think of everything, so I will waste no time in foolish self-recrimination. And now, I shall bestir myself to find my man Pierre-Édouard, to alert him as to our change in plans." Languidly he rose to his feet, pausing for a moment to look in a glass hung on one wall. "I observe that my neckcloth was disarranged as I attempted to catch you, my dear Helen. How very distressing. My appearance now smacks painfully of the uncouth. *Tant pis*, it cannot at the present moment be helped. If you will excuse me, *s'il vous plaît*, I shall very shortly return."

Gwendolyn sat for a few seconds absorbing this masterly speech, then jumped up and hurried after de Montmorency, swiftly catching up to him in the corridor. She took hold of him by the arm and he swung around at once. They were nearly of a height, and very calmly did he look into her eyes.

"Why?" Gwendolyn said, low and fierce. "Why did you do it? I don't believe she loves you, or that you love her."

"Oh no," he answered equably. "You are quite right, *mademoiselle*. To put it in the simplest of terms, I need money, and Helen—*eh bien*, Helen requires shelter from the storm. It seems to me a wonderfully benign transaction."

"What storm? I don't understand."

With a tinge of cynical amusement in his voice, he said, "Is it possible, *mademoiselle*, that you have failed to observe the unhappiness that rages within her? And you draw no inference from her reaction upon thinking you to be your brother Francis?"

Gwendolyn drew in a sharp breath. "You mean it's *Francis* she cares for? But he—why, he's clearly not at all interested in her that way!"

"Exactement."

"I thought—I thought she liked Christopher!"

"A stratagem, however clumsy and limited in scope, to evoke in Francis the response of a jealous lover. It failed, and spectacularly so, which is why she was not displeased to receive my proposal. Indeed, she welcomed it as her— if this is not too extravagant a word—salvation."

"Be good to her, *monsieur*," said Gwendolyn fiercely.

"I shall endeavor to do my best. I don't dislike her, you know. And I believe that I understand her. Too, you may be pleased to learn that in my letter to the Duchess I have begged her permission to have Helen's horse transported to my estate."

"That's something, at least."

"These are faint, very faint words of praise, but none-theless I welcome them in the spirit of amity. And may I extend to you my felicitations, *mademoiselle*?"

"Felicitations? What for?"

"On noticing the absence of both your pearl ring and the Earl himself, I have deduced that you and he are no longer betrothed."

"That's right. We're not. I broke it off earlier today."

"Hence my felicitations. It was my private opinion, at the very outset, that you were far too good for Julian, who is possessed of—how can I put it least offensively?—a pedestrian mind. You are, I believe, well shut of him, *mademoiselle*. *Enfin*, if you will kindly release from your surprisingly strong grip my poor arm—*merci beaucoup*—I shall be on my way." He bowed slightly, pleasantly, and strolled away down the corridor.

Christopher sat in one chair, Gwendolyn, looking pensive, even downcast, in another. They had the private parlor to themselves now; after some rather awkward farewells, de Montmorency and Helen were gone, off to board his yacht, there to spend the night and leave at sunrise the next morning. The fire, crackling and popping cheerfully in the parlor's hearth, was for some time the only sound in the room. Finally Gwendolyn said to him:

"Christopher, are you—are you dreadfully upset?"

"Am I upset that we didn't arrive in time to stop the marriage? I don't see how we could have, *signorina*. It seems clear that Helen wanted to marry de Montmorency."

"No, I mean—" Gwendolyn swallowed and went on in a strained voice, "I mean because Helen married some-one else."

Christopher looked hard at her. "Why would that bother

me? That is, I hope she'll be happy, but . . ." He trailed off. Into his mind came rushing little, baffling memories from these past weeks.

Gwendolyn, at Vauxhall: *Do you want to dance with Helen?* And then, a little later: *Should I feel guilty for taking you away from Helen?*

At Hyde Park, discussing Lady Jersey's evening-party later that day, Gwendolyn, with an odd, earnest look of resignation on her face: *Shall I make sure Helen knows you're going?*

And the next day, when he had gone early to the Egremont townhouse, to tell Gwendolyn he was leaving for Nottingham, and after Helen barely lifted her head from her breakfast to say goodbye, Gwendolyn saying, with obvious distress: *I'm so sorry about Helen.*

Christopher said, "Good God, Gwennie, is it possible—do you think I'm in love with her?"

Her eyes wide, Gwendolyn answered quickly, "Well, yes! The way you look at her, Christopher! So—well—*tenderly.* And all the time, de Montmorency says, she was in love with Francis! Which means she was only *using* you."

Christopher sat back in his chair, taking all this in. Helen, it seemed, had been doing her best to flirt with him, in a bid to get Francis's attention. To which he, Christopher, laughably oblivious to her agenda, had responded with all the simple courtesy he could muster. Meanwhile, Gwendolyn had believed he cared for Helen and had—with kindness, with sweetness, with generosity—been doing *her* best to promote the match. Lord, what a tangle. And the sooner unraveled, the better. Slowly he said to Gwendolyn:

"I wasn't in love with her. I never was. To own the truth, I felt sorry for her."

"Sorry for her?" echoed Gwendolyn. "That's what I saw in your face? Pity?"

"Yes. I sensed, perhaps, a little of her desperate struggle."

"You're not angry that she tried to deceive you?"

He shook his head. "No harm done—to me at least."

"Oh, Christopher, I've been so worried! All this time I thought Helen was going to break your heart!"

"She didn't. She won't." There was more he could say on the subject of his heart, but not now. Not now. In this moment, he was happy to be here with Gwendolyn. Happy to see the burden she'd been carrying lift away, the strain disappear, and to see her smile at him—in that singularly bright, sweet smile of hers not a shadow of anxiety now, or strain, or fear.

"Well, thank goodness!" she exclaimed, joy in her voice. "I'm so glad you're all right, *ma sherry moo*!" Then she leaned back comfortably in her own chair and stretched out her booted feet toward the fire. "Well! What a day this has been! Quite the longest day of my life, I think! What do we do now?"

He looked at her and smiled. "I think we should have dinner."

"Oh, yes, let's! I'm starving, aren't you?"

"Ravenous, *signorina*," he said, and went to get the waiter, and before too long he and Gwendolyn were sitting cozily at the table in what was now their very own private parlor, a veritable feast spread out between them, and so they ate, and drank, and talked, and laughed, well into the wee hours of the morning.

Chapter 18

With luxurious slowness Gwendolyn drifted up, up, into wakefulness, conscious of a wonderful feeling of well-being. Of being rested. Renewed. She had slept deeply and dreamlessly, without, she thought, stirring at all.

She turned onto her side and opened her eyes.

With a curious lack of surprise she saw Christopher. He lay three or four feet away in this large bed, still asleep, on his side as well and facing her. He was wearing his shirt from yesterday, open at the neck, revealing a little of the strong planes of his chest, and his long dark hair lay in gorgeous disarray about his face and on his pillow. Drowsily she admired the strong line of his jaw, a little shadowed with new beard, his dark lashes and brows, the sturdy column of his throat.

It was strange, but somehow she hadn't quite noticed—hadn't really appreciated—just how remarkably attractive he was. Uniquely distinguished, yes, and very good-looking, and definitely appealing, especially when she factored in his intelligence, his kindness, his honesty, his courage and his steadiness—but for some reason she hadn't, before, quite put it all together.

And there was another thing.

She was struck by how natural it felt to see him there.

It *shouldn't* have felt natural, to be in a bed with a man. But it wasn't just any man—it was Christopher.

She liked knowing that she could, if she wanted, reach out her hand and touch him.

Last night—or, rather, earlier this morning—she had insisted he share the room with her. Share the bed. *What, go off and sleep in the stables?* teasingly she had told him. *Absolutely not. Old Blue Alvin might get you.*

It had all happened without any silly awkwardness or discomfort. They had kept on their shirts and their breeches, she had climbed into bed, Christopher had blown out the candles and gotten in as well. They had said goodnight, just as if that was something they did all the time, and that was the last thing she remembered.

As if sensing her gaze upon him, Christopher stirred. Opened his eyes. Saw her, and smiled.

"Buongiorno, signorina."

"Good morning, *ma sherry moo.*"

"Come va?"

"Very well, *grazie.* And you?"

"Likewise." Christopher stretched, and lazily ran a hand through his hair. "God, did I sleep."

"So did I."

"Good. We both needed it, I think. Well, *signorina*, what's our plan?"

She thought. "Let's go check on the horses, to make sure they're all right. After that, breakfast. I'm hungry again! And then . . . oh, Christopher, wouldn't it be great fun to go on jaunting about like this? Outwitting robbers and climbing trees? But I think we should go directly back to London. I don't like to leave Lady Almira alone for much longer. And I don't even know how to break the news to her about Helen."

"We'll figure that out," he said, "when the time comes," and it occurred to Gwendolyn how much she liked his use of the word *we*.

"Yes," she said confidently, "we will." She smiled at him, he smiled back, and so their day began. After breakfast they stopped briefly at the water's edge, where the harbormaster confirmed that de Montmorency's yacht had indeed sailed away at daybreak.

"That's that, then," said Gwendolyn, and looked at Christopher. "On to London?"

"On to London," he confirmed, and they got onto their horses and rode away from Bournemouth. Their journey, this time, was uneventful, perhaps a little to Gwendolyn's regret. But she was glad when, arriving back at the Egremont townhouse where she quickly changed into a gown and slippers, she stopped in to see Lady Almira and found her no worse, and perhaps even a trifle improved in health.

"Tyndale's managed the whole thing beautifully," Gwendolyn said to Christopher, who had been waiting for her downstairs in the drawing-room. "Lady Almira has no idea that I was away, or that Helen's gone, or that Cousin Judith is in Great Yarmouth with Philip."

"Ignorance being a sort of bliss, I suppose, if only temporarily. Tyndale's had tea brought in. Would you like some?"

"Yes, please, with one of those little iced cakes. Thank you very much." She sat down next to him on the sofa and took the plate and cup he held out to her.

"You're welcome, *signorina*. Oh, and here's de Montmorency's letter to the Duchess." He pulled from his jacket pocket the letter, then set it on the table next to the tea-tray.

"Oh yes, I'll send it on to her right away, with a letter of my own. Thank you, Christopher." Thoughtfully she ate the little cake, and sipped at her tea. "I've been thinking that we should wait to say anything to Lady Almira until we've heard from Cousin Judith. Or does that seem unfair to Lady Almira?"

"No—if you think she won't notice their absence."

"I don't believe she will. She's anxious that they not visit her and risk getting ill again. So that buys us a little time." Gwendolyn put her plate on the table and turned to face him. "Christopher, if it's not a horrible inconvenience to you, would you mind very much staying in Town for a while longer? At least until we know how Philip is, and that Lady Almira can handle all this news."

"I don't mind at all."

Gwendolyn felt herself smiling with both relief and pleasure. "*Thank* you, *ma sherry moo*! I can't tell you how—how *comfortable* that will be."

And it was.

Over the next several days, Christopher spent a great deal of time at the Egremont townhouse, patiently waiting for Gwendolyn to emerge from Lady Almira's room and go with him for a walk or a ride, or to have nuncheon or tea together, or to play chess or simply talk. Day by day Lady Almira improved; and just as she began to speak of rising at last from her sickbed, an express came from Great Yarmouth.

Philip's surgery had been successful, wrote the Duchess, and he was recovering so well that she hoped to bring him to London within the week, where he might continue to convalesce under the watchful eye of the family's own doctor. Helen's elopement was shocking, but one must, she said philosophically, hope for the best, adding that she had sent a notice to the *Gazette* announcing the marriage, which (the announcement would say) had been privately celebrated due to an illness in the family—thereby quashing any ripples of scandal which might otherwise threaten to rise. As for telling Almira, the Duchess went on, she had full confidence in Gwendolyn and Christopher's judgment; she only asked they emphasize the fact that Philip was doing well and that Almira would soon be reunited with him.

So on the day that Lady Almira, supported on either side by Gwendolyn and Christopher, made her slow, tentative way downstairs and into the drawing-room, they together told her, in careful and measured terms, about Philip and about Helen. Gwendolyn sat next to her and held her hand as she burst into tears, and they both watched her closely, fearful of an abrupt relapse.

But Lady Almira, surprising them, soon dried her tears. She would, she declared, write at once to her dear impetuous Helen, congratulating her on what was, in fact, a decidedly brilliant match. And she would confer with the housekeeper about preparing a room for Philip, preferably one next to her own, so that she might be available day or night should he need her. She stuffed her damp handkerchief—Christopher's old one, actually—into her reticule, rose to her feet, and with astonishing energy went away to find the housekeeper, leaving behind in her wake two dropped shawls, a glove, and a small box of comfits.

A week later the Duchess arrived with a pale, weak, but irrepressibly breezy Philip Thane. Motivated by a keen desire to help nurse him, Lady Almira quickly returned to full health, as did also, thankfully, Lizzie and everyone else under the Egremont roof who had succumbed to this rather nasty bout of spring influenza. Gwendolyn and Christopher twice went to Almack's, where—under Lady Jersey's indulgent gaze (and a disapproving glare from the Honorable Mrs. Drummond-Burrell, which made them laugh to themselves)—together they danced a few more dances than was entirely proper, Christopher remarking at one point that the *pentozali* might be a delightful way to liven things up in the otherwise rather staid rooms. One evening they went to Bushy House and dined with the Duke of Clarence, several of his friends, and quite a few of his many children, altogether making for a noisy, lively supper-table which was, they both agreed, a great deal of fun and not in the least bit what one would expect from a senior member of the Royal Family.

Meanwhile the Westenburys had hastily betaken themselves back to Gloucestershire, and it may safely be said that few people in London, if any, missed the Honorable Rupert. There was—inevitably—talk about the broken betrothal between the Earl and Gwendolyn Penhallow, but it was soon overshadowed by more exciting events including a duel fought on Wimbledon Common between two high-ranking members of the Foreign Ministry (over a raging policy dispute), the release of a dozen kangaroos in the zoo (a nocturnal prank by an inebriated young nobleman), and the exploits of a dashing opera-dancer who was rumored to have received half a dozen proposals of marriage from a certain duke (and former war hero) who was becoming increasingly desperate to win her capricious hand.

At around this same time, Helen's beloved horse, under the tender care of no less than three grooms, was duly shipped off to France. Too, several of the more daring young ladies among the *ton* were going about with hair newly shorn to their jawlines, a style that swiftly became known as the *coiffeur à la Penhallow*, and was even featured in the newest issue of *La Belle Assemblée* which Gwendolyn passed along to Lizzie, who stared at the illustration with a kind of proud amazement.

"I tell *everyone* it was your brilliant idea, Lizzie," said Gwendolyn.

In due course Percy returned from Brighton, and reacted to the news of Helen's marriage with a surprise mingled so strongly with disapproval and anger that Gwendolyn looked at him with surprise of her own. Not long afterwards, the lurid London scandal-sheets were reporting that the delectable Viscountess of Tarrington, thought to be carrying on with a military gentleman (perhaps even a member of the Prince Regent's own Horse Guards), had been abruptly cast off; but, within a matter of days, had taken up with a certain Mr. R., newly arrived in Town, young, impecunious, and extremely good-looking. And Percy, offered the chance for a captaincy in Sumatra, where Sir Stamford Raffles governed, immediately accepted this new post and promotion, and within just a few days was on his way. Gwendolyn and Christopher went to the pier to say goodbye, both noticing in Percy a curious mixture of anticipation, excitement, and a certain bitter melancholy only partially suppressed.

Pleased with Philip's improvement, the Duchess began making plans for the family to return home to Hathaway Park. And Katherine and Hugo were coming to London to accompany Gwendolyn back to Whitehaven—as well as to allow Katherine to deliver in person her latest manuscript to her publisher, and also to give a talk about her provocative, best-selling book *A Vindication of the Novel*. This talk she gave in a large hall filled to overflowing, and was so well-received that she got a thundering ovation which went on for nearly five minutes. Gwendolyn, standing between Hugo and Christopher, clapped until her hands hurt, glowing with pride in her wonderful and talented sister-in-law.

Afterwards, the Duchess gave a reception at the townhouse in Katherine's honor which was so robustly attended that it was deemed a horrendous squeeze—the highest encomium any hostess could wish for, although it was doubtful whether the Duchess (whose preference for country living was well-known) really cared about such things. In the quietest corner of the drawing-room, Gwendolyn stood talking with Christopher.

"So you're leaving tomorrow, *signorina*?"

"Yes. Oh, Christopher, I'm looking forward to seeing everyone at home, but I'm going to miss you dreadfully! Are you still planning to go to Nottingham?"

"Yes. For a while."

"For a while? And after that?"

"I don't know."

"Good God, what a crush!" said Hugo. "It's splendid that Kate is so popular, but the crowds! Nearly got trampled by a pack of adoring book critics on my way over to you." As Hugo stood well over six feet tall in his stocking feet and was as strong as the proverbial ox, this was clearly an unlikely assertion, but they let it pass. He was looking with keen interest at Christopher. "Did I hear you say you're going to Nottingham? But only for a while?"

Christopher nodded, and Hugo went on:

"Well, if you've nothing better to do, come back to Whitehaven and work with me—for however long you like. Commissions for new ships are coming in faster than Will Studdart and I can build them, and I could use your help in managing the crews."

Come back to Whitehaven.

This was clearly the best, cleverest, most wonderful idea in all the world and Gwendolyn found herself holding her breath waiting for Christopher to reply. Then she saw that he was looking at her with his dark brows raised a little. It seemed a sufficiently inquiring look for her to burst out at once: "Oh, Christopher, please do! I'd like that so much."

"Would you, Gwennie? Then I will." Christopher

turned to Hugo and said, "Thanks, Captain Penhallow. I'll do my best for you."

Hugo clapped him on the shoulder. "Excellent! And call me 'Hugo,' won't you?"

This new and delightful development made it infinitely easier to say goodbye to Christopher the next morning, and Gwendolyn traveled home with Katherine and Hugo in the highest of spirits. Once back in Whitehaven, she plunged into her life there with enthusiasm. She spent a lot of time reading to and playing with her young nieces Cordelia and Rosalind, whose charming vocabularies seemed to enlarge by the hour. She went frequently to the parsonage on George Street where, in Aunt Claudia's cozy, light-filled studio, she worked hard at her painting. With Mama she helped at the indigents' charity, preparing and serving meals, and sometimes she went to the offices of Studdart & Penhallow, Shipbuilders, where she assisted their man of business in wading through the mountain of paperwork that was an inevitable aspect of running a thriving company.

And when, in July, Christopher arrived, they simply picked up where they left off. They went for long rides in the countryside, or on the wide beach. They played chess, cards, backgammon. They talked about books, they debated each other about art; occasionally they argued but would swiftly resolve their quarrels—neither of them, they learned, being one to hold onto a grudge. They went to the indigents' charity to help there. They walked to the harbor, looking at all the Studdart & Penhallow ships in various stages of construction. Sometimes they took the little sailboat Hugo had acquired a few years back and went skimming along the shore under the high, bright summer sky. And together they laughed a great deal.

Hugo and his partner Will were full of praise for Christopher's work, to which he applied himself with energy and growing skill. He discovered that he enjoyed managing and overseeing the crews, but he still liked to vigorously pitch in at the sawpits where, he said, the exercise did him considerable good.

Mama and Hugo had offered him a place to stay in the Penhallow home, as had Will and his wife Céleste in their house nearby on Duke Street, but Christopher had thanked them and instead taken up residence in his old house next door to the Penhallows. It had been left only meagerly furnished, but there was a bed and the necessary linens, a few tables and chairs, some dishes and cooking implements, and Christopher declared himself to be entirely comfortable.

Cook, however, being of an old-fashioned bent, was skeptical of any man's ability to prepare his own food and was quite vocal in urging the family to invite Christopher over to dine as frequently as possible, lest he starve, waste away, and crumble into dust. Invitations were tendered—by Mama, Katherine, Hugo, and of course Gwendolyn herself—and very often accepted, much to Cook's relief. The little twins took a great fancy to Christopher, demanding on all occasions that he pick them up and twirl them about, laughing with such exuberant glee that it was impossible not to laugh along with them.

And so the months passed from spring, to summer, and into autumn.

It was on a crisp, brilliantly clear afternoon in late November that Gwendolyn, in her bedroom at home, was sitting on her bed and leafing through her London sketchbook.

Here were all her drawings of the Earl, as well as those she'd made of the other, various things interesting her at the time. Some paintings and sculptures she had admired. Pretty gowns that caught her eye. Lady Jersey's funny little dog Purkoy. A whimsical caricature of Mrs. Drummond-Burrell, with wheels instead of feet. A bird's-eye view of how she had imagined the maze at Richmond Park would look. The stage at the Theatre Royal, lamp-lights blazing, with Edmund Kean playing the black-clad Hamlet. A cow in St. James's Park; a bucket of daffodils.

Gwendolyn turned another page and came across the odd wedding-scene on the moon. She looked at it, amused. Rupert's smelly hat was, she thought, quite well done. And she was pleased to see how nicely she had rendered the proportions of the flying unicorn—it actually looked realistic.

Without a single pang of regret or twinge of pain, she turned the page.

Now she came to some drawings of Christopher.

Dozens of them; pages of them.

Christopher in a thoughtful mood.

Christopher rather stormy-looking.

Christopher smiling, with his eyes crinkled up at the corners in the way she liked so much.

Christopher, soothing the Duke of Clarence's unhappy horse.

Christopher, very handsome in dark evening-clothes.

Christopher, in bed at the Lion's Head inn, his head on the pillow and his long hair tousled.

Gwendolyn stared at this particular drawing for a long time.

Then she got a pencil and, next to the drawing of Christopher in the Lion's Head bed, she sketched a tiny little seed.

After that, she drew the seed again, and added some delicate little roots.

Next, she drew a small plant growing up out of the ground: a stem, a few tentative leaves.

She drew the plant again, but bigger. A small, hardy tree now, with a thicker trunk, more developed roots, more leaves.

And again. Bigger.

And yet again. Bigger still.

Growing, growing. Flourishing.

Finally she drew a tree in full maturity, with deep roots extending into the welcoming earth, a wide sturdy trunk, and a large healthy canopy of leaves.

She looked at it for a while, as if it were a wonderful surprise.

A revelation.

The past, the present, and the future.

It was curious, Gwendolyn thought, how entirely certain she had been that she would go to London and find her one true love. And she had, though not at all in the way she'd believed she would. Instead she had found her one true *real* love in a very unexpected way.

She looked again—with pleasure, with hope, with a powerful surge of happiness—at this singular page of her sketchbook.

Then, satisfied, certain, she closed her sketchbook, got up, and went to the window of her room that looked out to the Becks' house and the long yard to the back. What she saw there made her smile. And then she went to get her pelisse.

"Christopher, may I talk with you, please?" Gwendolyn said, and Christopher brought his axe down with a *thunk* into a fat yew log and split it in two.

He turned to her and smiled, liking how the wind played with her hair and ruffled the hems of her white gown and rose-colored pelisse; admiring the grace and strength in her tall, slender body, the enduring beauty of her delicate features, the allure of her tenderly curved mouth, the exact shade of a ripe peach. A vivid memory rose up, from years ago, and in this very yard.

He answered, not curtly this time, but softly:

"Well?"

"You see, I've had an idea." Gwendolyn's face was bright with a kind of mischievous joy.

Christopher leaned on the axe handle, his smile growing. "I am, as they say, all attention."

"I must say that I think it's quite a brilliant idea. You know, of course, that I love you?"

I love you.

The words were like a bell resonating within him, rich, deep, sonorous, bringing forth the instant echo of his own love for her. The secret hope, the wild longing he'd carried all these months—answered.

I love you.

Three short, simple words which would change his life, his world, forever.

He looked down into Gwendolyn's lovely face and said, in his voice a new caress: "No, I didn't know."

"Well, I do love you, Christopher, and I thought that we could get married."

"Get married?" he said, teasingly repeating his own words from years ago. "Are you mad?"

"Of course I'm not mad," she answered, doing the same. Her eyes were sparkling like sapphires. "It seems to me a wonderfully clever plan."

"I thought girls were supposed to wait for a proposal."

"Oh, who cares? Besides, wouldn't it be a splendid adventure?"

At this Christopher tossed aside the axe and went to Gwendolyn, reaching down to take her hands in his. *"Sì, signorina,"* he softly said. "It would be the most splendid adventure."

"Oh, Christopher, do you mean it?"

"Yes."

"And—and do you love me too?"

"Yes. Mind, heart, body, and soul. Yes."

"Oh, I'm so *glad,"* Gwendolyn said, and pulled her hands away, but only to slide her arms around his neck, to come as close as one person could to another, and to bring her mouth up against his own.

Into Christopher's mind flashed the memory of that all-too-brief embrace at Vauxhall Gardens, the agony of self-control it took to not kiss Gwendolyn, to do the right and honorable thing while every part of him yearned to forget that she was engaged to the Earl.

But that was then, and this—this, by God, was now, in all its wonder and glory.

I love you.

I thought that we could get married.

Do you love me too?

Mind, heart, body, and soul.

He brought his own arms around Gwendolyn, and with a low, rough sound that was half a laugh, half a groan of pleasure, he kissed her. Slow, gentle, aware of a certain hesitancy on her part at first and keenly sensitive to her response. There was all the time in the world for them now, and her pleasure meant everything. Her pleasure, her joy, was his.

Slowly, slowly, their kiss deepened. Her mouth as delectable as a sweet, ripe peach—and he a man hungry in every part of him for it. For her. For Gwendolyn, his light, his love. The woman who was his friend and would be his wife. Who was, in fact, kissing him back, her arms tightening around his neck, and for a while—it could have been a minute, it could have been forever—he couldn't tell where he ended and Gwendolyn began. They were one, and it was right, so very right.

When finally they pulled apart a little, he saw that she was radiant.

"Oh, *Christopher*," she said, rather dazedly.

"Yes, Gwennie?"

"I wasn't thinking *anything* the whole time we were kissing."

"Is that good?"

"Very good! I was just—*being*. Feeling. Feeling you and me—*enjoying* from head to toe, and everywhere in between! Let's do it again."

"Yes," he said, "let's," and he cupped her face in his hands, leaning down just enough so that he could slant his mouth against hers. Her lips, soft, warm, parting at once. The taste of her, the feel of her, it was heaven here on earth: eagerness and passionate response, fire and silken wetness. He gave and she took; she gave and he received. Then she very provocatively bit at his upper lip and pleasure juddered through him so strongly that the breath audibly left him.

She withdrew, just a little, and looked up into his face. "Was that all right, what I did?"

"Oh God, yes."

"You liked it?"

"Hardly a strong enough word."

She smiled, glowing, radiant. "Really?"

"Really."

Gwendolyn brought up her hand and slowly she slid it along a lock of his hair that had fallen across his forehead. Dreamily she said, "Christopher, I don't mean to be boastful, but I don't think I'm half-bad at kissing."

"Gwennie," he answered, smiling back at her, "you're *excellent* at it."

"It's very reassuring. I had my doubts, as I think you

knew. Also, *ma sherry moo*, you're quite excellent yourself."

"We may as well admit it, *signorina*. We're perfect for each other."

She laughed. "Oh, we are! We are!"

He caught at the hand that had caressed his hair and brought it to his lips. "Gwennie, how long have you known?"

"How long have I known that I love you?" She was looking up at him, thoughtfully, with a kind of dreamy marvel in her beautiful bright eyes. "I've loved you as a friend since London. As for falling head over heels in love with you—it was a gradual thing, you know, a little seed that needed time to grow into something solid and sturdy and lasting and *real*. But I think it really began at the Lion's Head inn, the morning I woke up and saw you there right next to me." She smiled. "I've realized that I want to spend the rest of my life finding you there with me, every single morning."

"A brilliant plan indeed," he said, and kissed her hand again.

"I'm glad you think so! Christopher, how long have *you* known?"

"Since London also. But there were—impediments." She nodded, and he went on, "Thank God for Hugo inviting me to come back to Whitehaven. It was when you seconded his invitation—do you remember? You said, 'Please do. I'd like that so much.' Well, it gave me hope. The hope that you wanted me here, that our friendship might, perhaps, become something more. I'd have found some other way to come back to Whitehaven to see you—but Hugo made it easy for me."

"Hurray for Hugo! We'll have to tell him he played Cupid for us. Oh, how patient you've been, *ma sherry moo*! You've been yourself all this time—your *congruent* self—never trying to force things along, or rush me into a declaration before I was ready. For all you knew, I'd never be more than a friend to you."

"It was a risk I was willing to take."

"Do I really mean that much to you, Christopher?"

He caught her up in his arms again. "Yes. I love you, Gwennie, and I mean to show you just how much. Today, tomorrow, next week, next year—always. And now—to paraphrase Señor Rodrigo—kiss me again, you saucy wench."

She laughed, and she did.

And when, some time later, they drew apart, her face was rosy and smiling. "Oh, goodness, I feel like a human stove! I'm so hot I feel like taking off my pelisse. Actually," she added mischievously, "I feel like taking off *everything*."

"I'd like to see that."

"Would you? Well, you will. You're marrying a brazen woman, you know."

"I wouldn't have it any other way."

She twinkled up at him. "I'm almost tempted for us to run away to Gretna Green tonight, and be wed over the anvil. But no—I'll display superhuman restraint and wait till we can be married in Grandpapa's church. If that's all right with you?"

"It sounds perfect."

"I think so too! It will be absolutely *marvelous*. Hugo can give me away, and Katherine will be my matron of honor—and oh my goodness, Cordelia and Rosalind can be flower girls. How they'll *adore* that! Grandpapa will perform the ceremony, and he'll do it so beautifully that Mama and Aunt Claudia for certain will cry, and Cook will too, and I may burst into tears myself from sheer thankfulness and joy."

"I'll bring a handkerchief for you."

"Of *course* you will, dearest, most wonderful of men. It will be the best and most delightful wedding of all time! Because I'll be marrying *you*. Do you think we should have Señor Rodrigo there too, and try to persuade him to say 'You may now kiss the bride,' at just the right moment?"

Christopher laughed. "He's more likely to say 'Heave ho, you bilge-sucking scallywag.' As he did just yesterday when he was eyeing my scone."

Gwendolyn giggled. "Alas, too true! Perhaps not *quite* the tone we would like. Do you think your family will be able to come?"

"If they can't, what do you think about visiting them in Nottingham afterwards?"

"Oh yes, I love that idea! I can't wait to meet Cora, and the baby, too! And do you suppose we could go to Italy, and stay with Mauro for a while? I'd love to get to know him, and see all those lovely horses."

"By all means. I know he'd like it—and I would also, *signorina*. And after that?"

"Oh, the world is so wonderfully large and interesting, isn't it? I'd like to go to Greece—to Athens, and see the Acropolis, and of course the olive groves you worked in, out in the countryside, and I've always longed to visit Constantinople, and visit the famous Hippodrome—and Egypt, too. The Nile—the Pyramids—the Great Sphinx! Do you think we can? Would you like that too?"

"Very much. Because we'll be doing it together."

"Yes. How glorious! And how lucky we are, aren't we?"

He kissed her again. "Very. Extremely. Incredibly lucky, *signorina*."

"And what about when we get back? What shall we do?"

"Look around us. Figure out what we'd like to do with ourselves. But there's one thing I'm sure about. I'd like to

put Uncle Dan's fortune to good use, by way of philan-
thropy. Recently I've been invited to join some charity
boards in London—one is an animal protection society, and another's for impoverished ex-sailors and their
families—and I've accepted. When I was in Nottingham
I asked Father to teach me about business, and how to
wisely invest Uncle Dan's money, so that I'll be able to not
just keep giving it away, but also ensure that there's plenty
to go around, and for a long time."

"Oh, Christopher, what a wonderful idea! And do you
think we could also help with another endeavor? I noticed
in the London museums and galleries that nearly all the
artists whose work is being shown are men. It's so silly
and wrong, when there must be so many talented women
who aren't being given the chance to exhibit their paintings and sculptures. I'd like to help them if I can—with
financial support, for housing and food and supplies, and
perhaps fund a London gallery exclusively for the work of
women artists."

He took her hand in his. "I think that's a wonderful
idea also. Let's do it."

Gwendolyn beamed up at him. "Oh, Christopher, do
you know what? Life with you really *is* going to be a
splendid adventure. I can't wait to begin."

He smiled back at her. "Gwennie," he said, "I think we
already have."

Chapter 19

❧⚬❧

The wedding took place on a cold, cloudy winter morning in Whitehaven, but inside Grandpapa's little church it was warm and bright, illuminated by many candles and also, Gwendolyn thought, by all the love filling it.

As she had predicted, Grandpapa performed the marriage service with such simple, moving dignity that Mama, Aunt Claudia, and Cook wept copiously, and several other people in the packed pews dabbed at their eyes. As for herself, well, tears *did* come to her eyes once or twice, but being tears of joy they were easy to blink away. Besides, she knew that if she needed it, Christopher would have a handkerchief ready for her. He had promised, and therefore he would. Christopher, whom she could trust absolutely. Christopher, whom she liked, respected, loved, adored.

Christopher, her husband.

For Grandpapa had just said *You may now kiss the bride,* and so she and Christopher looked at each other, a smile flashing between them as they both thought of Señor Rodrigo (at present sulking at home on his perch), and then little Cordelia, standing proudly between Rosalind and Katherine, cried out:

"*Kiss* her, Uncle Kwistopher!"

A low laugh rumbled throughout the church, and Christopher, his dark eyes alight with humor, did indeed kiss her, and with so much tenderness that Gwendolyn, feeling as if her heart was overflowing with happiness, sent up to heaven a prayer of gratitude for the many, many blessings she had received.

"Kiss *me*, Uncle Kwistopher!" said Rosalind loudly, and laughter rose again.

Gallantly Christopher did, and kissed Cordelia on her plump cheek as well, and managed to tactfully decline their subsequent demands to be twirled about by mentioning that their cherished coronets of pink winter roses—which matched their Aunt Gwennie's exactly—might not emerge unscathed.

"Well done, Mr. Beck," Gwendolyn whispered approvingly, and he had just enough time to answer with a smile, "*Grazie*, Mrs. Beck," before they were enveloped in loving hugs, hearty handshakes, and congratulations from all sides.

After, there was a breakfast at home, with so much food and drink that Gwendolyn said to Christopher she was sure she heard the tables literally groaning under the weight of it all. Cook, near to bursting with excitement and pride, had brought on a cadre of helpers to produce a truly remarkable array of dishes including eggs in various forms, sausages and bacon, fried potatoes, delicately marinated asparagus, muffins and rolls, preserves of all kinds, tarts both savory and sweet, fresh fruit, cold meats and cheeses, several different types of biscuits, and dozens of little iced cakes in addition to a large and magnificent three-tiered butter-cake. Owen FitzClarence, who had come with Francis for the wedding and the winter holiday, opened his eyes wide at the sight of it all, and went on to earn in Cook's heart a lasting approbation by the sheer quantities he zestfully consumed.

It took an entire lemony Shrewsbury biscuit for Gwendolyn to coax Señor Rodrigo out of his sulks, but by the end of it, having scattered crumbs beneath him with abandon, he visibly cheered up and even cackled agreeably when Gwendolyn told him she loved him. "Blimey," he said, and in such outrageously dulcet tones that she couldn't help but laugh.

She went around the drawing-room, talking happily with Bertram, who had also come home from Oxford, and then with Katherine, Aunt Verena, Owen, Mrs. Studdart, and many other guests including several of Hugo and Will's employees, afterwards sitting with Cordelia and Rosalind for a quick sketch Aunt Claudia begged to make of them, and finally looked around for Christopher. He was talking with Grandpapa and Will Studdart, but as she came toward them he broke away with a smile and a pleasant word, and took her hand as together they went toward one of the windows.

They stood, fingers intertwined, looking out into the wintry afternoon. The sky was a soft pearly gray, and snow had begun to fall, drifting down in large, lacy flakes.

"How beautiful it is," Gwendolyn said dreamily.

"Not as beautiful as you, *signora*."

"*Signora*," she repeated, smiling. "*Signorina* no more. That's as it should be. But you'll always be *ma sherry moo*, you know—my dear friend."

"I'm glad." He smiled back at her. "And likewise."

"I wonder how the Viscountess of Tarrington would say 'my wonderful husband'? Probably something along the lines of *ma merry mervy yoo*. So that's what you'll be too. Oh, Christopher, I'll always remember that night at

Vauxhall. The beginning, I think, of my great unhappiness at being engaged to the Earl, but also the beginning of understanding myself better, and loving you."

His hand tightened on hers. "A night to remember indeed, *signora*."

"Yes. And there's something else, too." She smiled up at him. "The Viscountess said, 'Things work out for the best. We must always follow our dreams.' Do you remember that? I don't think I quite registered it at the time. But now I do. And now I believe she was right."

"Wisdom arrives in many forms, doesn't it?"

"Very true. Oh, I wish Percy were here! If only he hadn't gone so far away. Do you think we might go visit him sometime?"

"I'd like that."

"You would? I'm so glad. I've been reading up on Sumatra, and—"

"Aunt Gwennie!" It was Cordelia, tugging at the lilac-colored silk of Gwendolyn's gown, and she looked down at her niece with a smile.

"Yes, Cordelia?"

"Come see! Aunt Claudia's made a picture of Uncle Kwistopher and you!"

Gwendolyn and Christopher turned away from the window, and Cordelia led them to where Claudia, perched on the arm of a sofa, had been sketching them as they stood looking out into the soft winter sky. She showed them the drawing, and Gwendolyn exclaimed:

"It's wonderful, Aunt Claudia! Is that for us?"

"Yes, to be sure, and all the other little sketches I've been doing today. I even did one in the church, of the two of you together at the altar. Verena thought it rather irreverent of me, but I must say I think she's not quite right. For what could be a more beautiful, more sacred

moment? And the *light*!" A rapt look on her face, Aunt
Claudia gestured with one slender paint-splotched hand,
the slow, delicate movement expressive of a very real awe.
"Magical, my dears. Magical!"

"It seemed magical to us, too," said Christopher, and
Gwendolyn, with yet another rush of happiness, clasped
his warm strong hand in hers again. She said:

"What wonderful mementoes of our wedding-day, Aunt
Claudia! Thank you so much."

"I've enjoyed making them, my dear. So much joy
everywhere. While you're away, I thought I would add in
washes of color, and frame them, and have them placed
wherever you like in your house."

"Our house," murmured Gwendolyn, the phrase delightfully cozy, but still unfamiliar in her mouth. It was
hard to believe that Christopher's father had given them
the house next door as a wedding-gift, whether to keep
or to sell. Such extraordinary generosity! They both had
agreed to keep it; they didn't know where ultimately they
would settle down, but Whitehaven would always be in
some essential way their home, and certainly a place they
would visit regularly.

"I thought perhaps one of the hallways?" Aunt Claudia went on musingly. "When the painters are done, of
course. How fresh and new it will all look."

"I propose they go in the main drawing-room," said
Christopher, "in a place of honor," and Gwendolyn added
at once:

"Yes, I think so also! And how we shall shamelessly
brag, too, when people come over. Our very own artwork
by the brilliant and renowned artist Claudia Mantel!"

"Oh, my dears, you flatter me," murmured Claudia,
blushing modestly.

"Not a bit of it, Auntie," said Christopher, using this

new and affectionate sobriquet which only made Claudia blush the more.

"And you *are* going to work on something for my London gallery, Aunt Claudia, aren't you?" Gwendolyn said.

"Yes, if you like. I want to do a portrait of Verena, you know, making lace. If I can capture the absorption on her face, and do justice to her clever, clever hands, I'll be so pleased! But it would be only for show, my dear Gwendolyn, not for sale."

"Absolutely," answered Gwendolyn, and so the bargain was struck, and after that Rosalind came swaggering over with Señor Rodrigo riding jauntily on her shoulder, and she said in a loud, commanding voice to no one in particular:

"Walk the plink, you scarvy dig!"

At this Señor Rodrigo gave an extremely noisy laugh that went on for fully half a minute, and Hugo came over to catch up Rosalind in his arms, bearing Rodrigo up with her. "By Jove, isn't she splendid?" he said proudly. "As fierce as her mama."

"She is indeed," Gwendolyn agreed. "And may she stay that way forever."

"Papa's crown," said Rosalind, and put her coronet of roses on Hugo's golden head.

"Thank you, sweetheart," said Hugo. "I say, I feel quite regal."

Katherine came over, holding Cordelia in her arms, and so Cordelia generously put *her* coronet on her mother's head, and then the family's dogs, who had been shut into the library when the celebration began, somehow got out— it being Bertram's considered opinion that one of them, a mastiff whom Mama had found abandoned as a puppy a few years ago and brought home to nurse back into health, had figured out how to turn door-handles with its mouth— and they all came lolloping into the drawing-room where they proceeded to gaily greet everyone and also hunt down and eat every scrap of food that had fallen onto the floor. Nobody minded, and then Will Studdart brought out his fiddle, so furniture was pushed away to make room and there was some very lively dancing, followed by cake and champagne, and then, as afternoon gave way to evening, the guests began to leave, and the twins, who had fallen asleep on one of the sofas, were carried upstairs by Katherine and Hugo, Owen had one more giant slice of cake and then helped Christopher and Francis and Bertram push the furniture back into place, Gwendolyn let the dogs out into the yard for a run and called them all back inside, and hugged Mama for a very long time, and then, finally, she and Christopher went out into the dark snowy night and strolled next door to their house.

They went into the kitchen, where from the banked fire Christopher lit a candle, and they walked upstairs, hand in hand, and to the threshold of the small room he had been using as his bedchamber.

Christopher pushed open the door. "After you, *signora.*"

"Thank you, *ma merry mervy yoo*," Gwendolyn answered, took a step inside, then stopped, amazed.

In the room was only a bed, a chair, a small table with a couple of books upon it, and an old armoire which Christopher had brought up from the basement. Upon every surface, including the floor, had been scattered pink rose petals, the same shade as those Rosalind and Cordelia had gleefully strewn to left and right as they walked down the aisle in church, the same shade as the bouquet she herself had carried, the same shade as the coronet which she had just given to the young daughter of one of Hugo's employees, who had looked so very proud and happy to wear it.

"Christopher," Gwendolyn breathed, turning to him wide-eyed, "how *lovely.*"

He smiled. "The room seemed a little spartan for our first night together."

"I'd have spent it in a cave. All that matters is *you*. But rose petals! And the scent! It's heavenly."

"I'm glad you like it. I hoped you would." Christopher went to the fireplace and used the candle to set aflame the twigs and logs he had carefully prepared earlier. Light and warmth began to fill the room, and he put the candle on the little table. He looked at her, long and deeply, and softly said, with pure wonder in his voice:

"Bellissima."

It was dim here in this small bedroom, but Gwendolyn could very easily see the glow, the love, in Christopher's eyes. She smiled, and went to him, and lifted the hand upon which a new gold band gleamed, the mate to the one she now wore on *her* left hand. Lightly she pressed her lips to his wedding-band, the everlasting symbol of everything they were to one another.

"Mio amore," she whispered, and then took hold of a frill in his neckcloth. "May I?"

"Yes, please," Christopher answered, and so she began to untie his neckcloth. His breathing quickened, she could see it in the rise and fall of his chest, and it made her want to hurry, hurry.

Nonetheless she tried her best to be slow, leisurely, deliberate; she made herself pull the long strip of white linen from around Christopher's neck as if, in fact, her own breathing hadn't sped up, or as if she wasn't starting to feel very, very warm, or as if she could wait a long, long time for all that was to come.

Slowly she pulled free the linen strip and let it fall onto the floor. Onto the rose petals that smelled so sweet.

Then she tugged open the sides of his jacket and Christopher helped her by shrugging himself out of it.

The jacket, too, went onto the rose petals.

Gwendolyn tugged up the hem of his white shirt and her hands went to the warm, hard flesh of his torso, and up along the sides, lingering upon each slight rise and fall of rib-bone—a sensation so delicious, so intoxicating, it felt as if her fingers, her palms, were kissing his skin. A hot purl of pleasure went through her, settling low in her belly, between her legs, and suddenly all thoughts of a protracted disrobing vanished.

She ripped Christopher's shirt up and over his head and then her hands were at the fastenings of his breeches, struggling. He helped her with these, too, kicking off his shoes and drawing off his dark stockings, then slid his breeches down, past his narrow hips; he stepped out of them, pushed them aside, and she whipped around so that he could undo the many little silk-covered buttons of her gown.

"May I?" he said.

"Oh yes. *Yes.*" She was trembling, in an agony of impatience now, and though it seemed like years it was probably only a minute or two before Christopher had finished, sliding her gown away and down, and then her shift, and she turned to face him clad only in her gossamer-thin white stockings, garters, and lilac-colored slippers.

"*Mia cara,*" he said, his voice low and rough and eager, the very sound of it sending a delicious thrill cascading through her. Quickly Gwendolyn went to the bed, sat on the edge, shoved off her slippers and garters and stockings, and looked up at Christopher in all his masculine glory, the wiry strength of him, his muscled arms and shoulders, the taut planes of his chest, and more.

Oh, so much more.

She held out her hand to him and he came to her, swiftly, eagerly, matching her in urgency, and in a moment, they were lying together on the bed, body to body, his mouth on hers, and with a soft noise of the greatest satisfaction Gwendolyn wrapped her arms around Christopher and held him tight.

If within her were any lingering doubts about herself, about her capacity to give and receive pleasure, they were gone in just a few staccato beats of her heart, as she met Christopher kiss for kiss, caress for caress, and for every achingly sweet thrust of him inside her, she welcomed him, moved with him, effortlessly, in a timeless dance of love and shared joy. It was everything Gwendolyn could have dreamed of—yet, at the same time, it far exceeded what she had thought being with him would be like.

In Christopher she found a lover both tender and ardent, sensitive and generous, to whom she could open herself with trust and with freedom.

A lover with whom she could be herself, to whom she could whisper, or gasp, or cry out: *Yes, that, more, please, here, could we, oh again, again.*

And so the night went on.

Both of their voices, mingling: *I love you, yes, again, please, would you, shall we, yes let's, oh God, ti amo, ti amo . . .*

With the candle long since guttered out, the first soft intimations of dawn—just barely beginning to brighten the curtain drawn against the window—found them in each other's arms, languorous, contented, drowsy.

"Christopher," Gwendolyn said, lifting herself on one elbow.

"Sì, signora?"

"You have rose petals in your hair." Lazily she reached to pluck a few of them from amongst the dark strands and toss them, like confetti, into the air, where they drifted down onto the floor.

"So do you." He smiled. "They suit you. You look very much like a flower yourself."

"Do I? What sort of flower?"

"You remind me of a *strelitzia*."

"A what?"

"A crane lily. Sometimes they call it a bird of paradise. Do you know it?"

"No, but what a flattering comparison." She snuggled closer to him. "What does it look like?"

"It's got a very sturdy stem, with bright strong leaves almost in a kind of fan effect. With your hair all rumpled like that, and your throat bare, that's what reminded me. You look a little fragile, *signora*, but you're not. You're very strong."

"Cook always says it's because we eat fish all year round."

He laughed. "She may be right."

"Where have you seen crane lilies?"

"In Naples. A family from Madeira brought them over, and were hoping to cultivate them there."

"It sounds like such a lovely flower. I hope they succeeded."

"Shall we go find out?"

"Yes, let's." Gwendolyn reached up to stroke his shoulder, relishing the warmth of his skin, the powerful muscles and the bone beneath, then luxuriously ran her fingers down along his arm. "Oh, Christopher, how marvelous you are. I can hardly believe we can touch each other—feel each other—as much as we like."

"And for a lifetime." He kissed her, and pleasure shivered all throughout her body. A thought suddenly occurred to her and she giggled.

"What is it?" he asked, smiling.

"Oh, I was just remembering the ending of *Escape from Castle Killarney*. After the heroine runs away from home, she somehow manages to get to London and falls into the clutches of an evil woman who runs a—what is it called?—oh yes, a house of ill-repute, where she's sold to the highest bidder, a dreadful old roué who spends several pages rubbing his hands together and leering at the poor girl."

"If this is the ending, it's rather an unfortunate one."

"Oh, I've backtracked. She's rescued, you see, and at the very last moment, by a handsome duke who happens to be walking by and hears her screams."

"How does he find her? Let me guess. Does he scale the walls of the house, with stunning agility?"

"No, he goes in at the front door. First he has to fight at least half a dozen burly guards, and then he has the most magnificent confrontation with the evil proprietress, and then he dashes upstairs and bursts through the locked door of the room where the heroine is being held captive. And he just happens to have a great long whip concealed on his person, which he uses to wonderful effect on the old roué, who's promptly reduced to a blubbering mass of tears."

"Well, that's nice."

"Diana and I certainly found it so! And we thought the Duke the most delightful hero there ever was."

"I wish *I'd* thought of carrying a whip around," Christopher remarked. "You'd have fallen in love with me much faster, wouldn't you?"

Gwendolyn laughed. "Very likely."

"Don't leave me in suspense. What happens after that?"

"Well, after five or six chapters—or is it more? I can't remember. It seemed to take *forever*. In any event, the Duke finally proposes, and the heroine's so happy that she faints, and then they get married—it's a magnificent wedding in London, and somehow the Pope shows up to officiate—but they only have a very brief, chaste kiss at the altar, which Diana and I found very disappointing. And then we see them the next morning having breakfast, without even a paragraph about what happened between them the night before. No kissing—nothing."

"How unutterably dull."

"Wasn't it? And so that's the ending, except that the author includes a rather long homily about how the heroine achieves happiness despite having been so shockingly unfeminine and naughty as to run away from home wearing men's clothing, and that she deserves all the awful things that happened to her, and she's going to atone for it all by being a properly obedient wife to the Duke. And that, evidently, is the moral of the story. So you see, Christopher, by this logic, I don't deserve you at all." Gwendolyn laughed again.

"Good God, what a lot of nonsense. Why did you and Diana read it?"

"Well, for the happy ending, for one thing. We knew that no matter what dreadful things happened, everything would be all right in the end. Also, we read it for the good parts."

"The good parts?"

Gwendolyn smiled mischievously. "You know—the hugging and the kissing and especially what comes after that."

"Ah."

"Unfortunately, in *Escape from Castle Killarney* there were barely *any* good parts."

"How disappointing. Aren't you glad we can create our own?"

Gwendolyn slid her leg over his lean hip, and brought

herself close, so wonderfully and intimately close, to him. His response was immediate and satisfying, and with a purr in her voice she said:

"Oh, Christopher, I'm *so* glad. We already have, haven't we? And we'll create some more. Right now, in fact, if that's all right with you?"

"*More* than all right, *signora*," he said, with a lovely answering rasp of desire in his own voice, and she kissed him, and he kissed her, and then they did.

Several years later . . .

"**A**nd so," Gwendolyn said, "in April of 1818, the Earl and I were officially betrothed. He gave me a ring, too. It had been in his family for generations—it was a gift from Queen Elizabeth to a previous Lady Westenbury who served as her Mistress of the Robes. Oh, it was so beautiful! It was made of gold, with a large, milky-white pearl in the center. Around the pearl were tiny, perfect rubies which made it seem to absolutely *glow.*

"When I was alone, I'd hold up my hand and stare at the ring. A symbol of my future happiness. No—my *present* happiness. I was engaged, I would tell myself over and over, and to the most wonderful man in the world.

"Engaged to the Earl."

Gwendolyn looked down at her left hand, where on her fourth finger gleamed not a glittering ruby and pearl ring, but a simple gold band, and she smiled.

Cordelia and Rosalind Penhallow, who had been listening to their aunt tell the story of her long-ago engagement to the Earl of Westenbury with all the fascination fourteen-year-old girls feel for a romantic tale, exchanged wondering glances.

"How long did it last, Aunt Gwennie?" asked Rosalind.

"Long enough for me to realize it would have been a dreadful mistake. As it turned out, the Earl *wasn't* the most wonderful man in the world. At least, not to me, which was all that mattered. So one day I told him it was over, and gave him back his ring."

"Was he very upset?" Cordelia said.

"Yes, I'm afraid he was."

"And did he become a tragic figure after that, Aunt Gwennie? Did he shut himself away, hiding his broken heart from the world?"

"Did he become a hermit, living in a remote hut in the forest?" added Rosalind eagerly. "Forever weeping over his lost love, and growing an excessively long beard?"

"No," answered Gwendolyn, "he married a very nice young lady with whom he has, I believe, several children. I saw him and the Countess in London the last time your uncle Christopher and I were there. They seemed very happy together."

Both Rosalind and Cordelia looked disappointed, and Gwendolyn laughed. "But there *is* a moral to the story, my dears. It's this: I hope you'll always follow your dreams— and settle for nothing less than whatever is the best for *you*."

"That's a good moral, Aunt Gwennie," said Cordelia.

"Yes, Delia dear, it is. In fact, I think it's the best moral of all."

"Then I'll try to remember it," Cordelia said, and her twin added with a determined nod:

"I will, too."

The three of them were sitting together in the library of the Penhallow home in Whitehaven. It was a warm, bright summer day in July and all the windows were open to let the pleasant sea-breezes come wafting in. A couple of dogs were sleeping at Gwendolyn's feet, and a fluffy little gray cat was curled up in her lap, purring.

"Meow," suddenly said Señor Rodrigo from his perch on Rosalind's shoulder, looking with obvious affection at the cat, adding, as if an afterthought, "Blast and damnation."

"Wasn't it clever of Rodrigo to have found Kitty?" said Cordelia admiringly. "She had wandered onto the portico, you know, and Rodrigo simply *stalked* to the door and stood there squawking until we opened it. Poor Kitty had been in the most awful fight. Do you remember, Rosie? She was bloody all over and one of her ears was entirely gone. Papa went for Dr. Wilson, and how nice he was! Not a word about being a doctor only for humans. He stitched Kitty up beautifully, don't you think?"

"Yes, and you were a great help, Delia," replied Rosalind. "You held Kitty so gently, and didn't flinch once."

"Well, of course it was very difficult, but it was fascinating too. Dr. Wilson said I'd make a fine doctor someday. Or a veterinarian."

"I'd let you take care of me," Rosalind said loyally. "*And* all my animals."

There was a little knock on the open door, and Christopher came strolling into the library. He smiled at the charming tableau they three made: Gwendolyn, as slender and golden as ever and clad in soft violet, with a pretty, dark-haired young niece in white on either side of her.

"Am I interrupting, ladies?"

They all smiled back.

"We're having a lovely visit, Uncle Christopher," said Cordelia. "Do you need Aunt Gwennie?"

"Yes, your papa wants her at the harbor, to give her opinion on how the new sculpture's coming along. Want to come with us?"

"We'd love to," answered Rosalind. "But first I must tidy up this mess I've made, or Cook will be annoyed with me at tea-time. Will you wait?"

He glanced at the low table near the sofa on which they sat; it was entirely covered with a riot of paper and notes and scraps, all anchored against the breeze by beach-shells and little rounded stones, as well as by books and pencils and erasers. "Of course, Rosie. How's the latest poem coming along?"

"Splendidly. Although I simply *can't* think of anything that rhymes with either 'dangerous' or 'discombobulate.' Neither can Delia or Aunt Gwennie. Can you?"

He thought about it. "I'm afraid not. What's the topic of your poem?"

"Grace O'Malley."

"The Irish warrior-queen?"

"Yes. Supposedly she came to Whitehaven back in the seventeenth century."

Christopher nodded. "I once had a sailor friend named Barnabas, who said much the same thing. Well, I'd love to read it whenever you feel like sharing it, Rosie. Ready, *signora*?"

"Yes indeed." Gwendolyn gently set aside the little gray cat and rose to her feet. "Girls, we'll wait for you in the hall."

Rosalind got up and went over to Señor Rodrigo's perch, onto which he amiably climbed, and Cordelia got up too, saying, "I'll help you, Rosie."

They had gathered up most of the papers, when Rosalind paused and looked at a little stack of books on the table. At the bottom of the stack was Aunt Gwennie's book *Travels with Christopher*, which she had written and illustrated (and which King William, until only recently the Duke of Clarence, had publicly admired), and on top of that were three of her children's books of original fairy tales which she had also illustrated. Then Rosalind looked over to one of the bookshelves which held all of Mama's books, neatly lined up in a row.

"Delia," she said, "do you think there's room in the family for another writer?"

"Why not?" answered Cordelia, picking up the pencils and putting them in a silver mug. "There's not a limit, after all. Besides, it's about time we had a poet, don't you think?"

"Yes, maybe so."

They continued with their tidying-up, and Cordelia said, "It's so funny to think of Aunt Gwennie engaged to somebody else, isn't it? I can't imagine her not being married to Uncle Christopher."

"Nor can I. He's the dearest uncle there ever was." Rosalind picked up the pile of her papers, then went toward the writing-desk on the other side of the library. Passing by the open door, she glanced out into the hallway, then suddenly stopped and stared for a few moments. Then she turned around and hurried back to where Cordelia had stooped to pet Kitty, who was curling about her ankles.

"Delia!" Rosalind whispered, her eyes sparkling mischievously. "Guess what I just saw!"

"What?"

"Aunt Gwennie and Uncle Christopher *kissing*."

Cordelia nodded, and tickled Kitty's soft chin. "Love," she remarked sagely. "Isn't it grand?"

Keep reading for a sneak peek at the next
book in the Penhallow Dynasty series . . .

THE WORST DUKE IN
THE WORLD

. . . coming soon from Avon Books!

Somerset County, England
February 1817

His Grace the Duke of Radcliffe had reached the last of the wide marble steps that led from his house onto the graveled sweep and was just about to execute a gentle left turn when from above and behind him came a piercing voice which throbbed with annoyance and disapproval.

"Anthony."

He turned and looked up. On the broad covered portico stood his sister Margaret, clad in habitual black from the lacy cap on her head to the trailing draperies of her gown and sensible slippers. Her back was ramrod straight, her brows were drawn together, and her lips compressed into a thin, tight line. She had, in fact, the darkly ominous air of an avenging angel. All she lacked was a fiery sword. He said:

"Hullo, Meg."

Rather than responding to his civil greeting in kind, her frown only deepened. "Where do you think you're going?"

"To the stables."

"Why?"

"To get my horse."

"For what purpose are you getting your horse?"

He squinted up at her. Really, sometimes Margaret asked the most obvious of questions. "To go riding."

"Where?"

"To see Penhallow over at Surmont Hall. Apparently the enmity between our respective pigmen has been escalating."

"Indeed," said Margaret, although in a noticeably flat way.

"Yes, Johns says Cremwell has been threatening to sneak over from the Hall and put calomel in the Duchess's slops. Can't have that, you know. Very unsporting." Anthony watched with mild interest as Margaret's eyes began snapping with anger.

"Why you had to name that revolting pig 'Duchess' is beyond me."

"I didn't *have* to, Meg. And it was you who inspired me—don't you remember? Saying that I cared more for the new piglet than I did Selina. Which, of course, was not entirely untrue."

At this frank reference to his wife, dead these five years, and the unvarnished truth of his marriage—a dry, sepulchral, mutually loveless match of convenience—Margaret said, with more tartness than seemed strictly necessary:

"Your remarks, Anthony, are insupportable. Selina, may I remind you, was the daughter of an earl, and comported herself at all times with the dignity appropriate to her station in life. Moreover, if she had known you named a pig after her—"

"You're off the mark there, old girl. I didn't name the pig 'Selina,' after all."

"Off the *mark*? Why, you—you're—flippant—and

feckless—and—and—" Margaret actually sputtered, briefly fell silent, then gathered herself again for her *riposte*, as might a duelist prepare for the killing blow. "Your juvenile absence of seriousness on the subject is an affront to anyone with a particle of sensibility."

"I assure you, Meg, I'm very serious about my pigs."

"*And*," she went on, unheeding, "the manner in which you fraternize with your pigman is a complete betrayal of your rank."

"Is that what you came out onto the portico to tell me? Far be it from me to throw your own words back into your face, but you've said that many times before. Also, you'll get chilled standing there without a shawl."

"I came out to inform you," Margaret said, in the tone of one forced to call upon the last vestiges of extraordinary self-control in the face of unbearable provocation, "that instead of gallivanting off to Surmont Hall to chat about pigs with Gabriel Penhallow, you're shortly expected at tea, in your own drawing-room, where you are to carry on—if at all humanly possible—a polite conversation with the Preston-Carnabys."

"Who?"

"The Preston-Carnabys, whose daughter, as I have already explained to you twice today, you are to inspect with an eye toward matrimony."

Anthony groaned. "Oh, for God's sake, Meg, another one?"

"Yes, *another one*. It has evidently escaped your notice that you have but the one son, which leaves you in a very precarious position. You must marry again."

"Five years with Selina was enough."

"Your feelings in the matter, Anthony, are irrelevant. You have a duty to the family and to your ancient lineage. The Preston-Carnabys are our guests, and—"

"Your guests. I didn't invite them."

"They are our guests," Margaret said with steel in her voice, "who have come all the way from Yorkshire. Incidentally, Nurse tells me that Wakefield has not been seen since breakfast, *and* I got a note from the vicar saying that Wakefield didn't come for his lessons, *and* your tenant farmer Moore stopped by to complain that Wakefield was seen attempting to ride one of his bulls— all of which means, I daresay, that he could be anywhere by now."

"Oh, Wake's somewhere about, you know."

"Your only child and heir is missing."

"Not missing, Meg. Just not here. When I was his age I could spend half the day up a tree, or fishing by the river."

"And look how *you* turned out. When Wakefield returns, I expect you to discipline him with the utmost stringency. He's a marquis, after all, and ought to act like one."

"He's eight."

"And in line to inherit one of the most illustrious dukedoms in the country."

"Very well, stale bread and water for a week. Maybe a few turns on the rack, too."

In the silence that fell between them after this last utterance, Anthony would have sworn he could see actual flames shooting out from Margaret's eyes. Finally she hissed:

"You—you're—you're . . ."

"Yes?" he said, politely.

"You're a very bad duke!"

"Am I?" he said, still politely.

"Yes! In fact, you're the worst duke in the world!"

"Well then." Warm and comfortable in his wool greatcoat and tall hat, Anthony stood looking up at Margaret on the portico. The black hem of her gown fluttered in a sharp wintry wind, her nose had reddened in the cold, and her teeth were chattering ever so slightly. He knew from extensive experience that she would go on standing there until she gained her point, no matter how long it took. Little did he want on his conscience the nasty bout of pleurisy that might develop if she stayed like this much longer, so he said:

"I'll talk to Wakefield, Meg. Now, if you'll excuse me, I'll stop by the stables to tell them I don't want my horse after all. Then I'll come back for tea."

She eyed him narrowly, then nodded and turned around. A footman had obviously been awaiting her return to the house, for the door swung open wide to admit her, and then was closed very, very gently by the same invisible hand within. Had it not been beneath her, Anthony knew that Margaret would have loved nothing better than personally slamming the great oak door shut in a way that would have made her sentiments known to everyone within a fifty-foot radius.

He gave a little sigh.

Poor old Margaret.

He wished *she* would marry again.

At eighteen she had been wed to Selina's older brother, who had died after only two years of marriage. His heir, Selina's younger brother, had promptly booted the widowed Margaret out of the house, and so she had come back home to Hastings where she and Selina had— beneath a brittle veneer of civility—lived under the same roof as might two queens jockey for the same throne, an uneasy state of affairs which lasted until Selina's death, five long years later.

Now here they were. He a widower at thirty-one, she a widow at thirty-three. She still wore black for the late Viscount Peete, which was a mystery to Anthony, as Skiffy Featherington had not only been exceedingly stupid, he had also been vain, arrogant, and among the most extreme of the so-called Dandy set—notorious throughout half of England for the immense shoulder-padding in his coats, the soaring height of his shirt-points, the half-dozen fobs jangling from his waist, and the jeweled quizzing-glass he carried with him everywhere including (it was rumored) bed, bathtub, and privy.

Well, life was full of mysteries, wasn't it?

By way of further example, why had blight returned this past autumn to the northeastern apple orchards after a full decade of untroubled health and productivity?

And was it true that the long white blurry swath in the night sky wasn't a celestial sort of exhalation, as he'd been taught in his youth, but was instead, thanks to the revelations of modern telescopes, an immense grouping of distant stars?

Too, recently he had found himself wondering why the self-styled village oracle, Mrs. Roger, had come up to him the last time he was in Riverton and said, nodding her head in a highly significant manner, *You're next, Yer Grace.*

Also, would Margaret ever stop presenting him with marital candidates, or would this dispiriting parade of hopeful females go on forever?

Anthony turned away from the marble steps and began walking toward the stables, and as he passed a large and perfectly rounded shrub, a small form leaped out from behind it and onto the graveled path, shouting in a high-pitched childish treble:

"Boo!"

Anthony paused and calmly regarded his son, who in turn looked very disappointed.

"Oh, Father, you *never* jump."

"Nerves of iron," explained Anthony. "Only way a

chap could survive in this family. How long have you been hiding behind that shrub?"

"Ages. I heard everything you and Aunt Margaret said. I say, Father, are you going to marry Miss Thingummy?"

"Who?"

"You know, the lady from Yorkshire."

"Doubtful."

"Well, that's good. I saw her in the drawing-room, Father, and she asked who I was, and when I told her, she said I ought to be away at school, and then I told her I didn't want to go, and she said I was a foolish little boy and that *you're* a nonglickful father."

"Do you mean neglectful?"

"Yes, that's what I said. And then *she* said that the first thing she'll do after she marries you will be to pack me off to Eton."

"Fat chance of that. You'd run away and join the Navy."

"Yes, that's what I told her! And guess what she said then, Father?"

"She complimented you on your patriotic spirit."

"No, she said I was not only a foolish little boy, but a horrid one too."

"Hardly an endearing strategy to get me to marry her," remarked Anthony. "I wonder why she didn't think you'd repeat what she said to you."

Wakefield smiled a distinctly gleeful smile. "I *told* her I would, Father, and then she gave me a half-crown to keep my mouth shut."

"And yet here you are, telling me."

"Aren't you glad I did?"

"Well, yes," Anthony admitted. "You've given me all the insight I need into Miss Thingummy's character."

"I think *you* ought to give me a half-crown for that."

"Don't push your luck. You're already deep into morally

ambiguous territory. By the way, what were you doing in the drawing-room?"

"Hiding from Nurse."

"Why?"

"She keeps wanting to give me castor oil, and it's *foul*."

Anthony nodded, and resumed walking again. "She dosed me with that when I was a lad. Said it would fatten me up."

Briskly taking two or three strides to one of his own, Wakefield kept pace alongside him. "It didn't work, Father."

"No, it only made me bilious. Does she think you're too thin also?"

"Yes. She says I'll grow up to be a scarecrow like you if I don't watch out."

"A scarecrow? How unkind of Nurse to say that."

"I stuck up for you, Father."

"Did you, Wake? That was ripping of you."

"Yes, I told her you don't look like a scarecrow—you're more like a crane. Because your legs are awfully long, you know."

"They may be long, my boy, but at least they reach the ground."

Wakefield thought this over, and grinned. "I say, Father, you're the most complete hand."

"One does try."

"So will you talk to Nurse, then?"

"Yes. Henceforth no drop of castor oil is to pass betwixt your unwilling lips. This is my ducal decree. Let no man—or nurse—flout it with impunity."

Wakefield gave a joyful skip. "That's capital, Father, thanks ever so much."

"You're welcome. Speaking of hiding in the drawing-room, why didn't you go to the vicarage today for your lessons?"

"I wanted to, of course," said Wakefield, looking up at him with brown eyes that had somehow gotten all big and glistening, like those of a sweet, vulnerable fawn. "But there were so many more important things I had to do, Father."

"Like what?"

"Well, for one, yesterday I told Johns I'd stand guard over the Duchess for a few hours, so he could go get his breakfast. He'd told me about Cremwell's evil plan, you see, and he stayed by the Duchess's pig-cote all night. And when he got back, *I* was hungry, so I went to Mrs. Gregg's cottage. Because she makes the most dilickable muffins, Father."

"Do you mean delectable?"

"Yes, that's what I said. You ought to try them. So I had nuncheon with Mrs. Gregg, and then I *was* going to the vicarage, but I passed Mr. Moore's field and saw that bull of his, Old Snorter, and thought I'd give it a go. So after I fell off, I had to run away from Old Snorter *and* Mr. Moore, who was shouting like anything. Then I tripped over a tree-root and scraped away half the skin on my arm—"

"Did you really?"

"Well, no, but I *was* bleeding a bit, and luckily Miss Trevelyan came by on one of her walks, and she took me back to her house and put a sticking-plaster on it, and then I was hungry again, so Miss Humphrey made some sandwiches for me, and then we all went into the library so Miss Trevelyan could read aloud to us from the book she's writing, which was jolly good fun, and Miss Humphrey also brought in some biscuits. I saved one for you, Father."

Wakefield pulled from the pocket of his coat a vaguely circular object. "See? It's only a tiny bit crumbled."

He offered it to Anthony, who accepted it, blew off what looked like some dog hairs, and took a bite. "I say, it *is* good."

Wakefield looked pleased. "Isn't it? I ate five of them."

Anthony took another bite, then said, "Look here, old chap, these are all very worthy activities, but you and I made a bargain. I agreed to let you stay at home and not go off to school, and you agreed to have lessons with Mr. Pressley. So you ought to stick to the bargain, don't you think?"

Wakefield opened his mouth, closed it, kicked at the gravel, hopped on one foot, lagged behind, ran to catch up, and finally said, "Yes, Father."

"Splendid. Want the last bite?"

"Yes, please." Wakefield took what was left of the biscuit and ate it, and said, "I say, Father, I don't think Aunt Margaret meant it when she said you're the worst duke in the world."

"Oh yes, she did," answered Anthony dispassionately.

"There's probably worse ones in China, Father, or in the Colonies, or Antarctica."

"You're a great comfort to me, my boy."

"One does try."

Anthony ruffled his son's tawny hair, repressed a sigh at the thought of the predictably ghastly tea that lay ahead of him, and then the two of them passed into the stables which smelled so pleasantly of horse, hay, liniment, cheroot, and manure.

Meanwhile, over at Surmont Hall . . .

Jane Kent stood on the porch of the intimidatingly vast old house, gazing with some trepidation at the massive door of dark knotted wood and the polished knocker

which was just a little above her eye-level. She was uncomfortably aware that the hem of her shabby old gown
was rather short, showing far too much of her scrawny
ankles in equally shabby stockings and also entirely fail-
ing to conceal the fact that her dark half-boots, though
sturdy, were—unfortunately—shabby too.

She tightened her grip on the small battered valise she
held in both hands, additionally aware that she was raven-
ously hungry, underdressed for the winter weather, not as
clean as she would like after traveling in various dingy
coaches for four days, and that in the tatty reticule she
carried looped around her bony wrist was all the money
she had left in the world.

Three pounds, four shillings, and sixpence.

No, wait, that was wrong.

She had given the shillings to a nice old man named
John Roger who had conveyed her from the village—
Riverton—in his gig. He hadn't wanted to take the money,
but she had insisted.

It was his wife, curiously enough, who had helped her
find her way here.

Jane had just climbed out of the coach from Bristol,
and was standing, stiff and cold and bewildered, on the
high street, when a stout old lady had come marching up
and said in a satisfied way:

You're right on time.

Of course, the old lady, who then introduced herself as
Mrs. Roger, could have been referring to the coach's traveling schedule, but somehow Jane didn't think that was
quite what she had meant. Still, before she could gather
her scattered wits to try and frame a rational inquiry, Mrs.
Roger had taken her over to where her husband happened
to be standing with his gig and horse, hustled Jane up onto
the high front seat, and said:

You're to ask for old Mrs. Penhallow.

More bewildered than ever, Jane had thought about the fragile, yellowed letter she had in her possession, and only said:

At Surmont Hall?

Mrs. Roger had looked up at her and calmly answered, *Well, of course.*

And just for a second Jane felt like she had asked a stupid question.

A loud complaining rumble from her empty stomach abruptly reminded her that she'd been standing on the wide gracious porch of Surmont Hall like a wax dummy. Well, it was now or never, she supposed.

So Jane lifted her hand and rapped the knocker in a way that sounded, she hoped, neither too assertive nor too timid—the easy, casual knock of a person who was certainly going to be admitted into this very, very grand house despite looking as if she really ought to be going around the back to the servants' entrance and begging for a bowl of soup.

Which she might, in fact, shortly be doing.

A blast of cold sharp wind whipped at the hems of Jane's gown and pelisse and, as if embodied in an unseen malevolent hand, it also ripped from her head her old flat-crowned straw bonnet, which flew high into the air, did three or four jaunty somersaults, and landed gracefully into the tranquil waters of the large ornamental pond which lay beyond the curving graveled carriage sweep.

Jane was just about to go darting after it (as it was her only hat) when the big dark door opened. A beautifully dressed, well-fed, very clean young footman stood there, looking inquiringly at her.

"May I help you, miss?"

"Yes, please." Jane realized that her voice had emerged

rather weak and croaky, like that of a despairing frog, per-haps, and hastily she cleared her throat. "I've—I've come to see Mrs. Penhallow."

"Which one, miss?"

Jane gaped at the footman. Was this a trick question? How many Mrs. Penhallows could there possibly be? A dozen—a hundred—a thousand? Into her muddled mind came Mrs. Roger's instructions and she said rather wildly, "The—ah—older Mrs. Penhallow, if you please."

A little doubtfully, the footman said, "Is she expecting you, miss?"

"I—I have a letter." This was true, although Jane was miserably conscious that her answer was more than a little opaque. Her stomach rumbled again, as if to helpfully remind her of just how miserable things were.

"Very well, miss. Won't you please come inside?" The footman stepped aside, and gratefully Jane went into the light and warmth of an immense high-ceilinged hall, catching quick glimpses of an enormous fireplace flanked by gleaming suits of armor, a coat of arms carved into the massive chimney-piece, a large and unnerving display of old weapons on one wall, a wide curving staircase leading to the upstairs.

Everything was so big—and it made her feel so very small.

Jane shrank a little inside her pelisse, feeling extremely out of place among all this elegance and grandeur, and also hoping she hadn't tracked mud inside. Her idea back in Nantwich, to upend her life because of a yellowy old letter discovered by chance, had seemed so brilliant and important at the time, but now it struck her as reckless, demented, asinine, ruinous folly.

Still, maybe there would be soup.

She thought of a nice fragrant steaming hot bowl of

it, filled with, say, chunks of beef, and with carrots and parsnips and onions. Maybe some celery and diced potatoes, too.

Then she pictured a lovely thick slice of fresh bread, with a spongy tender crumb and a crisp chewy crust.

No, *two* slices. Why not?

In her mind's eye she pictured herself lavishly spreading onto the bread as much butter as she liked.

Lots and lots of it, fresh-churned and creamy, with a little sprinkle of salt, perhaps.

Covering every bit of the slice, all the way to the crust.

She would eat these two buttery slices very methodically—it would give her soup a chance to cool a little.

Next, she imagined *another* slice of bread, which she wouldn't butter, but would instead dip into her soup. It would soak up the rich beefy broth, and get all soft and drippy, and she'd have to carefully bite at it so as not to waste a single drop.

After that, she'd spoon up everything else.

Then, when she had nearly finished the bowl, she would use some more bread to mop up the last of the broth, wiping her bowl clean.

Of course, there would be plenty more soup and bread, and it would be perfectly all right for her to have seconds, so—

Jane realized that she was salivating, and that drool was just about to start spooling out of the side of her mouth. Quickly she swallowed. As she did, she heard, from within a corridor off the hall, a man say, in a deep, cool, aristocratic-sounding voice tinged with faint amusement:

"Cremwell's been telling me that Johns—the Hastings pigman—has been grossly insulting him in the Riverton pubs, denigrating his professional expertise, mocking his appearance, and casting aspersions on his mother's fidelity."

"Dear me," said another voice, a woman's, also very cool and aristocratic. "The passions of these pigmen! You ought, perhaps, to speak with Radcliffe, before they come to actual blows."

Nervously Jane turned toward these new voices and, her fingers clenched tight on the handle of her valise, watched as from the corridor came two people walking side by side.

One was a tall, broad-shouldered, excessively good-looking man in his early thirties, with neatly cropped brown hair and penetrating dark eyes, dressed very fine in a dark blue jacket, dark breeches, and tall glossy boots.

The other person was a handsome, slender old lady, very straight and graceful, with silvery curls and sharp blue eyes, and clad in a soft dove-gray gown of marvelous elegance and simplicity.

Jane stared at her, her heart thumping hard within her chest, hearing in her mind once again Mrs. Roger's firm voice:

You're to ask for old Mrs. Penhallow.

She took a few tentative steps forward. "Please, ma'am—are you—may I speak with you, please?" Her voice felt to her as if it were being swallowed up in this enormous hall, but apparently it was loud enough to attract the attention of the handsome man and the elegant old lady, for they both paused and turned to look at her.

The old lady's reaction was more intense—far, far more intense—than Jane could ever have anticipated.

At first moving over Jane with mild curiosity, those sharp blue eyes suddenly widened, her mouth went slack, and the old lady gasped out:

"Titus!"

Her face gone white as snow, she staggered back and would have fallen, if not for the swift action of the man beside her, who wrapped his arm around her to keep her upright.

The old lady didn't faint, but she certainly looked as if she had seen a ghost.